Hatter M

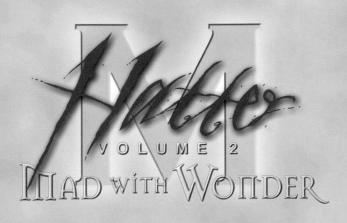

VOLUME 2

Mad with Wonder

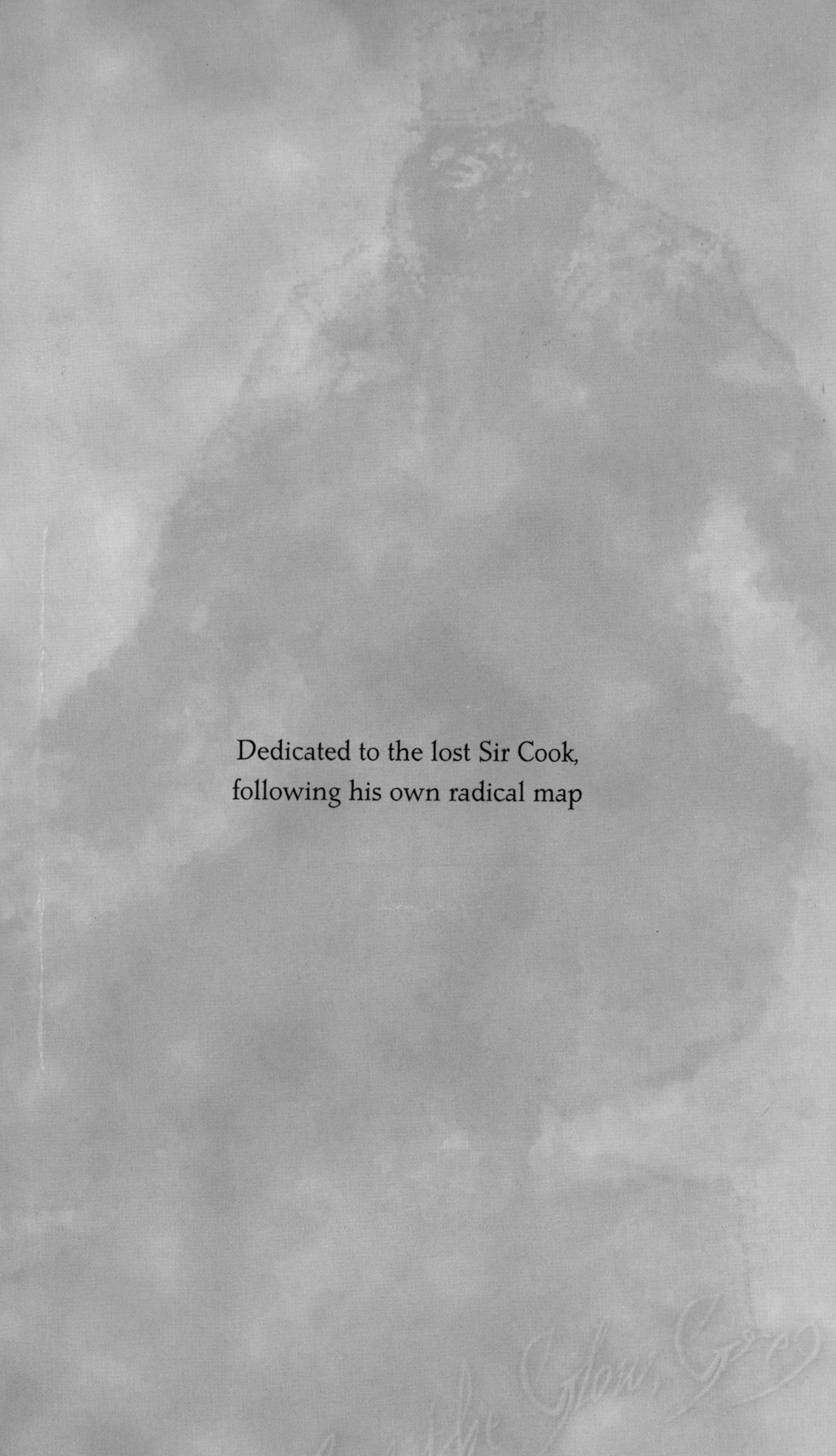

Dedicated to the lost Sir Cook,
following his own radical map

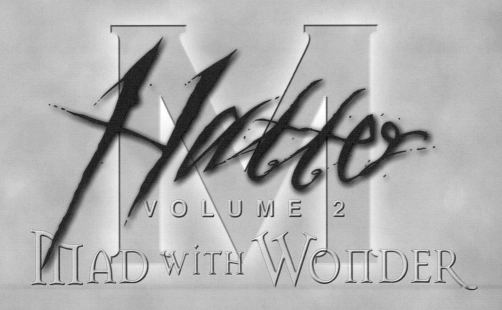

Hatter M
VOLUME 2
MAD with WONDER

Written by Frank Beddor & Liz Cavalier
Art by Sami Makkonen

AUTOMATIC
PICTURES
PUBLISHING

Hatter M: Mad With Wonder
Volume 2

Writers
Frank Beddor
Liz Cavalier

Art
Sami Makkonen

Cover Art
Tae Young Choi

Letterer
Tom B. Long

Editor
C.J. Wrobel

Reconnaissance & Analysis
Nate Barlow

Civil War Raconteur
Miss Emily McGuiness

Logo Designed by
Christina Craemer

Interiors Designed by
Vera Milosavich

Institute Artists
Chris Appelhans
Catia Chien
Tae Young Choi
Brian Flora
Vance Kovacs

www.lookingglasswars.com

The Looking Glass Wars® is a trademark of Automatic Pictures, Inc.
Copyright © 2009 Automatic Pictures, Inc. All rights reserved.

Excerpts from *ArchEnemy: The Looking Glass Wars, Book Three* used with permission of Penguin Books for Young Readers. All rights reserved.

From *Princess Alyss of Wonderland* by Frank Beddor, illustrated by Catia Chien and Vance Kovacs, Copyright © 2007 by Frank Beddor. Used by permission of Dial Books for Young Readers, A Division of Penguin Young Readers Group, A Member of Penguin Group (USA) Inc., 345 Hudson Street, New York, NY 10014. All rights reserved

Printed in Korea

ISBN 978-0-9818737-1-8

This is ~~not~~ the story
of a Mad Hatter

"Everyone is more or less mad on one point." —RUDYARD KIPLING

Thank You

Scholars, Antiquarians,
Reasoners, Logicians, Rationalists,
and Knights Errant

Contents

The Quest

The Rest

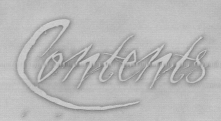

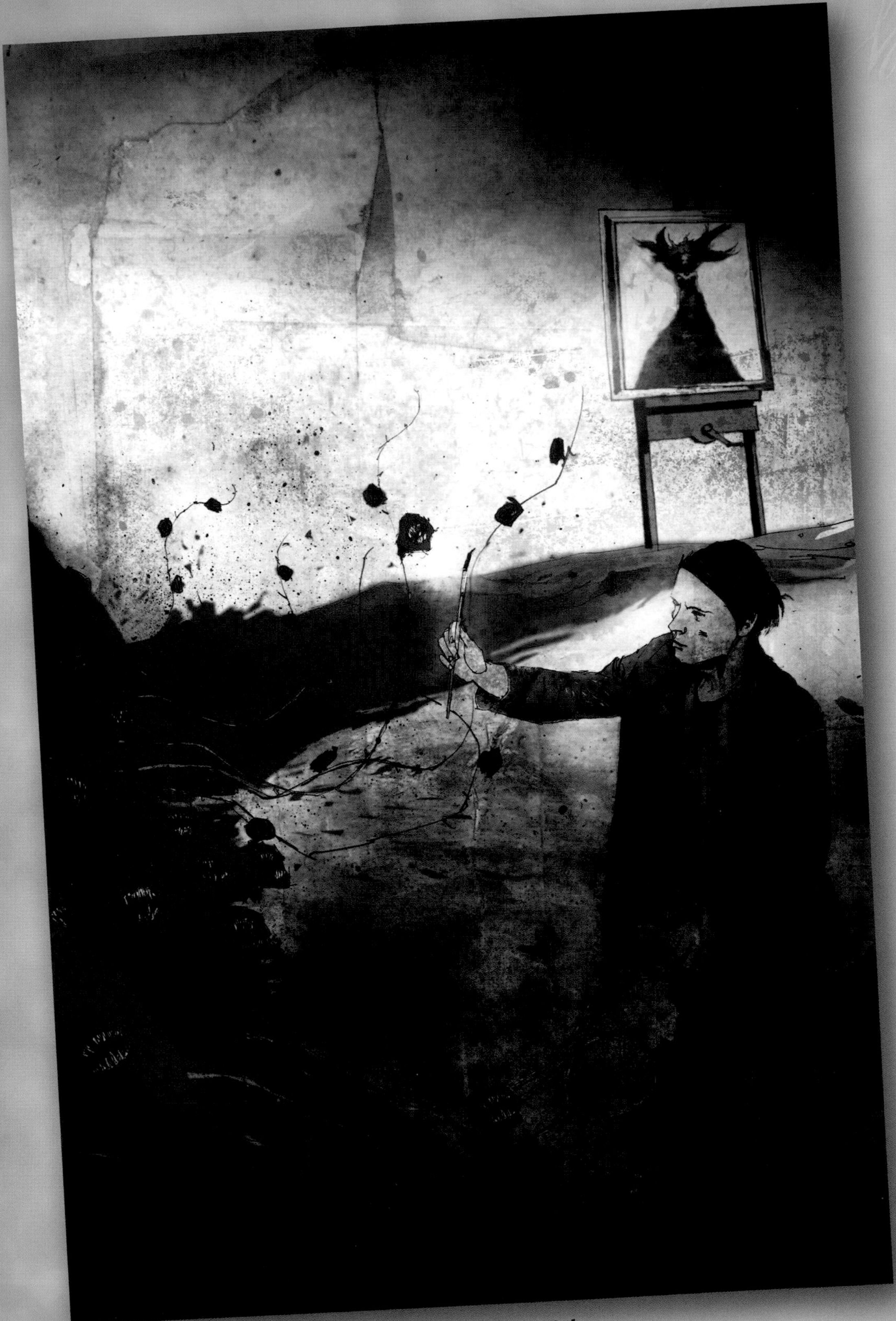

Sami's Imagination at Work

Much like Royal Bodyguard Hatter Madigan, I too have been on a non-stop quest following the Glow of Imagination. The object of my search was not, however, a lost princess but the artist to whom Ben Templesmith would pass the hallowed scepter of visual documentation. For over a year I trekked across continents in the hope of finding the paint-stained partner that would illustrate the volume you now hold in your hands. I did not limit my search to celebrated schools or established professionals but instead wandered the alleys claimed by Rio de Janeiro's muralists and the unmarked galleries of Shanghai looking for the *ONE*. Finally, exhausted and disillusioned, I was about to return to Los Angeles when I received a cryptic email from Joe Pruett of Desperado Comics. The email contained only the latitude and longitude of a small town in Finland and the name *Sami Makkonen*. Boarding a plane at midnight for the redeye to Finland I had a premonition that within hours I would be seated at a café table with the artist who would illustrate geo-graphic novel Hatter M Volume 2. My second sight proved correct and for the next several weeks Sami and I sat together at a scarred table in a forgotten café debating and analyzing the visuals that would bring this volume to life. I would watch as Sami intuitively pulled colors from the Wonderland spectrum and mixed them with his Finnish sensibility for an inter-realm artistry and silently marvel at my good fortune in finding one so talented and Imaginative! Thanks to Joe Pruett and Sami Makkonen I am now able to share with you Volume 2 of Hatter M's search — *Mad with Wonder*.

Frank Beddor

"In a completely sane world, madness is the only freedom!" —J. G. BALLARD

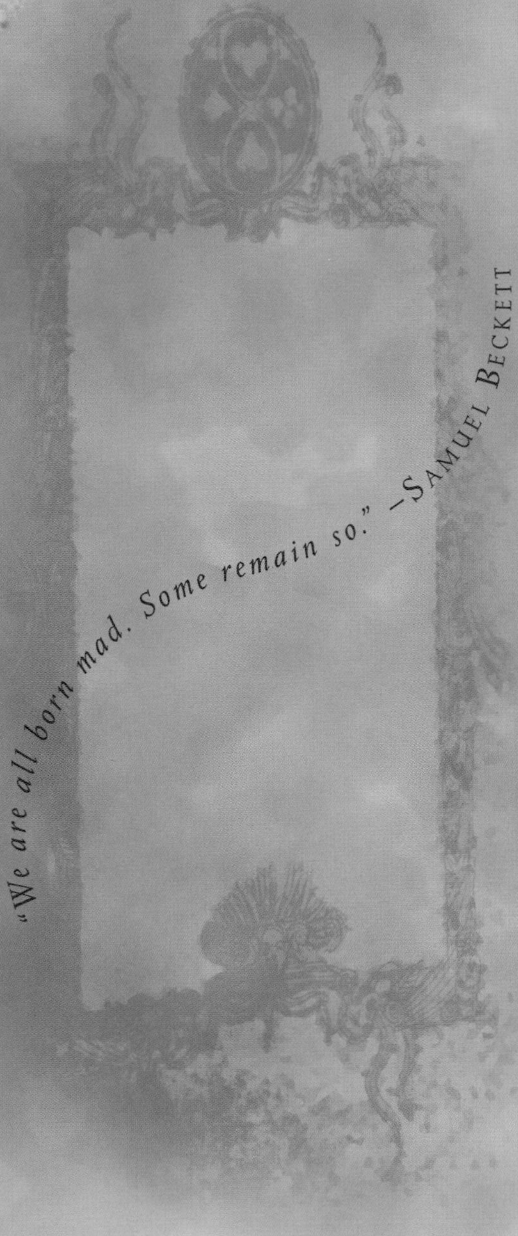

“We are all born mad. Some remain so.” –Samuel Beckett

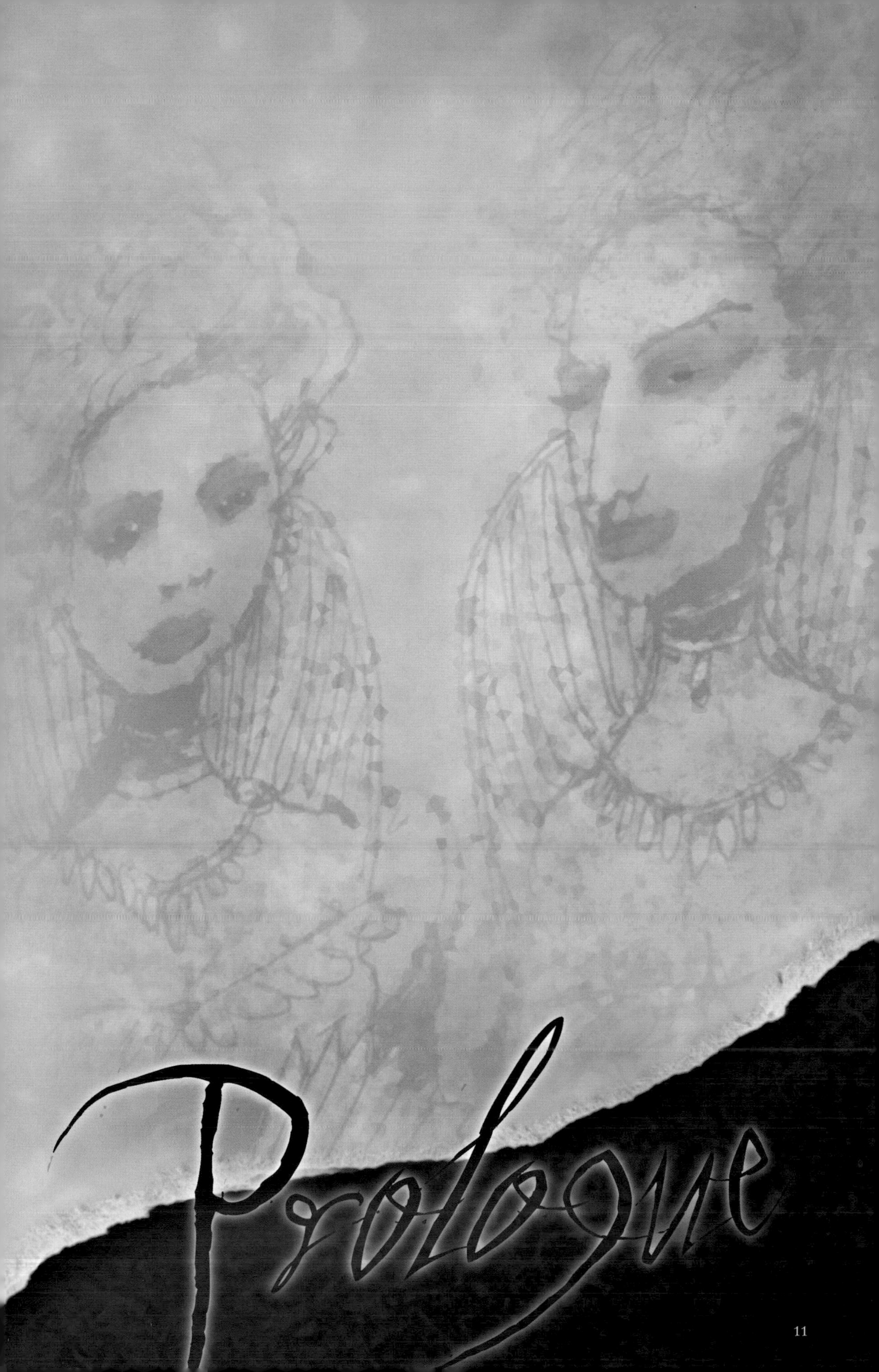

Prologue

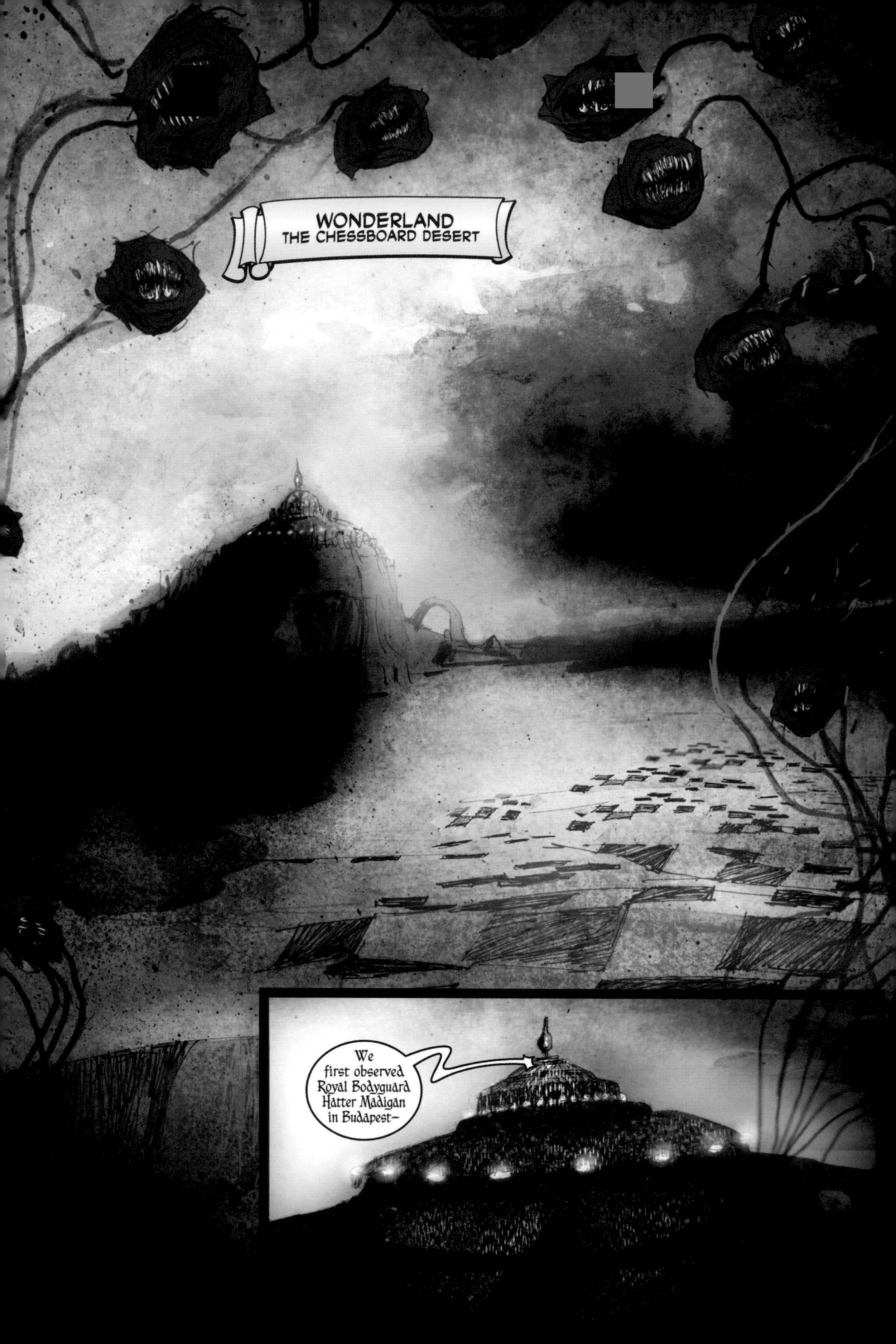
WONDERLAND
THE CHESSBOARD DESERT
We first observed Royal Bodyguard Hatter Madigan in Budapest~

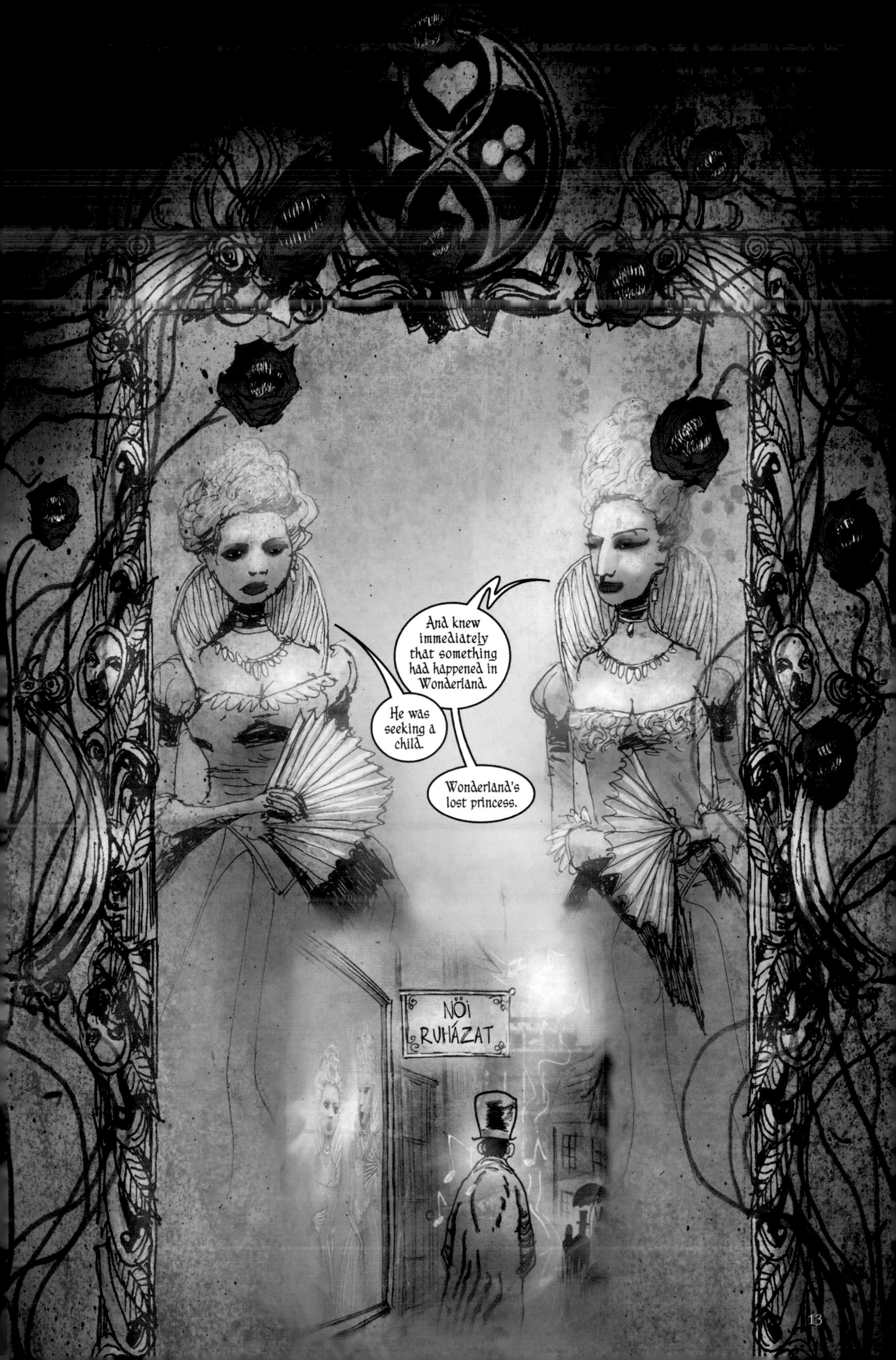
He was seeking a child.
And knew immediately that something had happened in Wonderland.
Wonderland's lost princess.
NÖi RUHÁZAT

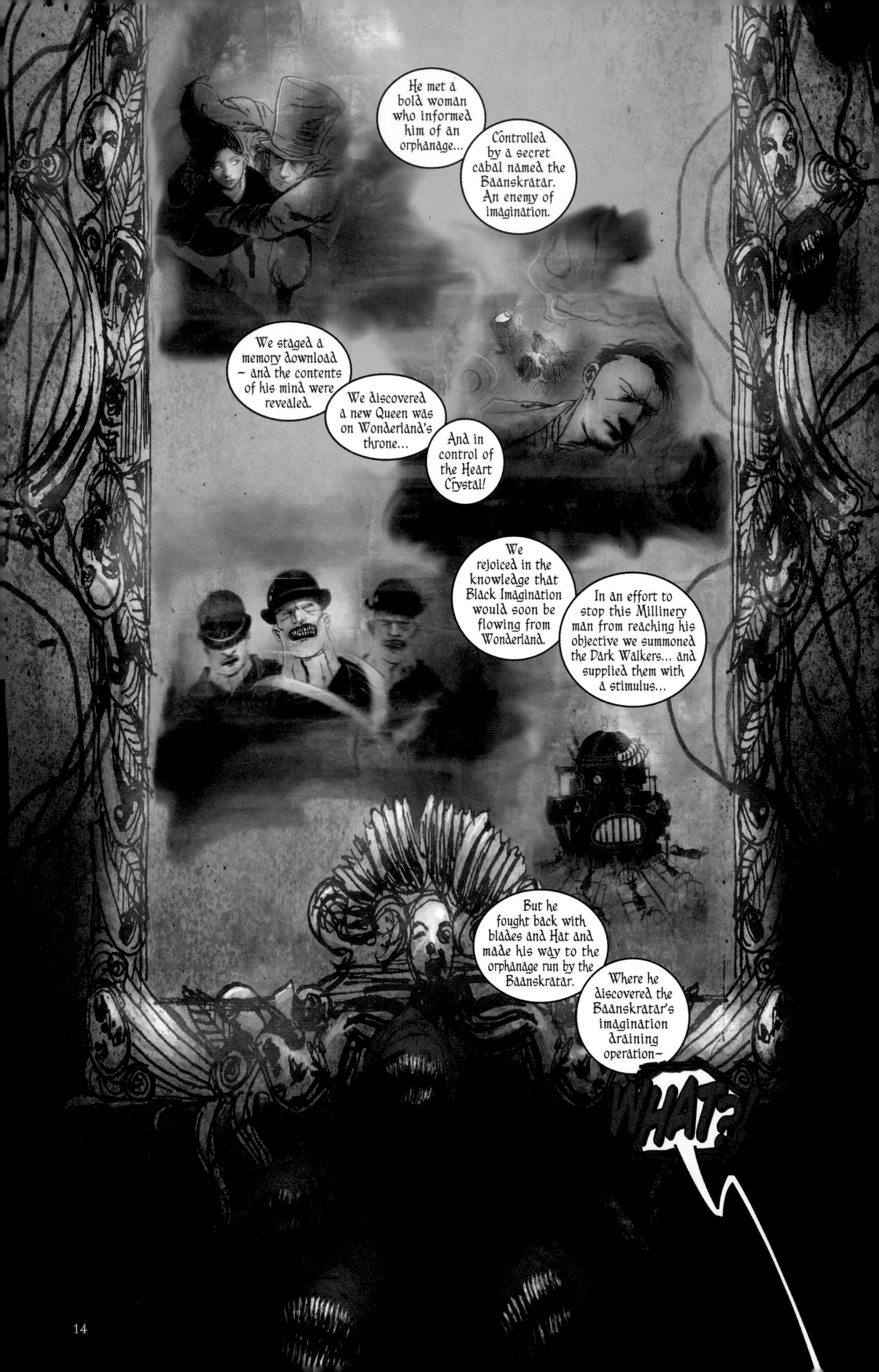
He met a bold woman who informed him of an orphanage...
Controlled by a secret cabal named the Baanskratar. An enemy of imagination.
We staged a memory download – and the contents of his mind were revealed.
We discovered a new Queen was on Wonderland's throne...
And in control of the Heart Crystal!
We rejoiced in the knowledge that Black Imagination would soon be flowing from Wonderland.
In an effort to stop this Millinery man from reaching his objective we summoned the Dark Walkers... and supplied them with a stimulus...
But he fought back with blades and Hat and made his way to the orphanage run by the Baanskratar.
Where he discovered the Baanskratar's imagination draining operation–
WHAT?!

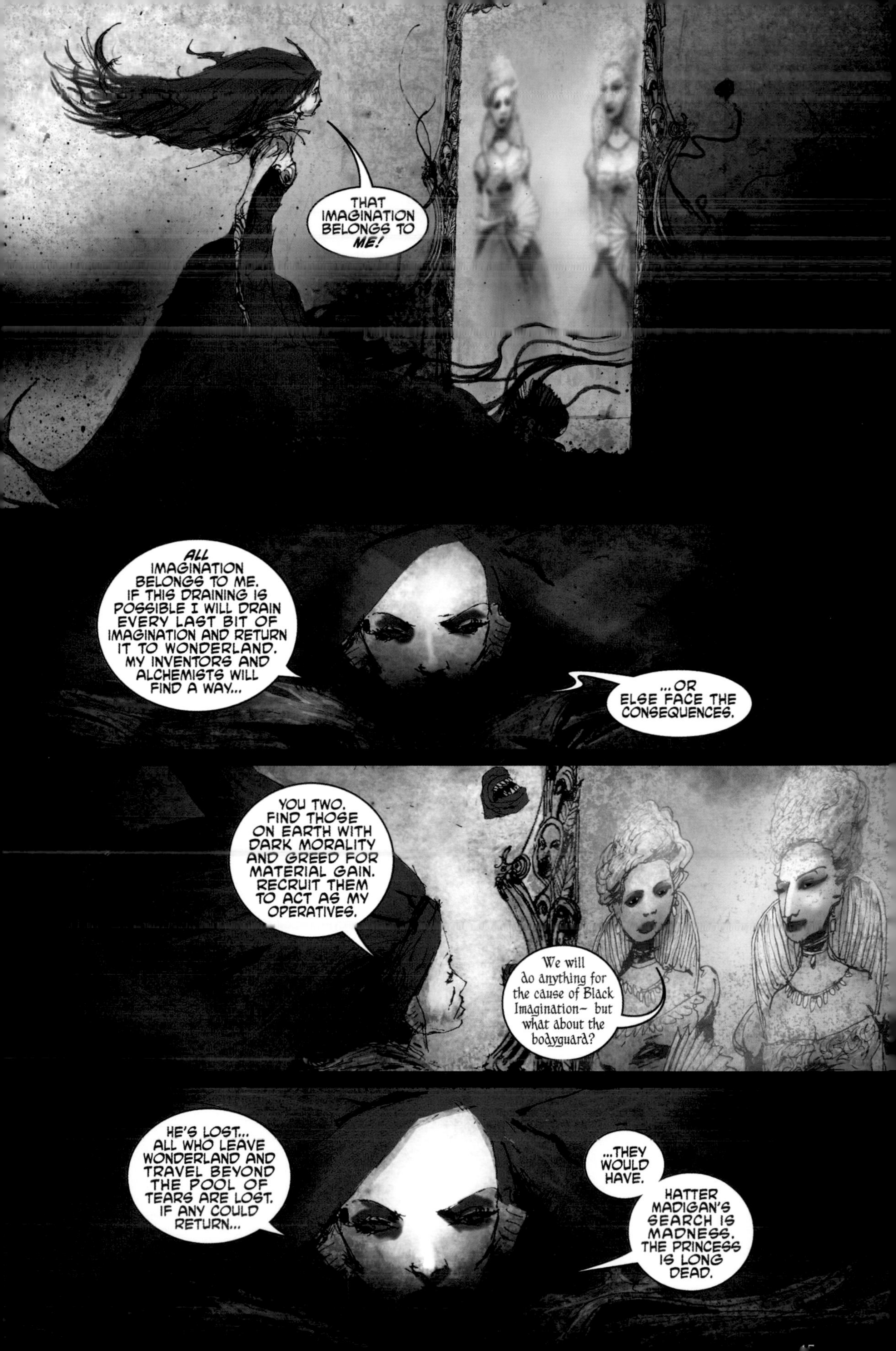
THAT IMAGINATION BELONGS TO *ME!*
ALL IMAGINATION BELONGS TO ME. IF THIS DRAINING IS POSSIBLE I WILL DRAIN EVERY LAST BIT OF IMAGINATION AND RETURN IT TO WONDERLAND. MY INVENTORS AND ALCHEMISTS WILL FIND A WAY...
...OR ELSE FACE THE CONSEQUENCES.
YOU TWO. FIND THOSE ON EARTH WITH DARK MORALITY AND GREED FOR MATERIAL GAIN. RECRUIT THEM TO ACT AS MY OPERATIVES.
We will do anything for the cause of Black Imagination~ but what about the bodyguard?
HE'S LOST... ALL WHO LEAVE WONDERLAND AND TRAVEL BEYOND THE POOL OF TEARS ARE LOST. IF ANY COULD RETURN...
...THEY WOULD HAVE.
HATTER MADIGAN'S SEARCH IS MADNESS. THE PRINCESS IS LONG DEAD.

Imperfect…I wander an imperfect world in search of Alyss. Daunting and vast.

197 million square miles…70.8% aqua…29.2% terra.

If not for the Glow that appears to beckon and guide me I would be as lost as she. How can one so small have a mission so great? One by one…doors keep opening…and I must carry on.

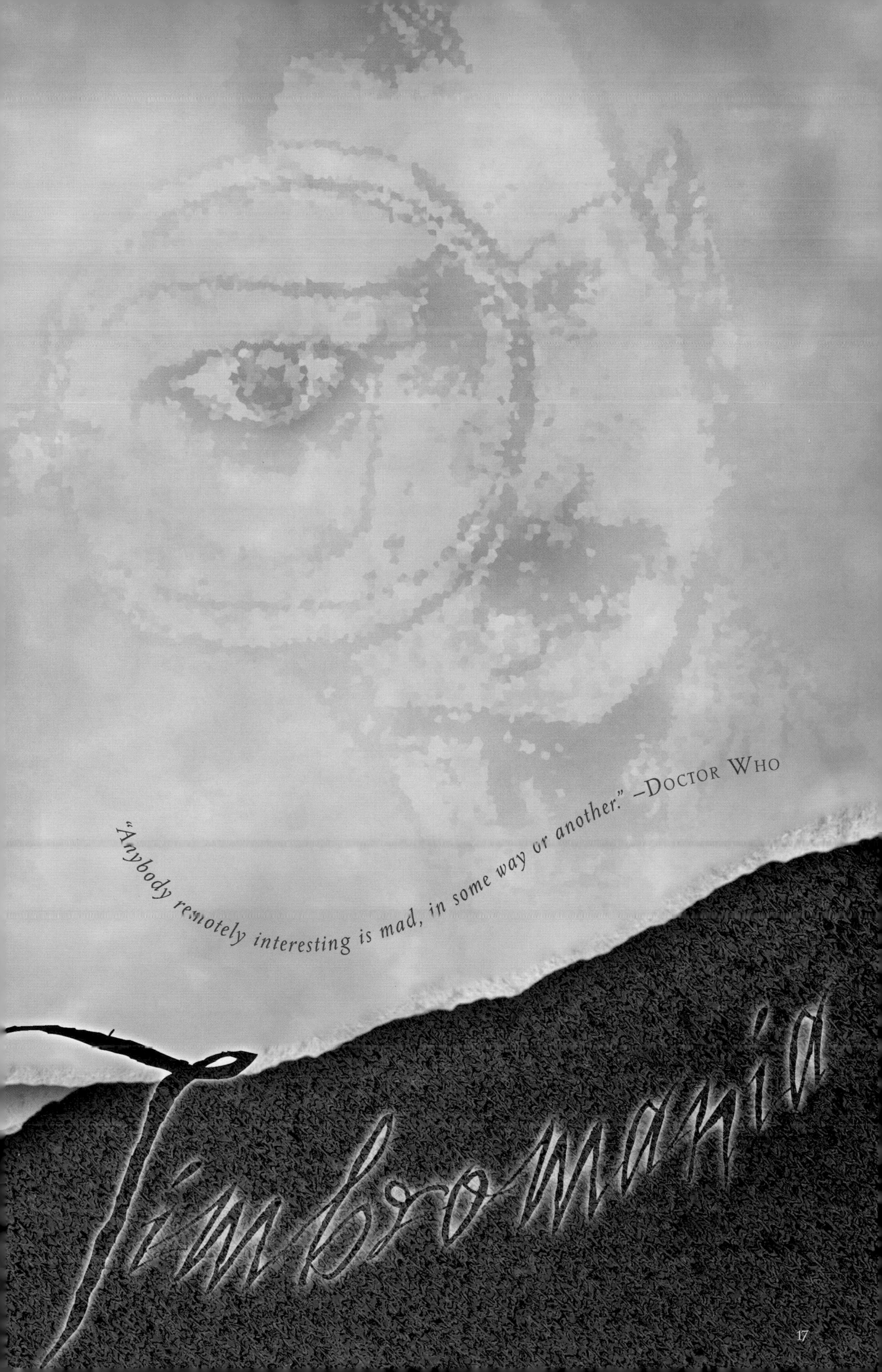

"Anybody remotely interesting is mad, in some way or another." –Doctor Who

Timbromania

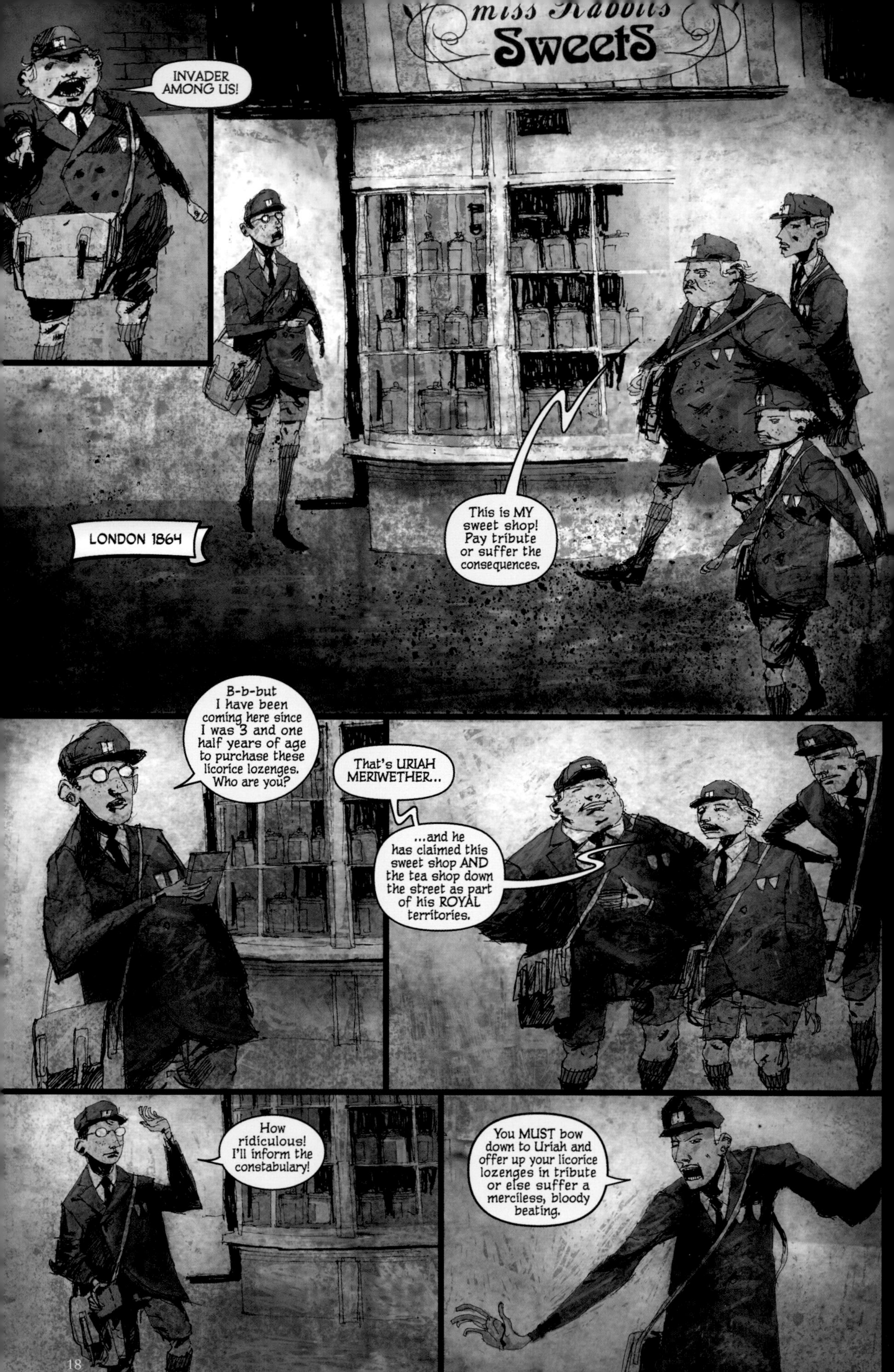
Sweets
INVADER AMONG US!
LONDON 1864
This is MY sweet shop! Pay tribute or suffer the consequences.
B-b-but I have been coming here since I was 3 and one half years of age to purchase these licorice lozenges. Who are you?
That's URIAH MERIWETHER...
...and he has claimed this sweet shop AND the tea shop down the street as part of his ROYAL territories.
How ridiculous! I'll inform the constabulary!
You MUST bow down to Uriah and offer up your licorice lozenges in tribute or else suffer a merciless, bloody beating.

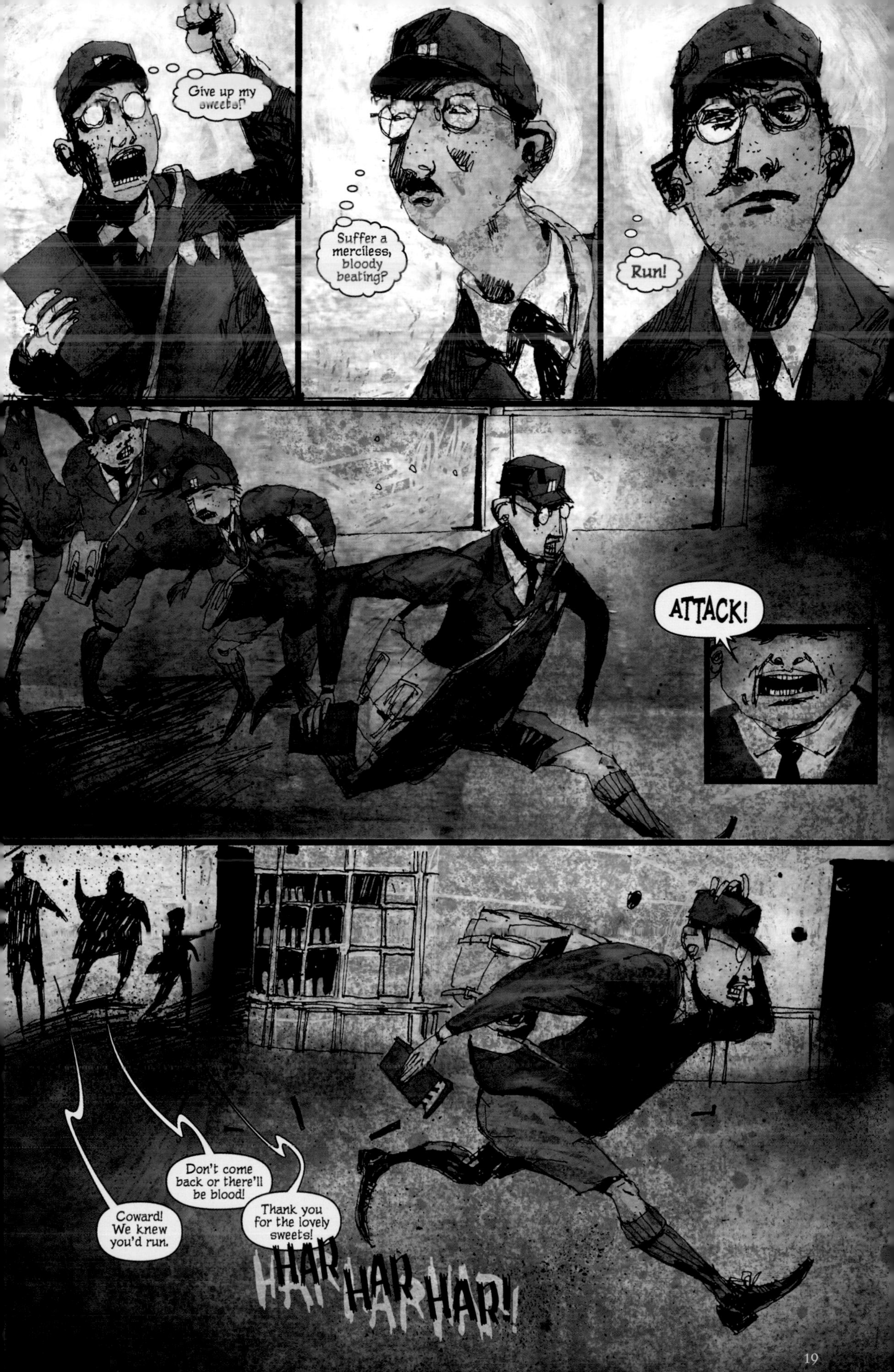
Give up my sweets?
Suffer a merciless, bloody beating?
Run!
ATTACK!
Coward! We knew you'd run.
Don't come back or there'll be blood!
Thank you for the lovely sweets!
HAR HAR HAR!

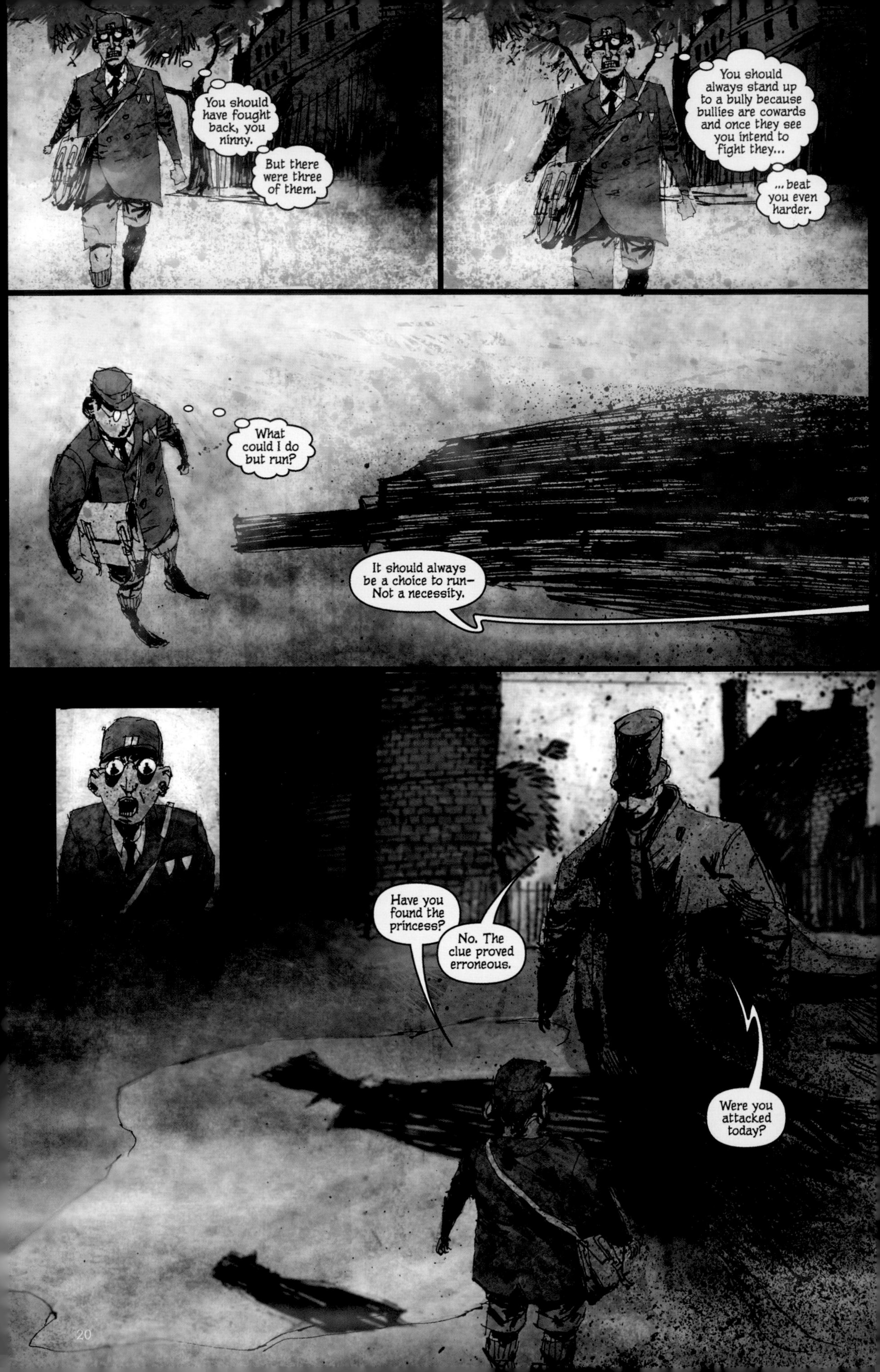
You should have fought back, you ninny.
But there were three of them.
You should always stand up to a bully because bullies are cowards and once they see you intend to fight they...
...beat you even harder.
What could I do but run?
It should always be a choice to run–Not a necessity.
Have you found the princess?
No. The clue proved erroneous.
Were you attacked today?

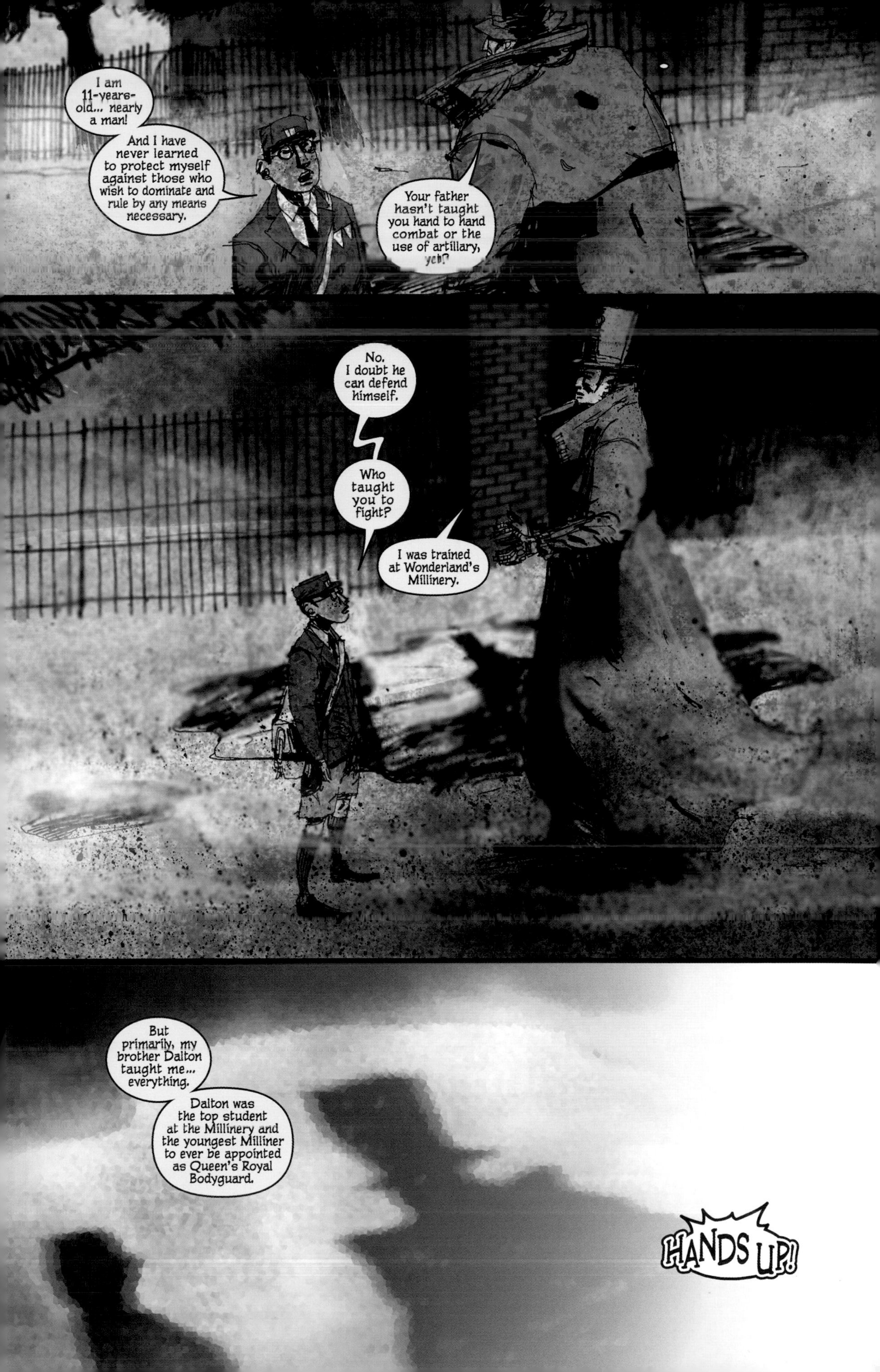
I am 11-years-old... nearly a man!
And I have never learned to protect myself against those who wish to dominate and rule by any means necessary.
Your father hasn't taught you hand to hand combat or the use of artillary, yeh?
No. I doubt he can defend himself.
Who taught you to fight?
I was trained at Wonderland's Millinery.
But primarily, my brother Dalton taught me... everything.
Dalton was the top student at the Millinery and the youngest Milliner to ever be appointed as Queen's Royal Bodyguard.
HANDS UP!

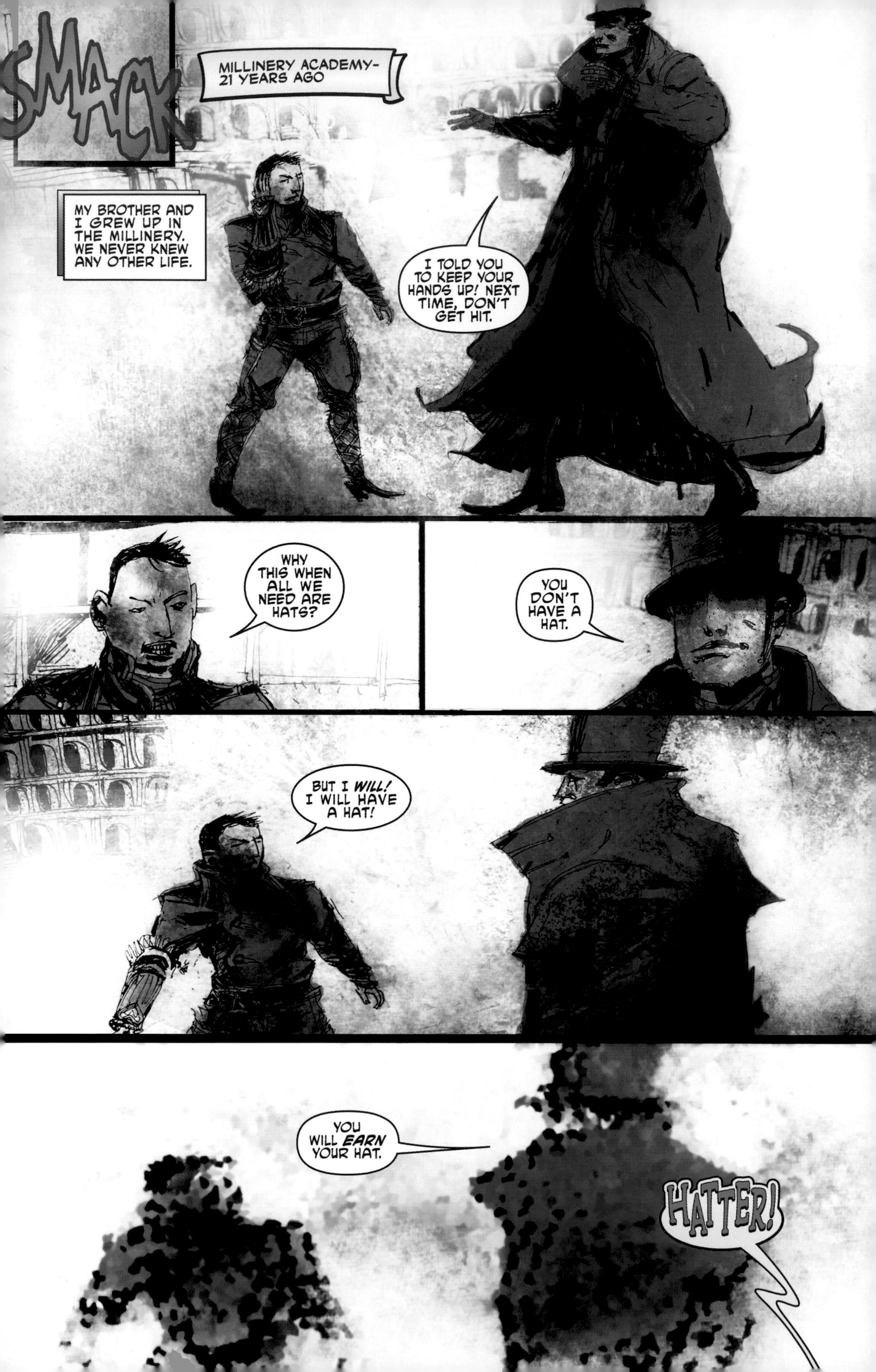
SMACK
MILLINERY ACADEMY-
21 YEARS AGO
MY BROTHER AND I GREW UP IN THE MILLINERY. WE NEVER KNEW ANY OTHER LIFE.
I TOLD YOU TO KEEP YOUR HANDS UP! NEXT TIME, DON'T GET HIT.
WHY THIS WHEN ALL WE NEED ARE HATS?
YOU DON'T HAVE A HAT.
BUT I WILL! I WILL HAVE A HAT!
YOU WILL EARN YOUR HAT.
HATTER!

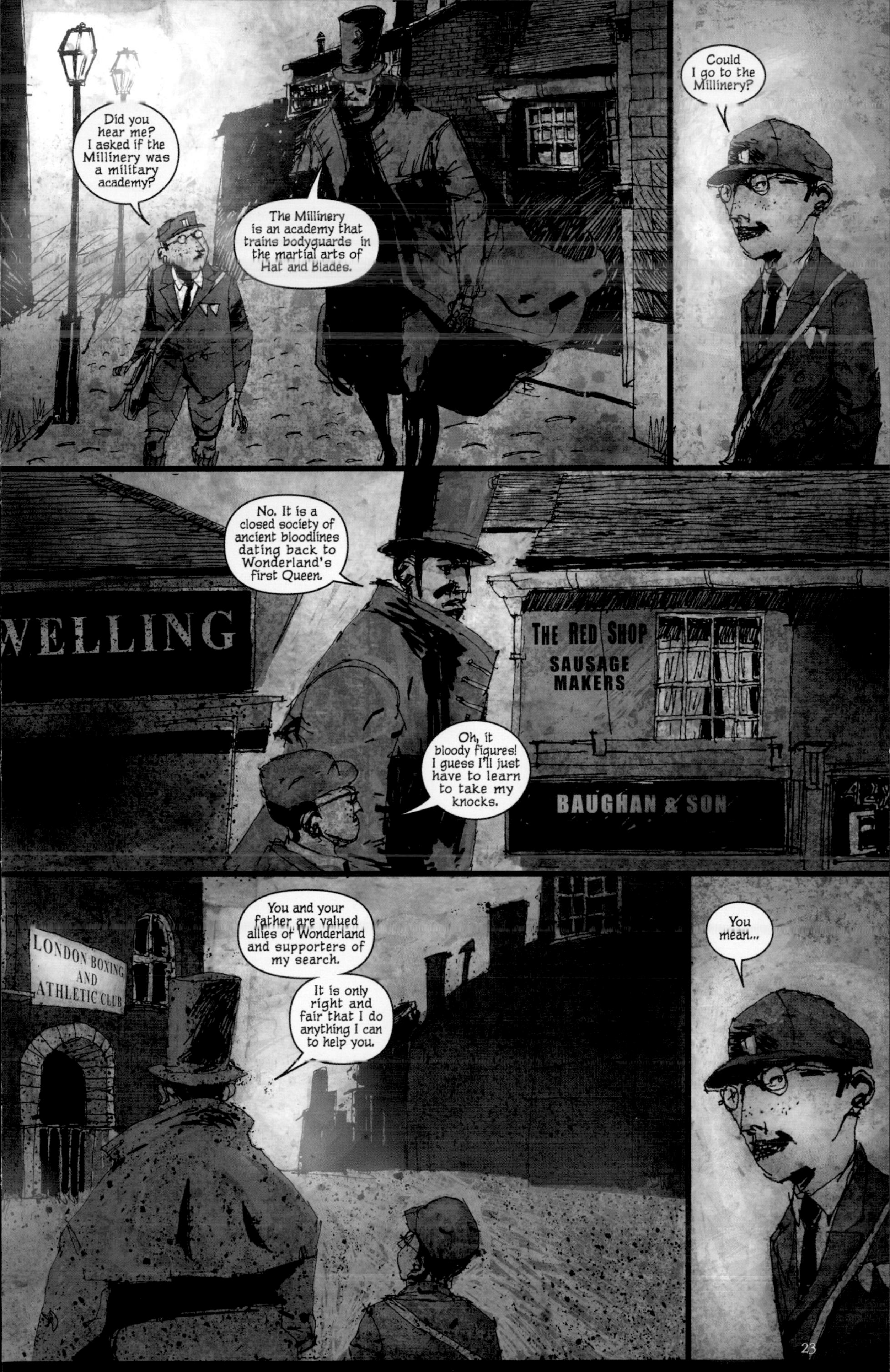
Did you hear me? I asked if the Millinery was a military academy?
The Millinery is an academy that trains bodyguards in the martial arts of Hat and Blades.
Could I go to the Millinery?
No. It is a closed society of ancient bloodlines dating back to Wonderland's first Queen.
WELLING
THE RED SHOP
SAUSAGE MAKERS
Oh, it bloody figures! I guess I'll just have to learn to take my knocks.
BAUGHAN & SON
LONDON BOXING AND ATHLETIC CLUB
You and your father are valued allies of Wonderland and supporters of my search.
It is only right and fair that I do anything I can to help you.
You mean...

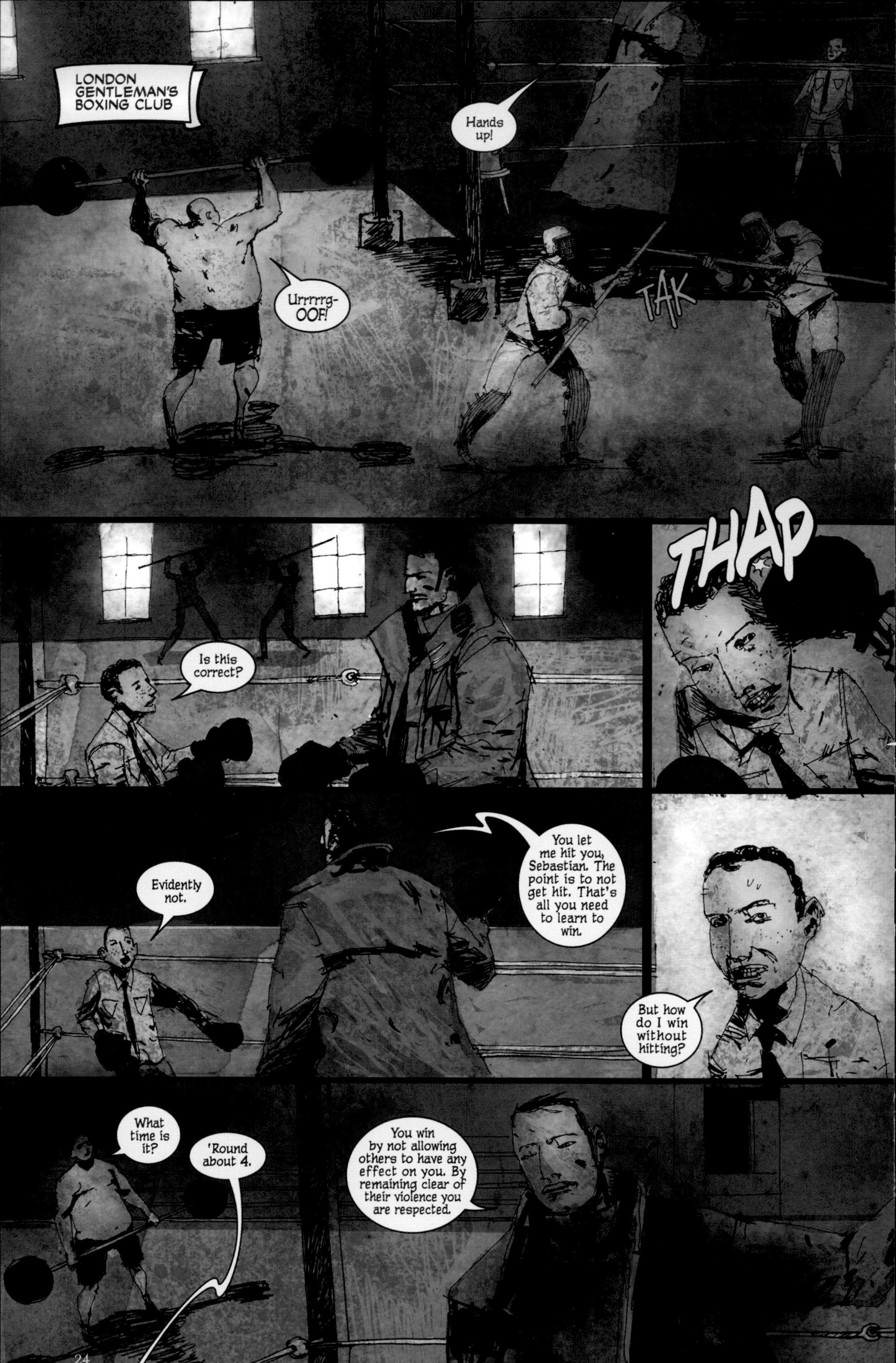
LONDON GENTLEMAN'S BOXING CLUB
Hands up!
Urrrrrg-OOF!
TAK
Is this correct?
THAP
Evidently not.
You let me hit you, Sebastian. The point is to not get hit. That's all you need to learn to win.
But how do I win without hitting?
What time is it?
'Round about 4.
You win by not allowing others to have any effect on you. By remaining clear of their violence you are respected.

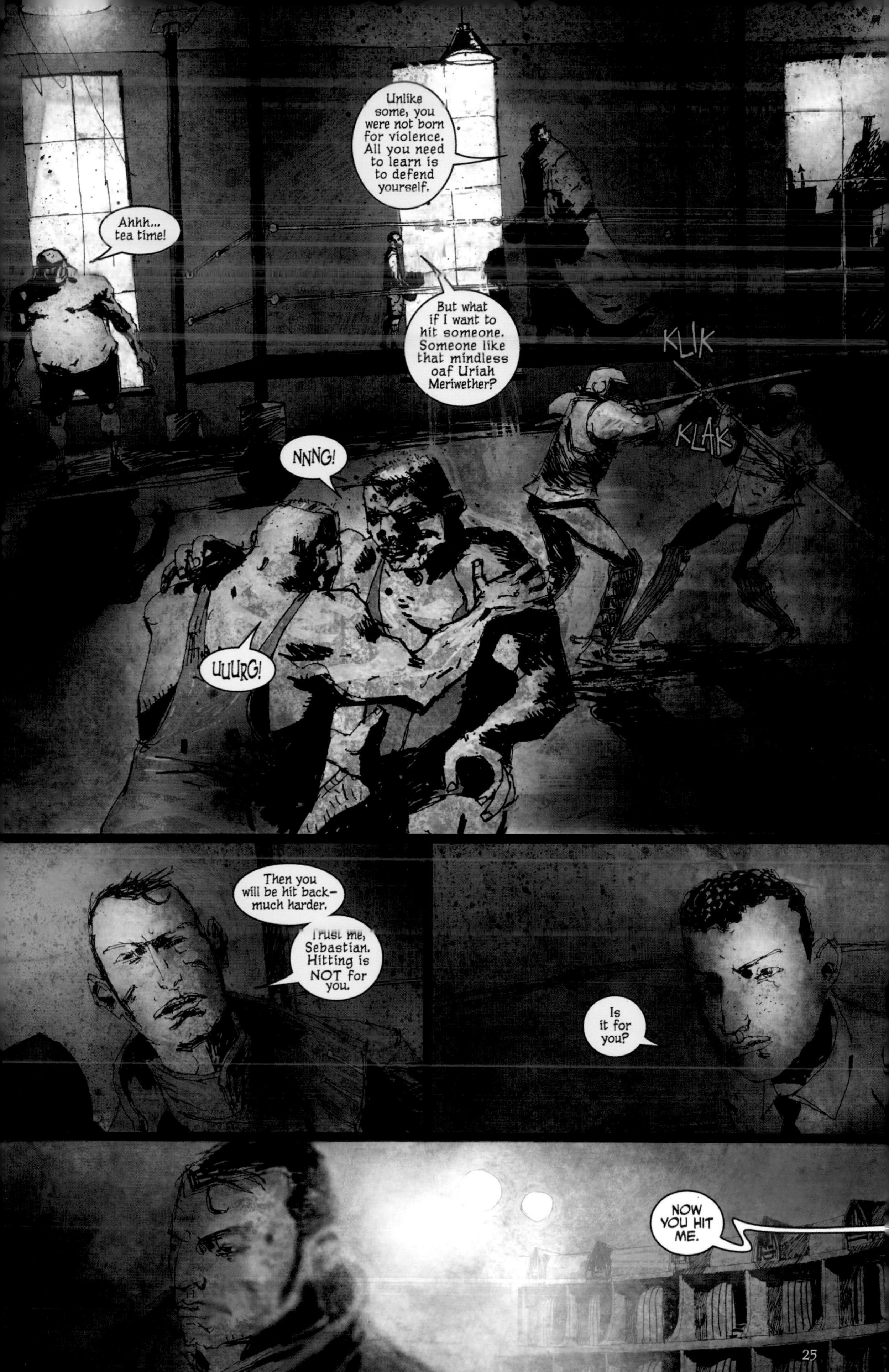
Unlike some, you were not born for violence. All you need to learn is to defend yourself.
Ahhh... tea time!
But what if I want to hit someone. Someone like that mindless oaf Uriah Meriwether?
KLIK
KLAK
NNNG!
UUURG!
Then you will be hit back- much harder.
Trust me, Sebastian. Hitting is NOT for you.
Is it for you?
NOW YOU HIT ME.

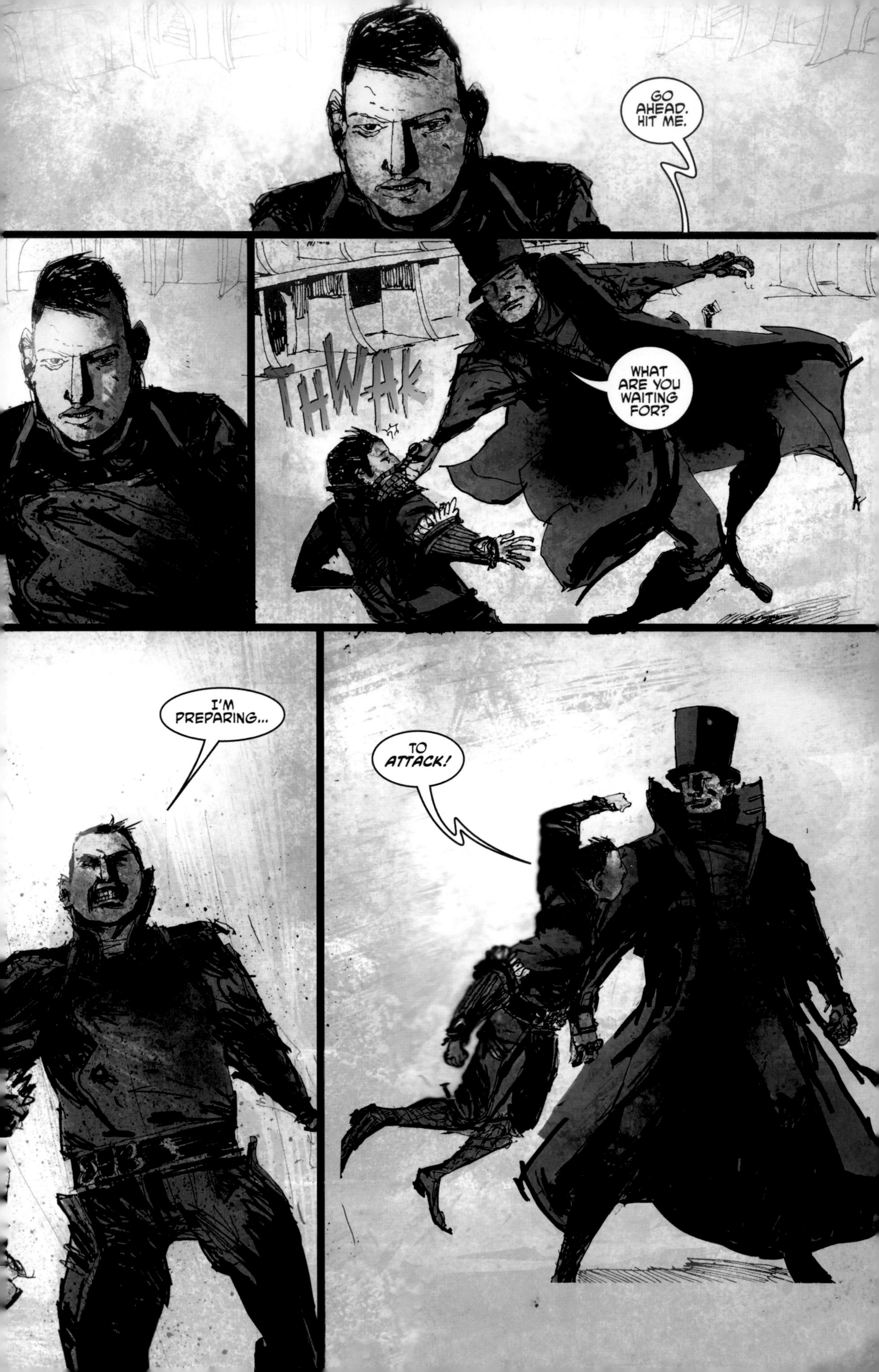
GO AHEAD. HIT ME.
THWAK
WHAT ARE YOU WAITING FOR?
I'M PREPARING...
TO *ATTACK!*

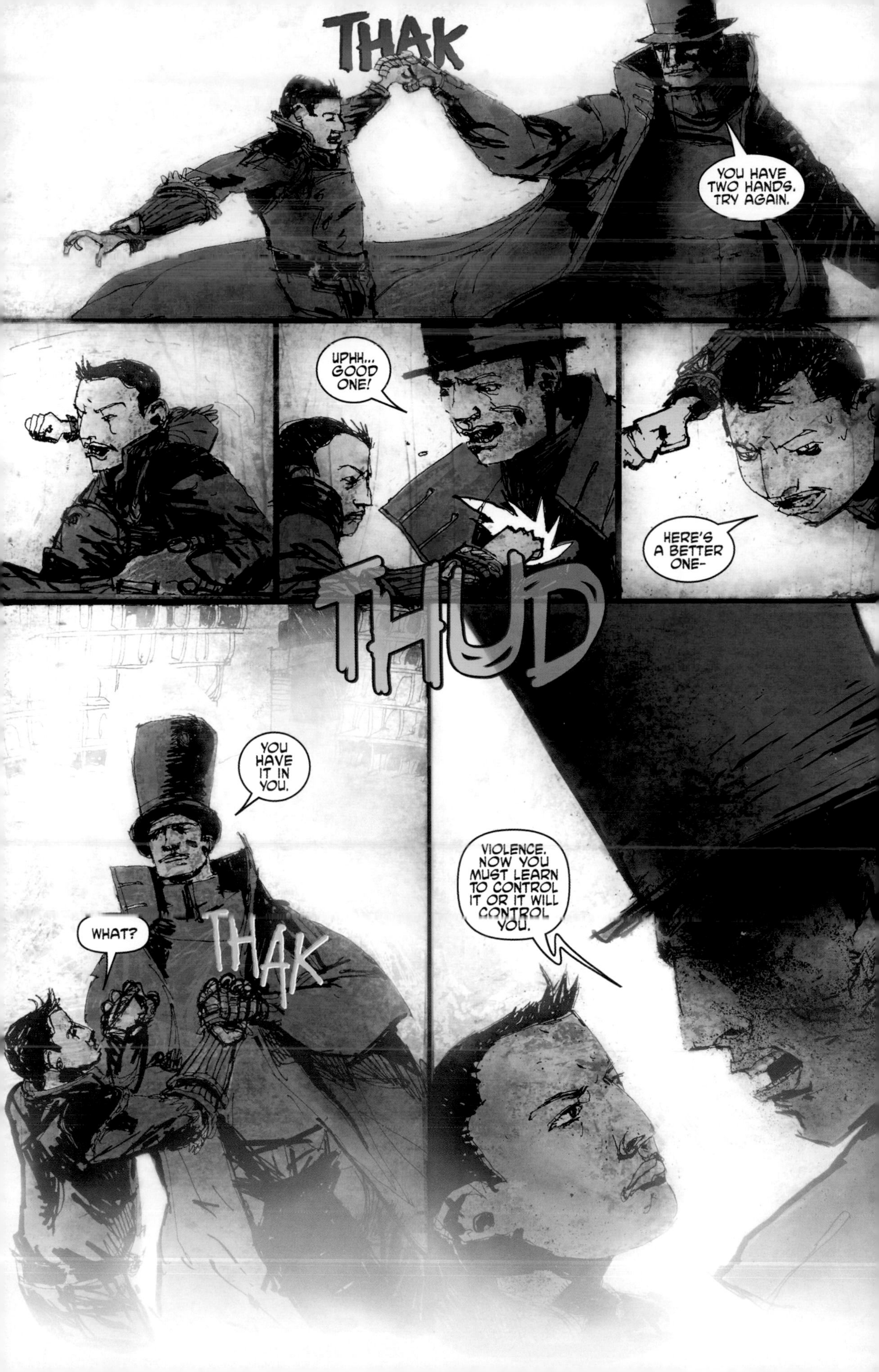
THAK
YOU HAVE TWO HANDS. TRY AGAIN.
UPHH... GOOD ONE!
HERE'S A BETTER ONE-
THUD
YOU HAVE IT IN YOU.
WHAT?
THAK
VIOLENCE. NOW YOU MUST LEARN TO CONTROL IT OR IT WILL CONTROL YOU.

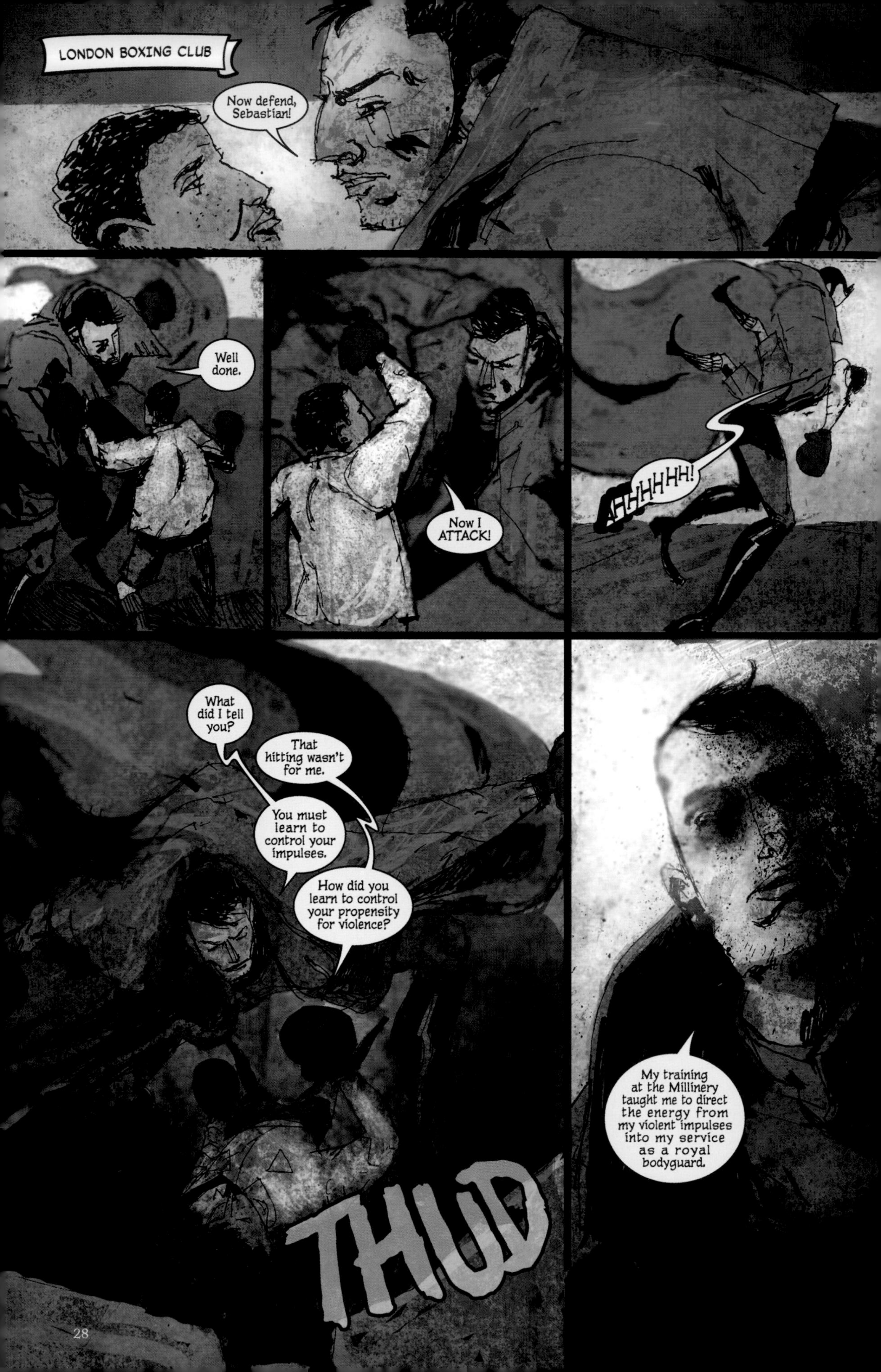
LONDON BOXING CLUB
Now defend, Sebastian!
Well done.
Now I ATTACK!
AHHHHHH!
What did I tell you?
That hitting wasn't for me.
You must learn to control your impulses.
How did you learn to control your propensity for violence?
THUD
My training at the Millinery taught me to direct the energy from my violent impulses into my service as a royal bodyguard.

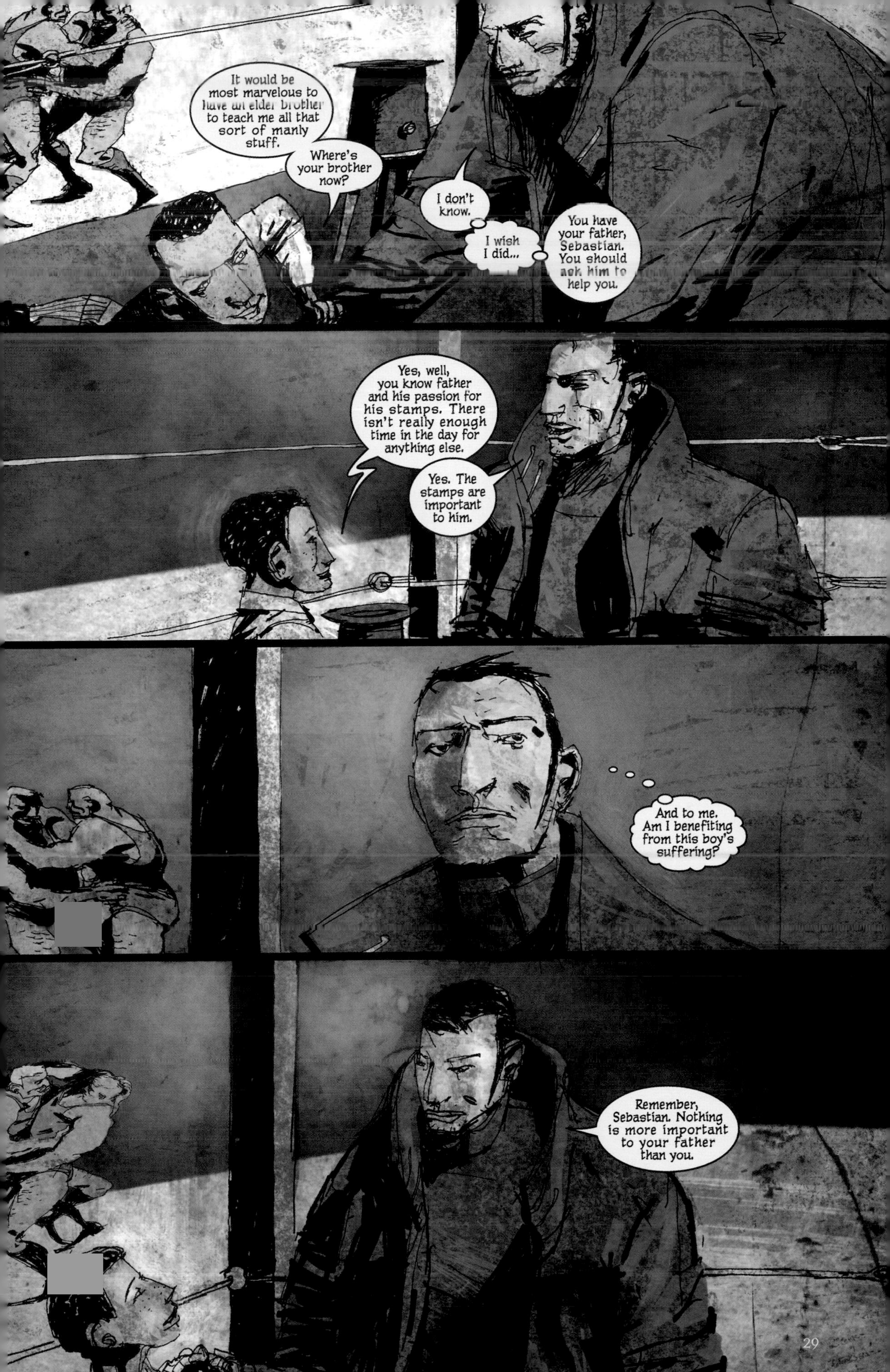
It would be most marvelous to have an elder brother to teach me all that sort of manly stuff.
Where's your brother now?
I don't know.
I wish I did...
You have your father, Sebastian. You should ask him to help you.
Yes, well, you know father and his passion for his stamps. There isn't really enough time in the day for anything else.
Yes. The stamps are important to him.
And to me. Am I benefiting from this boy's suffering?
Remember, Sebastian. Nothing is more important to your father than you.

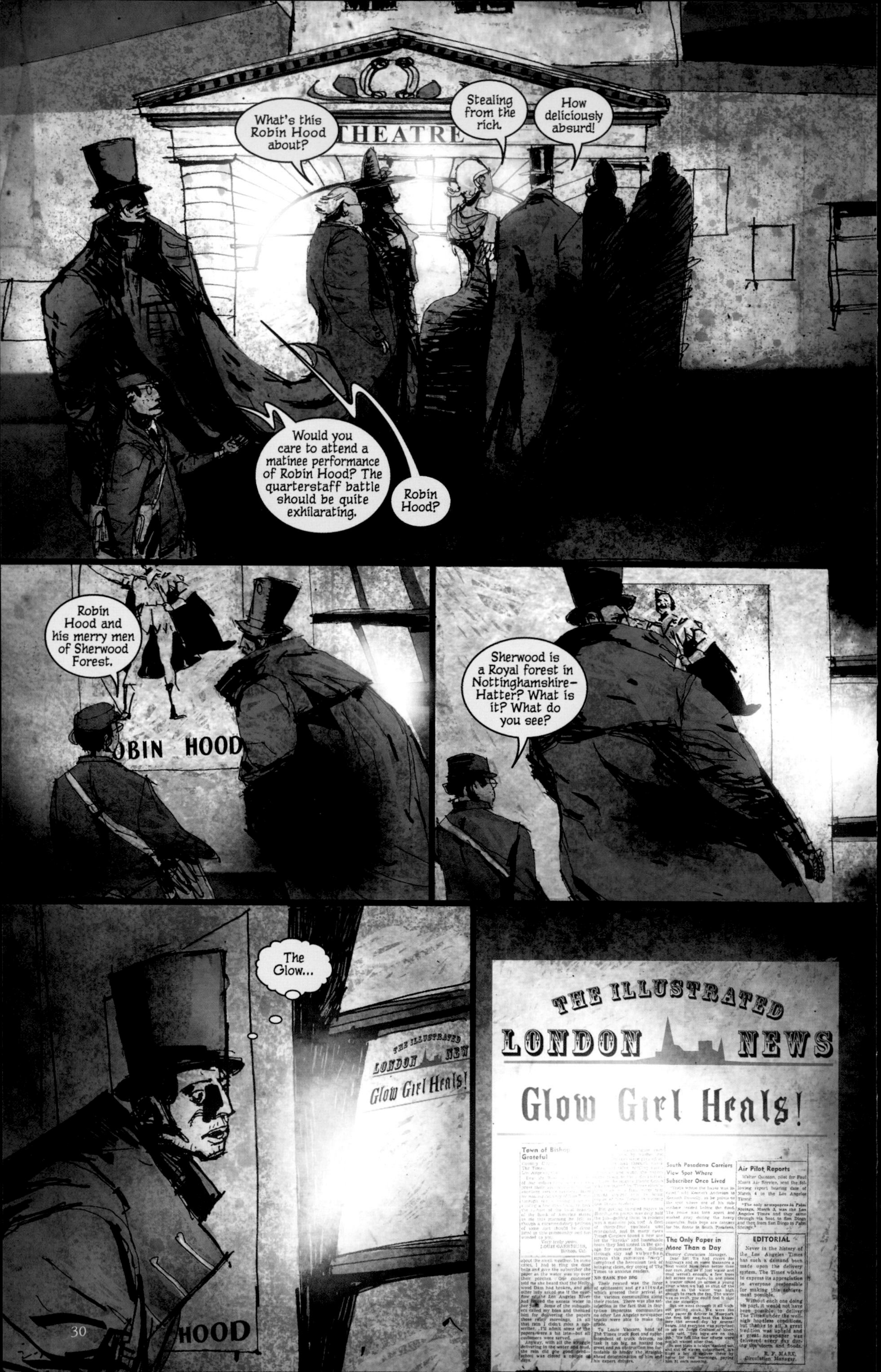
THEATRE
What's this Robin Hood about?
Stealing from the rich.
How deliciously absurd!
Would you care to attend a matinee performance of Robin Hood? The quarterstaff battle should be quite exhilarating.
Robin Hood?
Robin Hood and his merry men of Sherwood Forest.
OBIN HOOD
Sherwood is a Royal forest in Nottinghamshire– Hatter? What is it? What do you see?
The Glow...
THE ILLUSTRATED LONDON NEWS
Glow Girl Heals!
HOOD
THE ILLUSTRATED LONDON NEWS
Glow Girl Heals!
Town of Bishop Grateful
South Pasadena Carriers View Spot Where Subscriber Once Lived
Air Pilot Reports
The Only Paper in More Than a Day
NO TASK TOO BIG
EDITORIAL

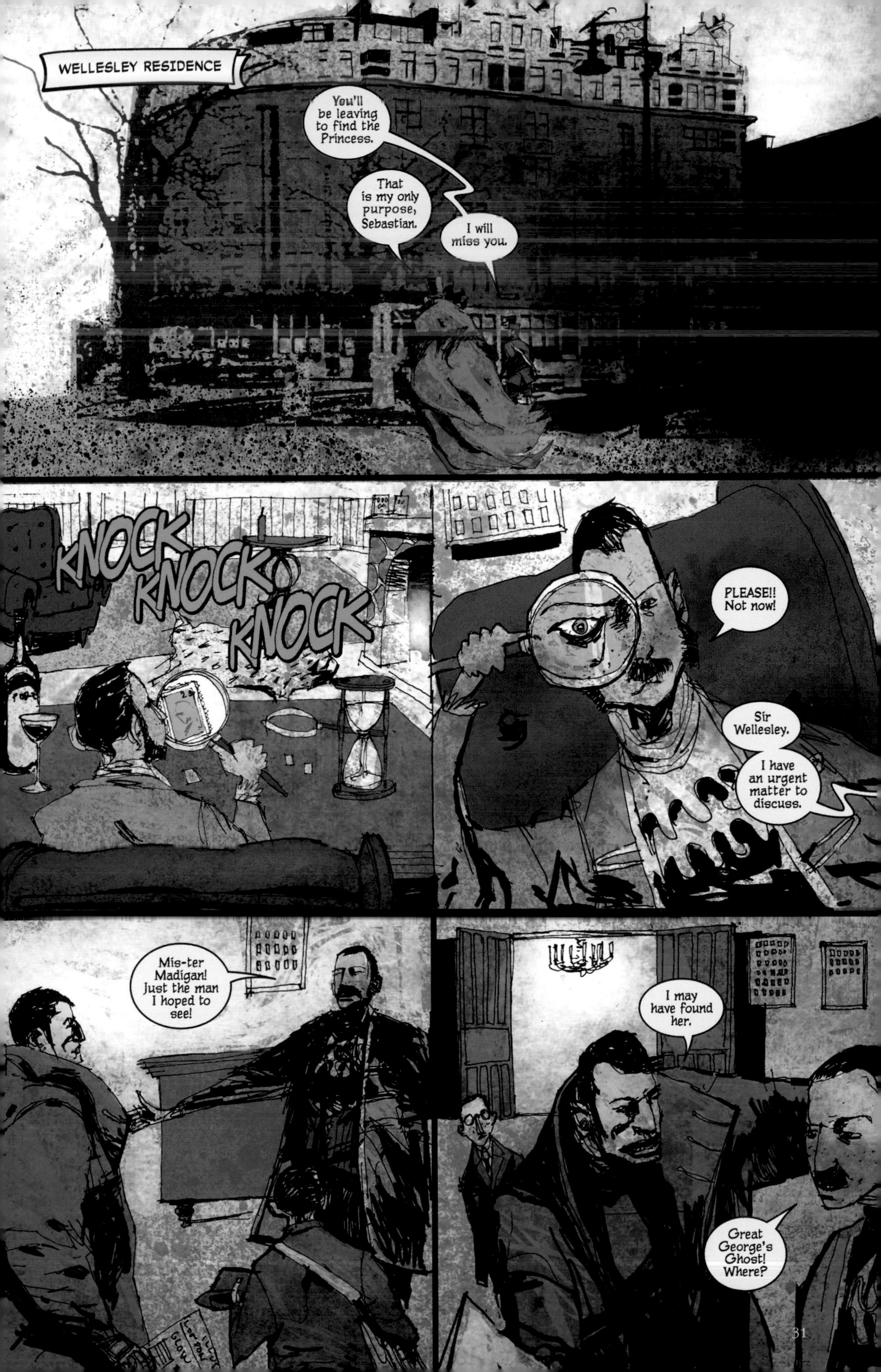
WELLESLEY RESIDENCE
You'll be leaving to find the Princess.
That is my only purpose, Sebastian.
I will miss you.
KNOCK KNOCK KNOCK
PLEASE!! Not now!
Sir Wellesley.
I have an urgent matter to discuss.
Mis-ter Madigan! Just the man I hoped to see!
I may have found her.
Great George's Ghost! Where?

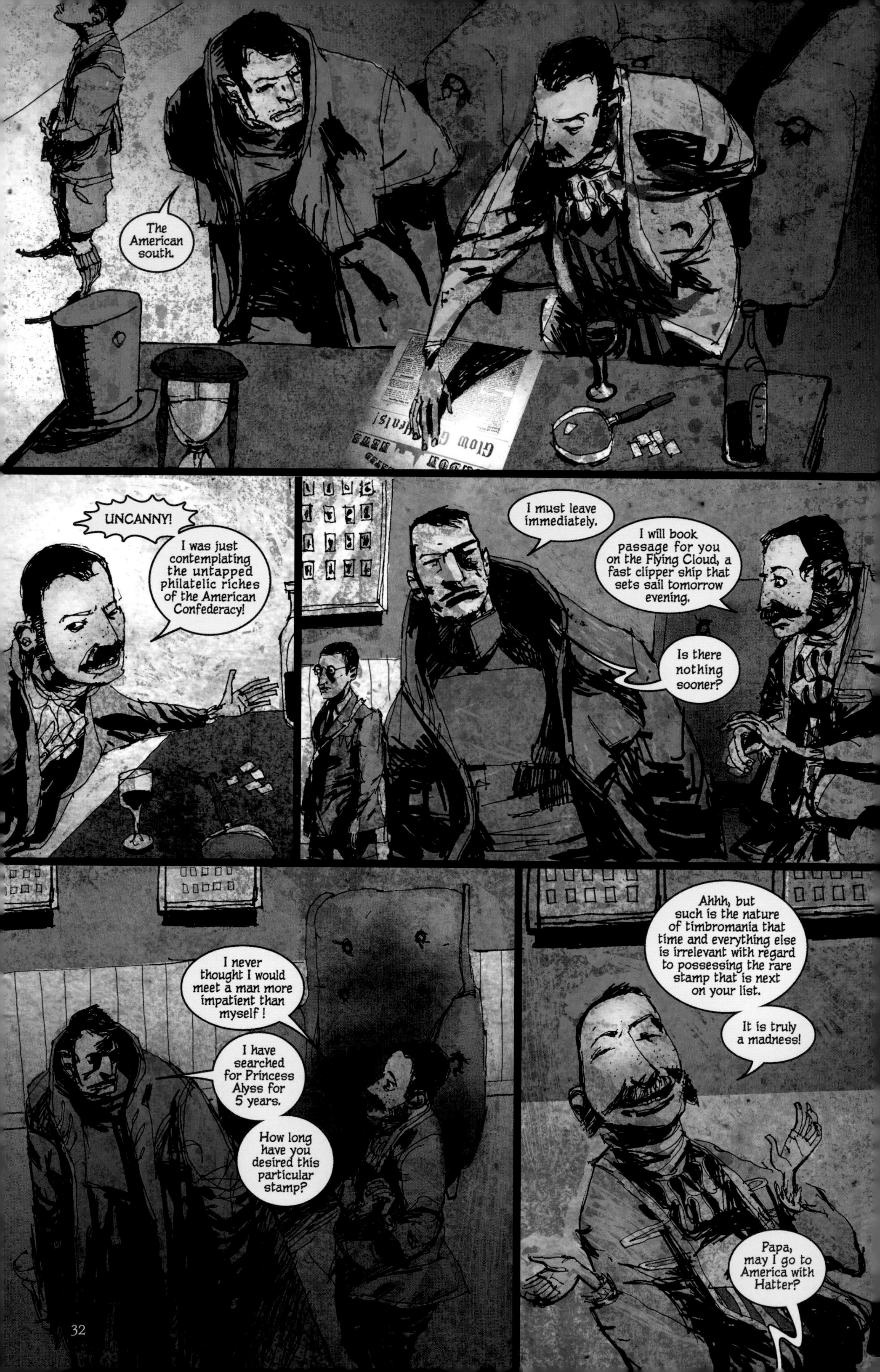
The American south.
UNCANNY!
I was just contemplating the untapped philatelic riches of the American Confederacy!
I must leave immediately.
I will book passage for you on the Flying Cloud, a fast clipper ship that sets sail tomorrow evening.
Is there nothing sooner?
I never thought I would meet a man more impatient than myself !
I have searched for Princess Alyss for 5 years.
How long have you desired this particular stamp?
Ahhh, but such is the nature of timbromania that time and everything else is irrelevant with regard to possessing the rare stamp that is next on your list.
It is truly a madness!
Papa, may I go to America with Hatter?

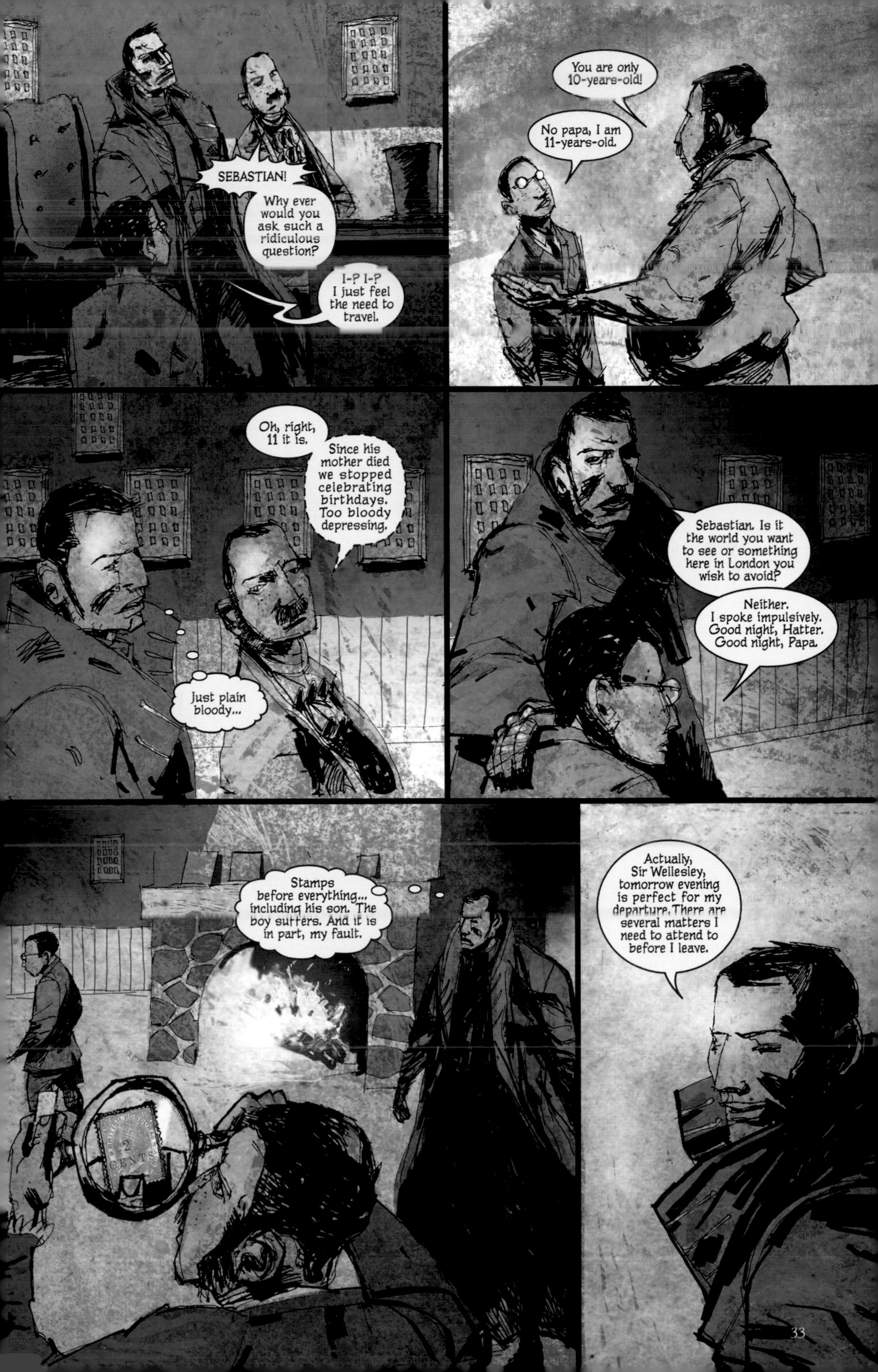
SEBASTIAN!
Why ever would you ask such a ridiculous question?
I-? I-? I just feel the need to travel.
You are only 10-years-old!
No papa, I am 11-years-old.
Oh, right, 11 it is.
Since his mother died we stopped celebrating birthdays. Too bloody depressing.
Just plain bloody...
Sebastian. Is it the world you want to see or something here in London you wish to avoid?
Neither. I spoke impulsively. Good night, Hatter. Good night, Papa.
Stamps before everything... including his son. The boy suffers. And it is in part, my fault.
Actually, Sir Wellesley, tomorrow evening is perfect for my departure. There are several matters I need to attend to before I leave.

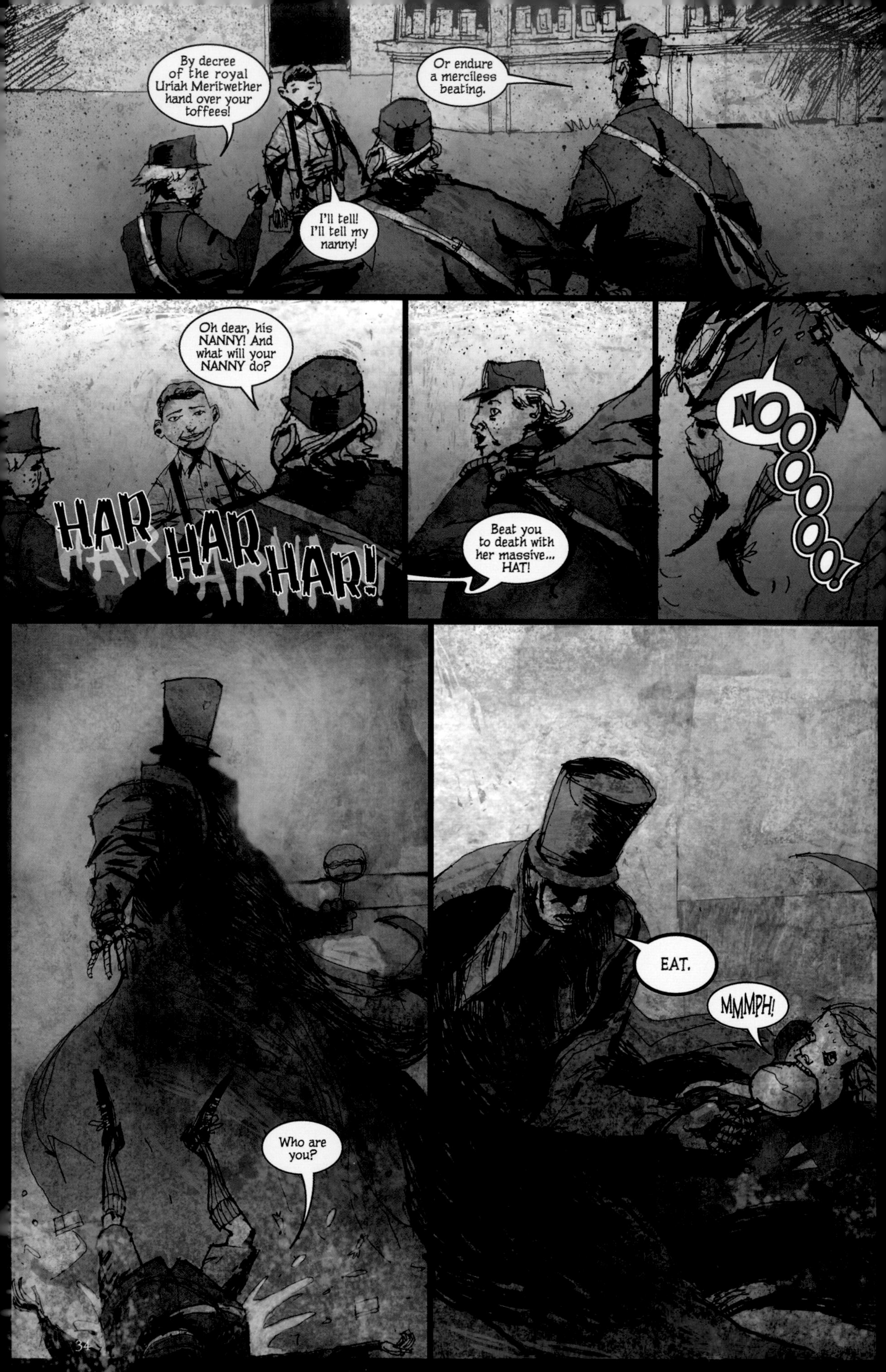

By decree of the royal Uriah Meritwether hand over your toffees!
Or endure a merciless beating.
I'll tell! I'll tell my nanny!
Oh dear, his NANNY! And what will your NANNY do?
HAR HAR HAR!
Beat you to death with her massive... HAT!
NOOOOOO!
Who are you?
EAT.
MMMPH!

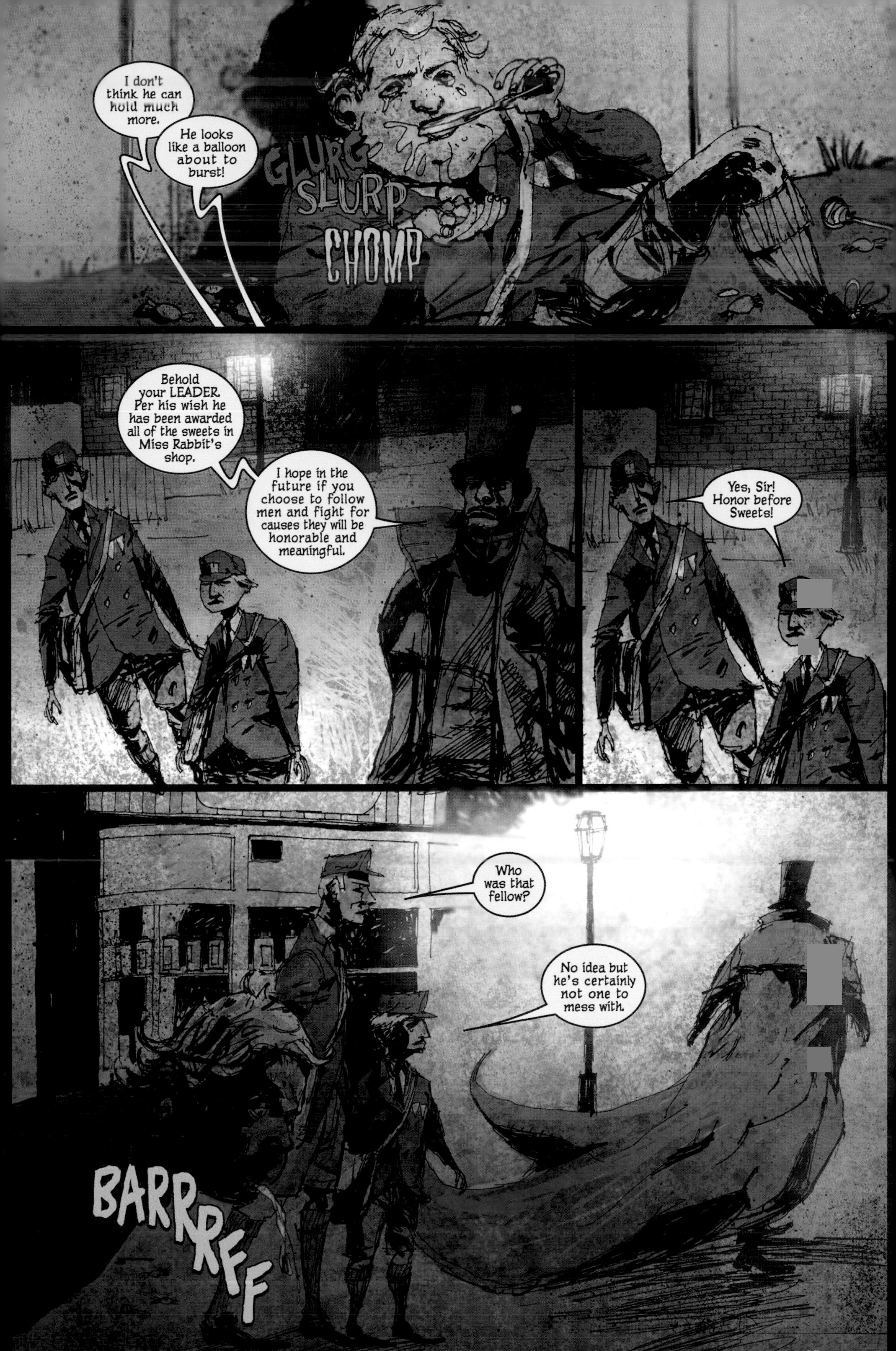
I don't think he can hold much more.
He looks like a balloon about to burst!
GLURG
SLURP
CHOMP
Behold your LEADER. Per his wish he has been awarded all of the sweets in Miss Rabbit's shop.
I hope in the future if you choose to follow men and fight for causes they will be honorable and meaningful.
Yes, Sir! Honor before Sweets!
Who was that fellow?
No idea but he's certainly not one to mess with.
BARRRFF

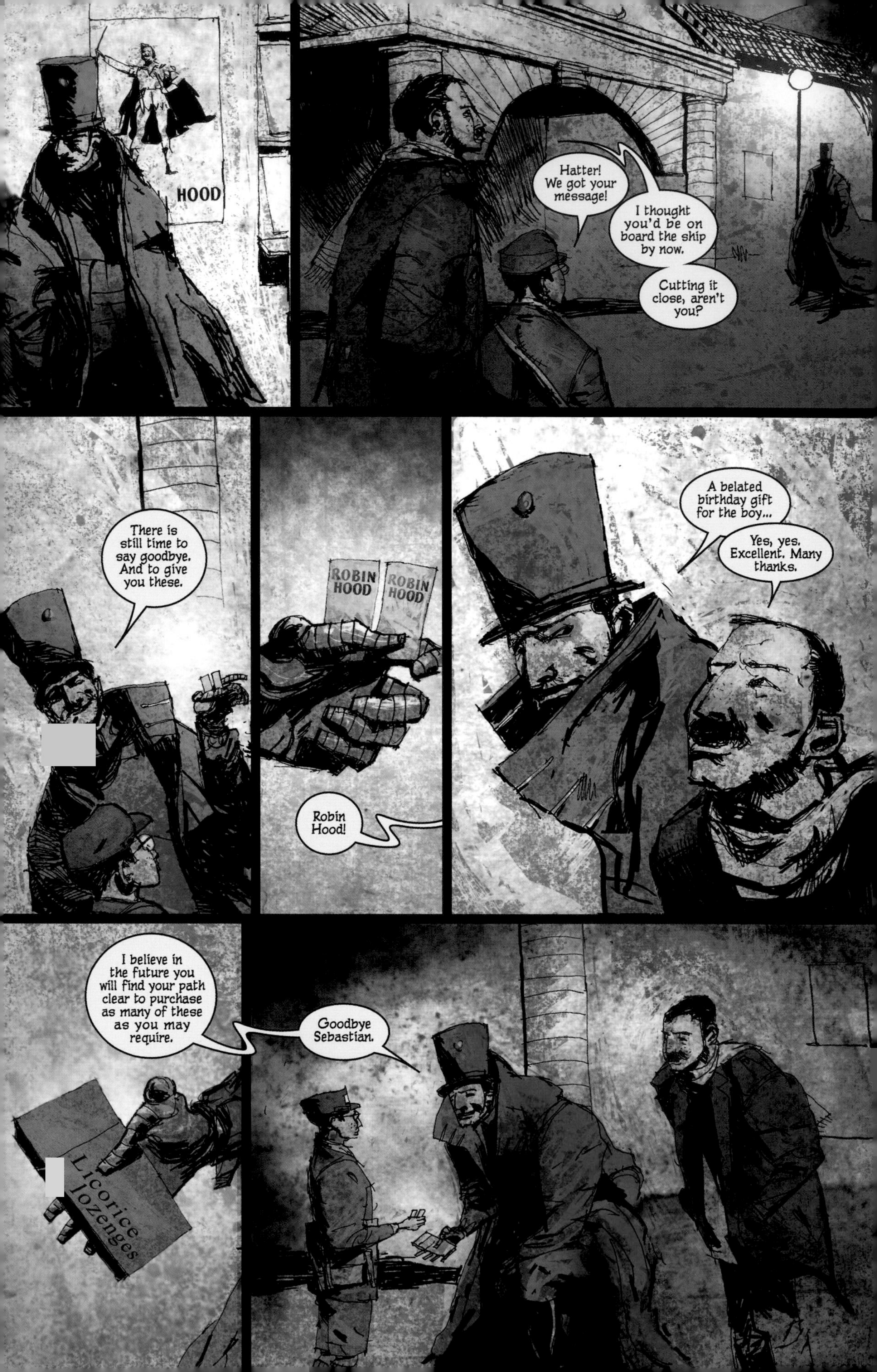
HOOD
Hatter! We got your message!
I thought you'd be on board the ship by now.
Cutting it close, aren't you?
There is still time to say goodbye. And to give you these.
ROBIN HOOD
ROBIN HOOD
Robin Hood!
A belated birthday gift for the boy...
Yes, yes. Excellent. Many thanks.
I believe in the future you will find your path clear to purchase as many of these as you may require.
Goodbye Sebastian.
Licorice lozenges

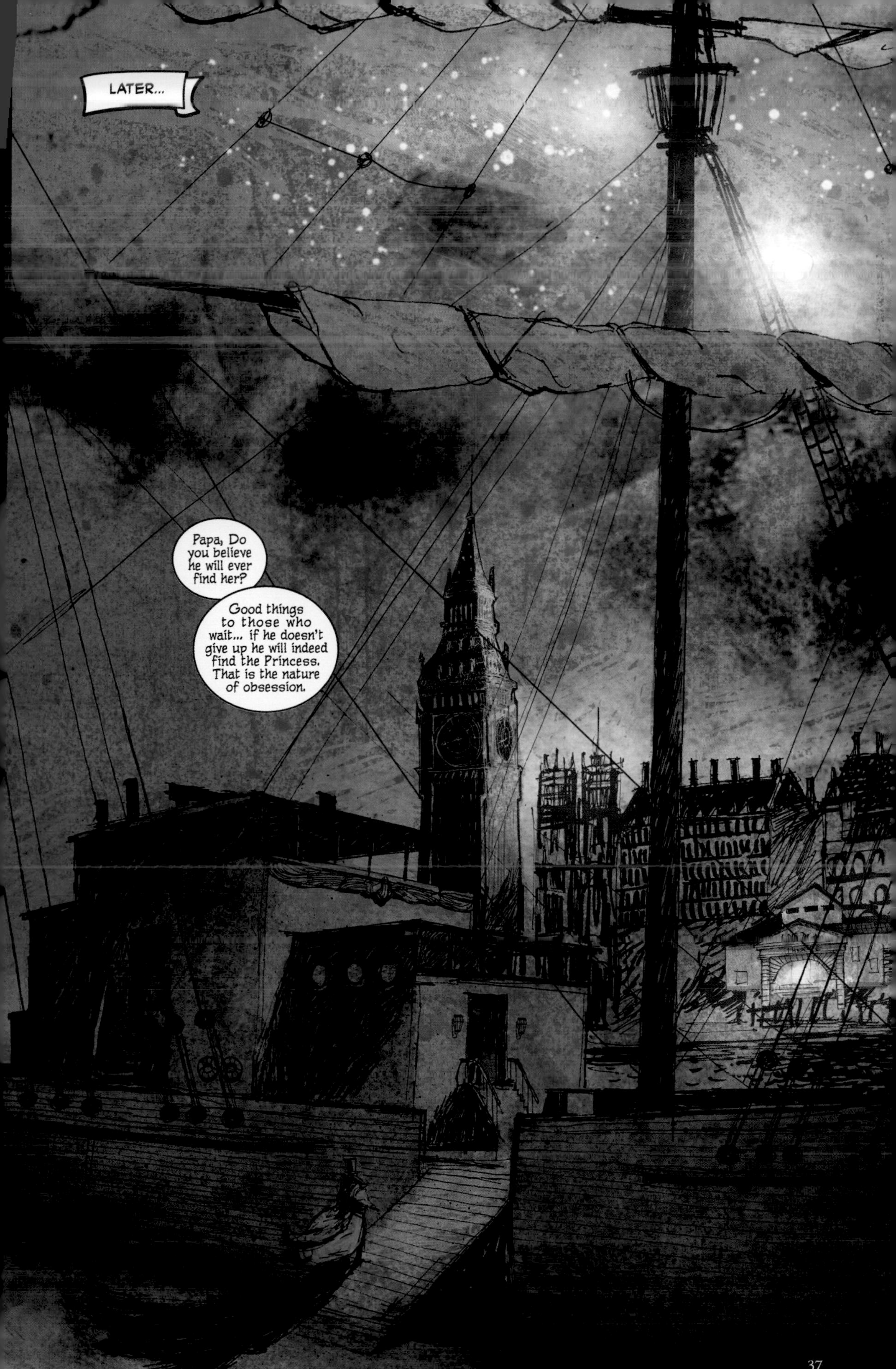
LATER...
Papa, Do you believe he will ever find her?
Good things to those who wait... if he doesn't give up he will indeed find the Princess. That is the nature of obsession.

A Flying Cloud transports me to the Land of Opportunity. The people say anything is possible there. That anything you can dream can be made manifest. Is America this world's Wonderland?

"The worst of madmen is a saint run mad." —ALEXANDER POPE

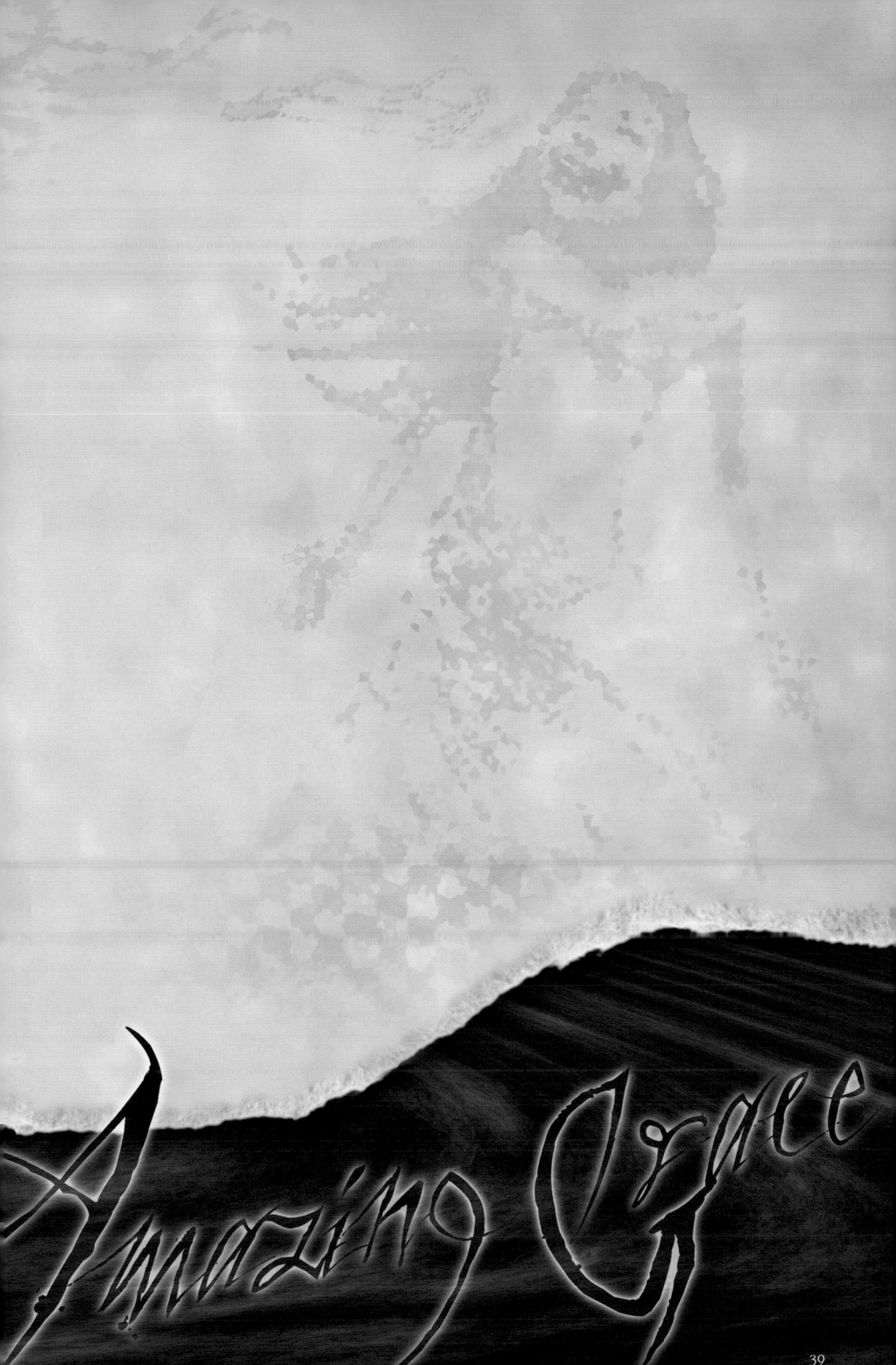

Amazing Grace

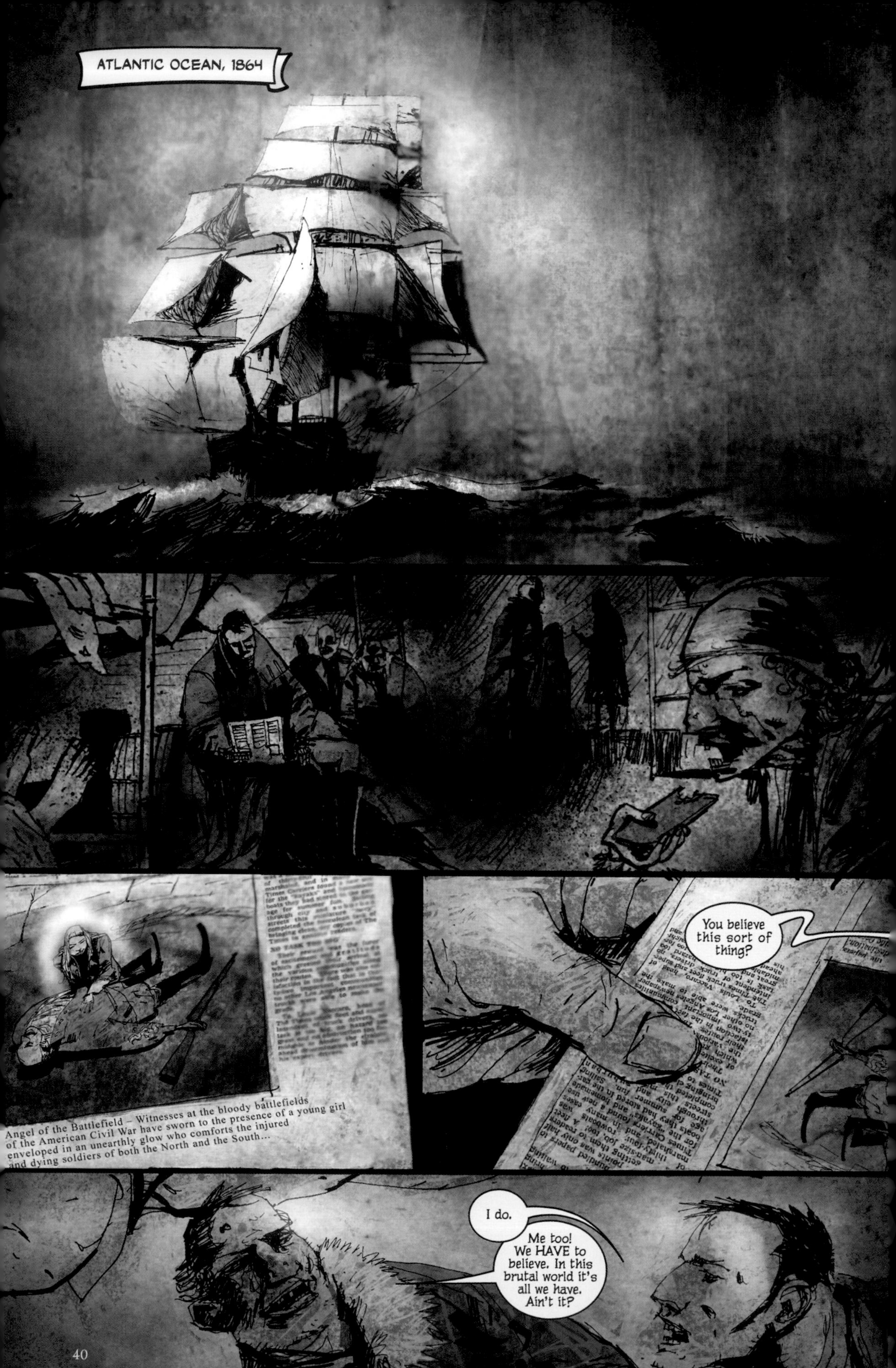
ATLANTIC OCEAN, 1864
Angel of the Battlefield – Witnesses at the bloody battlefields of the American Civil War have sworn to the presence of a young girl enveloped in an unearthly glow who comforts the injured and dying soldiers of both the North and the South…
You believe this sort of thing?
I do.
Me too! We HAVE to believe. In this brutal world it's all we have. Ain't it?

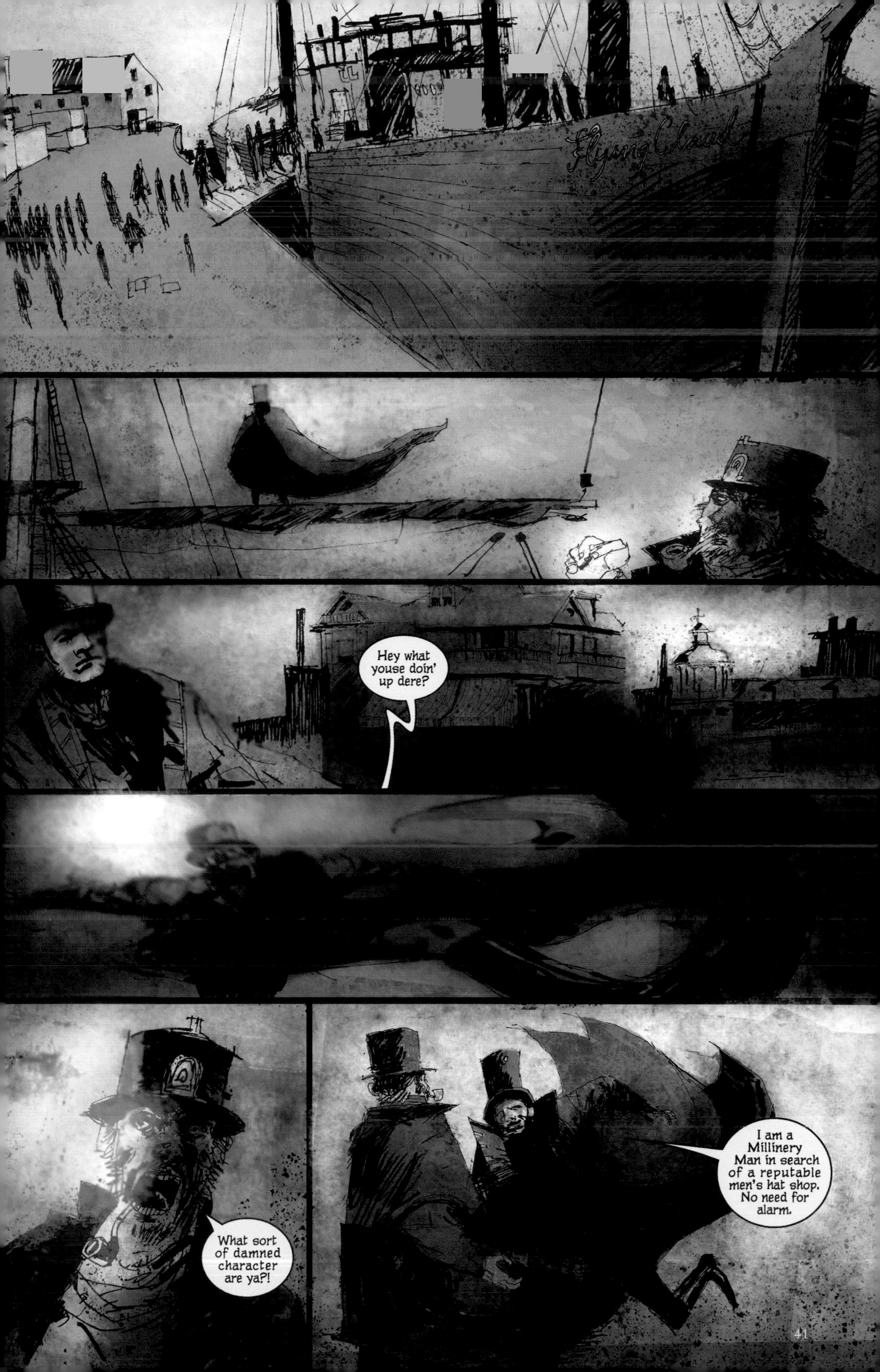
Flying Cloud
Hey what youse doin' up dere?
What sort of damned character are ya?!
I am a Millinery Man in search of a reputable men's hat shop. No need for alarm.

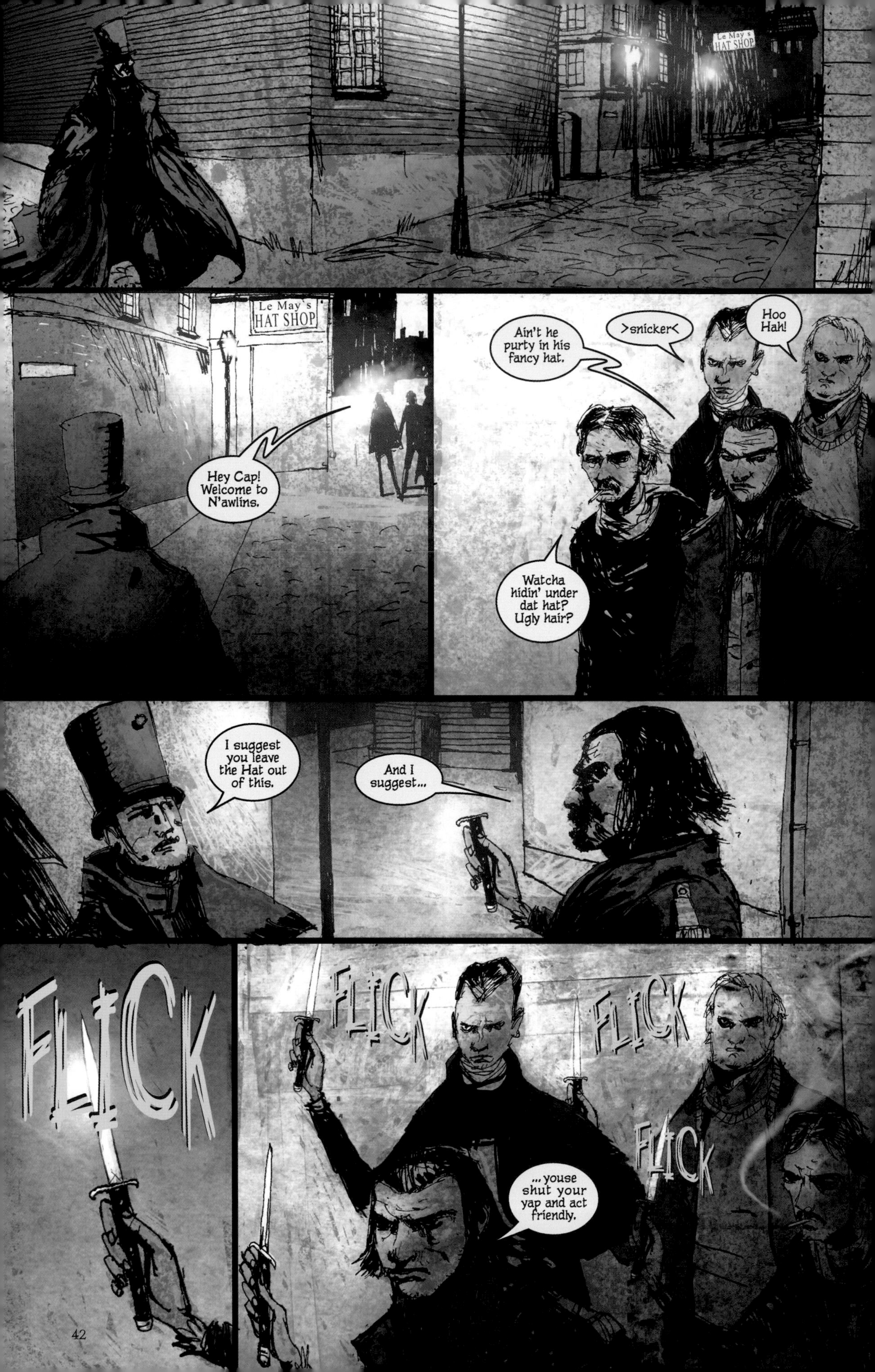
Le May's HAT SHOP
Le May's HAT SHOP
Hey Cap! Welcome to N'awlins.
Ain't he purty in his fancy hat.
>snicker<
Hoo Hah!
Watcha hidin' under dat hat? Ugly hair?
I suggest you leave the Hat out of this.
And I suggest...
FLICK
FLICK
FLICK
FLICK
...youse shut your yap and act friendly.

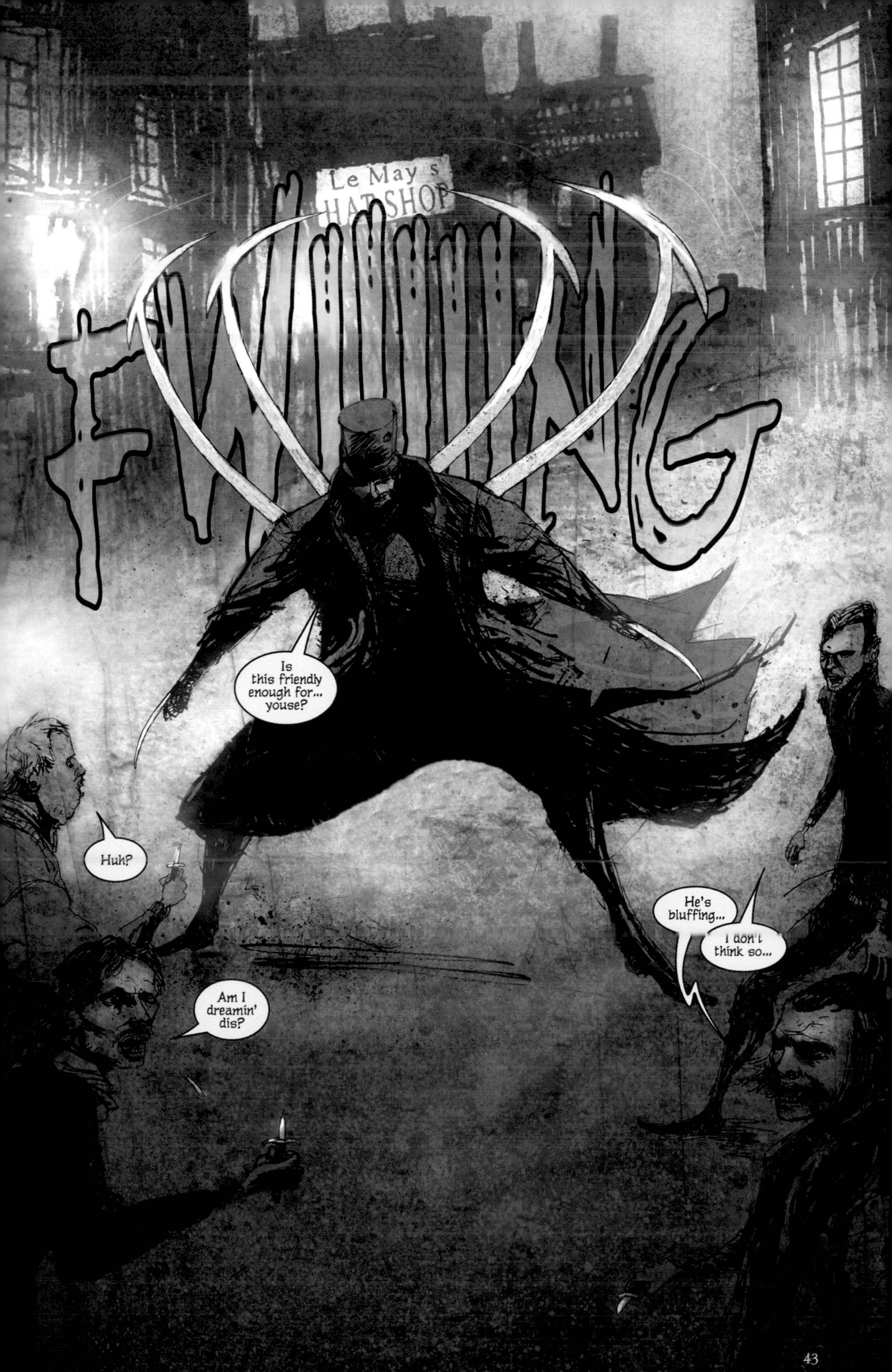
Le May s
HAT SHOP
FWIIIING
Is this friendly enough for... youse?
Huh?
Am I dreamin' dis?
He's bluffing...
I don't think so...

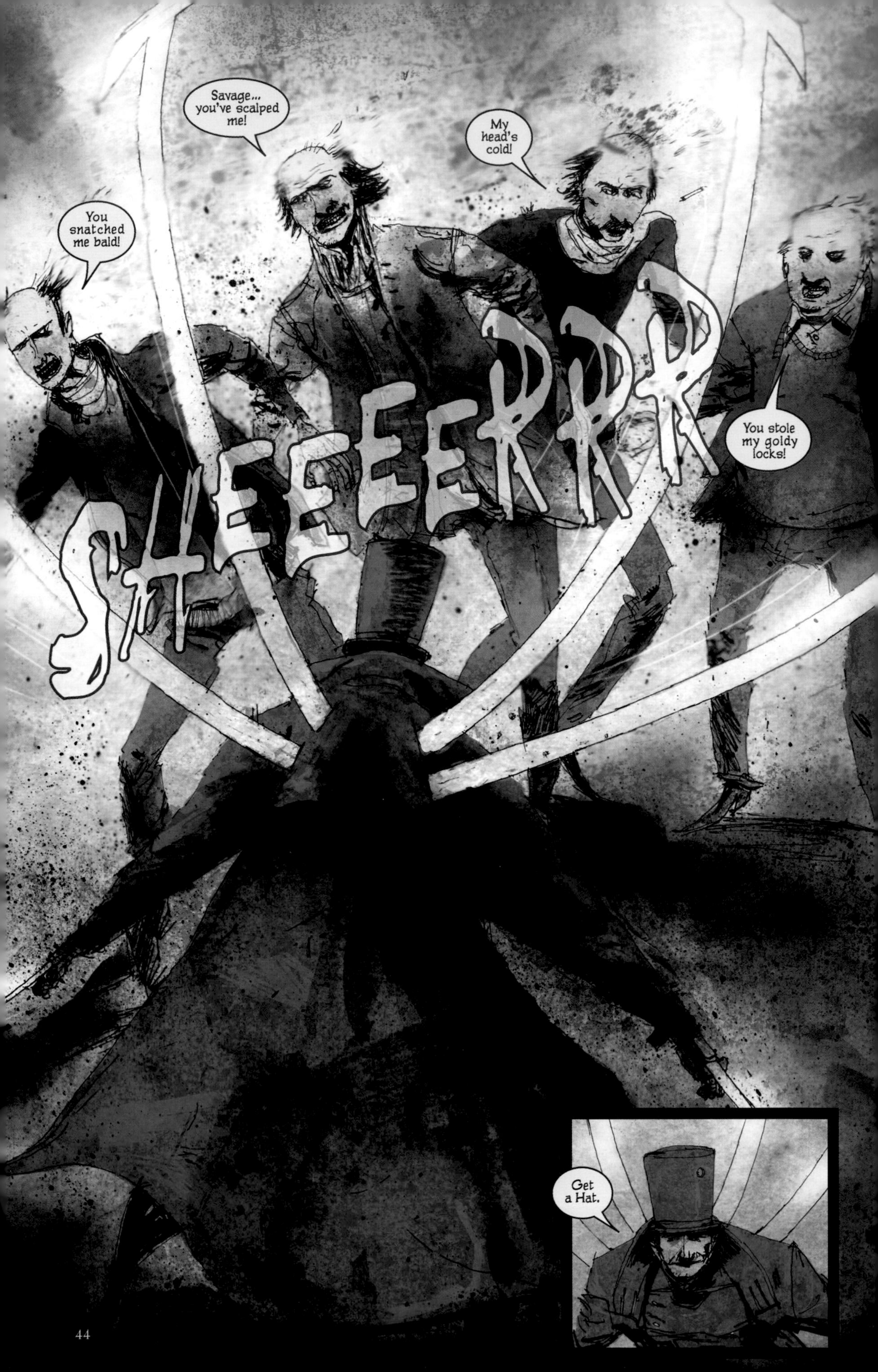
You snatched me bald!
Savage... you've scalped me!
My head's cold!
SHEEEERRRR
You stole my goldy locks!
Get a Hat.

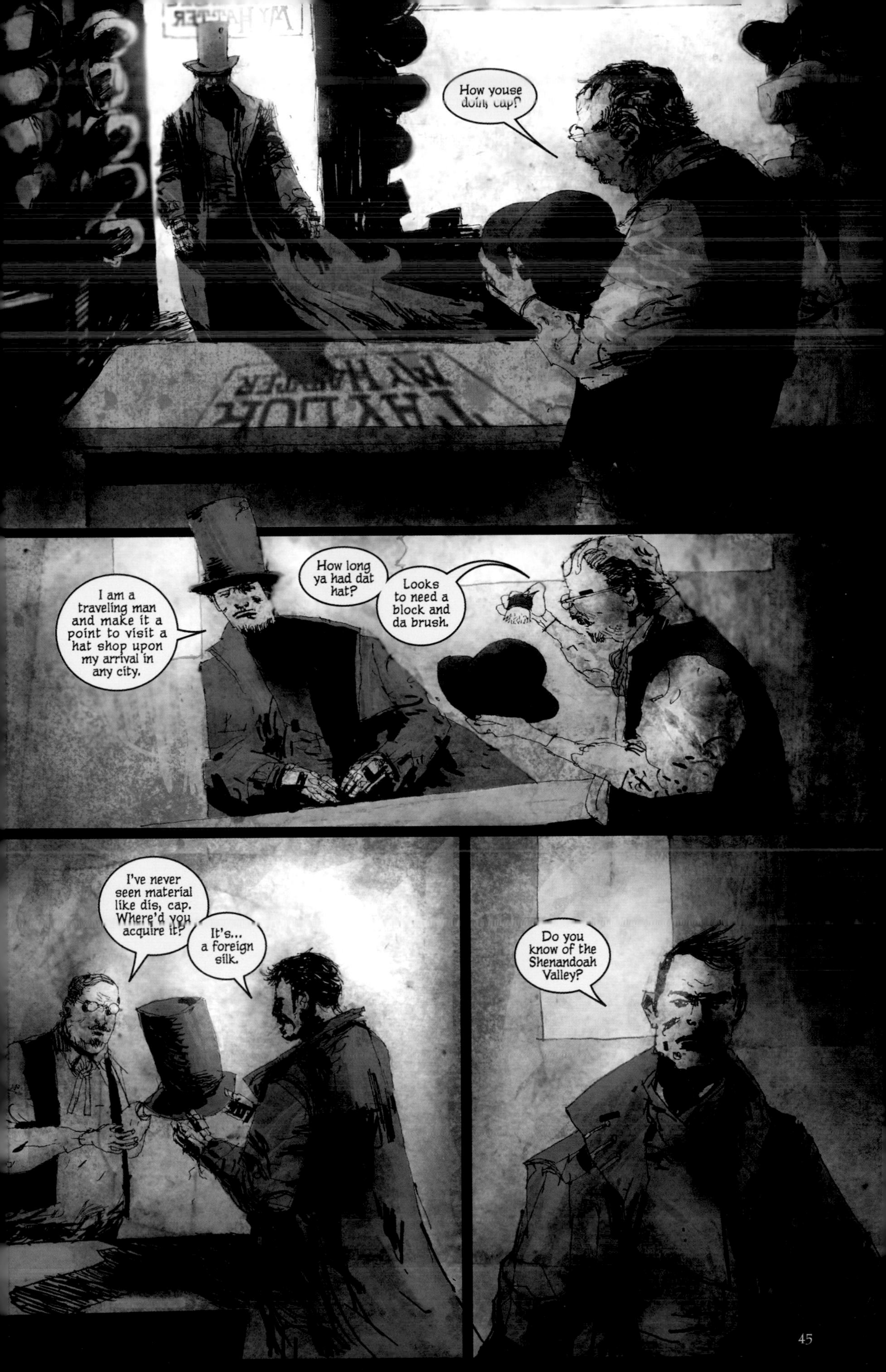

MY HATTER
How youse doin, cap?
TAYLOR MY HATTER
I am a traveling man and make it a point to visit a hat shop upon my arrival in any city.
How long ya had dat hat?
Looks to need a block and da brush.
I've never seen material like dis, cap. Where'd you acquire it?
It's... a foreign silk.
Do you know of the Shenandoah Valley?

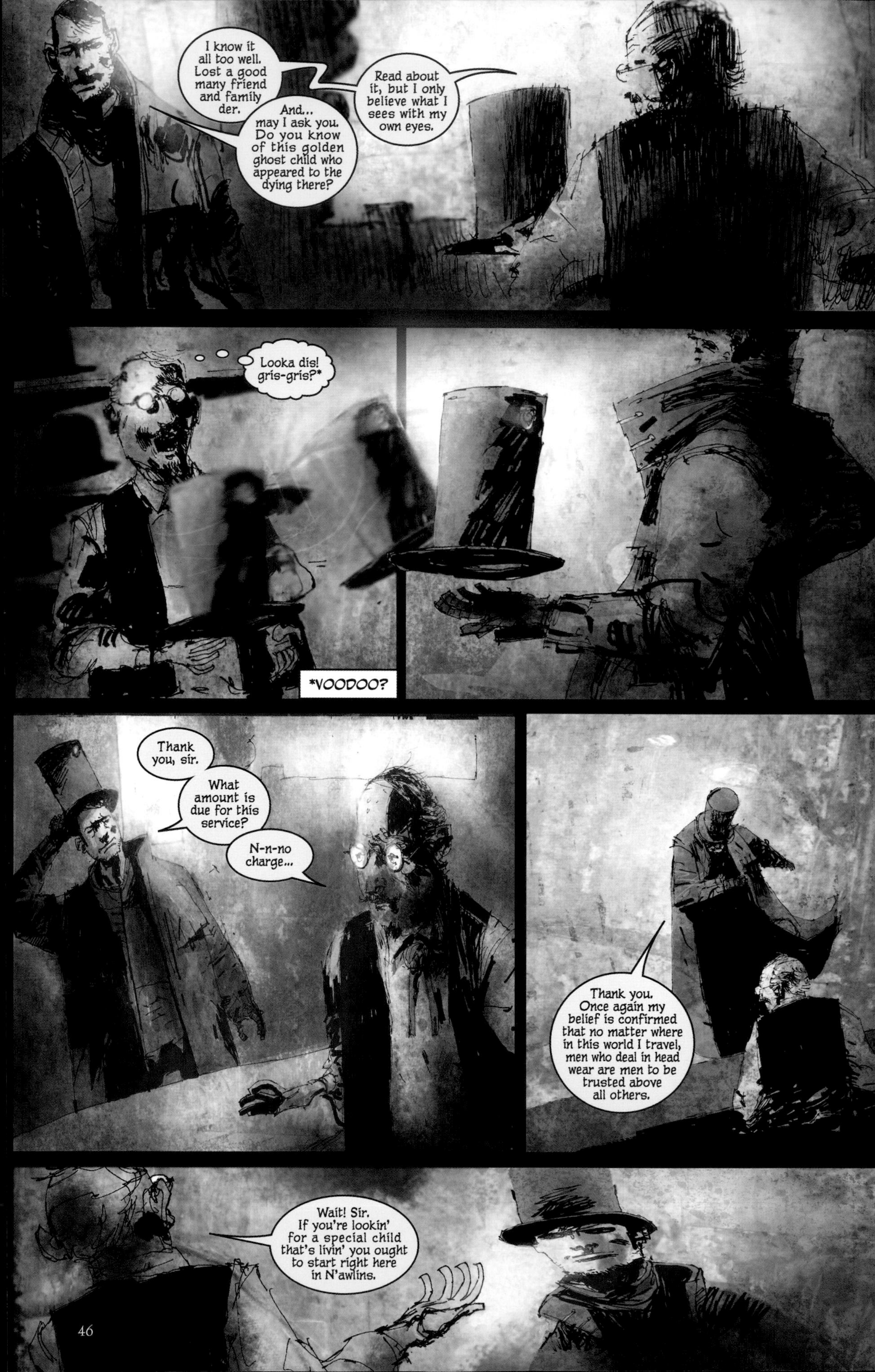
I know it all too well. Lost a good many friend and family der.
Read about it, but I only believe what I sees with my own eyes.
And... may I ask you. Do you know of this golden ghost child who appeared to the dying there?
Looka dis! gris-gris?*
*VOODOO?
Thank you, sir.
What amount is due for this service?
N-n-no charge...
Thank you. Once again my belief is confirmed that no matter where in this world I travel, men who deal in head wear are men to be trusted above all others.
Wait! Sir. If you're lookin' for a special child that's livin' you ought to start right here in N'awlins.

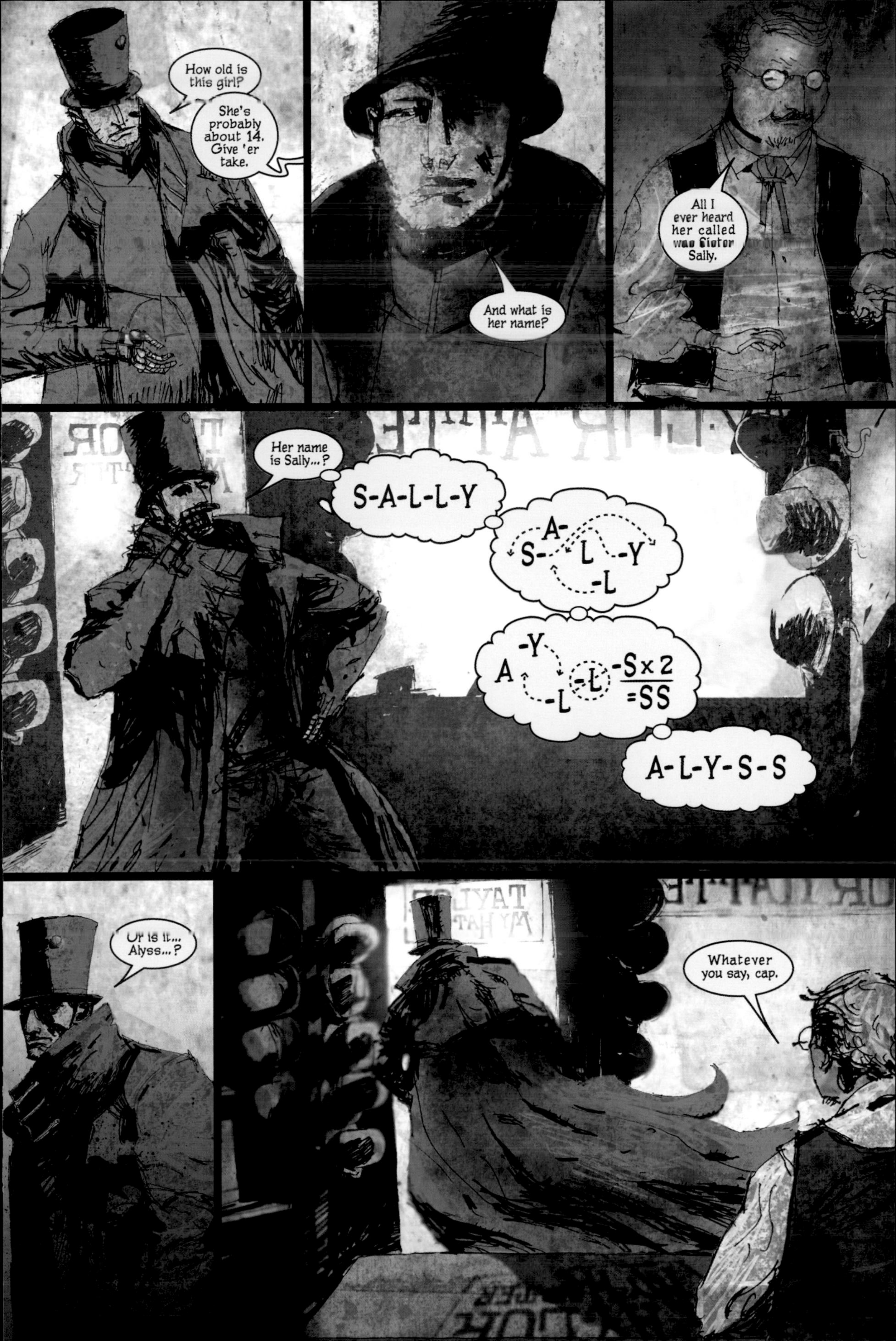
How old is this girl?
She's probably about 14. Give 'er take.
And what is her name?
All I ever heard her called was Sister Sally.
Her name is Sally...?
S-A-L-L-Y
-A- S- L -Y -L
A -Y -L -L -S x 2 =SS
A-L-Y-S-S
Or is it... Alyss...?
Whatever you say, cap.

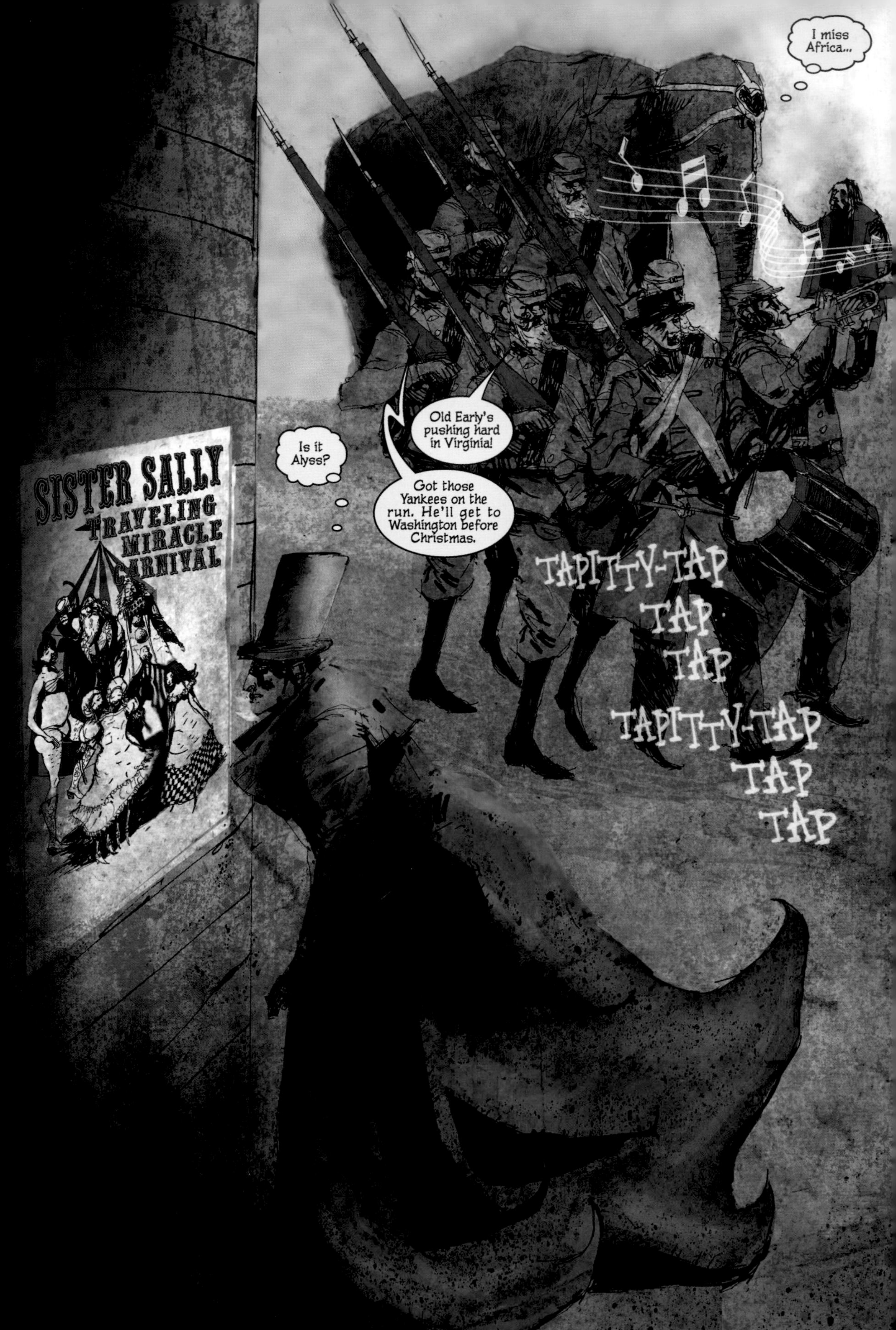
I miss Africa...
Is it Alyss?
Old Early's pushing hard in Virginia!
Got those Yankees on the run. He'll get to Washington before Christmas.
TAPITTY-TAP
TAP
TAP
TAPITTY-TAP
TAP
TAP
SISTER SALLY
TRAVELING MIRACLE CARNIVAL

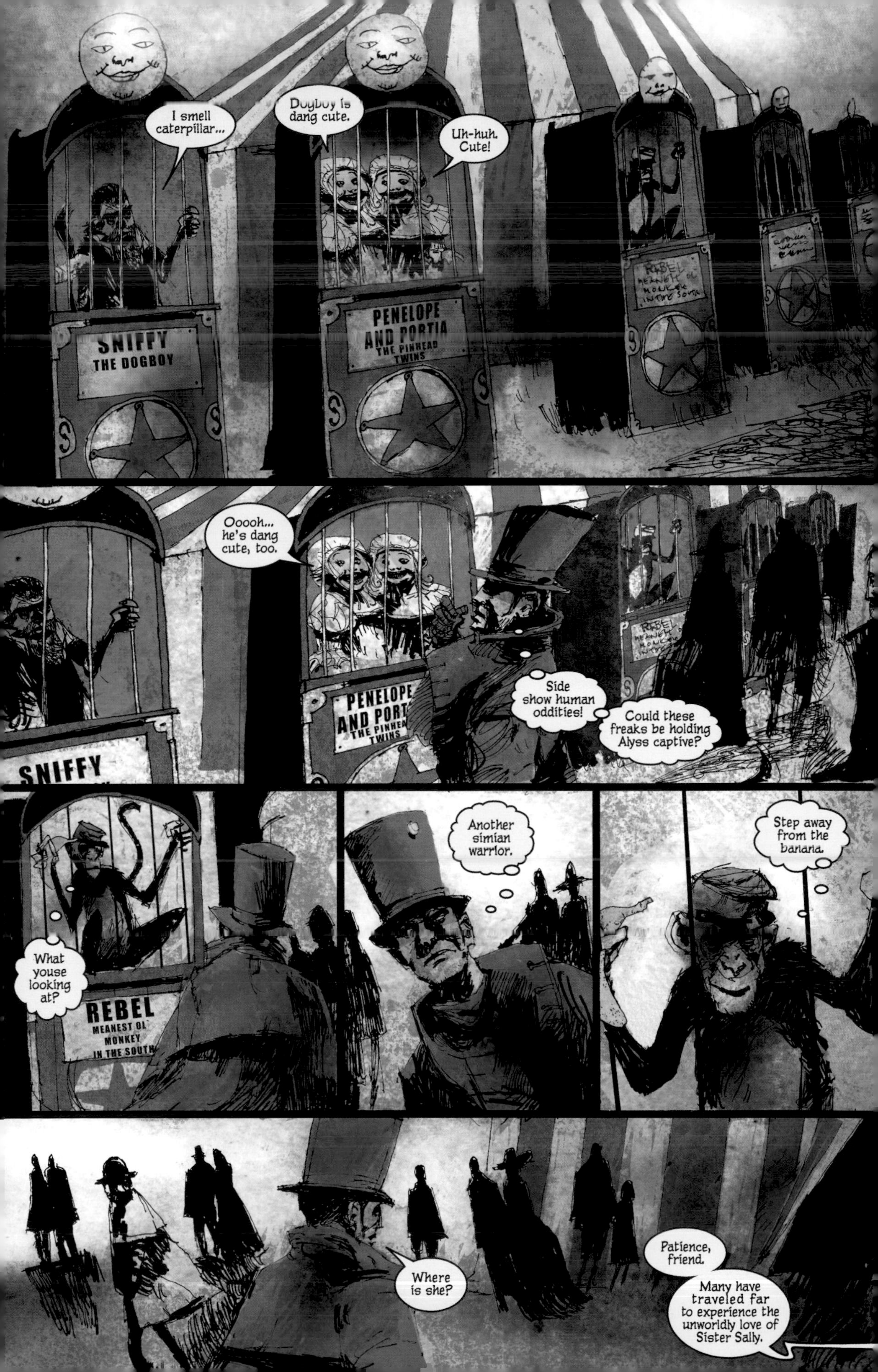
I smell caterpillar...
Dogboy is dang cute.
Uh-huh. Cute!
SNIFFY THE DOGBOY
PENELOPE AND PORTIA THE PINHEAD TWINS
Ooooh... he's dang cute, too.
Side show human oddities!
Could these freaks be holding Alyss captive?
What youse looking at?
REBEL MEANEST OL MONKEY IN THE SOUTH
Another simian warrior.
Step away from the banana.
Where is she?
Patience, friend.
Many have traveled far to experience the unworldly love of Sister Sally.

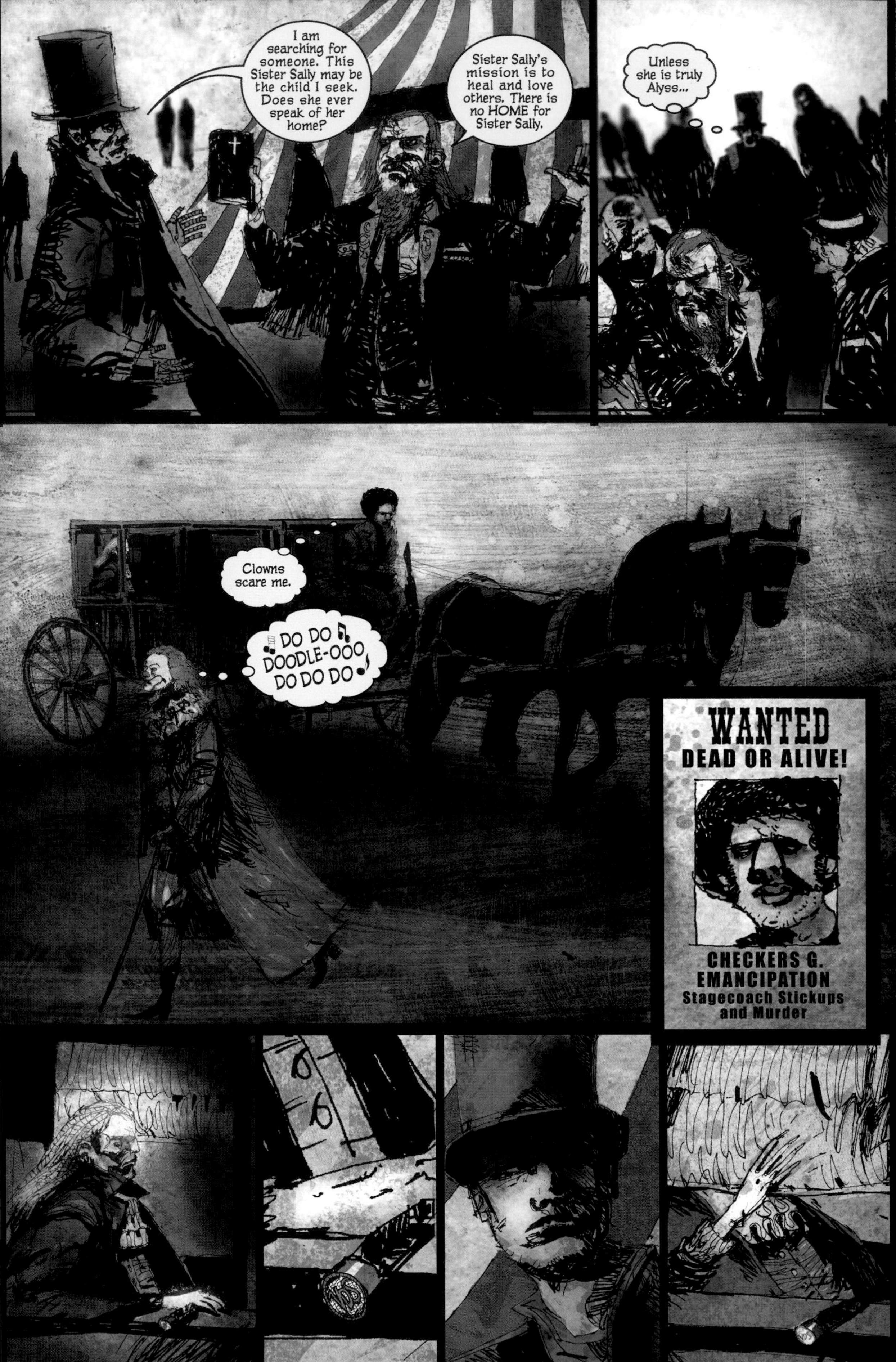
I am searching for someone. This Sister Sally may be the child I seek. Does she ever speak of her home?
Sister Sally's mission is to heal and love others. There is no HOME for Sister Sally.
Unless she is truly Alyss...
Clowns scare me.
DO DO DOODLE-OOO DO DO DO
WANTED
DEAD OR ALIVE!
CHECKERS G. EMANCIPATION
Stagecoach Stickups and Murder

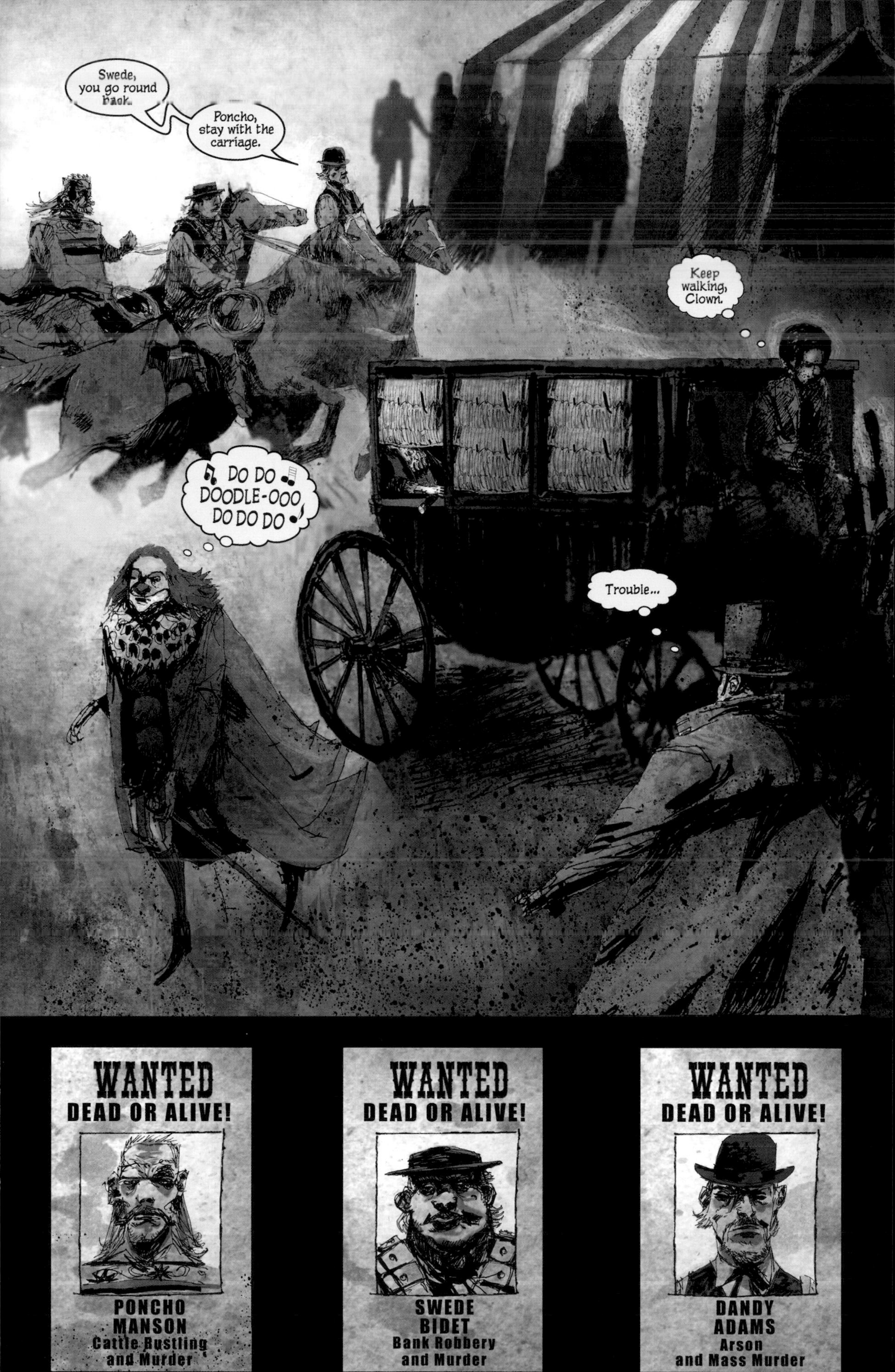
Swede, you go round back.
Poncho, stay with the carriage.
Keep walking, Clown.
DO DO DOODLE-OOO DO DO DO
Trouble...
WANTED
DEAD OR ALIVE!
PONCHO MANSON
Cattle Bustling and Murder
WANTED
DEAD OR ALIVE!
SWEDE BIDET
Bank Robbery and Murder
WANTED
DEAD OR ALIVE!
DANDY ADAMS
Arson and Mass Murder

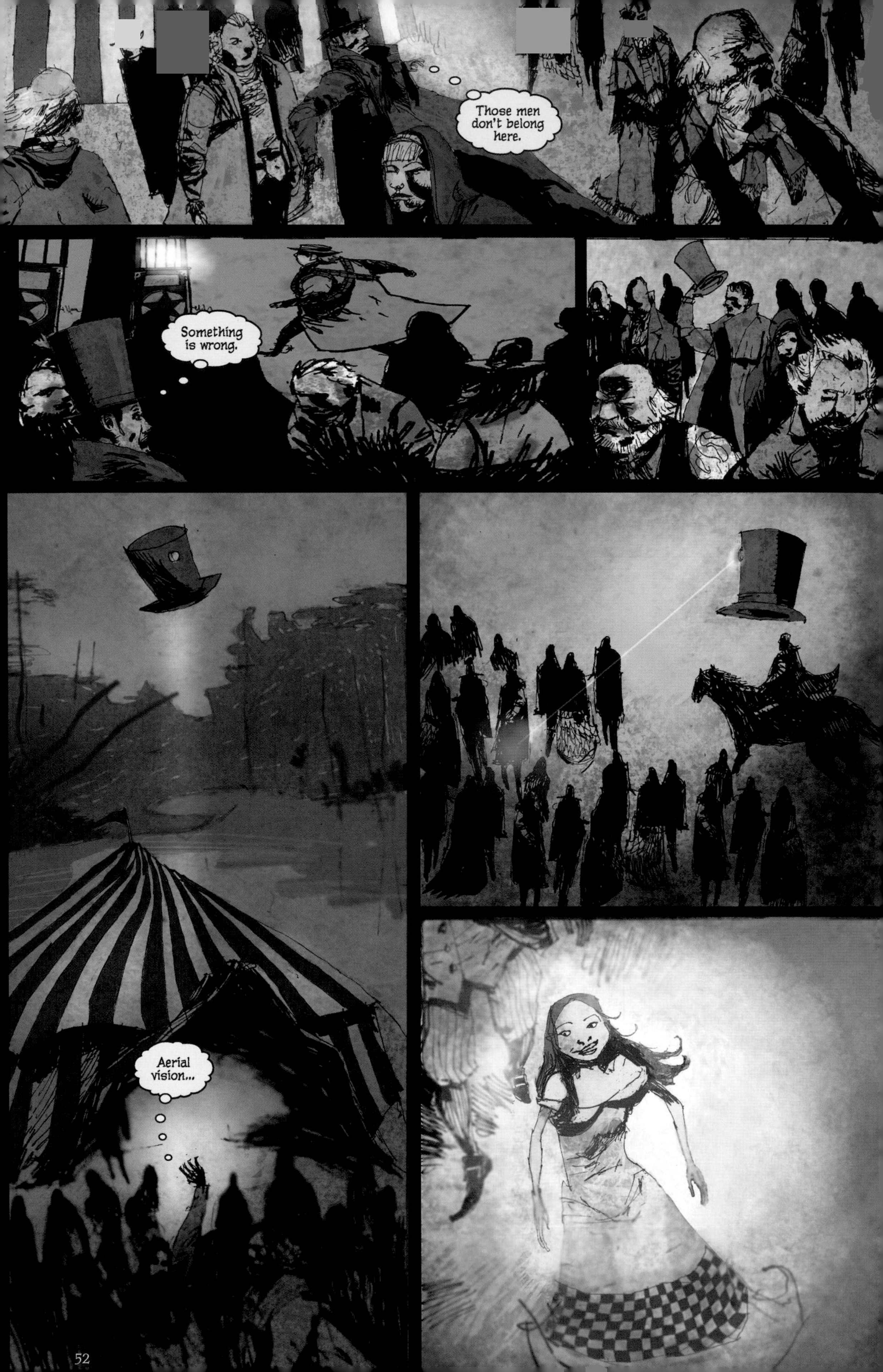
Those men don't belong here.
Something is wrong.
Aerial vision...

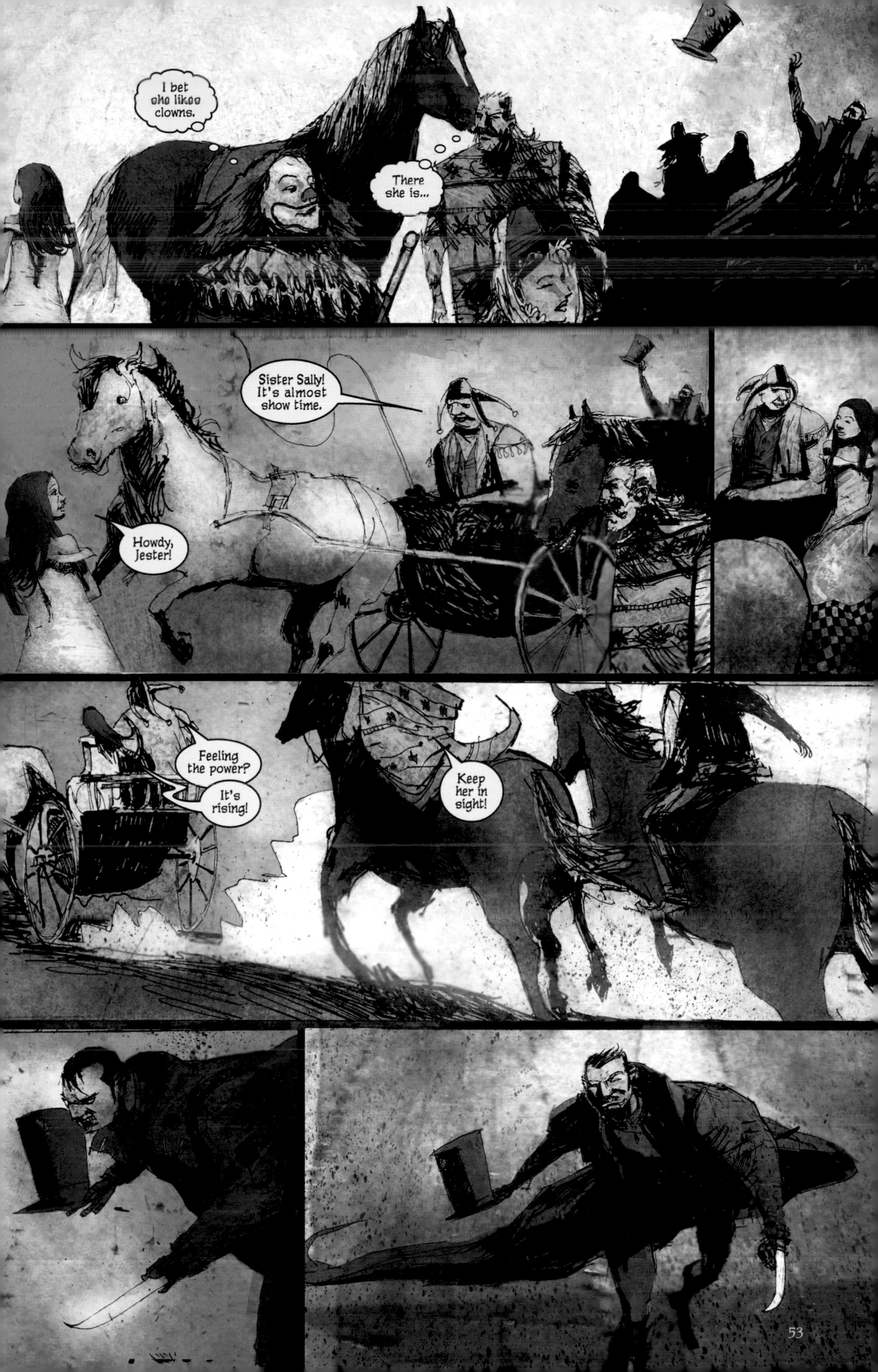
I bet she likes clowns.
There she is...
Sister Sally! It's almost show time.
Howdy, Jester!
Feeling the power?
It's rising!
Keep her in sight!

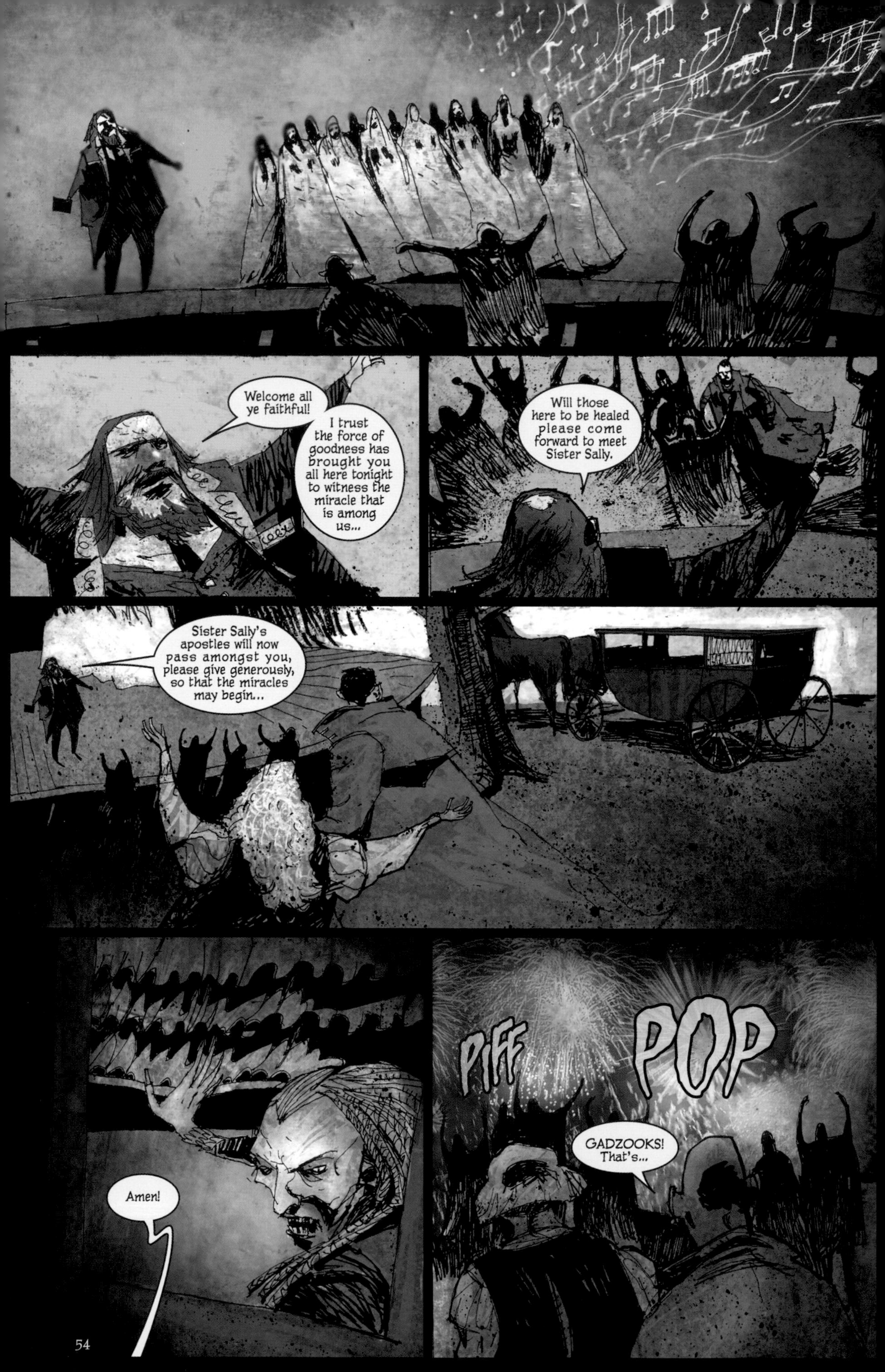
Welcome all ye faithful!
I trust the force of goodness has brought you all here tonight to witness the miracle that is among us...
Will those here to be healed please come forward to meet Sister Sally.
Sister Sally's apostles will now pass amongst you, please give generously, so that the miracles may begin...
Amen!
PIFF
POP
GADZOOKS! That's...

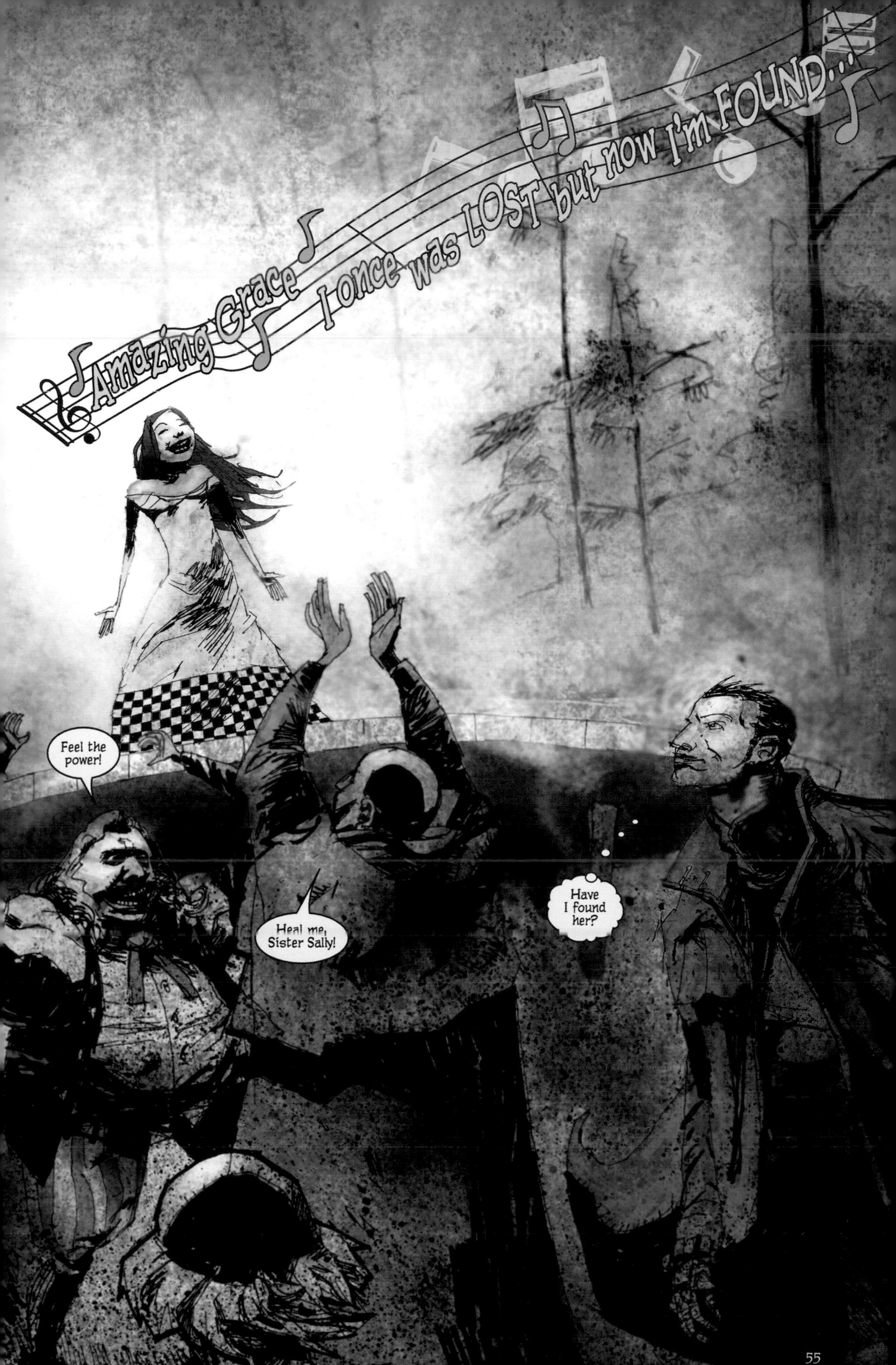
Amazing Grace
I once was LOST but now I'm FOUND...
Feel the power!
Heal me, Sister Sally!
Have I found her?

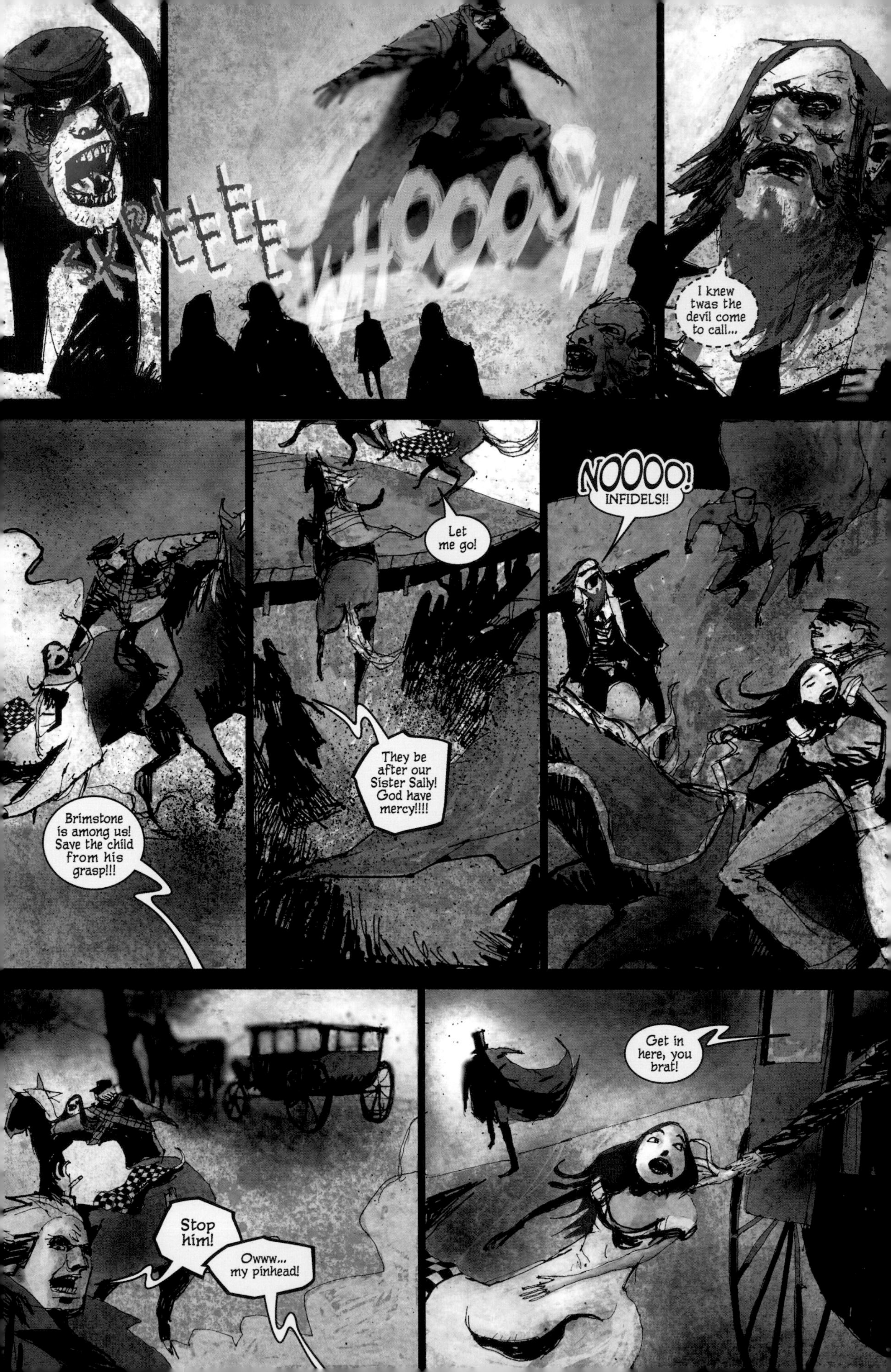
SKREEEEEE
WHOOOOSH
I knew twas the devil come to call...
Brimstone is among us! Save the child from his grasp!!!
Let me go!
They be after our Sister Sally! God have mercy!!!!
NOOOO! INFIDELS!!
Stop him!
Owww... my pinhead!
Get in here, you brat!

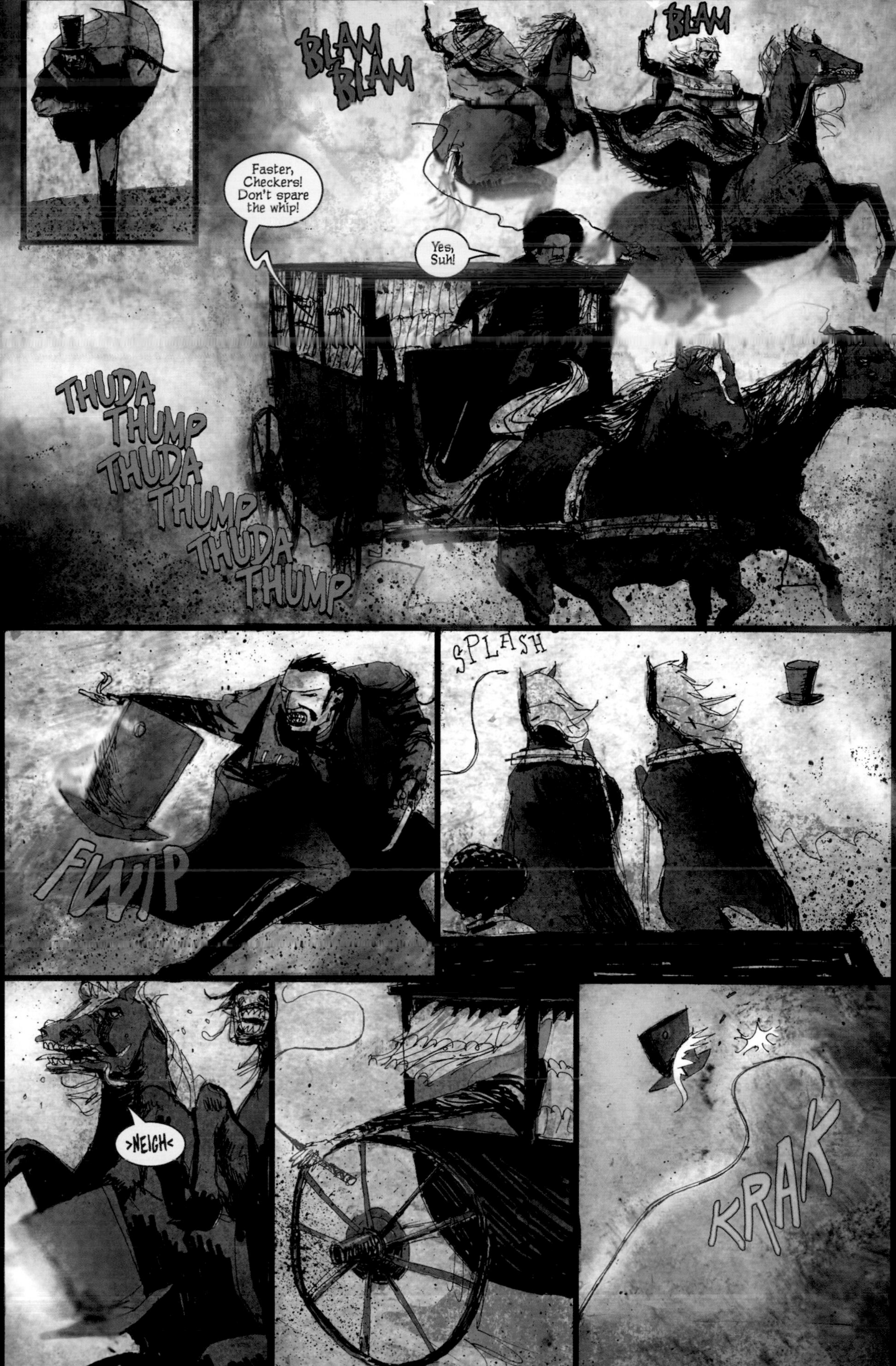
BLAM BLAM
BLAM
Faster, Checkers! Don't spare the whip!
Yes, Suh!
THUDA THUMP THUDA THUMP THUDA THUMP
FWIP
SPLASH
>NEIGH<
KRAK

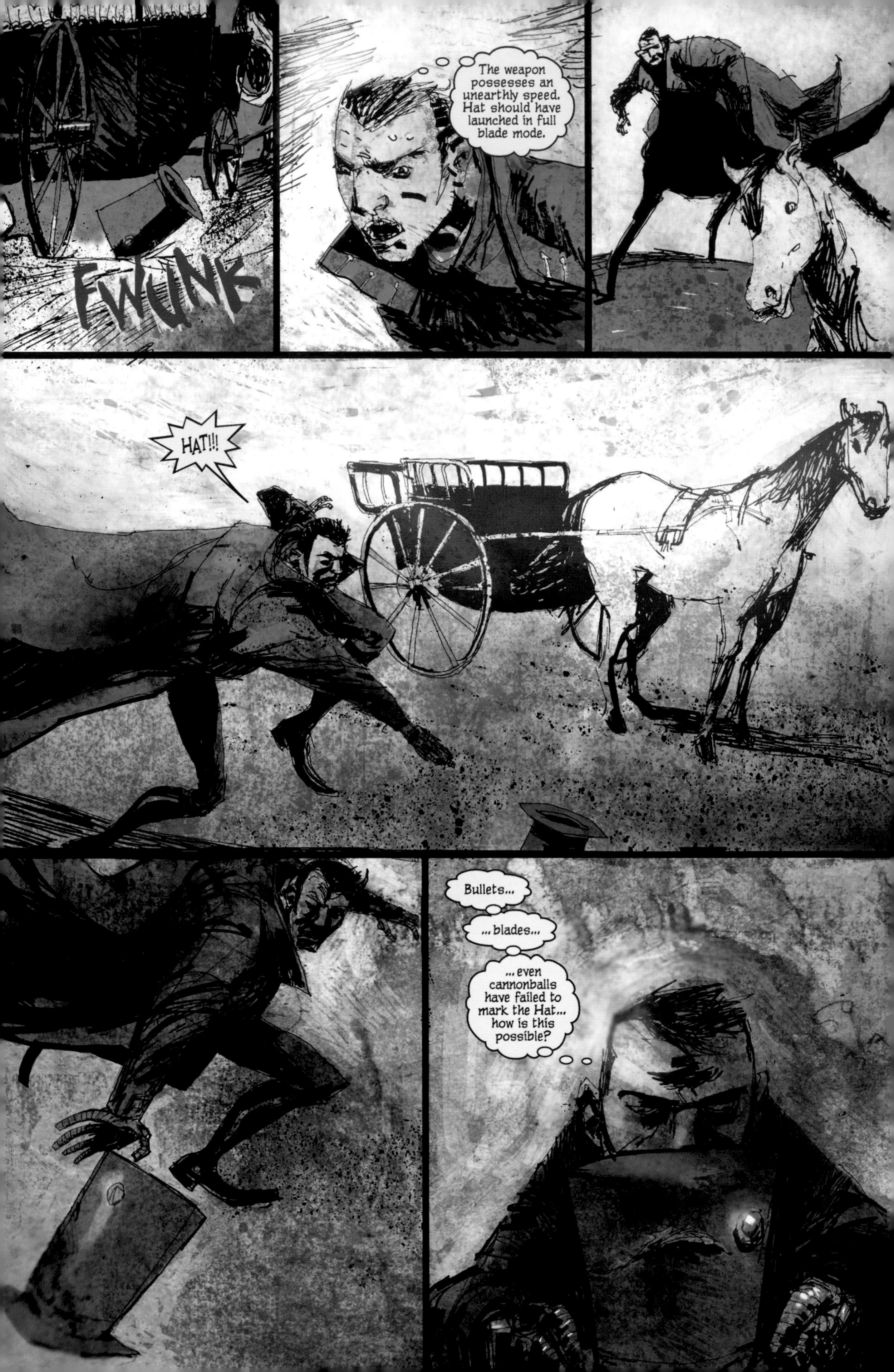

FWUNK
The weapon possesses an unearthly speed. Hat should have launched in full blade mode.
HAT!!!
Bullets...
...blades...
...even cannonballs have failed to mark the Hat... how is this possible?

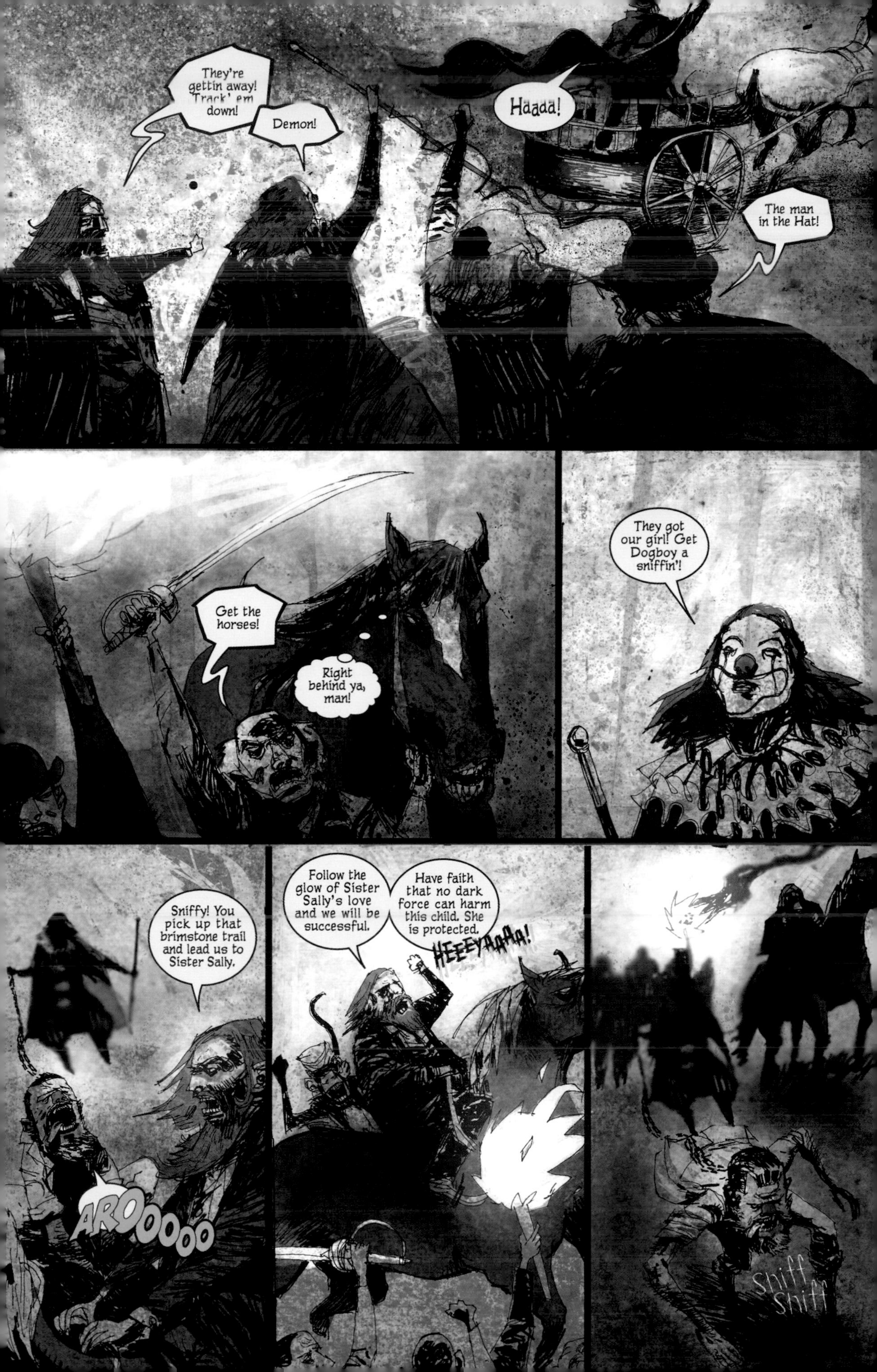
They're gettin away! Track' em down!
Demon!
Haaaa!
The man in the Hat!
Get the horses!
Right behind ya, man!
They got our girl! Get Dogboy a sniffin'!
Sniffy! You pick up that brimstone trail and lead us to Sister Sally.
AROOOOO
Follow the glow of Sister Sally's love and we will be successful.
Have faith that no dark force can harm this child. She is protected.
HEEEYAAAA!
Shiff Shiff

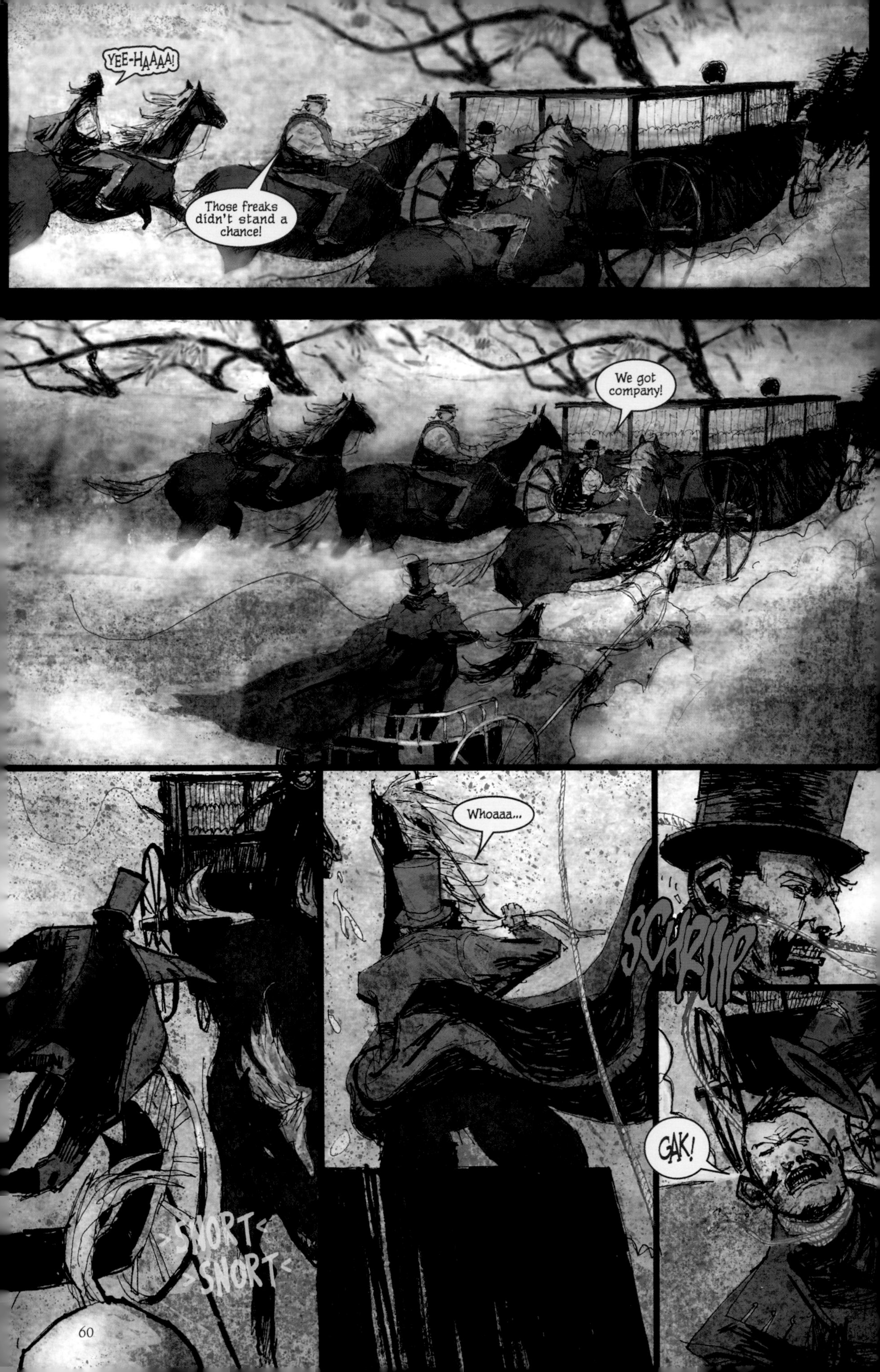
YEE-HAAAA!
Those freaks didn't stand a chance!
We got company!
Whoaaa...
SCHRIIP
GAK!
>SNORT<
>SNORT<

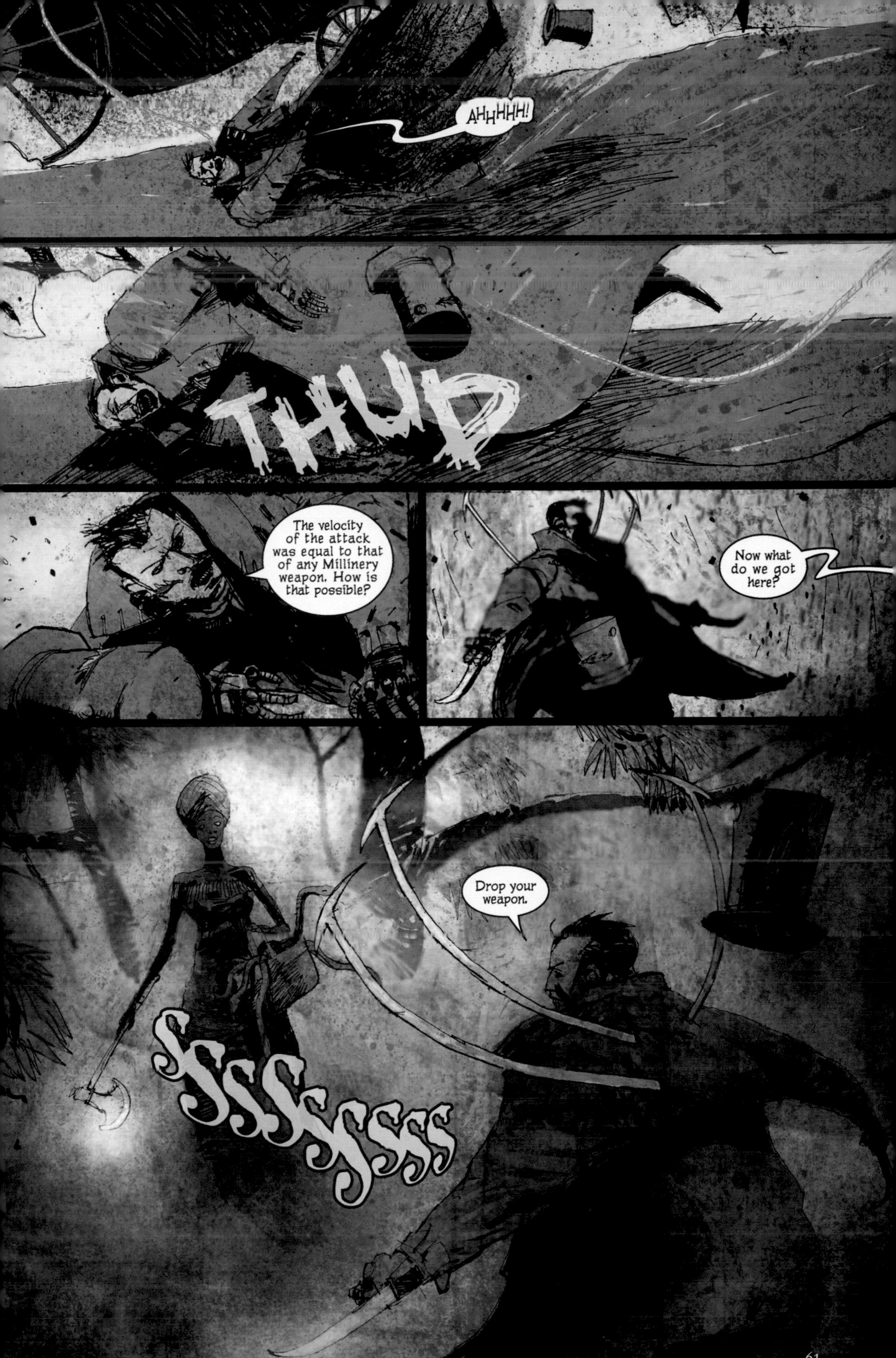
AHHHHH!
THUD
The velocity of the attack was equal to that of any Millinery weapon. How is that possible?
Now what do we got here?
Drop your weapon.
SSSSSSSS

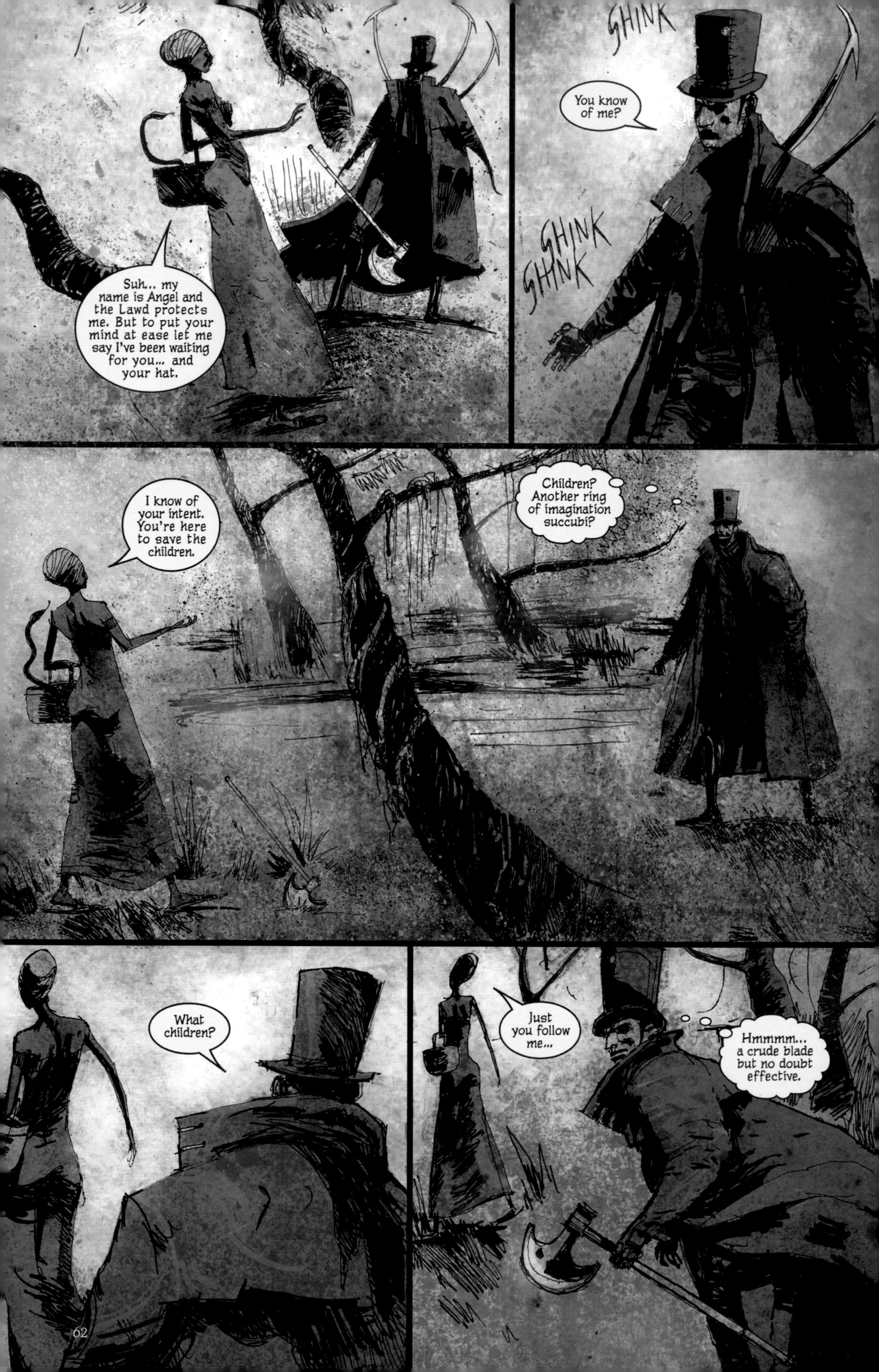
Suh... my name is Angel and the Lawd protects me. But to put your mind at ease let me say I've been waiting for you... and your hat.
SHINK
You know of me?
SHINK
SHINK
I know of your intent. You're here to save the children.
Children? Another ring of imagination succubi?
What children?
Just you follow me...
Hmmmm... a crude blade but no doubt effective.

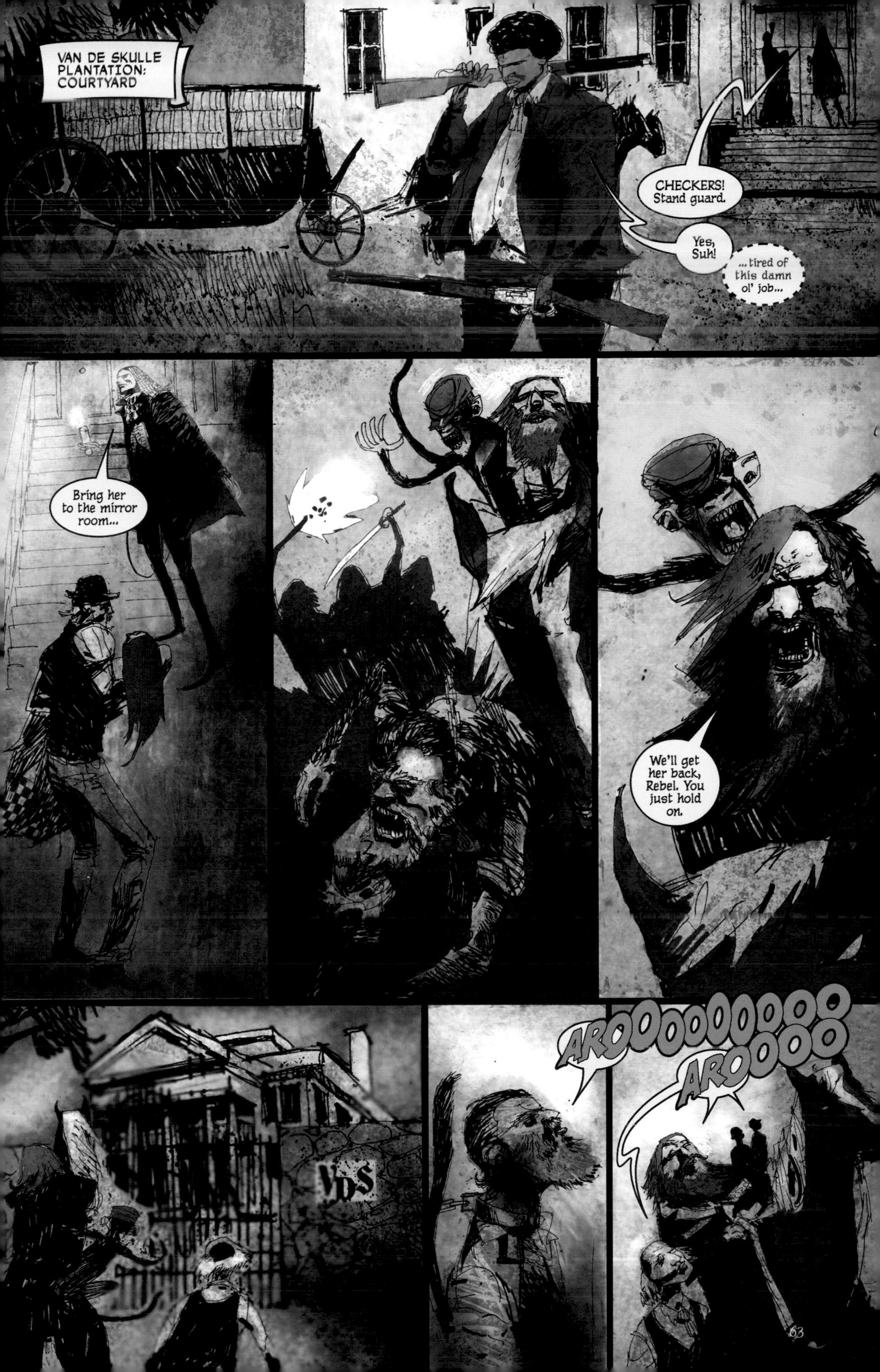
VAN DE SKULLE PLANTATION: COURTYARD
CHECKERS! Stand guard.
Yes, Suh!
...tired of this damn ol' job...
Bring her to the mirror room...
We'll get her back, Rebel. You just hold on.
VDS
AROOOOOOOOOO
AROOOOO

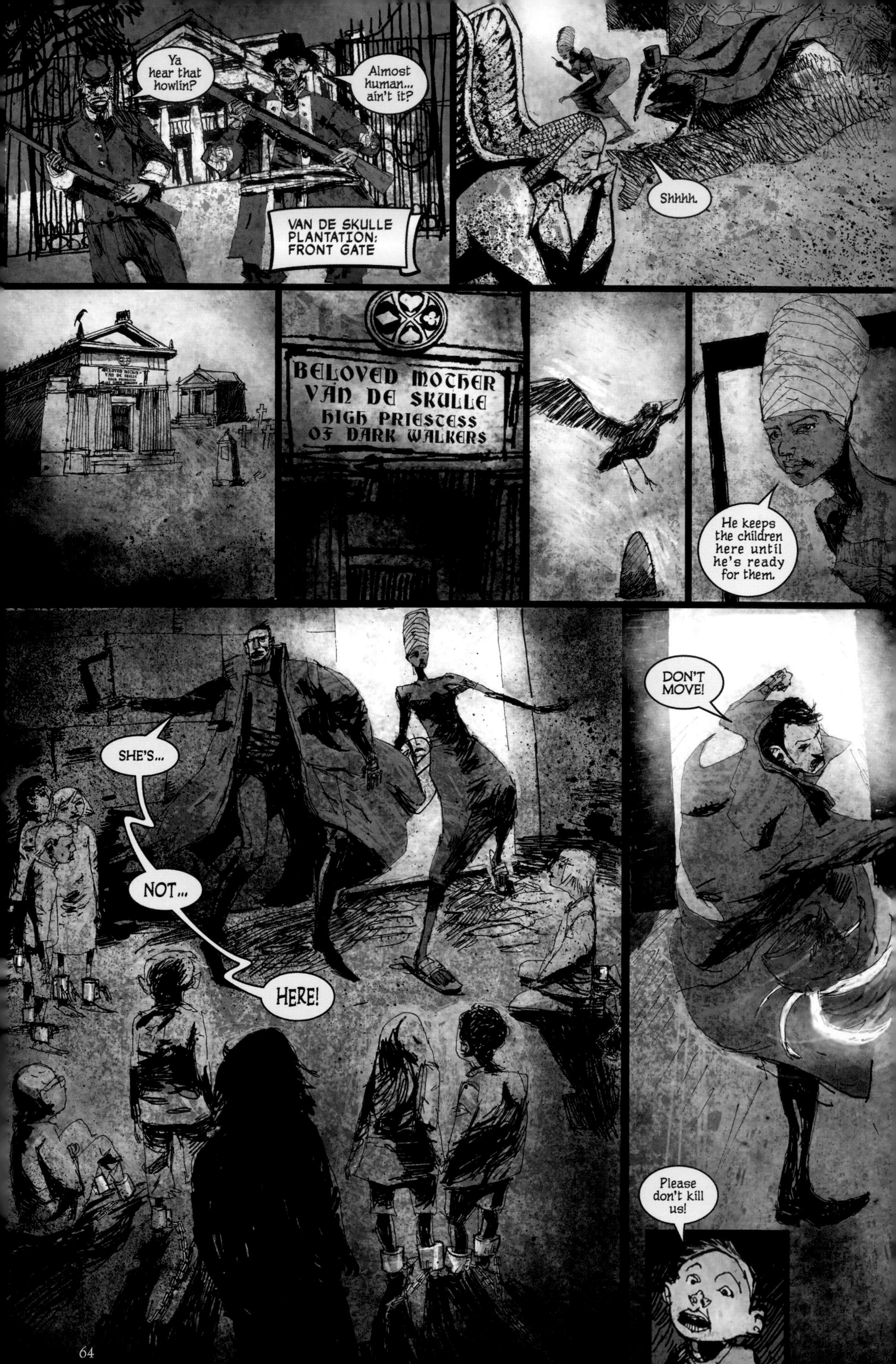
Ya hear that howlin?
Almost human... ain't it?
VAN DE SKULLE PLANTATION: FRONT GATE
Shhhh.
BELOVED MOTHER VAN DE SKULLE HIGH PRIESTESS OF DARK WALKERS
He keeps the children here until he's ready for them.
SHE'S...
NOT...
HERE!
DON'T MOVE!
Please don't kill us!

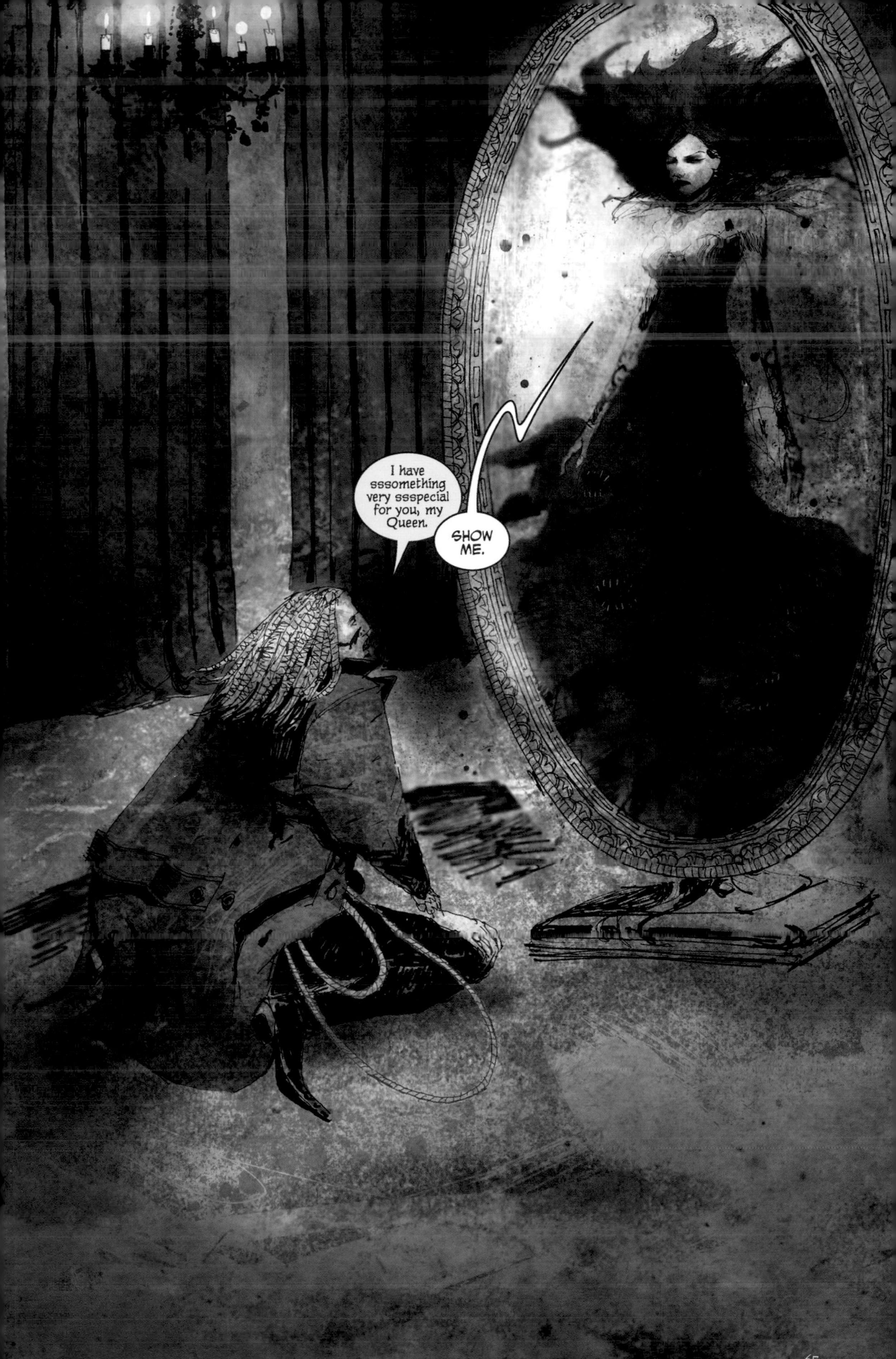
I have sssomething very sssspecial for you, my Queen.
SHOW ME.

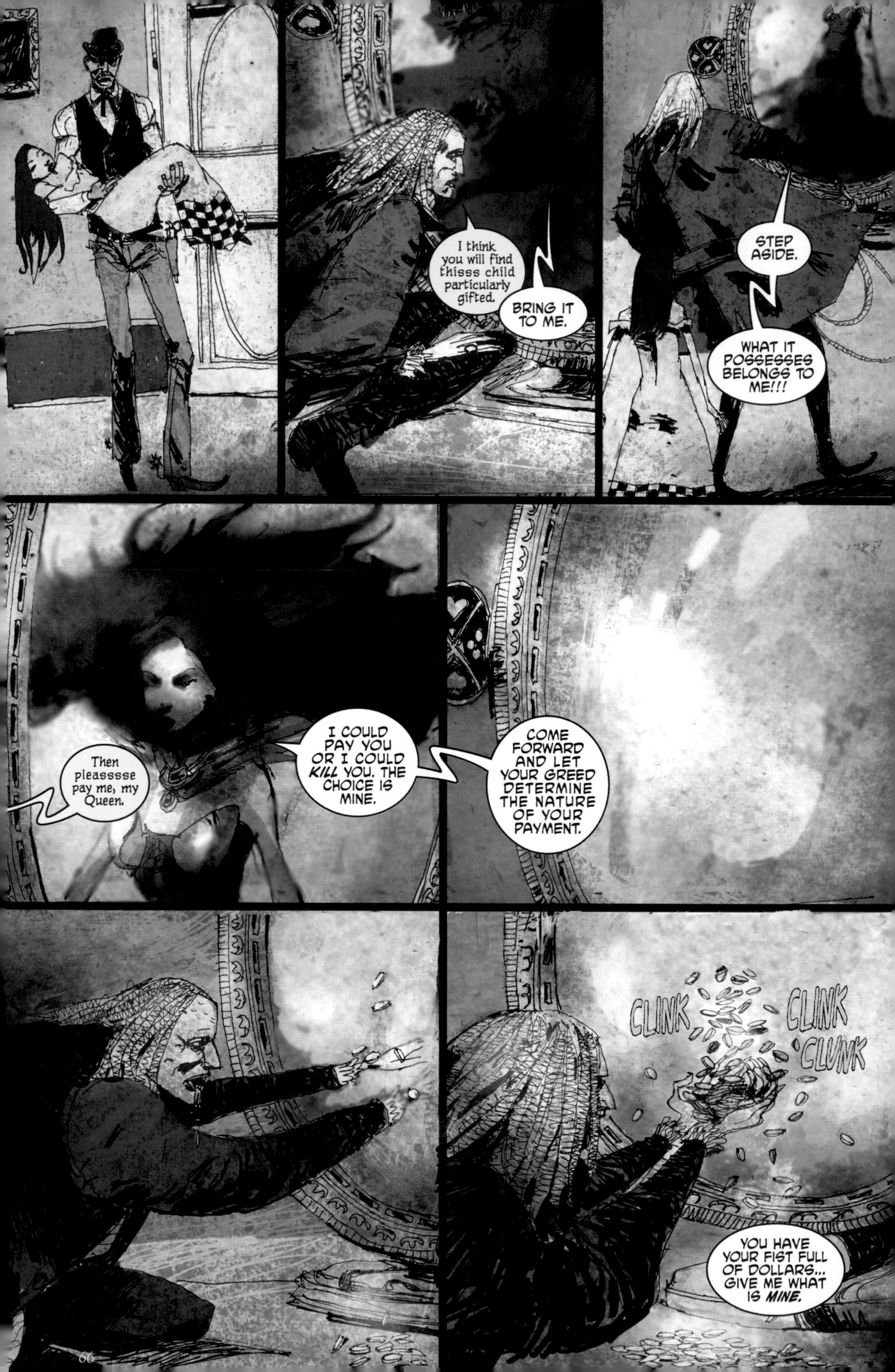
I think you will find thisss child particularly gifted.
BRING IT TO ME.
STEP ASIDE.
WHAT IT POSSESSES BELONGS TO ME!!!
Then pleasssse pay me, my Queen.
I COULD PAY YOU OR I COULD KILL YOU. THE CHOICE IS MINE.
COME FORWARD AND LET YOUR GREED DETERMINE THE NATURE OF YOUR PAYMENT.
CLINK
CLINK
CLUNK
YOU HAVE YOUR FIST FULL OF DOLLARS... GIVE ME WHAT IS MINE.

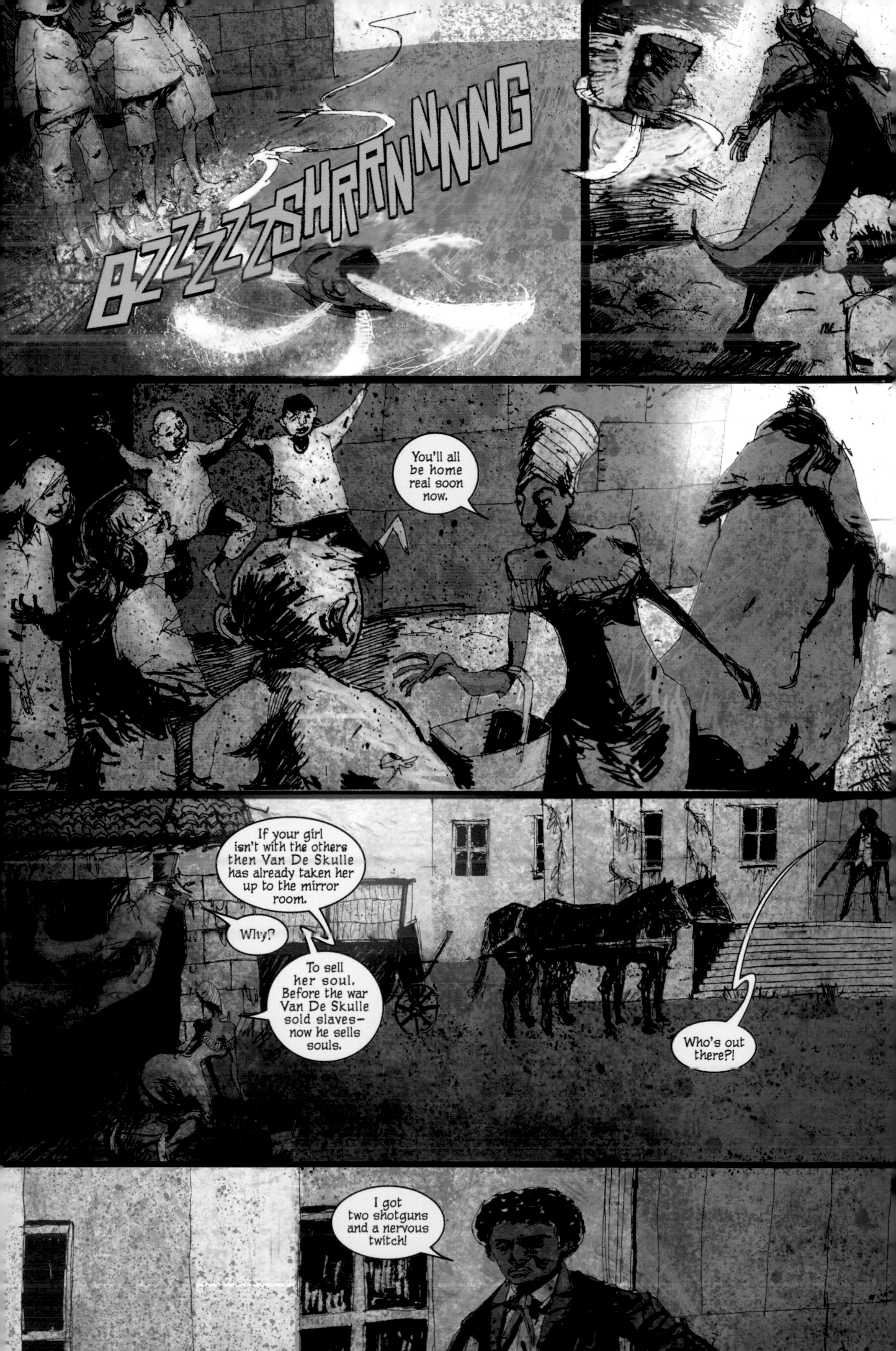
BZZZZZSHRRNNNNG
You'll all be home real soon now.
If your girl isn't with the others then Van De Skulle has already taken her up to the mirror room.
Why?
To sell her soul. Before the war Van De Skulle sold slaves— now he sells souls.
Who's out there?!
I got two shotguns and a nervous twitch!

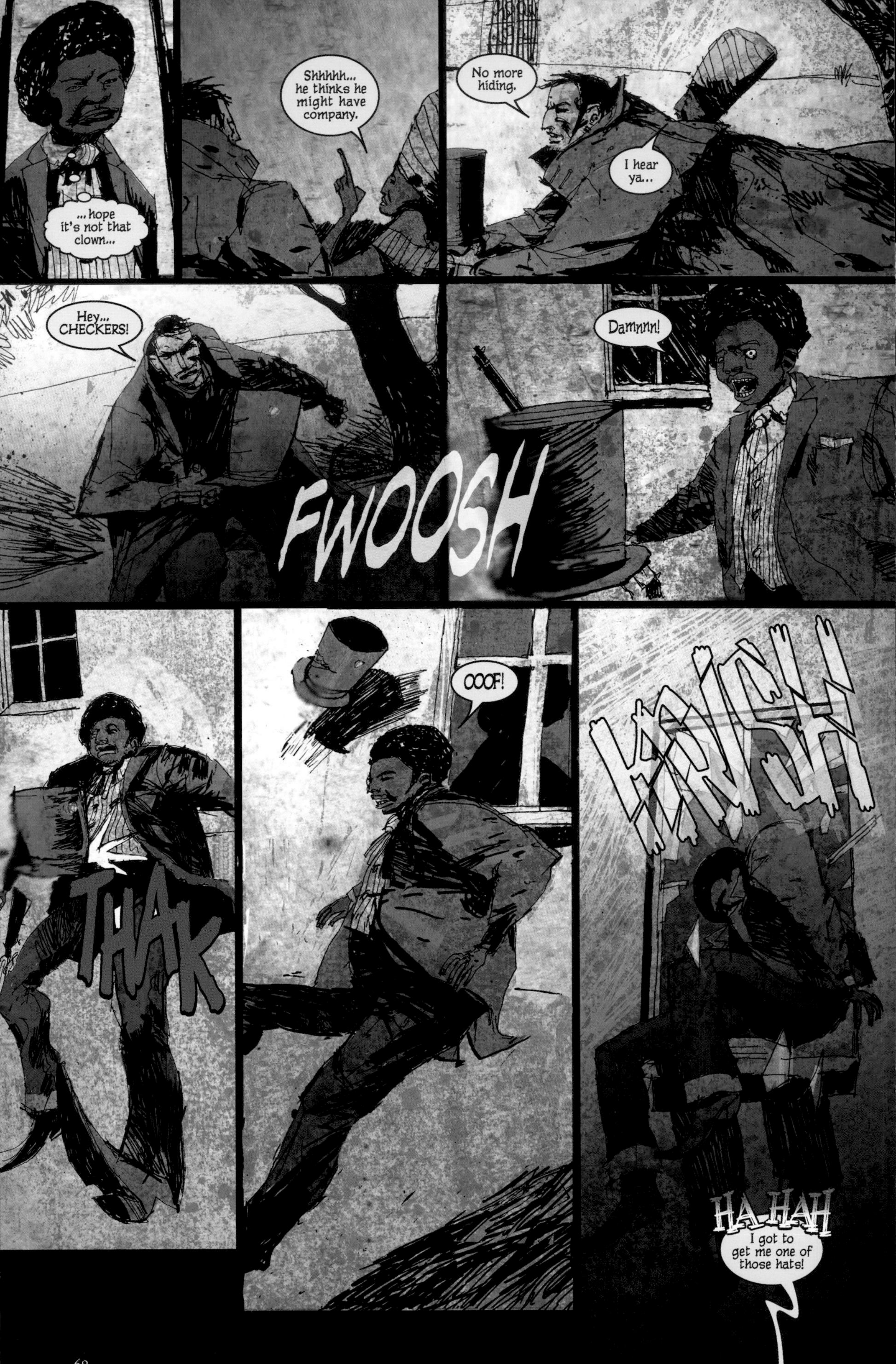
...hope it's not that clown...
Shhhhh... he thinks he might have company.
No more hiding.
I hear ya...
Hey... CHECKERS!
Damnnn!
FWOOSH
THAK
OOOF!
KRASH
HA-HAH
I got to get me one of those hats!

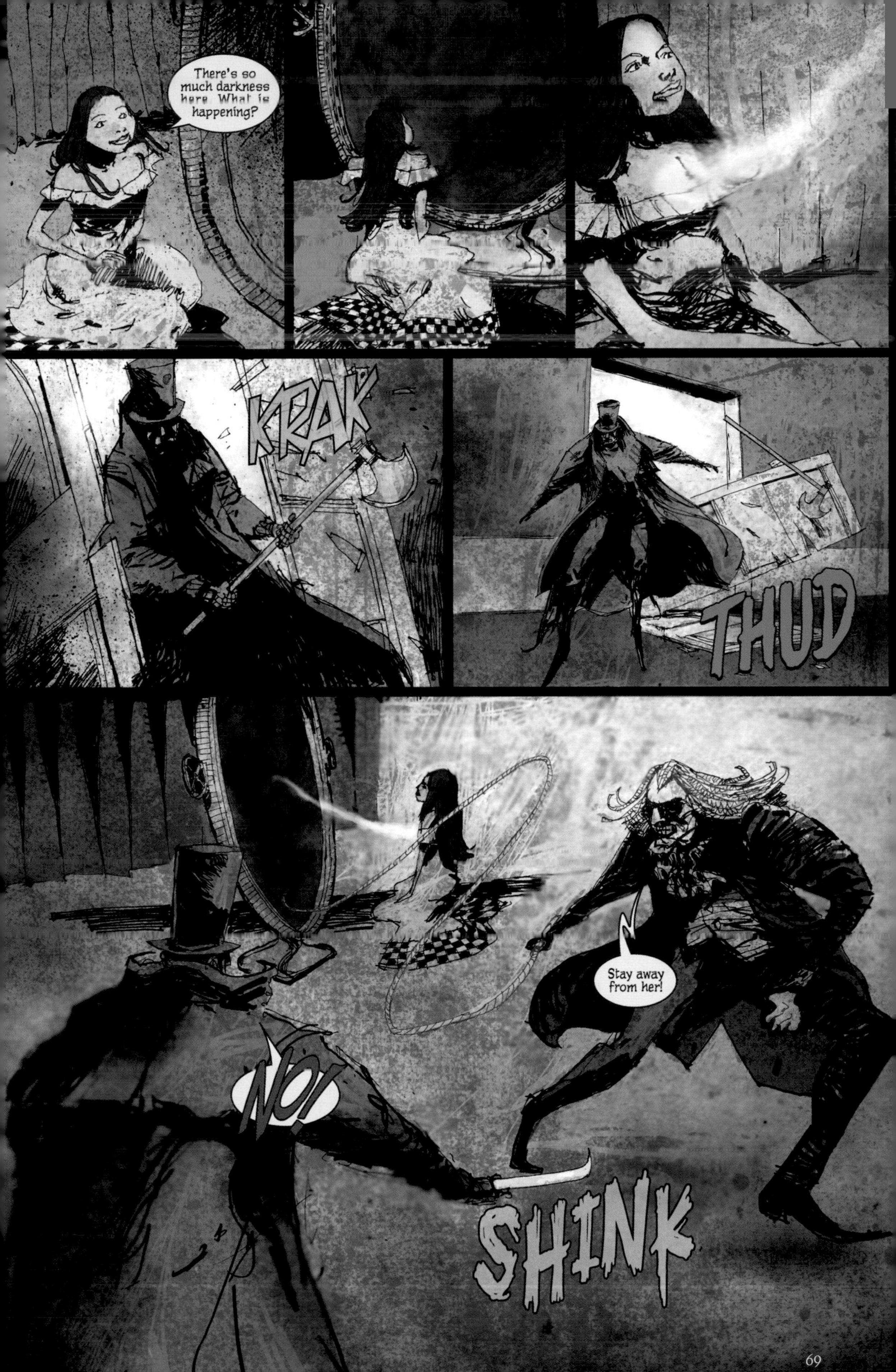
There's so much darkness here. What is happening?
KRAK
THUD
Stay away from her!
NO!
SHINK

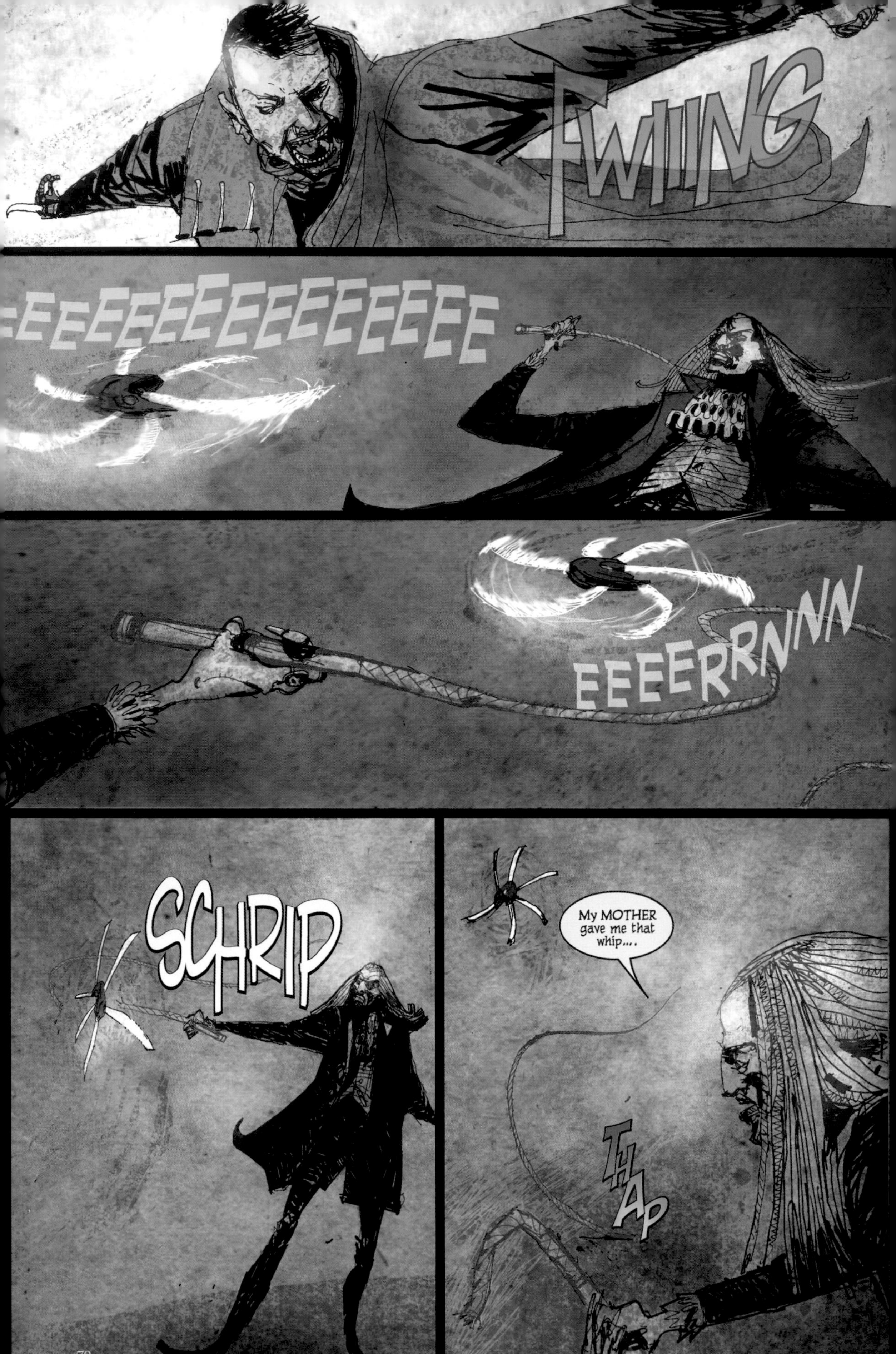
FWIING
EEEEEEEEEEEEEEE
EEEERRNNN
SCHRIP
My MOTHER gave me that whip....
THAP

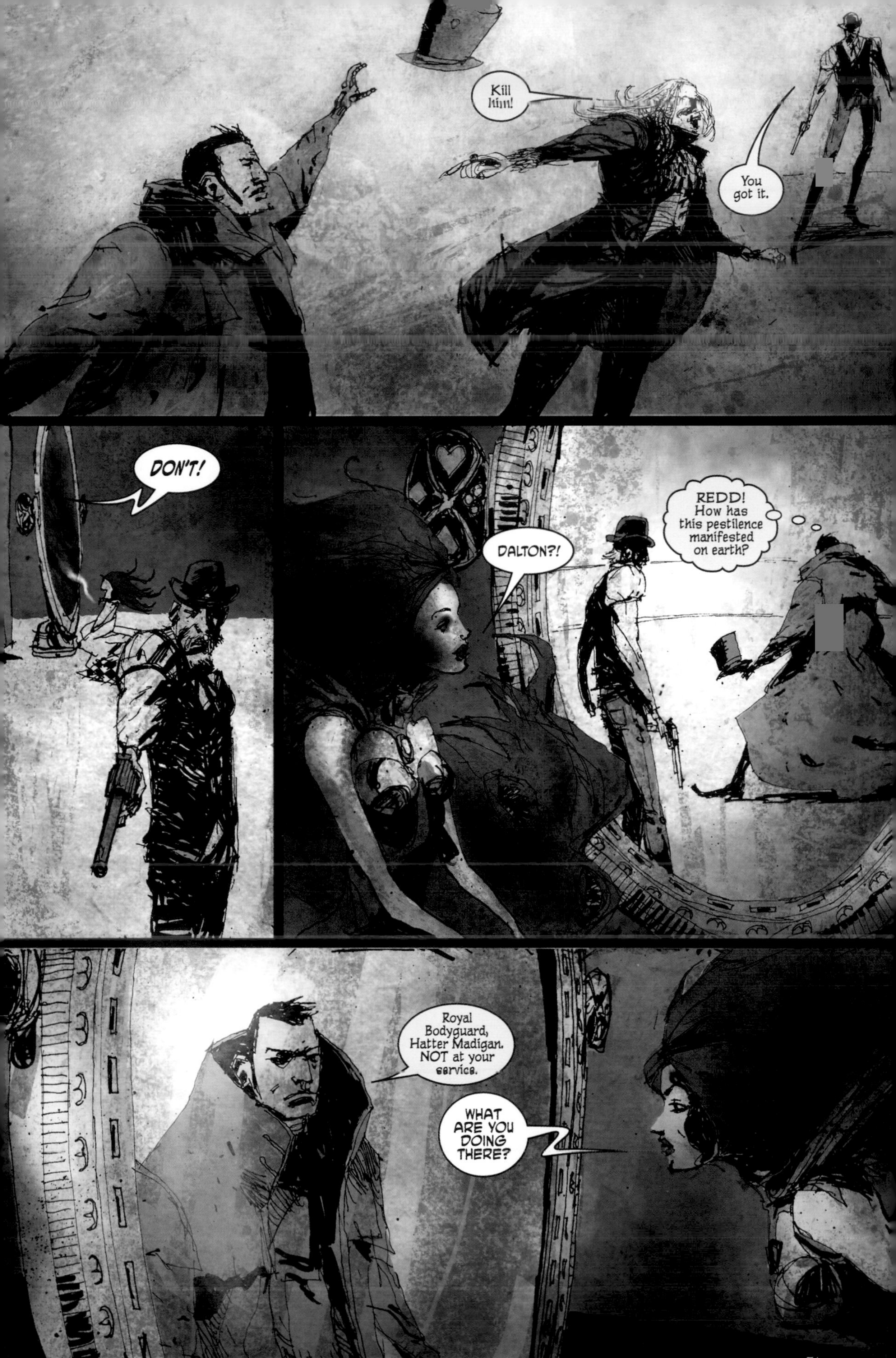
Kill him!
You got it.
DON'T!
DALTON?!
REDD! How has this pestilence manifested on earth?
Royal Bodyguard, Hatter Madigan. NOT at your service.
WHAT ARE YOU DOING THERE?

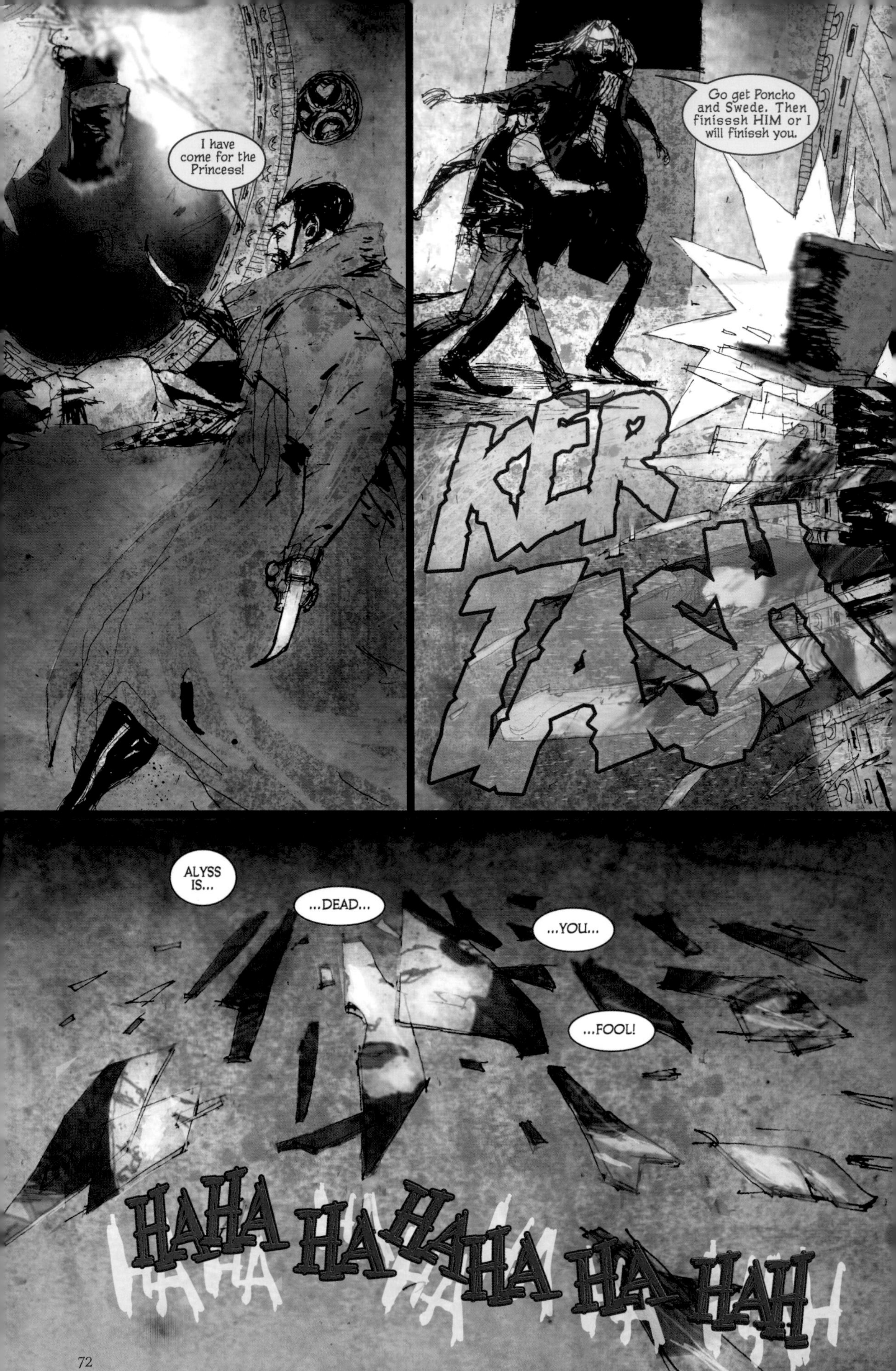
I have come for the Princess!
Go get Poncho and Swede. Then finisssh HIM or I will finissh you.
KER TASH
ALYSS IS...
...DEAD...
...YOU...
...FOOL!
HAHA HA HAHA HA HAH

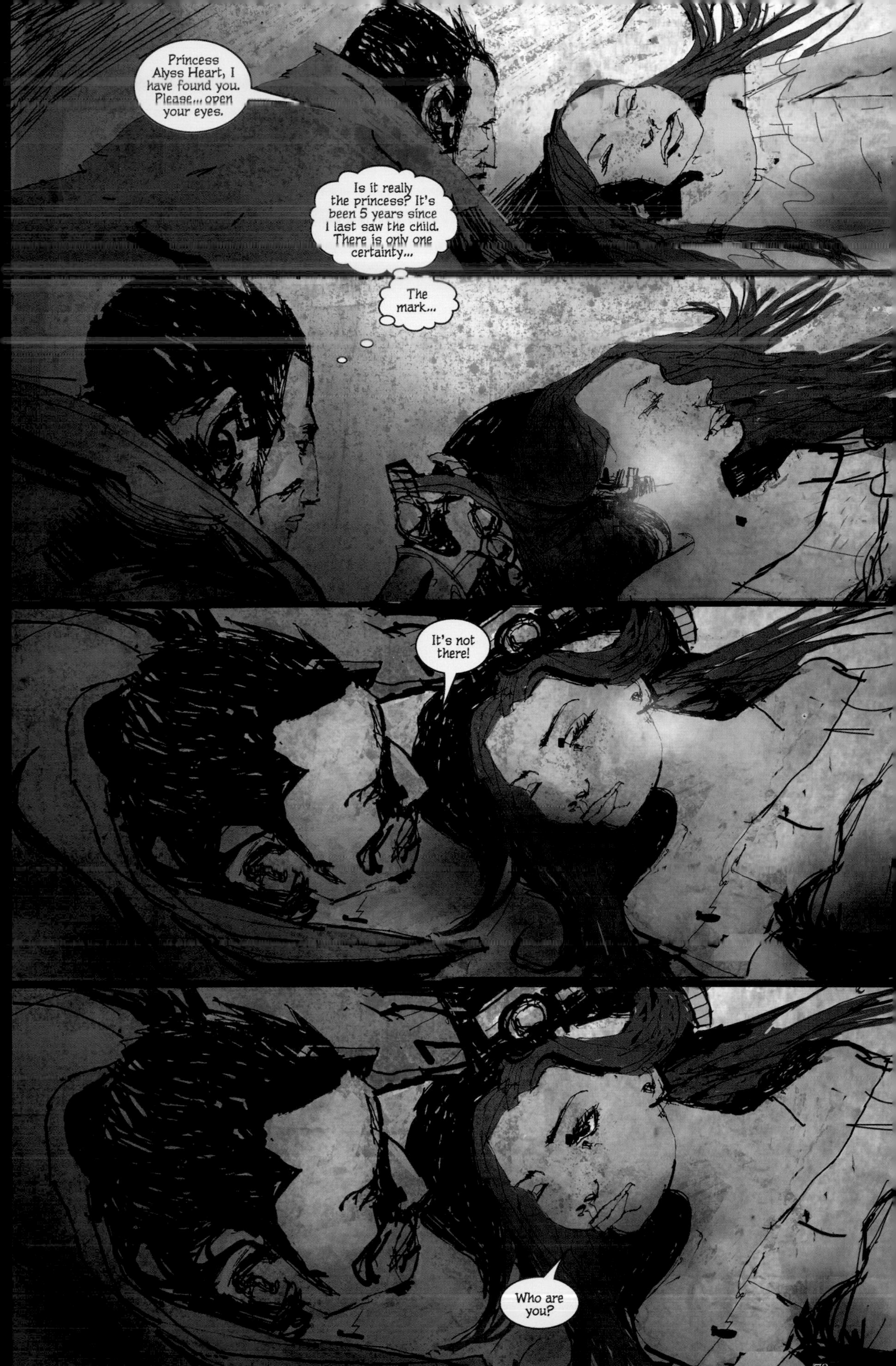
Princess Alyss Heart, I have found you. Please... open your eyes.
Is it really the princess? It's been 5 years since I last saw the child. There is only one certainty...
The mark...
It's not there!
Who are you?

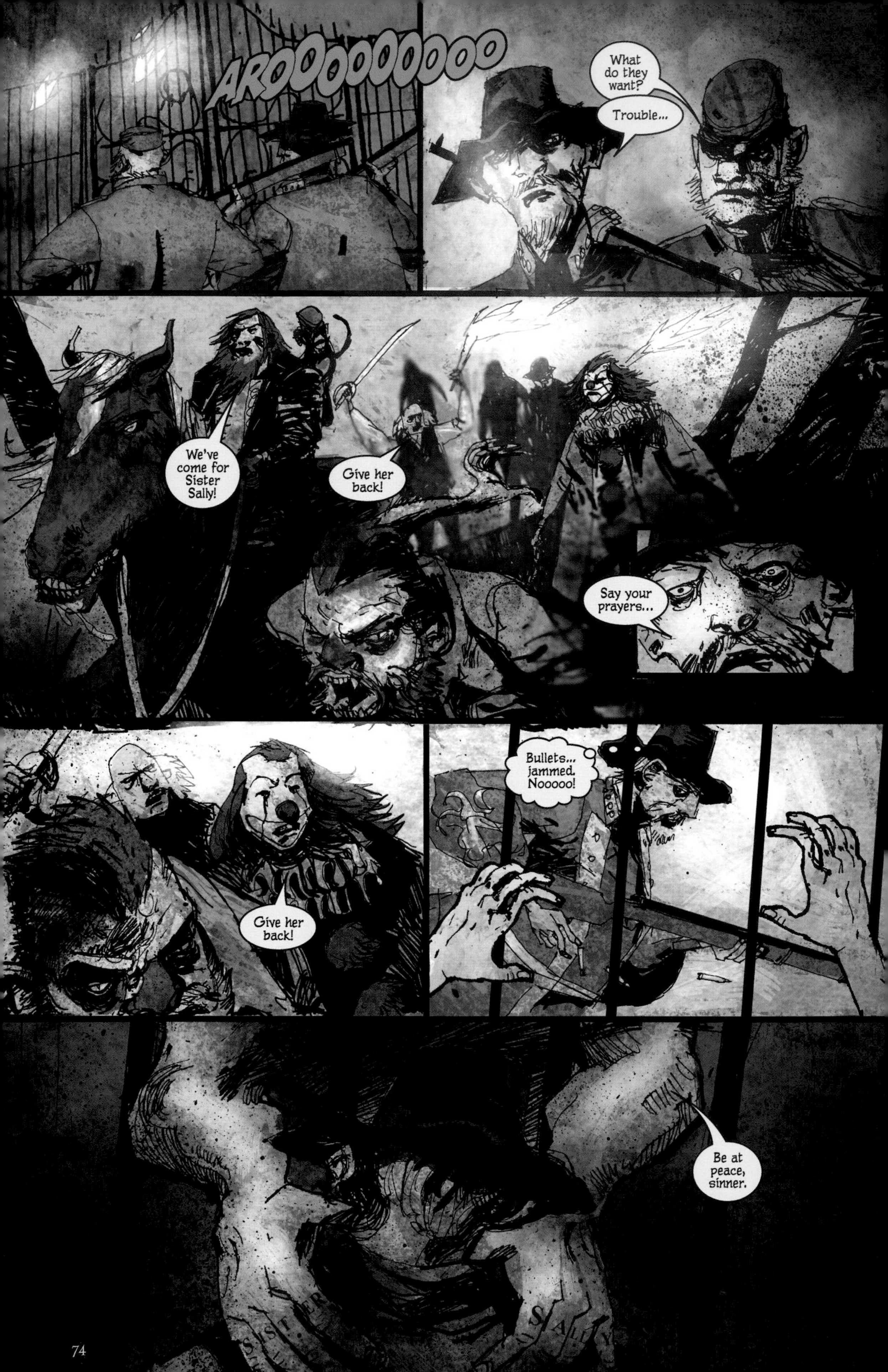
AROOOOOOOOO
What do they want?
Trouble...
We've come for Sister Sally!
Give her back!
Say your prayers...
Give her back!
Bullets... jammed. Nooooo!
Be at peace, sinner.
SISTER SALLY

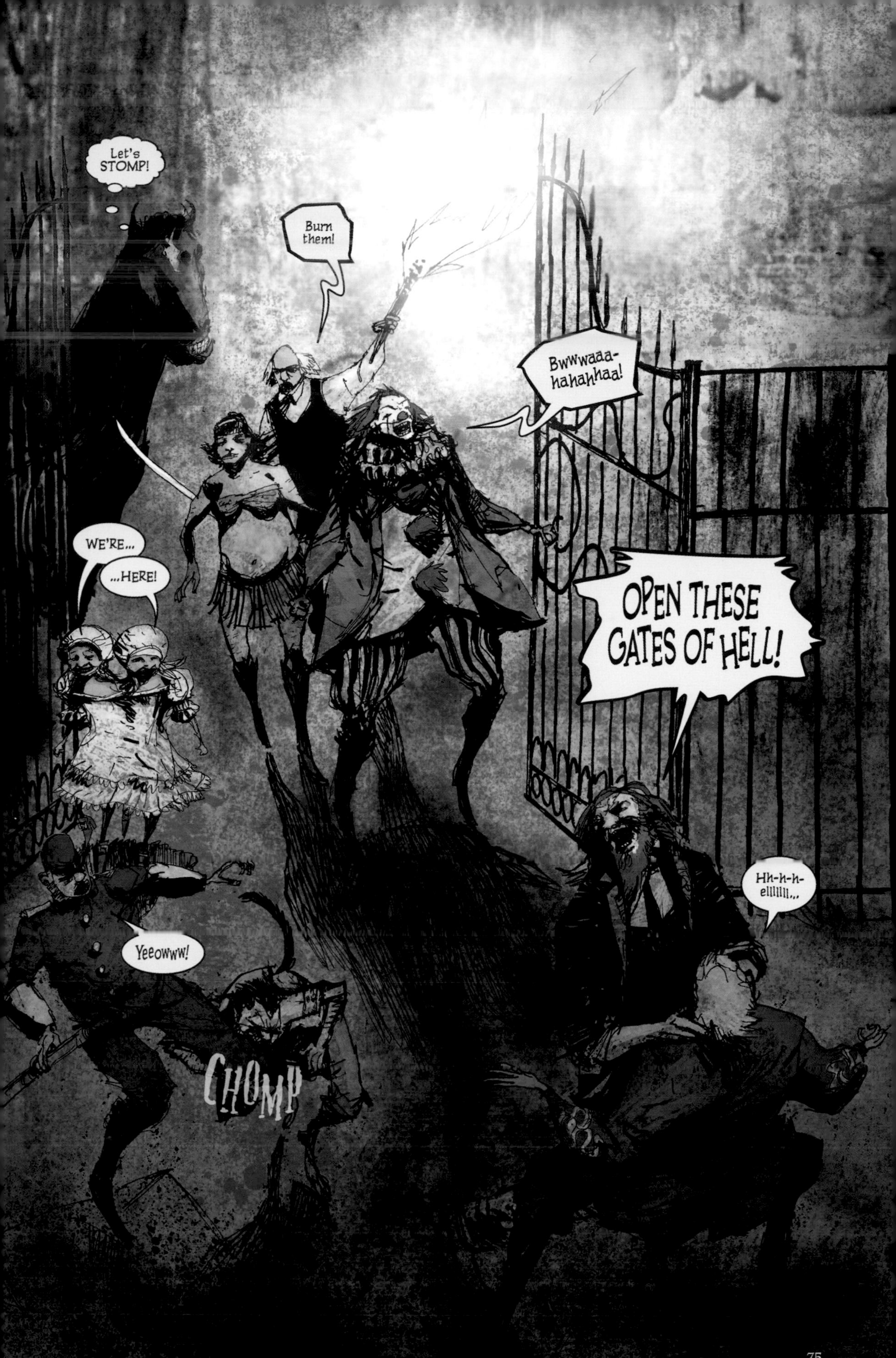
Let's STOMP!
Burn them!
Bwwwaaa-hahahhaa!
WE'RE...
...HERE!
OPEN THESE GATES OF HELL!
Hh-h-h-elllllll...
Yeeowww!
CHOMP

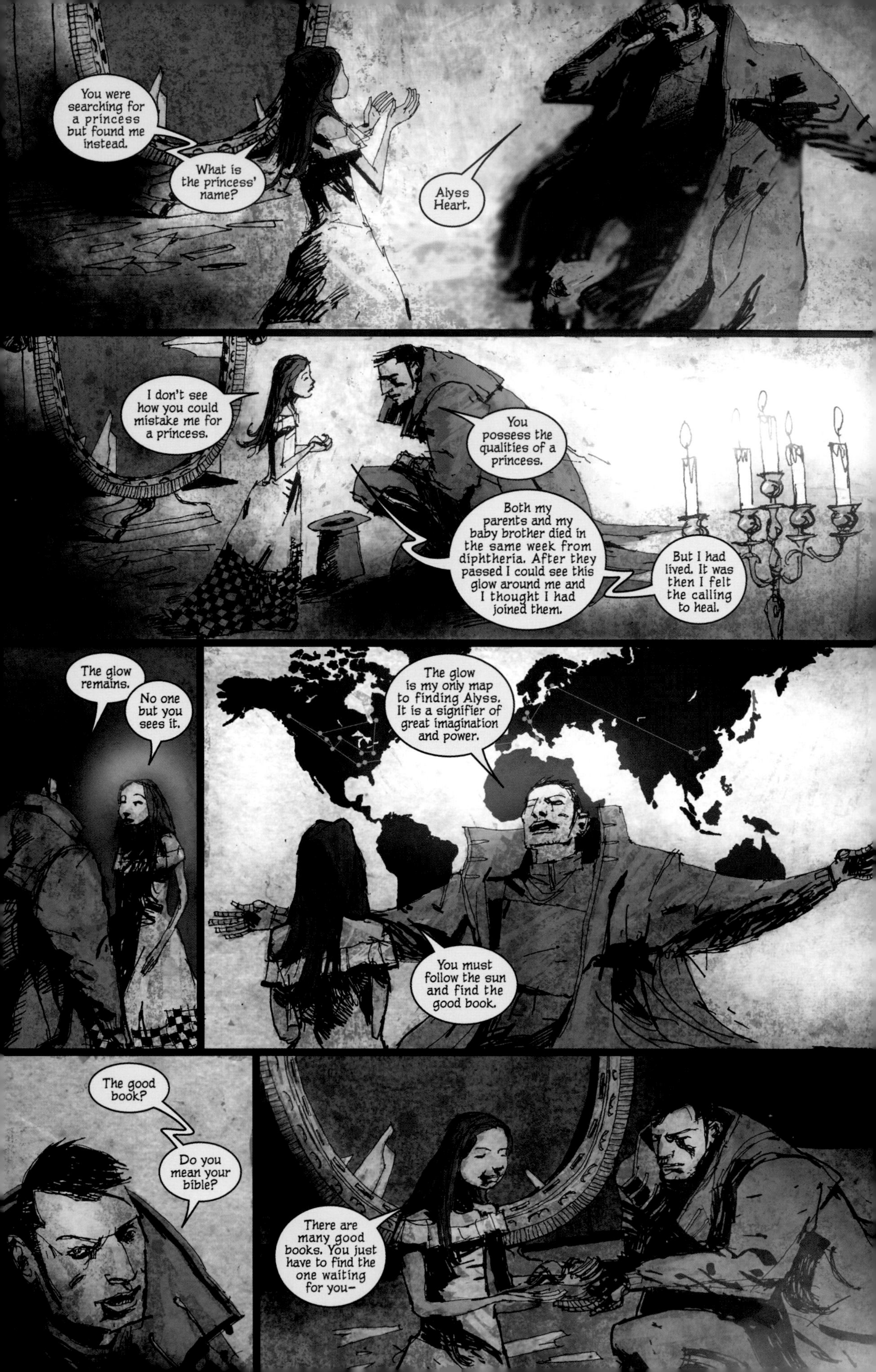
You were searching for a princess but found me instead.
What is the princess' name?
Alyss Heart.
I don't see how you could mistake me for a princess.
You possess the qualities of a princess.
Both my parents and my baby brother died in the same week from diphtheria. After they passed I could see this glow around me and I thought I had joined them.
But I had lived. It was then I felt the calling to heal.
The glow remains.
No one but you sees it.
The glow is my only map to finding Alyss. It is a signifier of great imagination and power.
You must follow the sun and find the good book.
The good book?
Do you mean your bible?
There are many good books. You just have to find the one waiting for you–

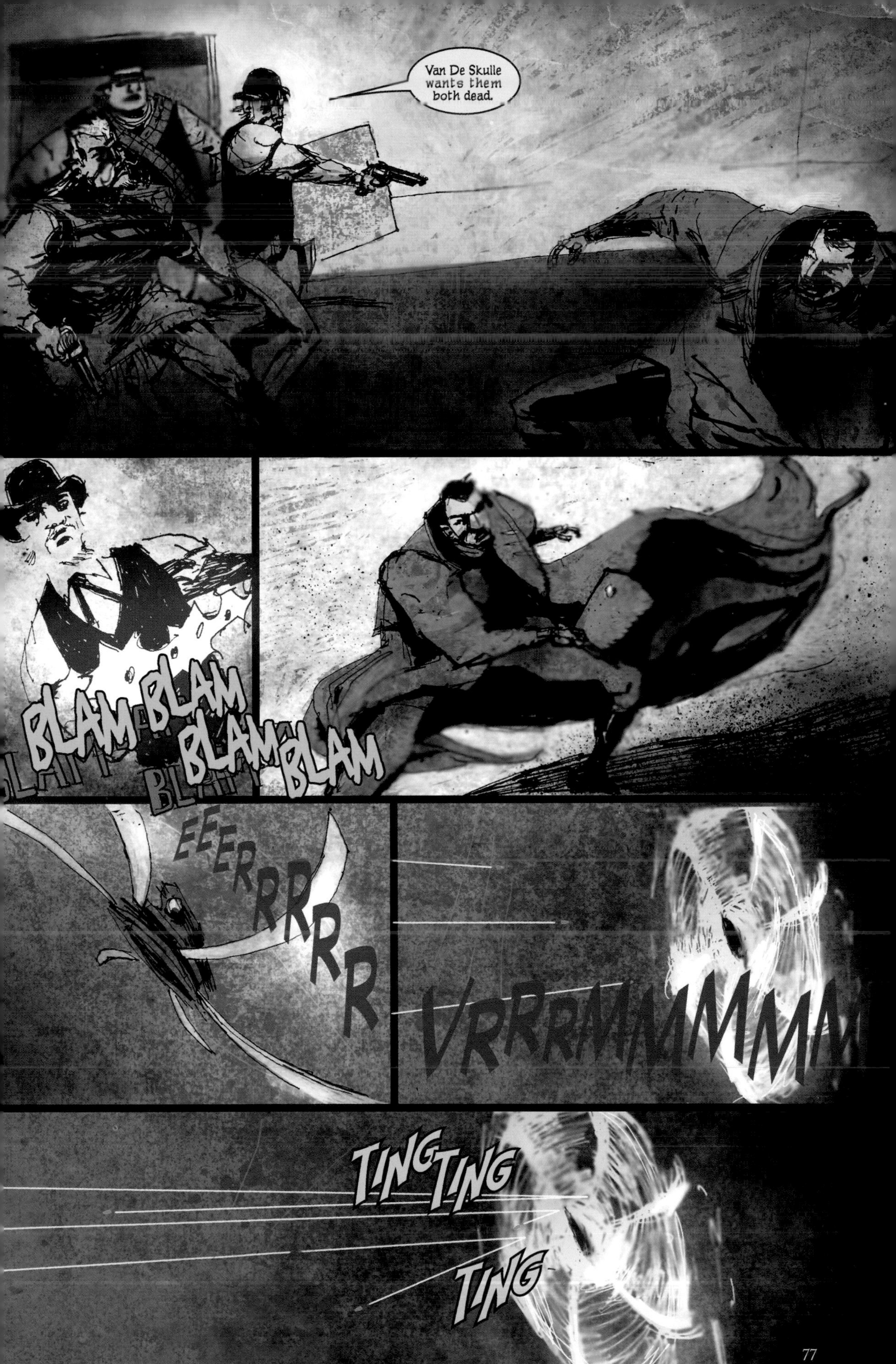

Van De Skulle wants them both dead.
BLAM BLAM BLAM BLAM
EEERRRRR
VRRRMMMMMM
TING TING
TING

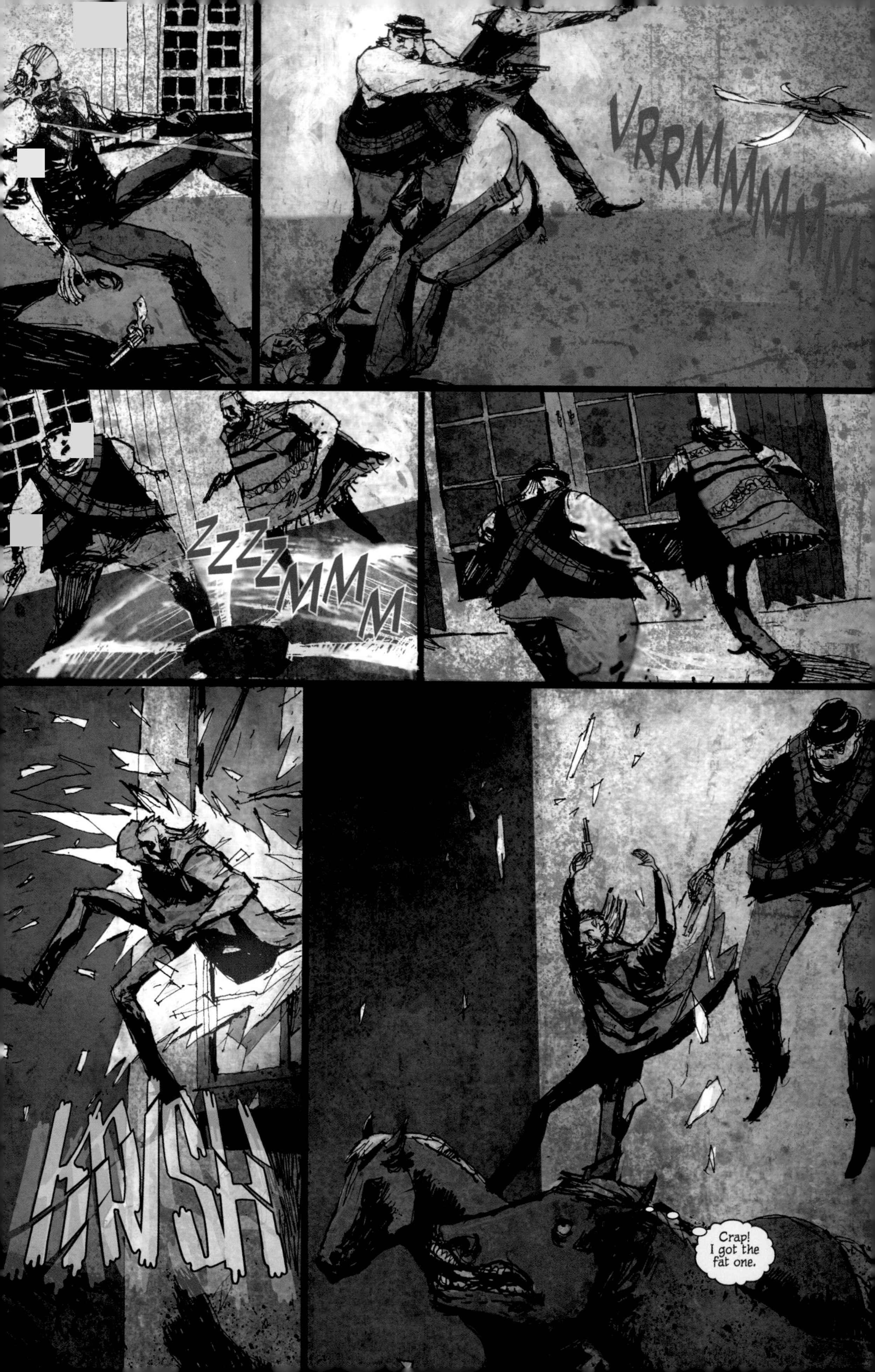
VRRMMMMMM
ZZZZMMMM
KRSH
Crap! I got the fat one.

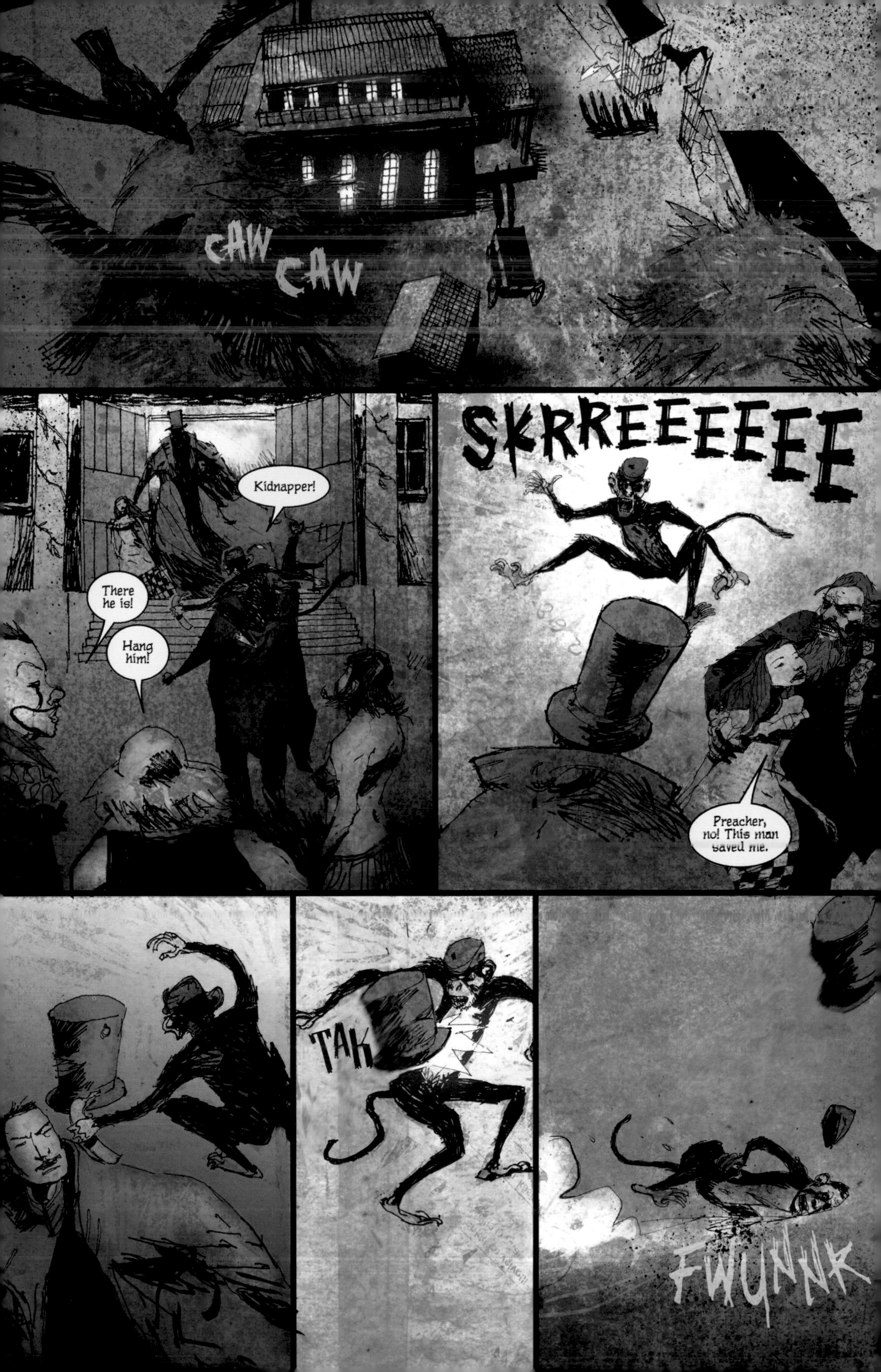
CAW
CAW
Kidnapper!
There he is!
Hang him!
SKRREEEEEEE
Preacher, no! This man saved me.
TAK
FWUNNK

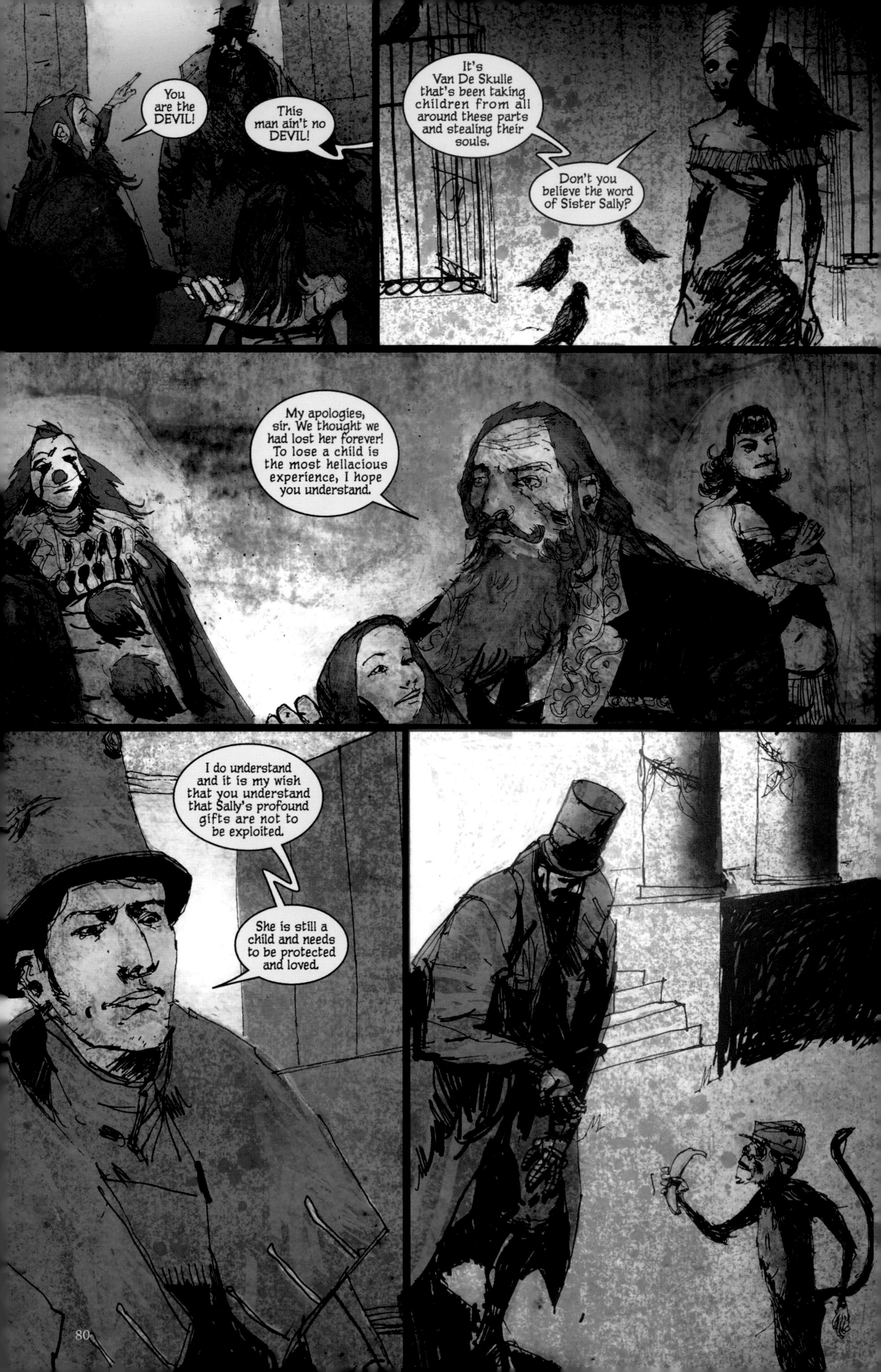
You are the DEVIL!
This man ain't no DEVIL!
It's Van De Skulle that's been taking children from all around these parts and stealing their souls.
Don't you believe the word of Sister Sally?
My apologies, sir. We thought we had lost her forever! To lose a child is the most hellacious experience, I hope you understand.
I do understand and it is my wish that you understand that Sally's profound gifts are not to be exploited.
She is still a child and needs to be protected and loved.

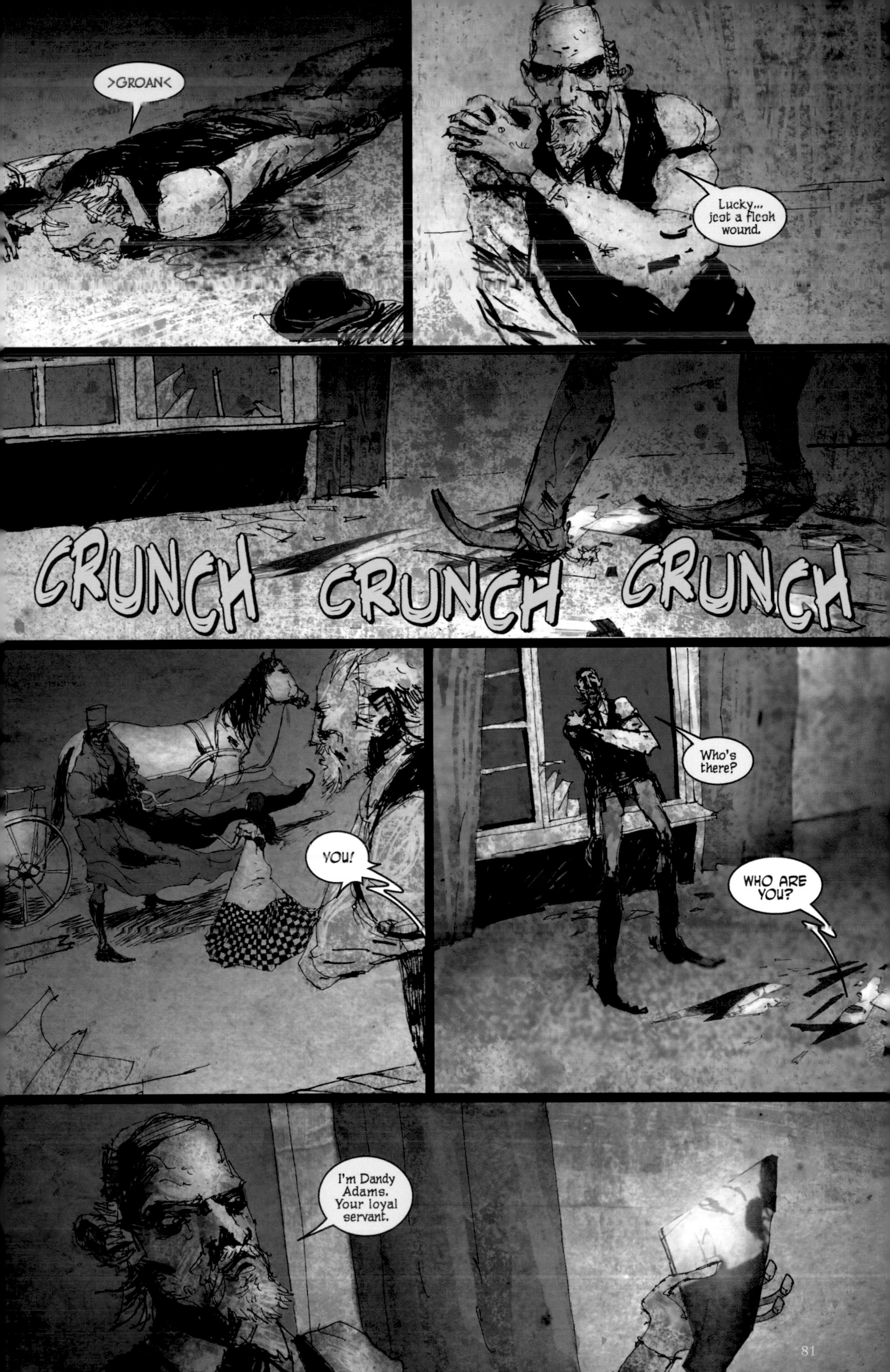
>GROAN<
Lucky... jest a flesh wound.
CRUNCH CRUNCH CRUNCH
YOU!
Who's there?
WHO ARE YOU?
I'm Dandy Adams. Your loyal servant.

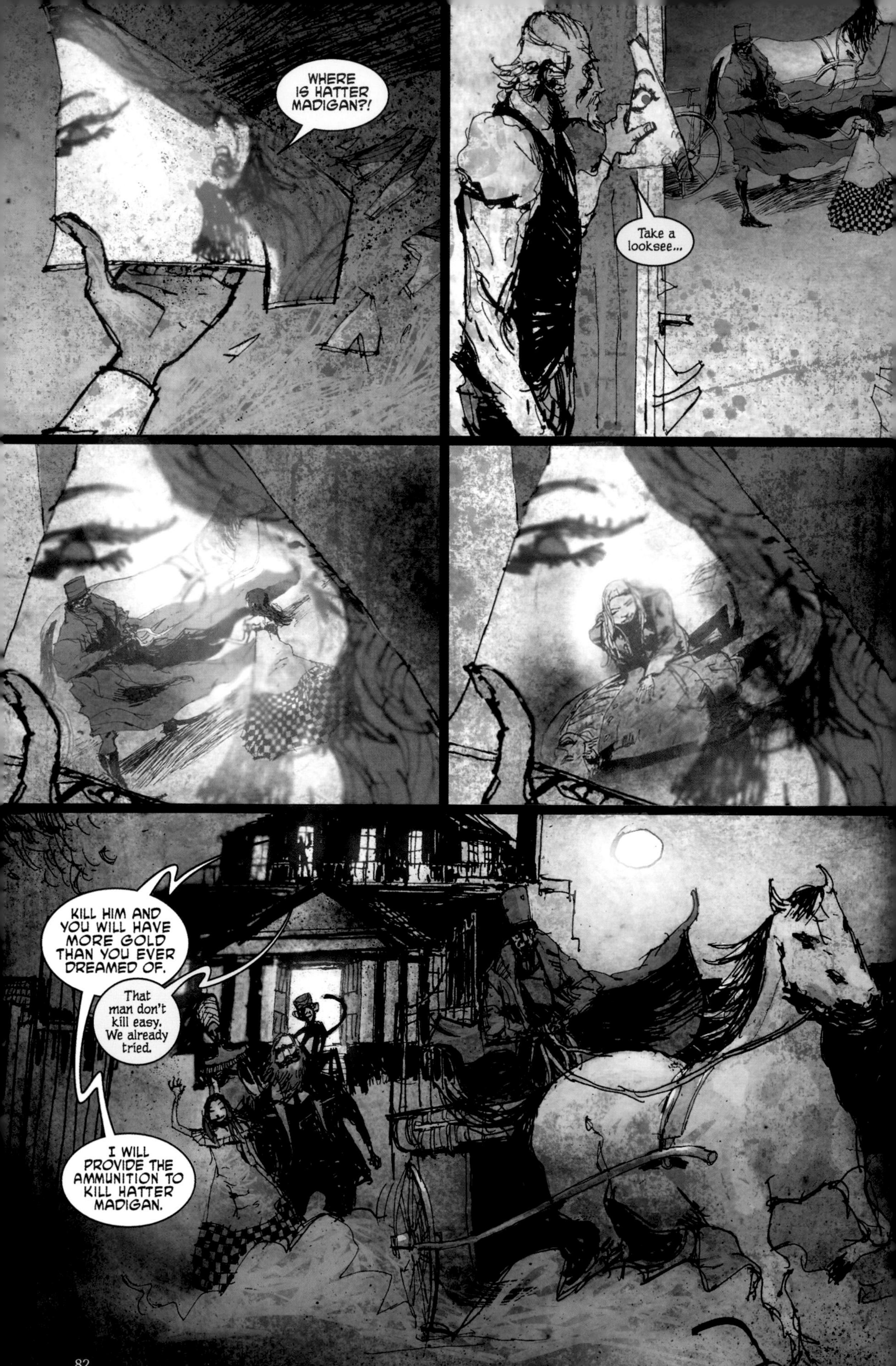
WHERE IS HATTER MADIGAN?!
Take a looksee...
KILL HIM AND YOU WILL HAVE MORE GOLD THAN YOU EVER DREAMED OF.
That man don't kill easy. We already tried.
I WILL PROVIDE THE AMMUNITION TO KILL HATTER MADIGAN.

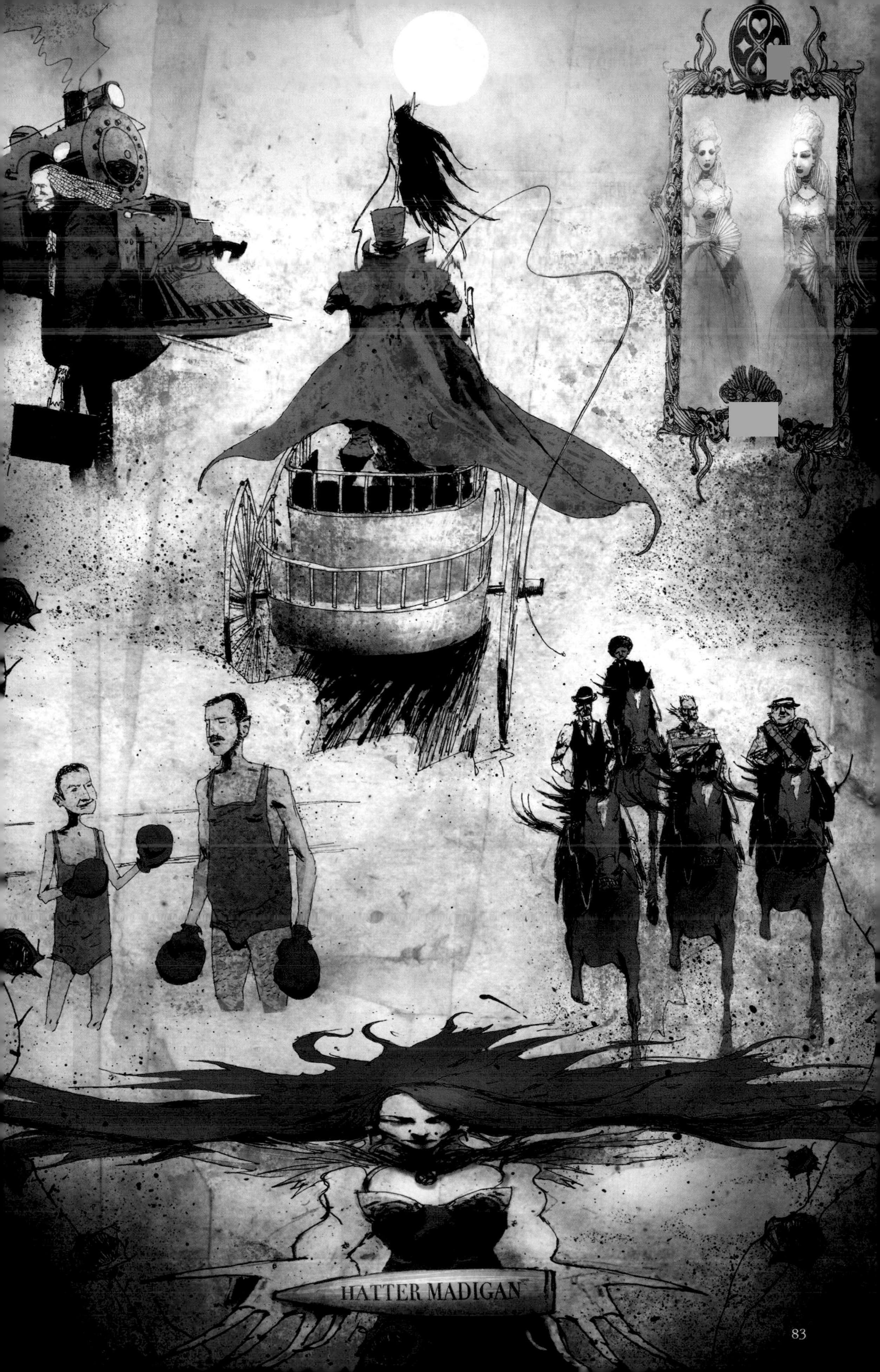
HATTER MADIGAN

Civil War in Wonderland...Civil War in America.
What world doesn't have war? Someday I should
like to travel there and perhaps...retire.

"The great proof of madness is the disproportion of one's designs to one's means." —NAPOLEON BONAPARTE

War

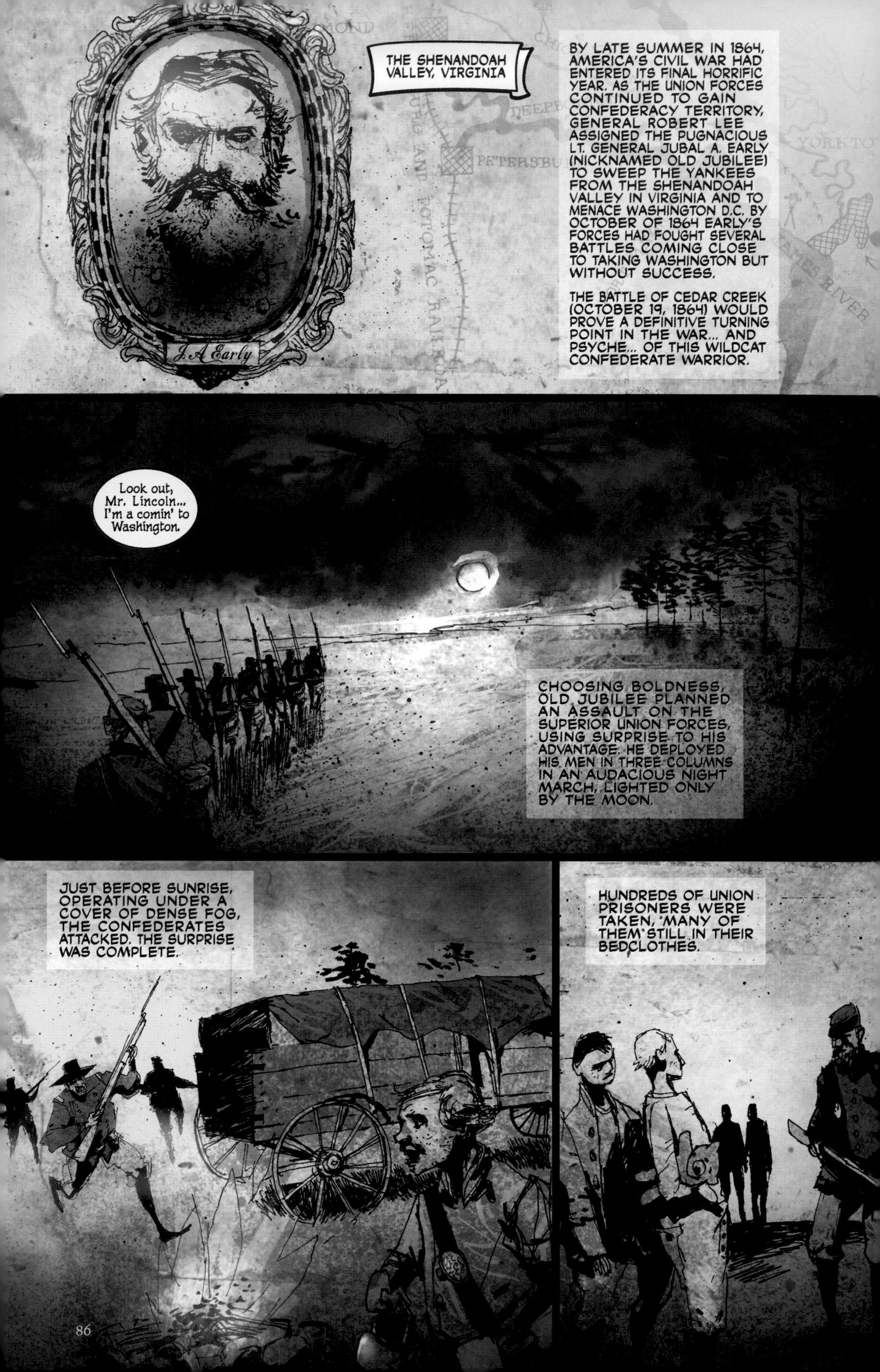
J.A Early
THE SHENANDOAH VALLEY, VIRGINIA
BY LATE SUMMER IN 1864, AMERICA'S CIVIL WAR HAD ENTERED ITS FINAL HORRIFIC YEAR. AS THE UNION FORCES CONTINUED TO GAIN CONFEDERACY TERRITORY, GENERAL ROBERT LEE ASSIGNED THE PUGNACIOUS LT. GENERAL JUBAL A. EARLY (NICKNAMED OLD JUBILEE) TO SWEEP THE YANKEES FROM THE SHENANDOAH VALLEY IN VIRGINIA AND TO MENACE WASHINGTON D.C. BY OCTOBER OF 1864 EARLY'S FORCES HAD FOUGHT SEVERAL BATTLES COMING CLOSE TO TAKING WASHINGTON BUT WITHOUT SUCCESS.
THE BATTLE OF CEDAR CREEK (OCTOBER 19, 1864) WOULD PROVE A DEFINITIVE TURNING POINT IN THE WAR... AND PSYCHE... OF THIS WILDCAT CONFEDERATE WARRIOR.
Look out, Mr. Lincoln... I'm a comin' to Washington.
CHOOSING BOLDNESS, OLD JUBILEE PLANNED AN ASSAULT ON THE SUPERIOR UNION FORCES, USING SURPRISE TO HIS ADVANTAGE. HE DEPLOYED HIS MEN IN THREE COLUMNS IN AN AUDACIOUS NIGHT MARCH, LIGHTED ONLY BY THE MOON.
JUST BEFORE SUNRISE, OPERATING UNDER A COVER OF DENSE FOG, THE CONFEDERATES ATTACKED. THE SURPRISE WAS COMPLETE.
HUNDREDS OF UNION PRISONERS WERE TAKEN, MANY OF THEM STILL IN THEIR BEDCLOTHES.

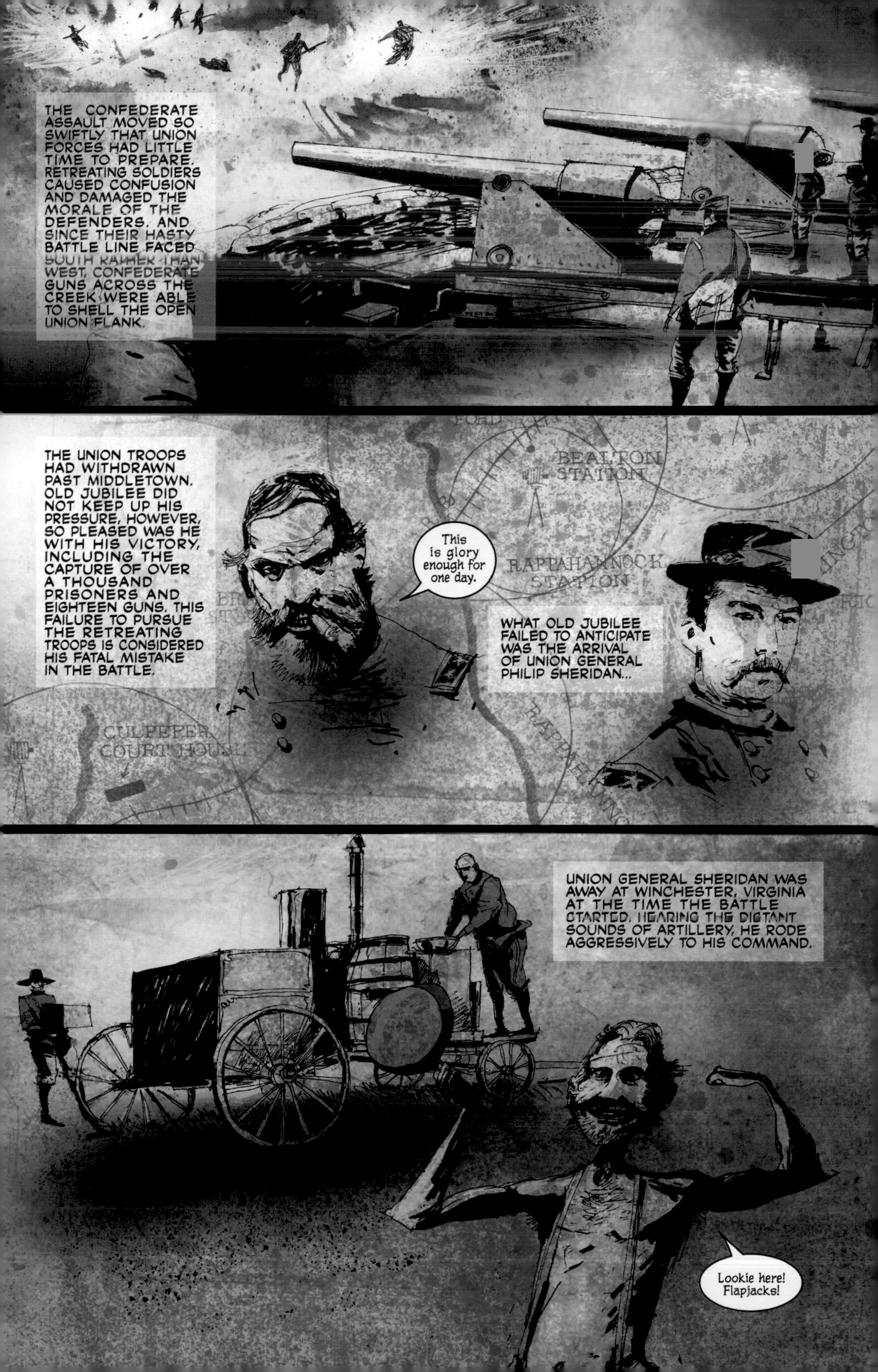
THE CONFEDERATE ASSAULT MOVED SO SWIFTLY THAT UNION FORCES HAD LITTLE TIME TO PREPARE. RETREATING SOLDIERS CAUSED CONFUSION AND DAMAGED THE MORALE OF THE DEFENDERS. AND SINCE THEIR HASTY BATTLE LINE FACED SOUTH RATHER THAN WEST, CONFEDERATE GUNS ACROSS THE CREEK WERE ABLE TO SHELL THE OPEN UNION FLANK.
FORD
BEALTON STATION
THE UNION TROOPS HAD WITHDRAWN PAST MIDDLETOWN. OLD JUBILEE DID NOT KEEP UP HIS PRESSURE, HOWEVER, SO PLEASED WAS HE WITH HIS VICTORY, INCLUDING THE CAPTURE OF OVER A THOUSAND PRISONERS AND EIGHTEEN GUNS. THIS FAILURE TO PURSUE THE RETREATING TROOPS IS CONSIDERED HIS FATAL MISTAKE IN THE BATTLE.
This is glory enough for one day.
WHAT OLD JUBILEE FAILED TO ANTICIPATE WAS THE ARRIVAL OF UNION GENERAL PHILIP SHERIDAN...
UNION GENERAL SHERIDAN WAS AWAY AT WINCHESTER, VIRGINIA AT THE TIME THE BATTLE STARTED. HEARING THE DISTANT SOUNDS OF ARTILLERY, HE RODE AGGRESSIVELY TO HIS COMMAND.
Lookie here! Flapjacks!

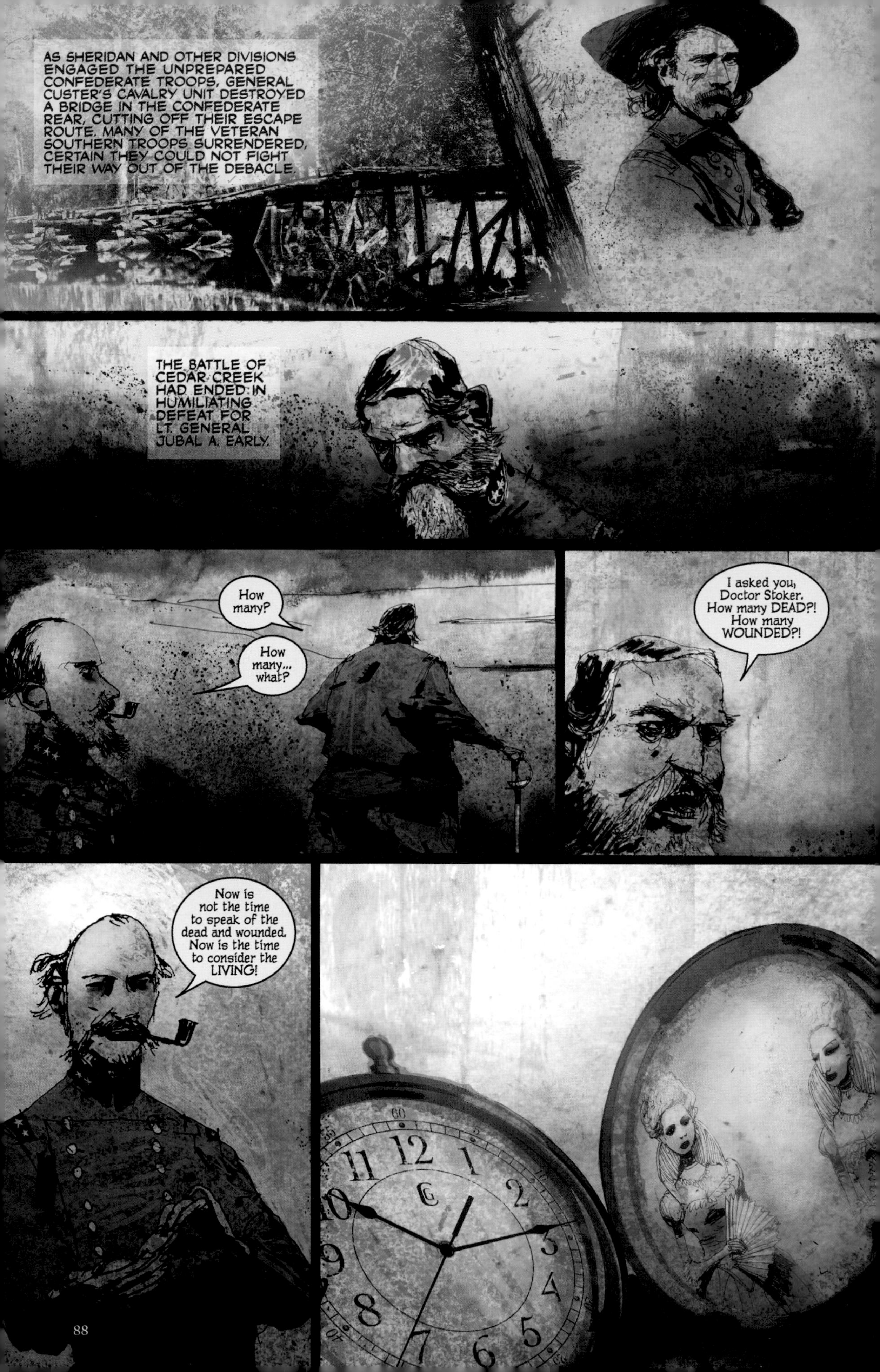
AS SHERIDAN AND OTHER DIVISIONS ENGAGED THE UNPREPARED CONFEDERATE TROOPS, GENERAL CUSTER'S CAVALRY UNIT DESTROYED A BRIDGE IN THE CONFEDERATE REAR, CUTTING OFF THEIR ESCAPE ROUTE. MANY OF THE VETERAN SOUTHERN TROOPS SURRENDERED, CERTAIN THEY COULD NOT FIGHT THEIR WAY OUT OF THE DEBACLE.
THE BATTLE OF CEDAR CREEK HAD ENDED IN HUMILIATING DEFEAT FOR LT. GENERAL JUBAL A. EARLY.
How many?
How many... what?
I asked you, Doctor Stoker. How many DEAD?! How many WOUNDED?!
Now is not the time to speak of the dead and wounded. Now is the time to consider the LIVING!

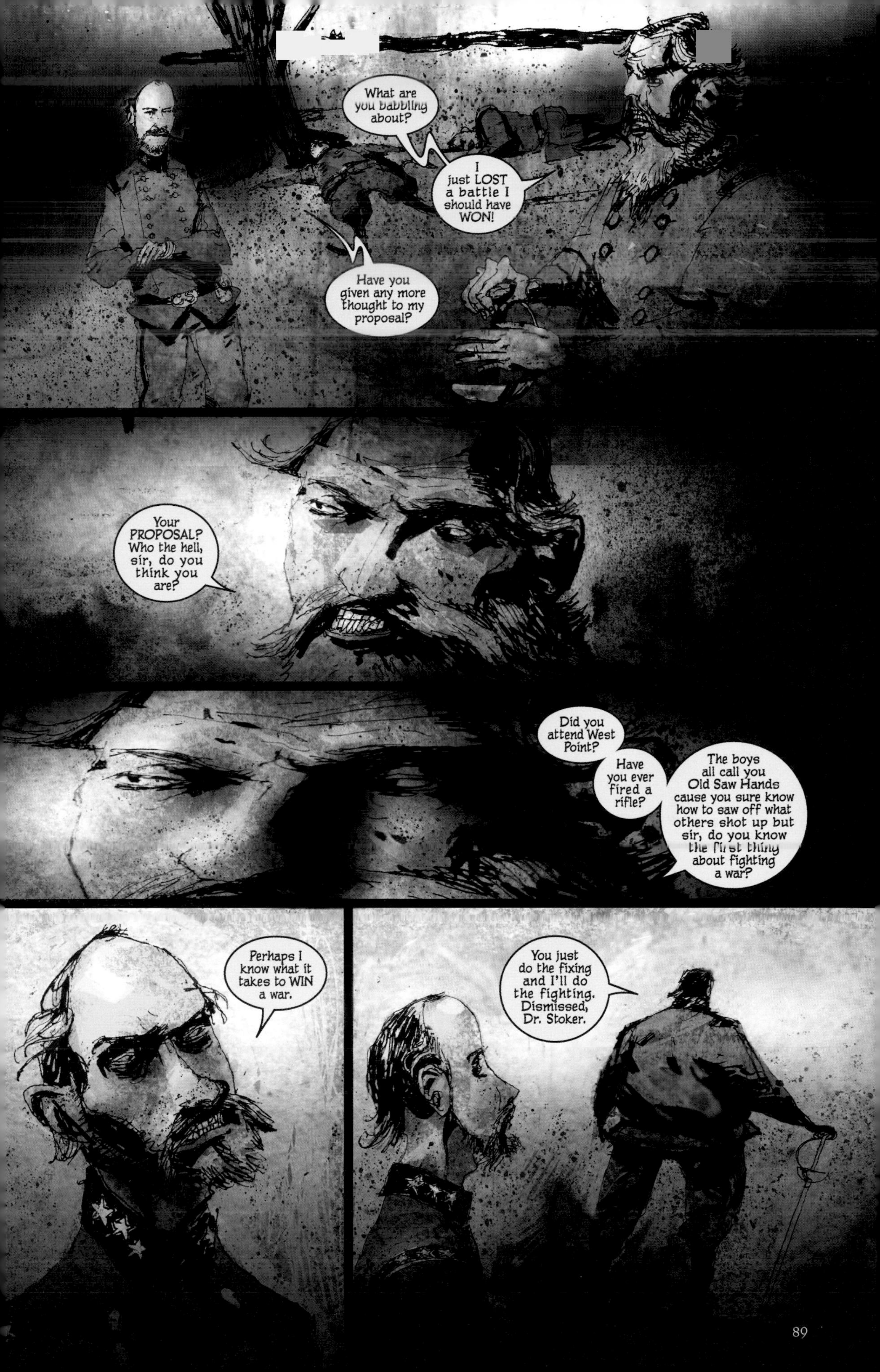
What are you babbling about?
I just LOST a battle I should have WON!
Have you given any more thought to my proposal?
Your PROPOSAL? Who the hell, sir, do you think you are?
Did you attend West Point?
Have you ever fired a rifle?
The boys all call you Old Saw Hands cause you sure know how to saw off what others shot up but sir, do you know the first thing about fighting a war?
Perhaps I know what it takes to WIN a war.
You just do the fixing and I'll do the fighting. Dismissed, Dr. Stoker.

I fear I feel too much. Emotions are inappropriate to my sworn duty. And yet...I feel love and loss and rage and...fear. What does a bodyguard become who has given up the right to feel?

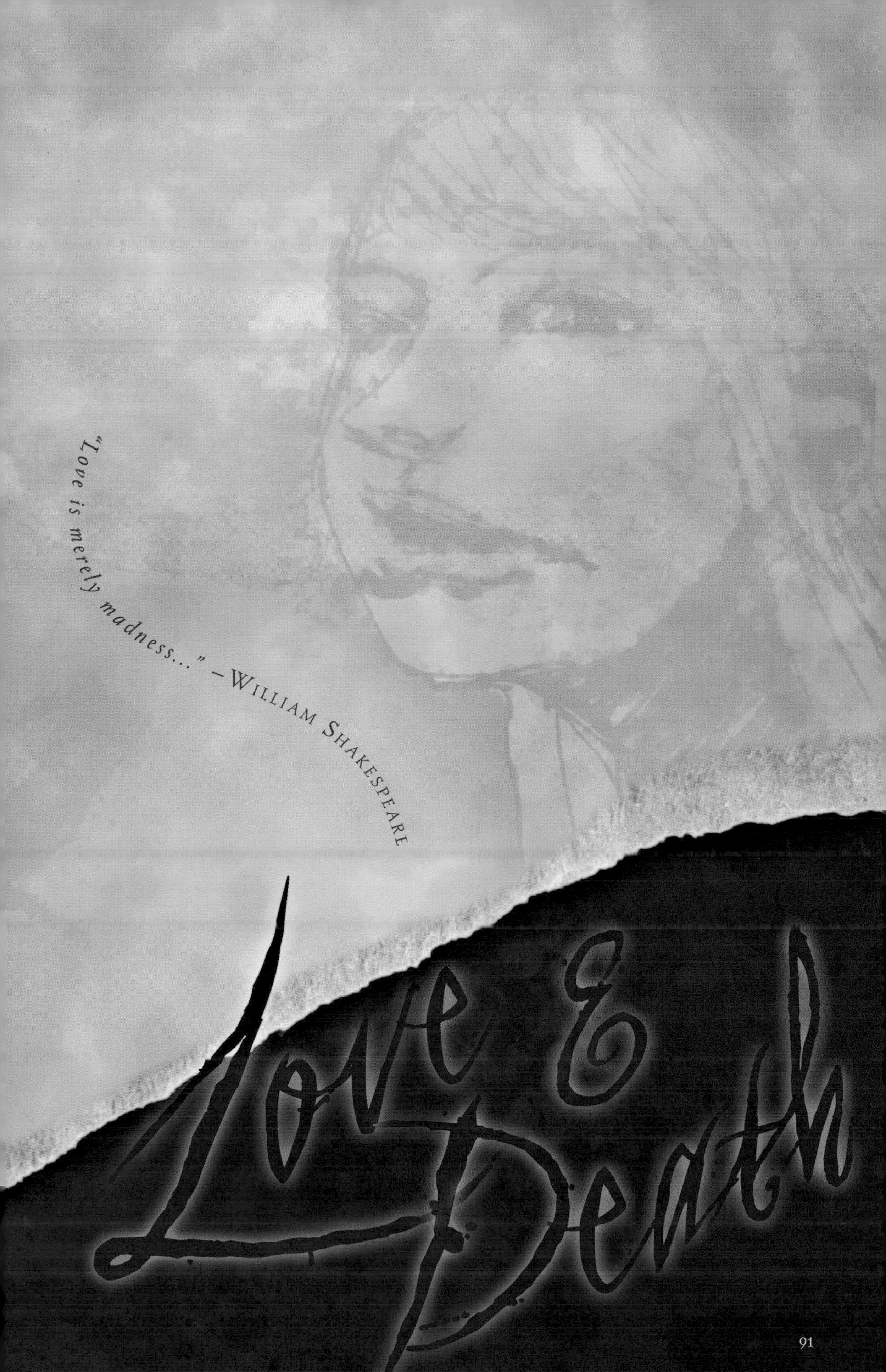

"Love is merely madness..." —William Shakespeare

Love & Death

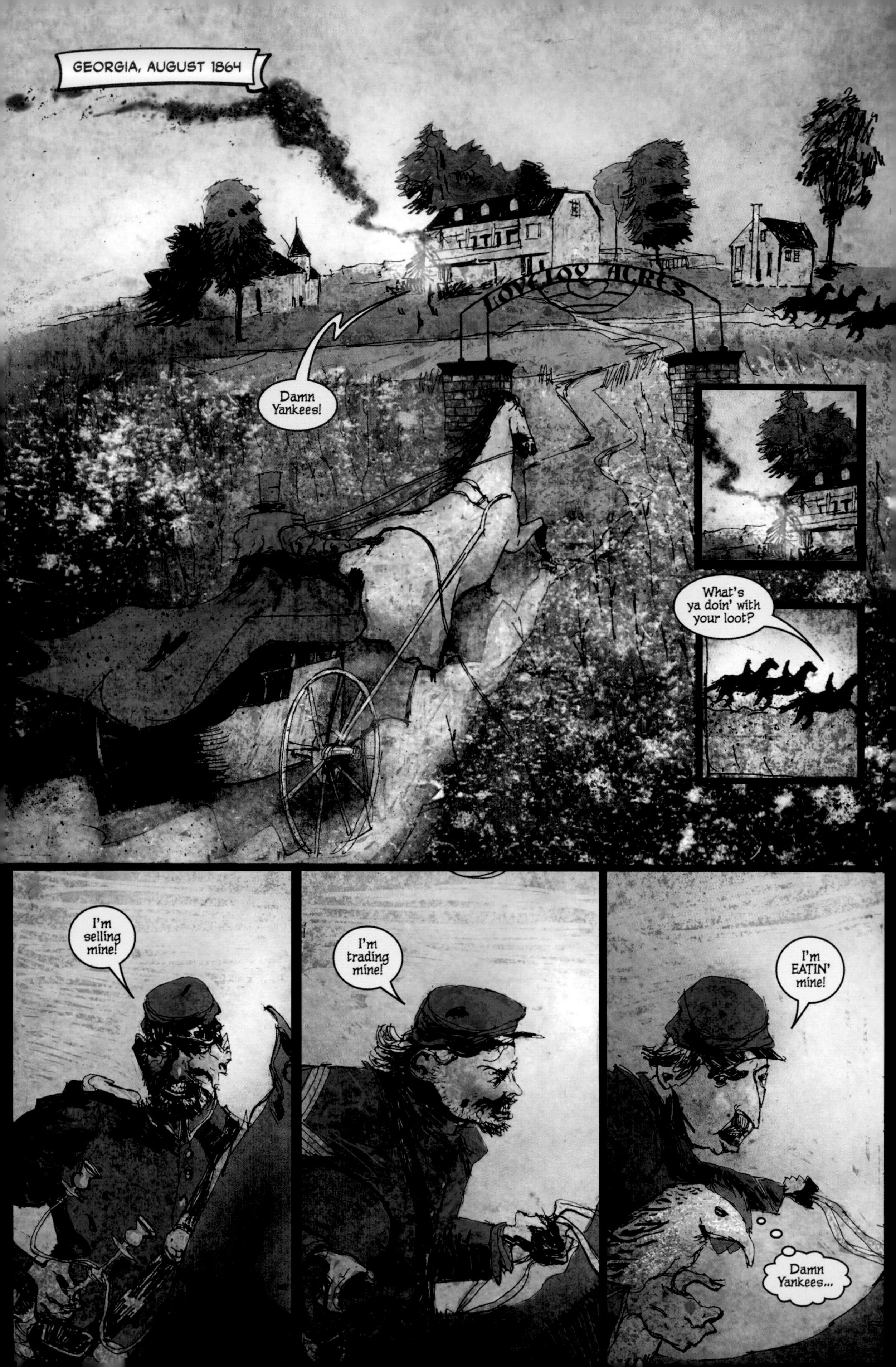

GEORGIA, AUGUST 1864
LOVEJOY ACRES
Damn Yankees!
What's ya doin' with your loot?
I'm selling mine!
I'm trading mine!
I'm EATIN' mine!
Damn Yankees...

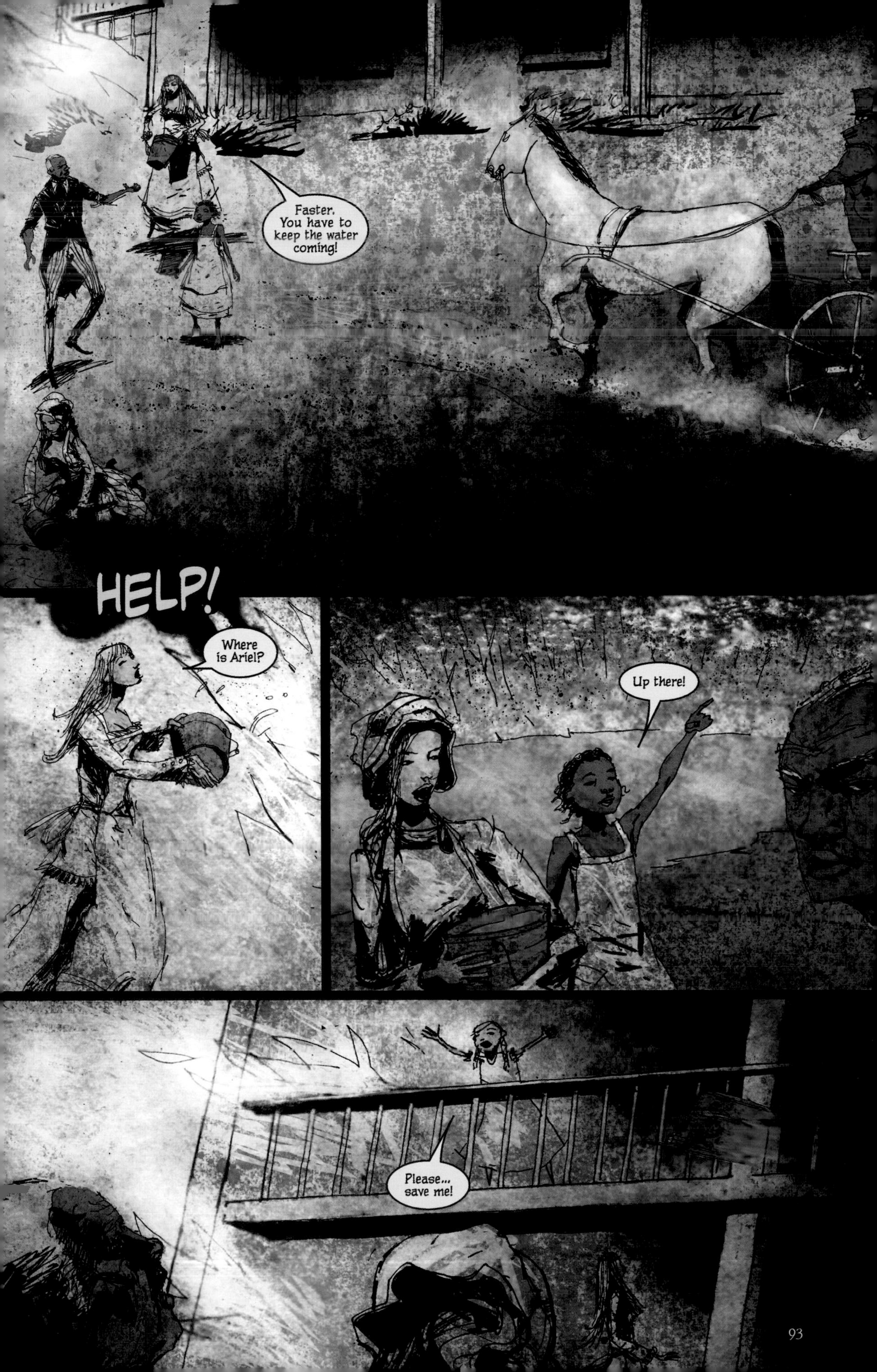
Faster. You have to keep the water coming!
HELP!
Where is Ariel?
Up there!
Please... save me!

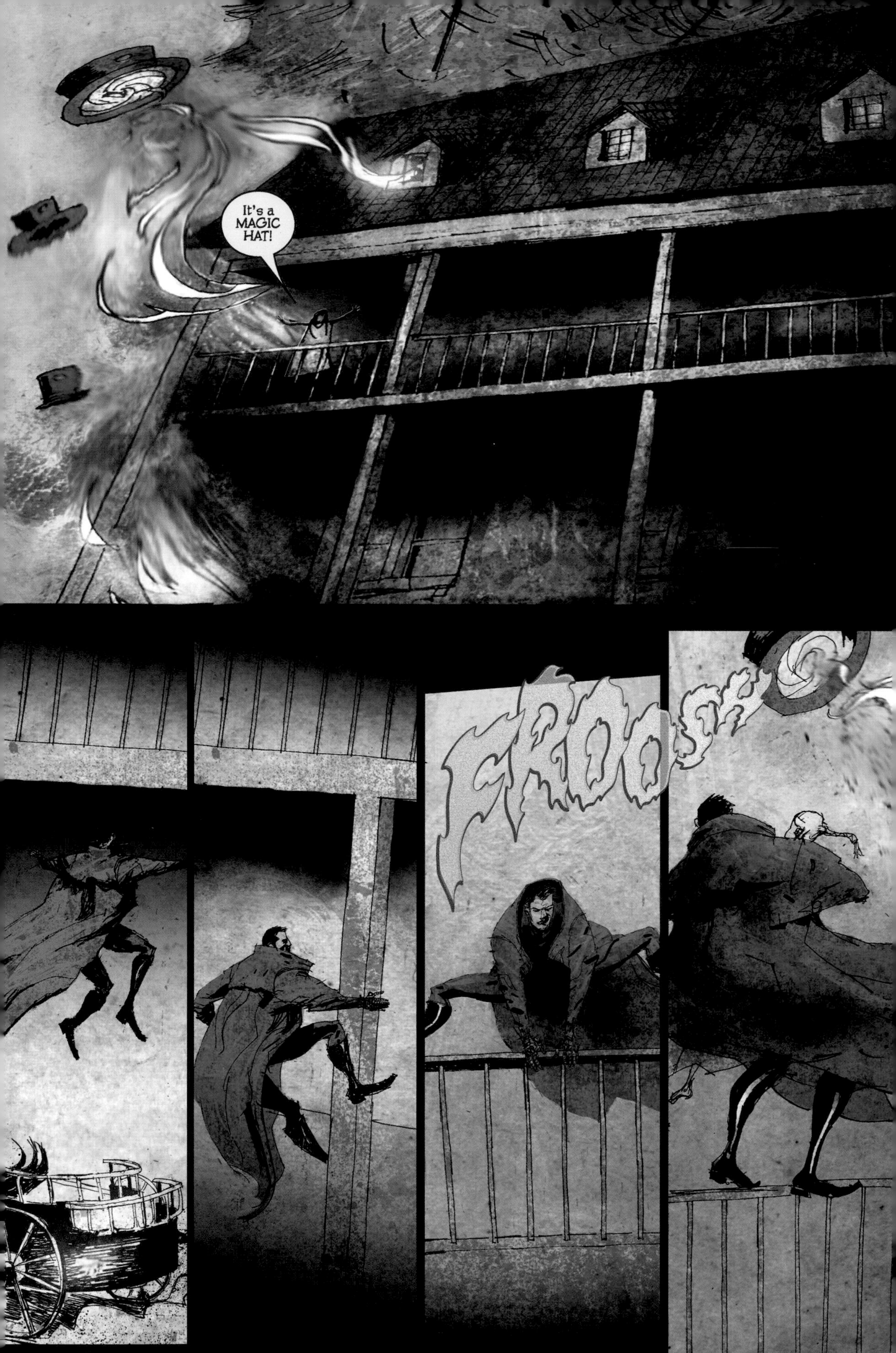
It's a MAGIC HAT!
FROOSH

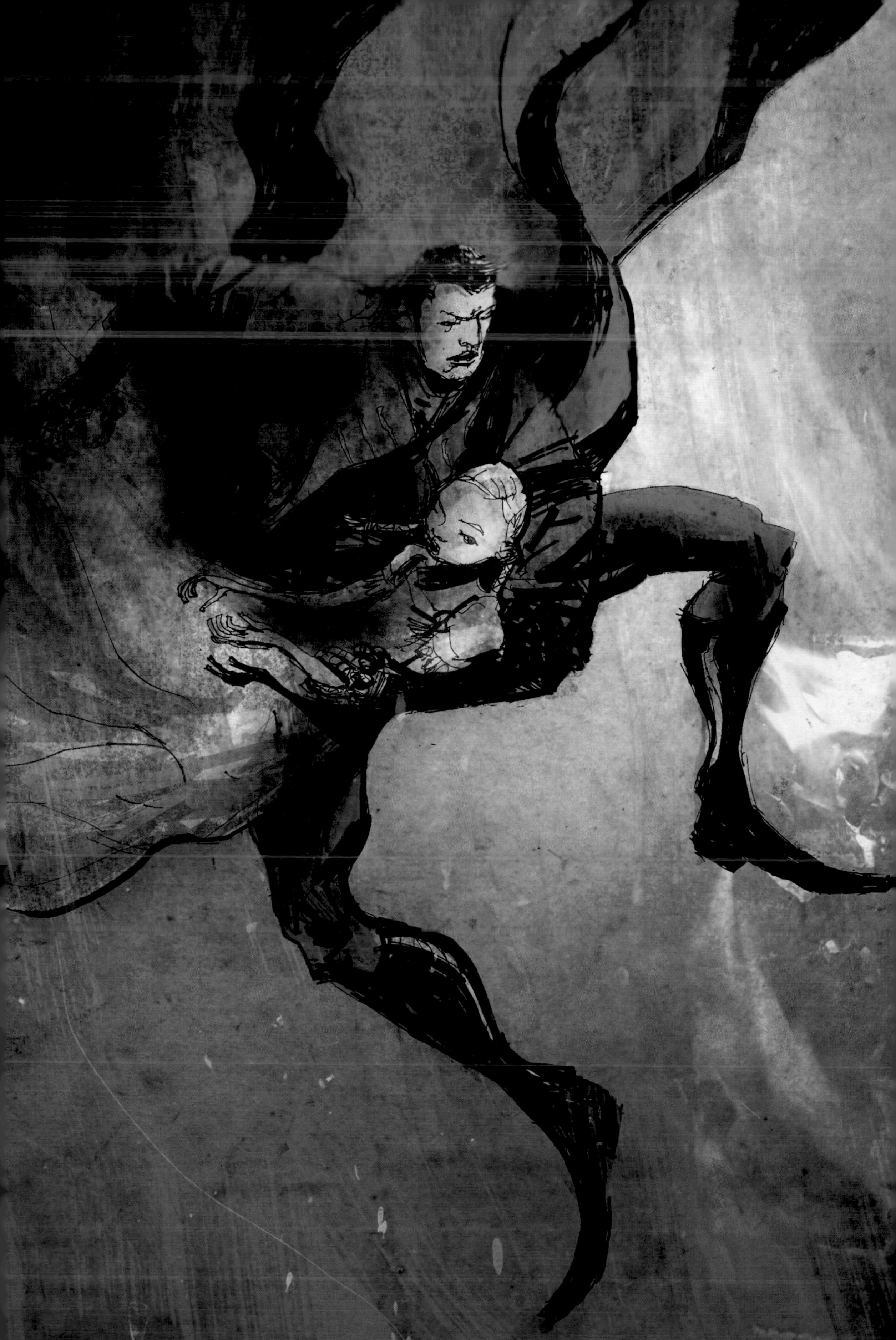

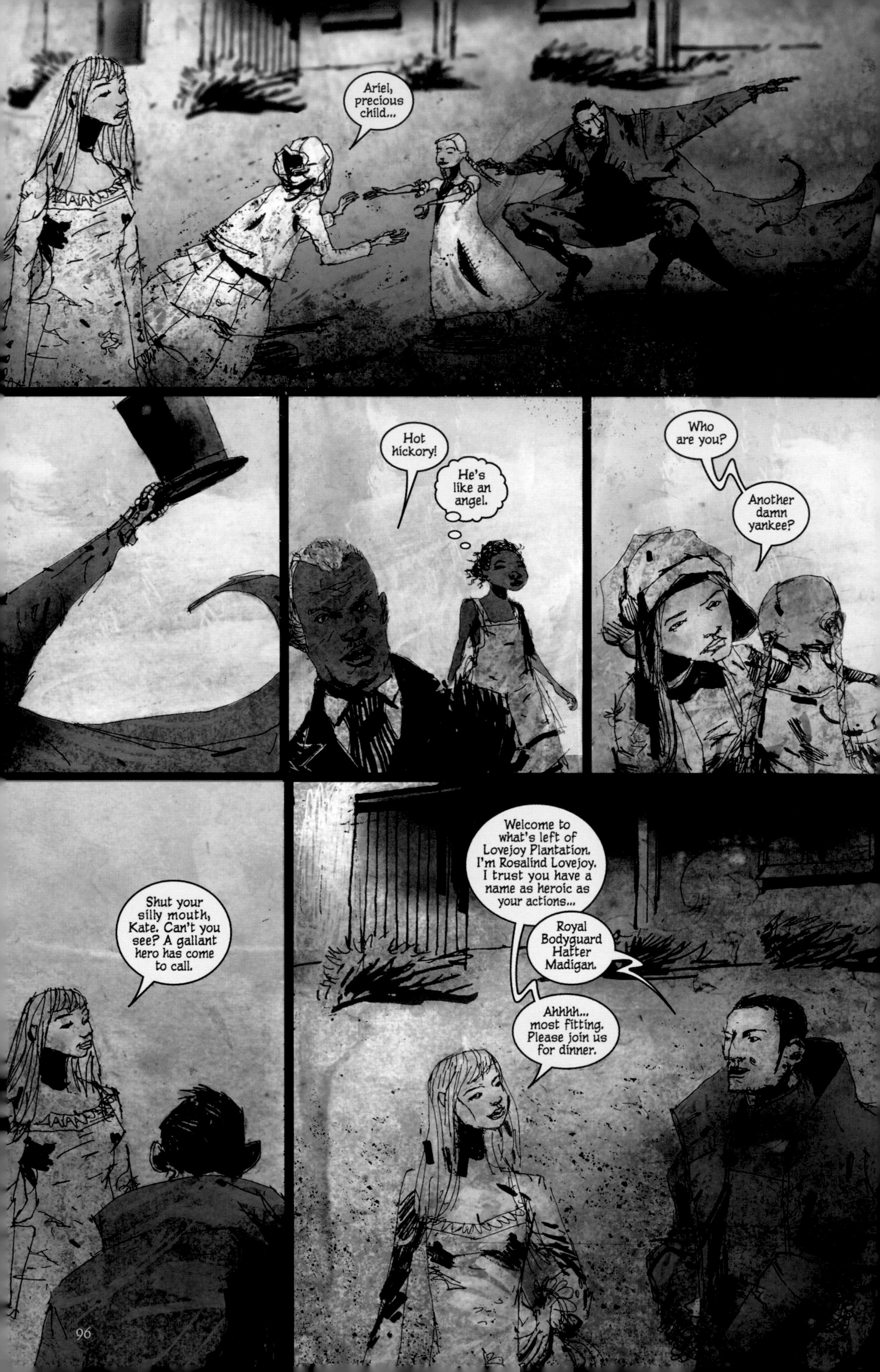
Ariel, precious child...
Hot hickory!
He's like an angel.
Who are you?
Another damn yankee?
Shut your silly mouth, Kate. Can't you see? A gallant hero has come to call.
Welcome to what's left of Lovejoy Plantation. I'm Rosalind Lovejoy. I trust you have a name as heroic as your actions...
Royal Bodyguard Hatter Madigan.
Ahhhh... most fitting. Please join us for dinner.

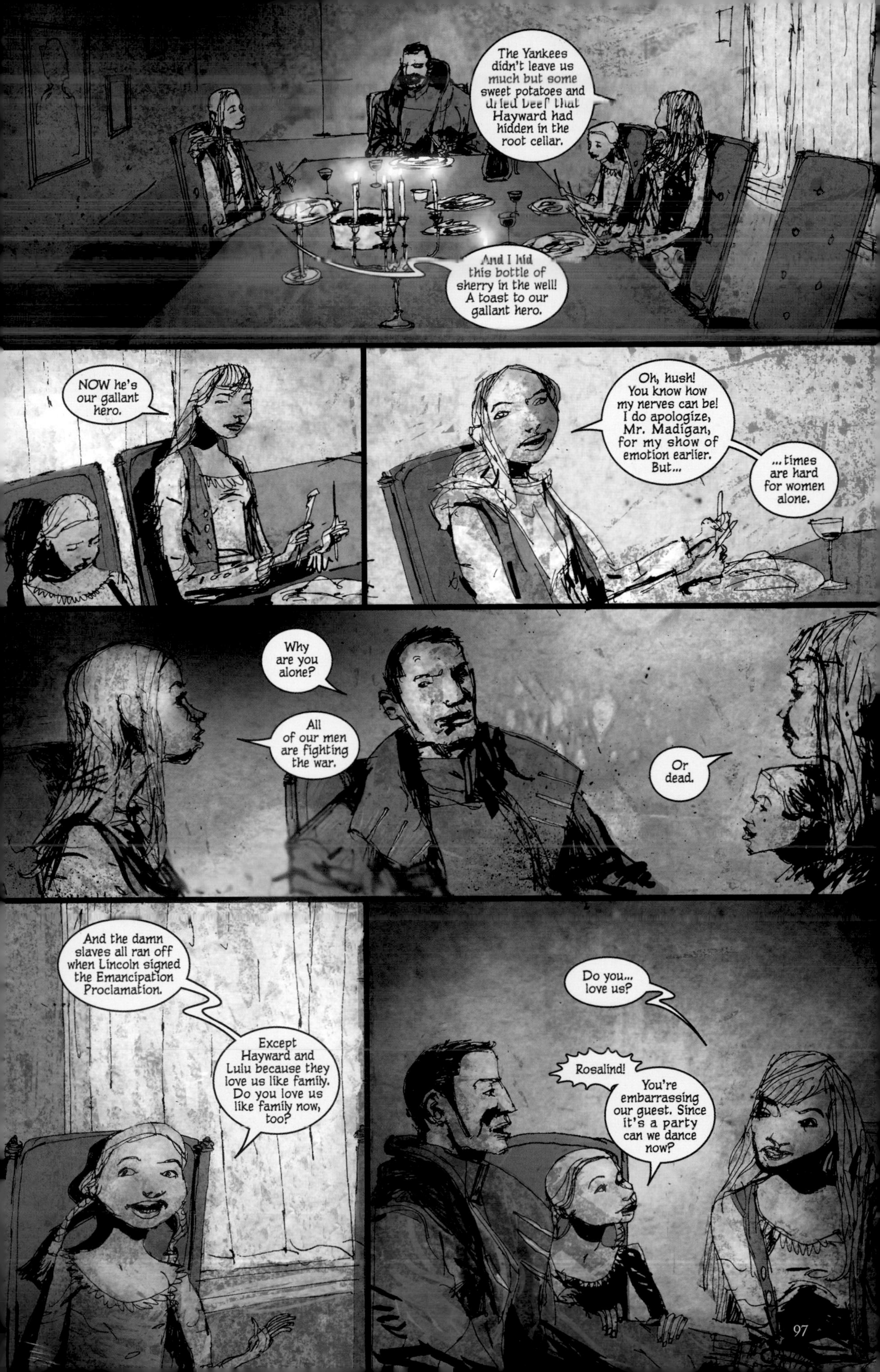
The Yankees didn't leave us much but some sweet potatoes and dried beef that Hayward had hidden in the root cellar.
And I hid this bottle of sherry in the well! A toast to our gallant hero.
NOW he's our gallant hero.
Oh, hush! You know how my nerves can be! I do apologize, Mr. Madigan, for my show of emotion earlier. But...
...times are hard for women alone.
Why are you alone?
All of our men are fighting the war.
Or dead.
And the damn slaves all ran off when Lincoln signed the Emancipation Proclamation.
Except Hayward and Lulu because they love us like family. Do you love us like family now, too?
Do you... love us?
Rosalind!
You're embarrassing our guest. Since it's a party can we dance now?

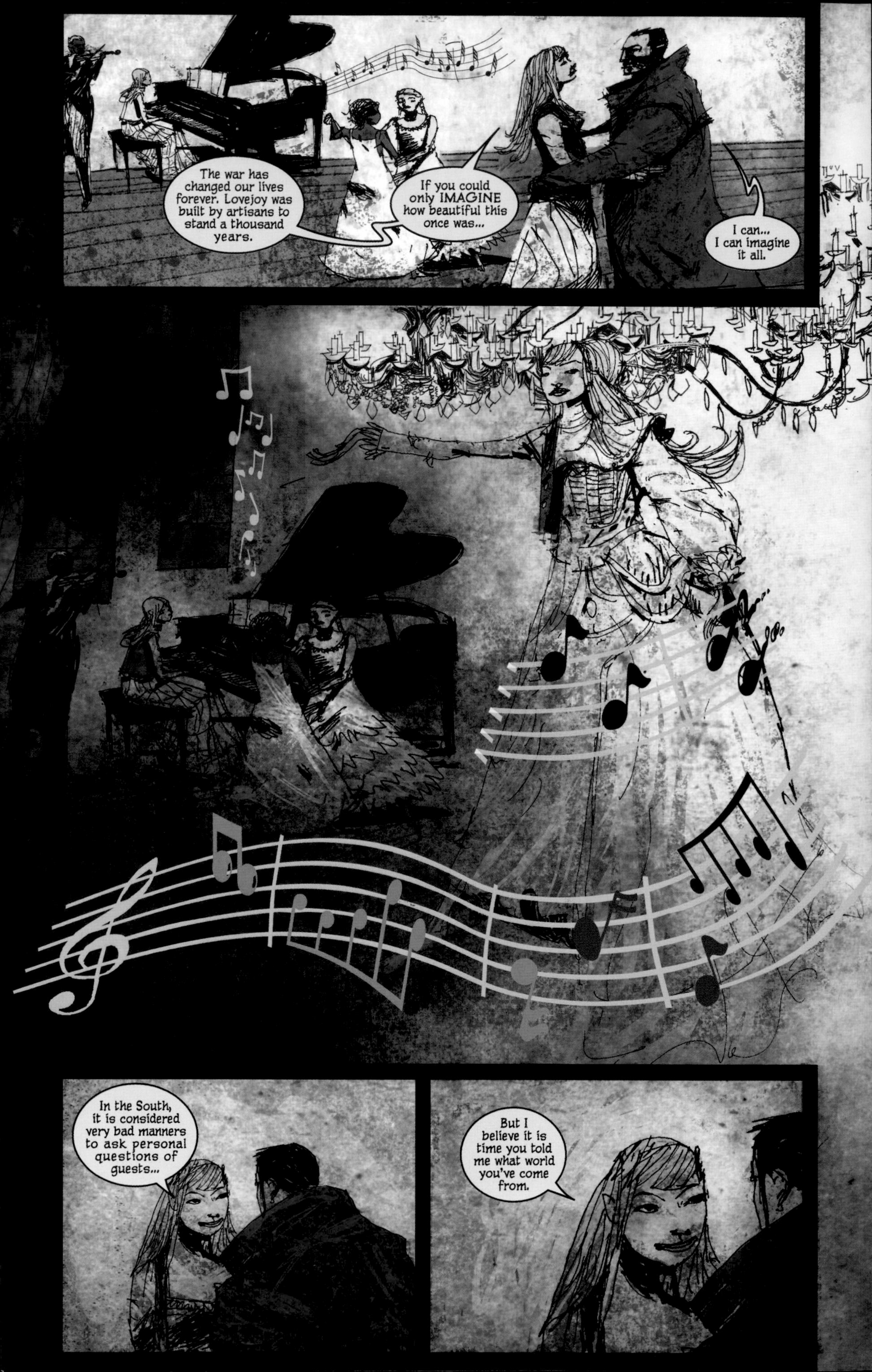
The war has changed our lives forever. Lovejoy was built by artisans to stand a thousand years.
If you could only IMAGINE how beautiful this once was...
I can... I can imagine it all.
In the South, it is considered very bad manners to ask personal questions of guests...
But I believe it is time you told me what world you've come from.

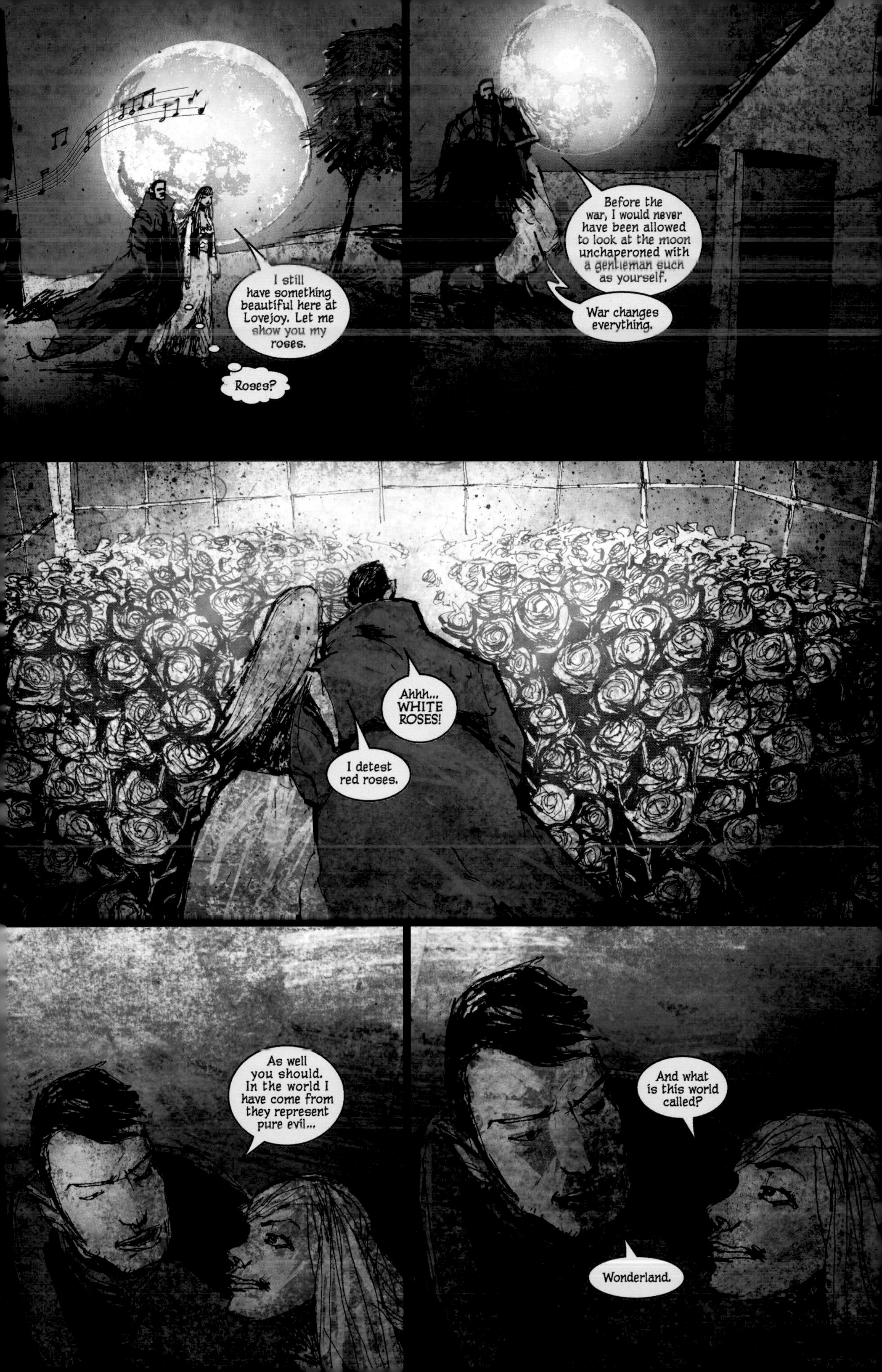
I still have something beautiful here at Lovejoy. Let me show you my roses.
Roses?
Before the war, I would never have been allowed to look at the moon unchaperoned with a gentleman such as yourself.
War changes everything.
Ahhh... WHITE ROSES!
I detest red roses.
As well you should. In the world I have come from they represent pure evil...
And what is this world called?
Wonderland.

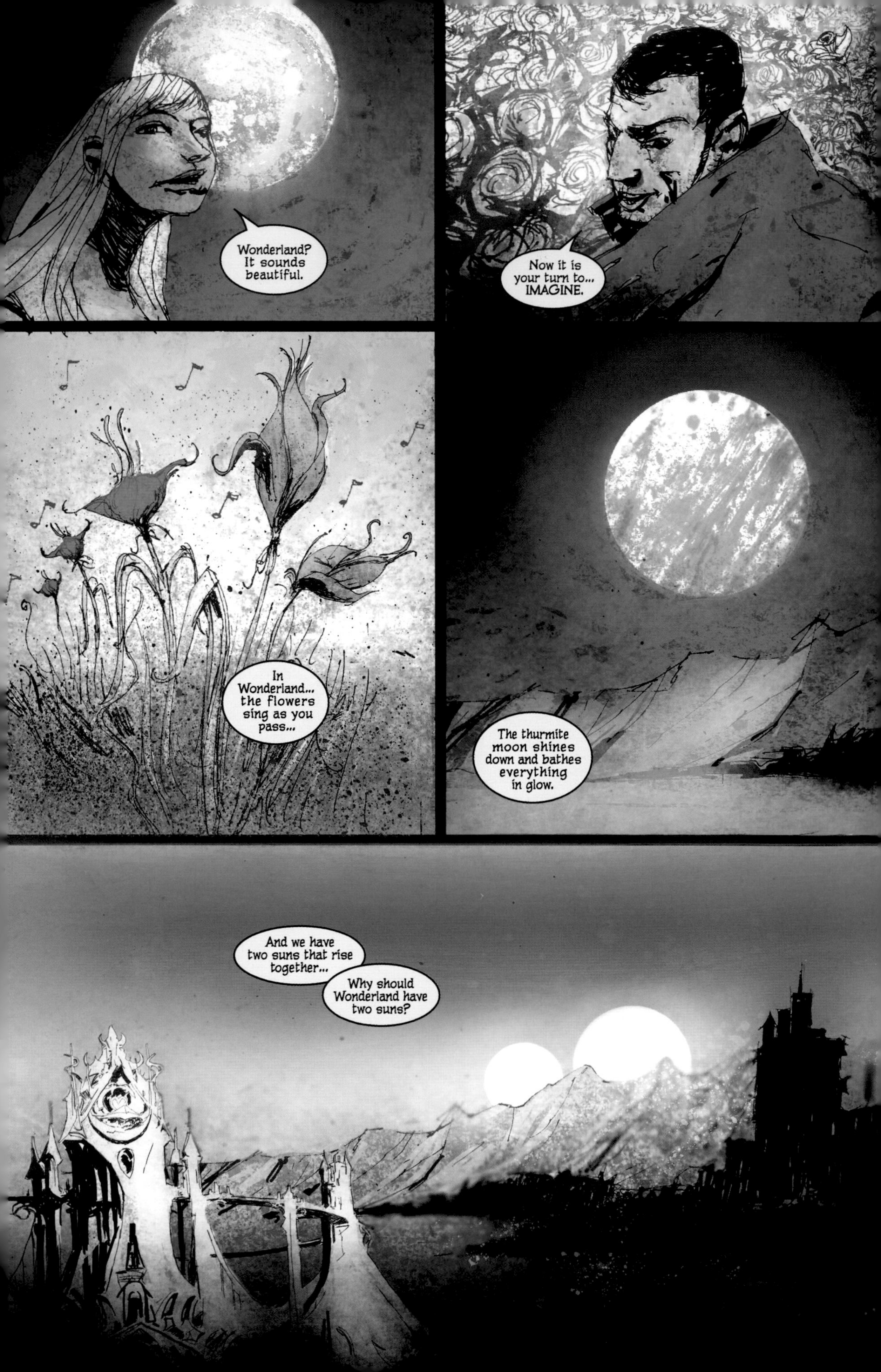
Wonderland? It sounds beautiful.
Now it is your turn to... IMAGINE.
In Wonderland... the flowers sing as you pass...
The thurmite moon shines down and bathes everything in glow.
And we have two suns that rise together...
Why should Wonderland have two suns?

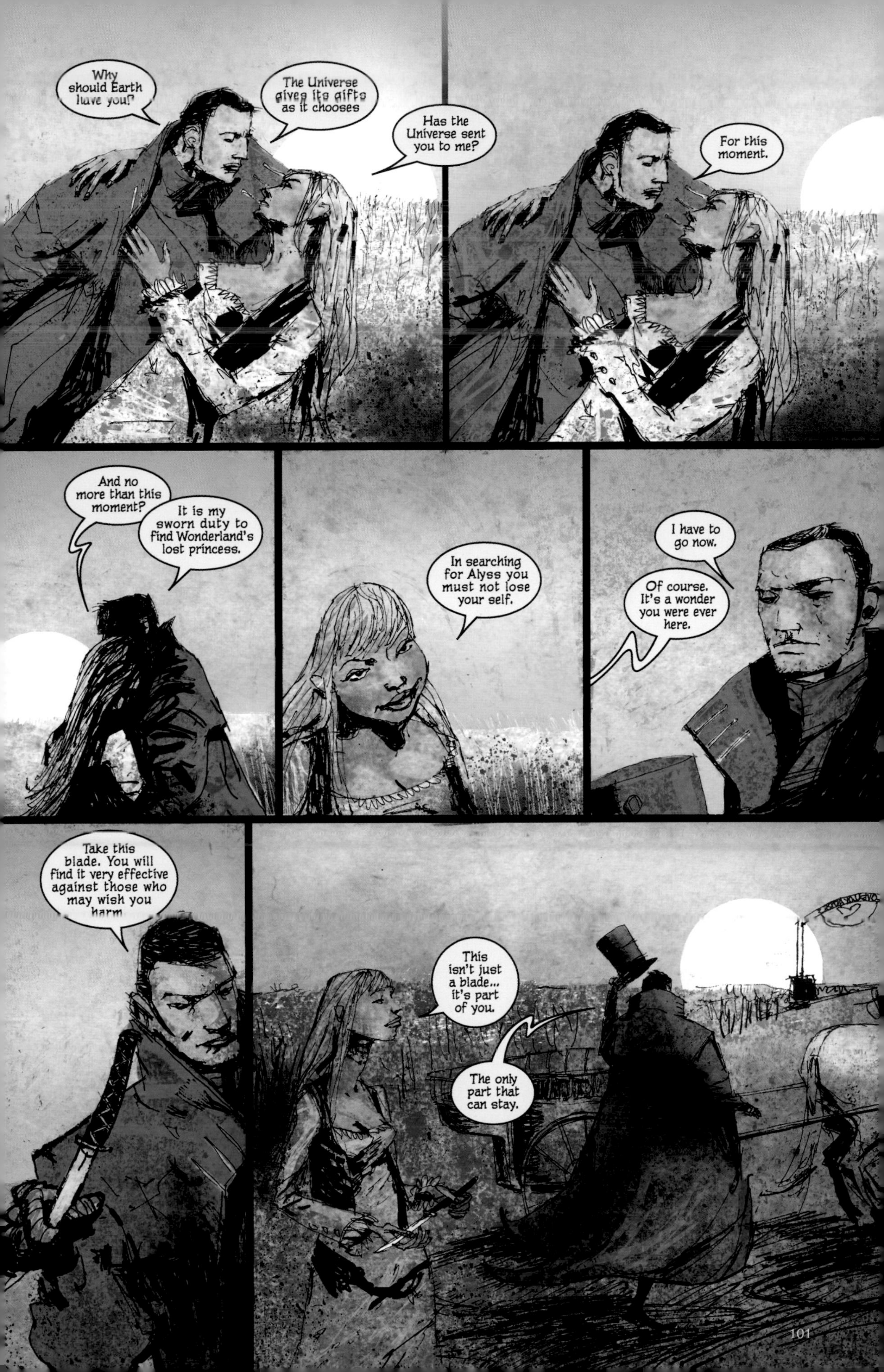
Why should Earth have you?
The Universe gives its gifts as it chooses
Has the Universe sent you to me?
For this moment.
And no more than this moment?
It is my sworn duty to find Wonderland's lost princess.
In searching for Alyss you must not lose your self.
I have to go now.
Of course. It's a wonder you were ever here.
Take this blade. You will find it very effective against those who may wish you harm.
This isn't just a blade... it's part of you.
The only part that can stay.

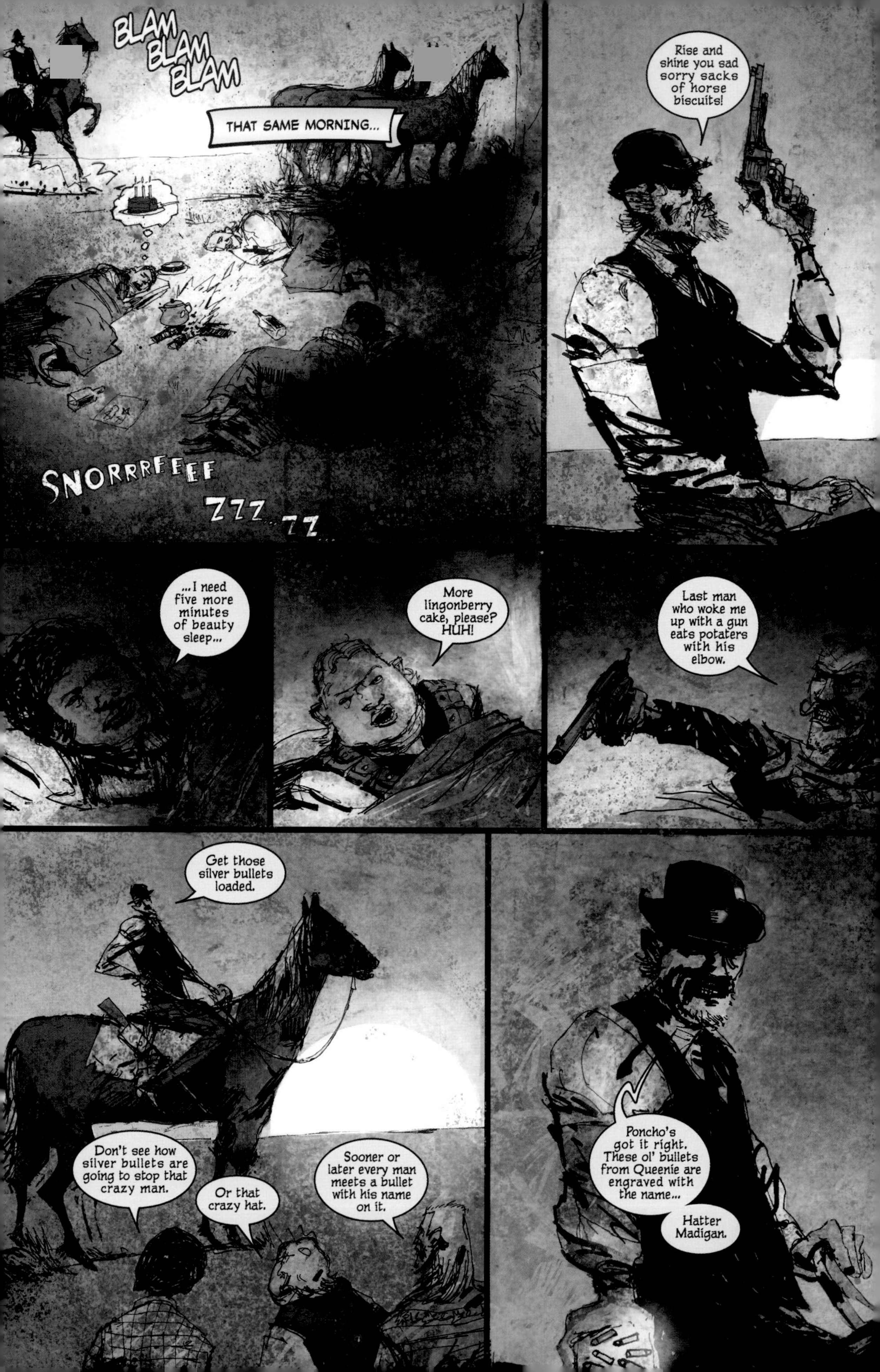
BLAM BLAM BLAM
THAT SAME MORNING...
SNORRRFEEEF
ZZZ...ZZ...
Rise and shine you sad sorry sacks of horse biscuits!
...I need five more minutes of beauty sleep...
More lingonberry cake, please? HUH!
Last man who woke me up with a gun eats potaters with his elbow.
Get those silver bullets loaded.
Don't see how silver bullets are going to stop that crazy man.
Or that crazy hat.
Sooner or later every man meets a bullet with his name on it.
Poncho's got it right. These ol' bullets from Queenie are engraved with the name...
Hatter Madigan.

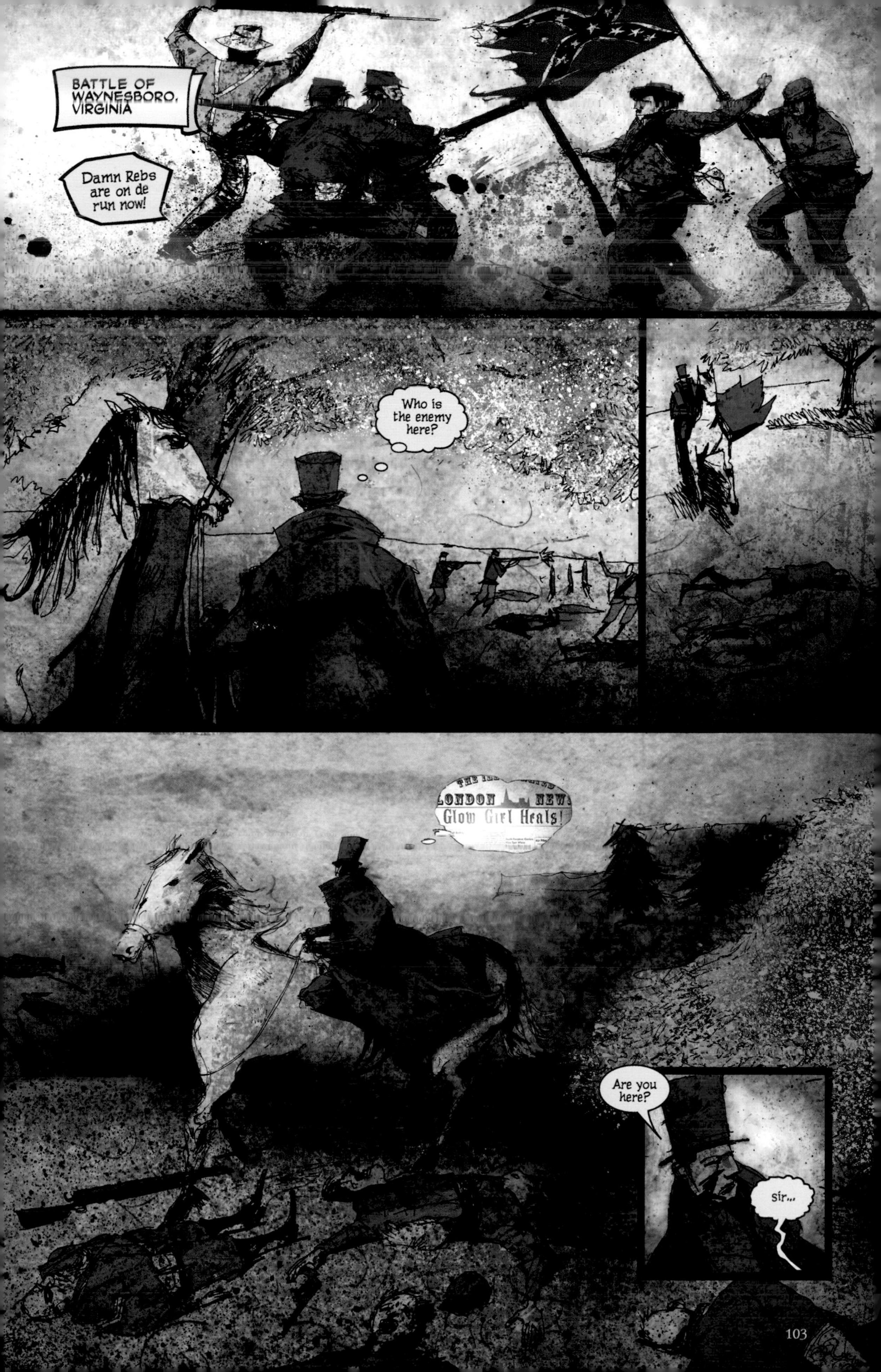
BATTLE OF WAYNESBORO, VIRGINIA
Damn Rebs are on de run now!
Who is the enemy here?
THE ILLUSTRATED LONDON NEWS
Glow Girl Heals!
Are you here?
sir...

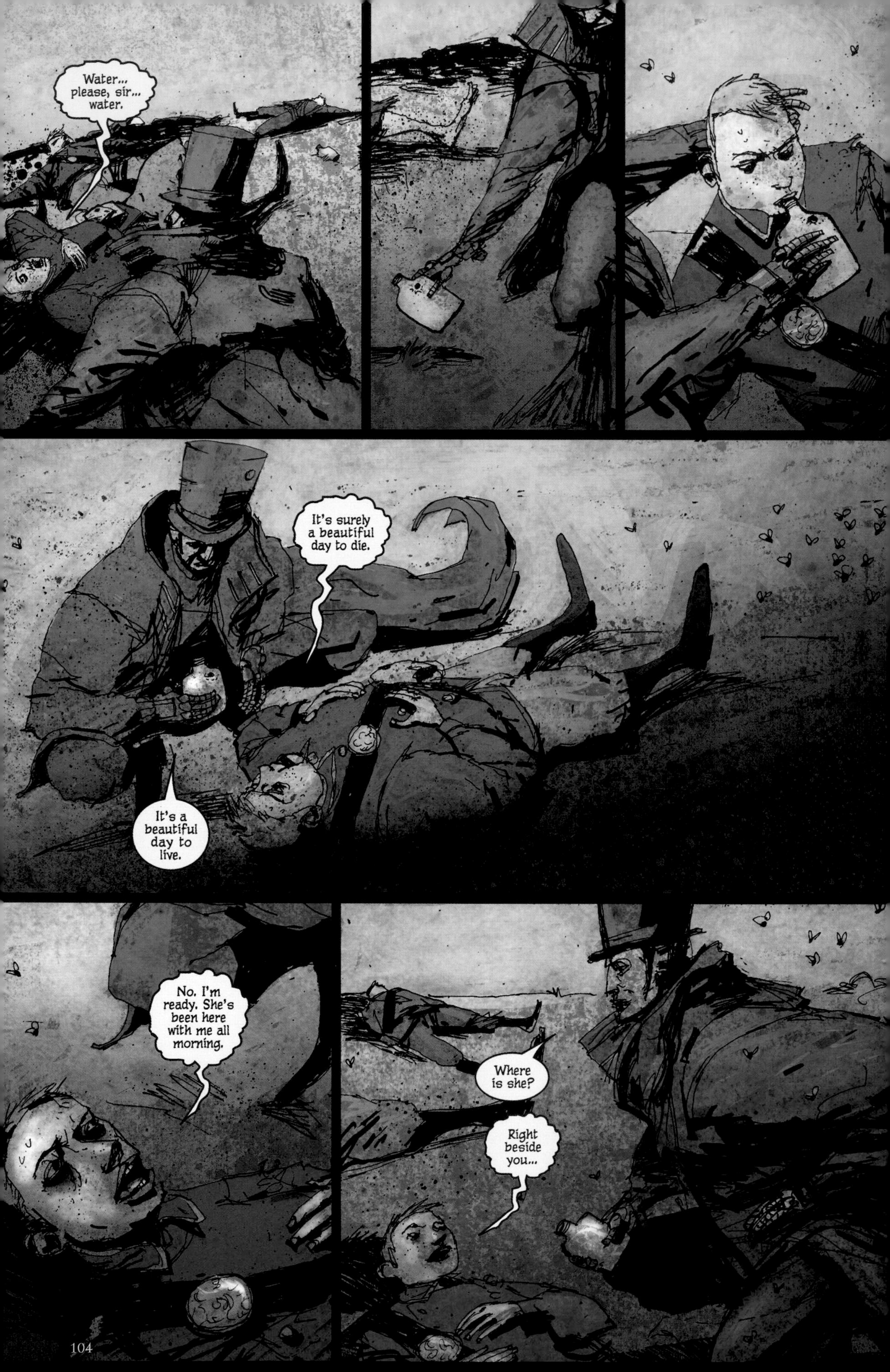
Water... please, sir... water.
It's surely a beautiful day to die.
It's a beautiful day to live.
No. I'm ready. She's been here with me all morning.
Where is she?
Right beside you...

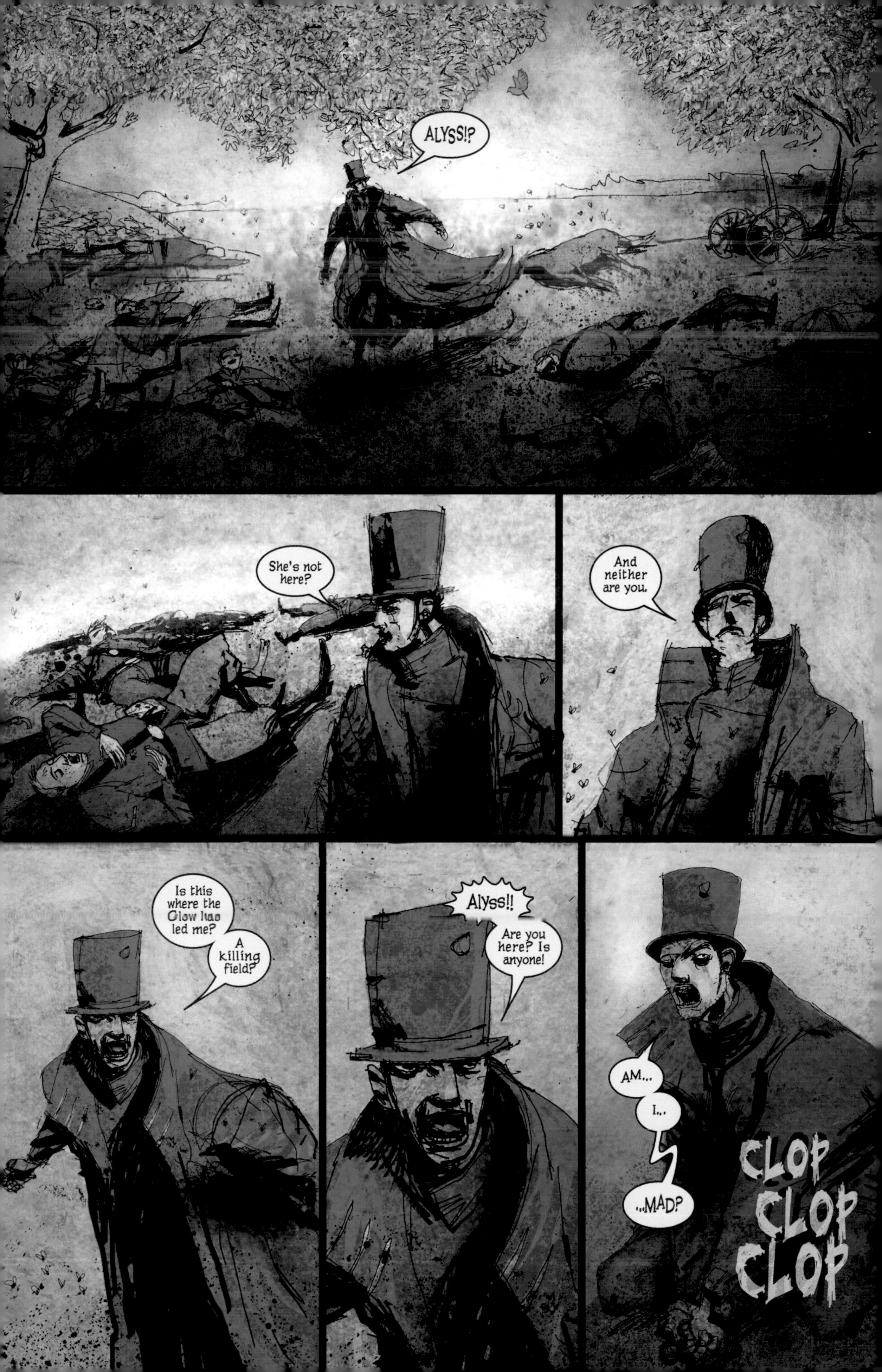
ALYSS!?
She's not here?
And neither are you.
Is this where the Glow has led me?
A killing field?
Alyss!!
Are you here? Is anyone!
AM...
I...
...MAD?
CLOP CLOP CLOP

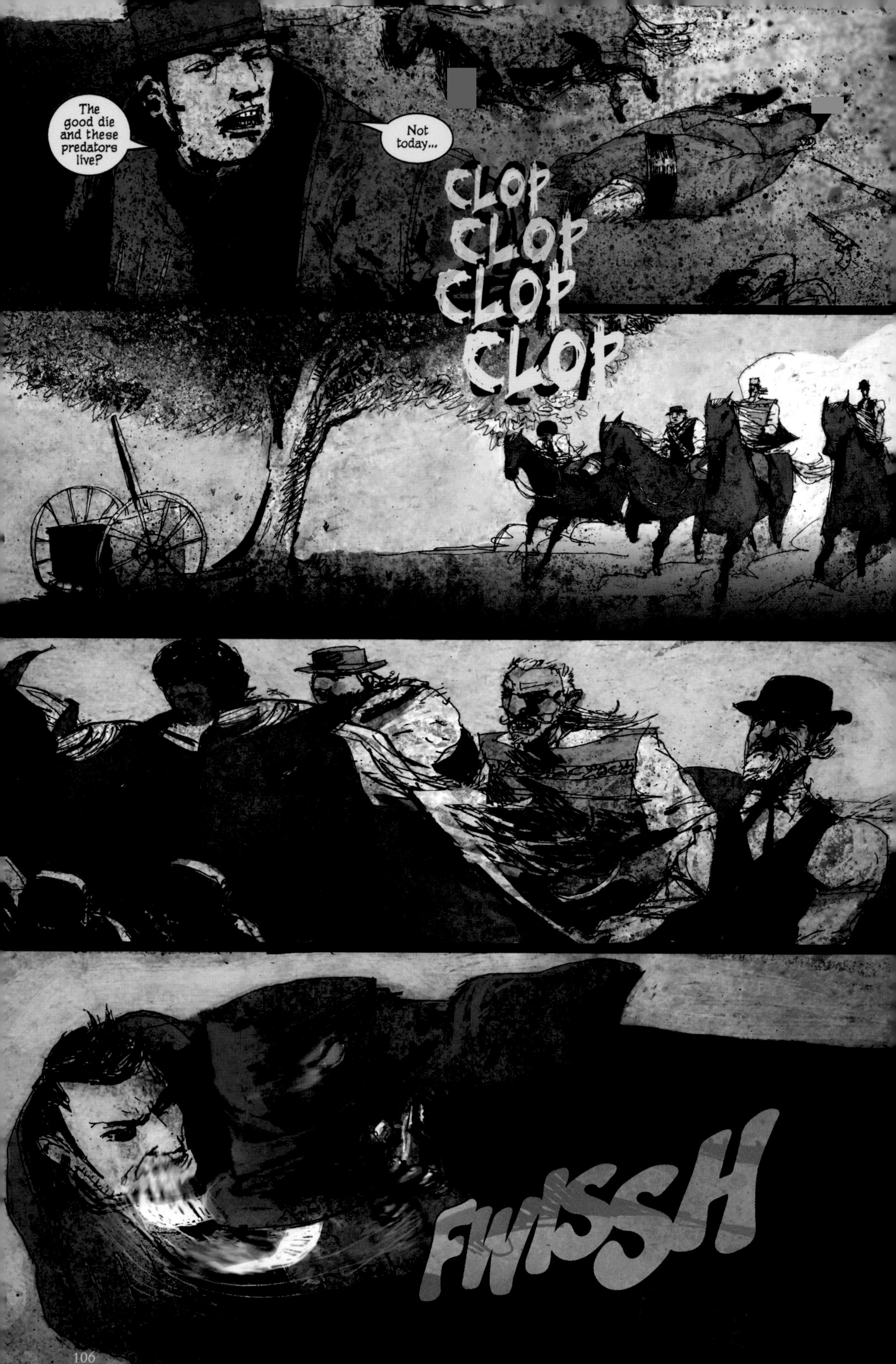
The good die and these predators live?
Not today...
CLOP
CLOP
CLOP
CLOP
FWSSH

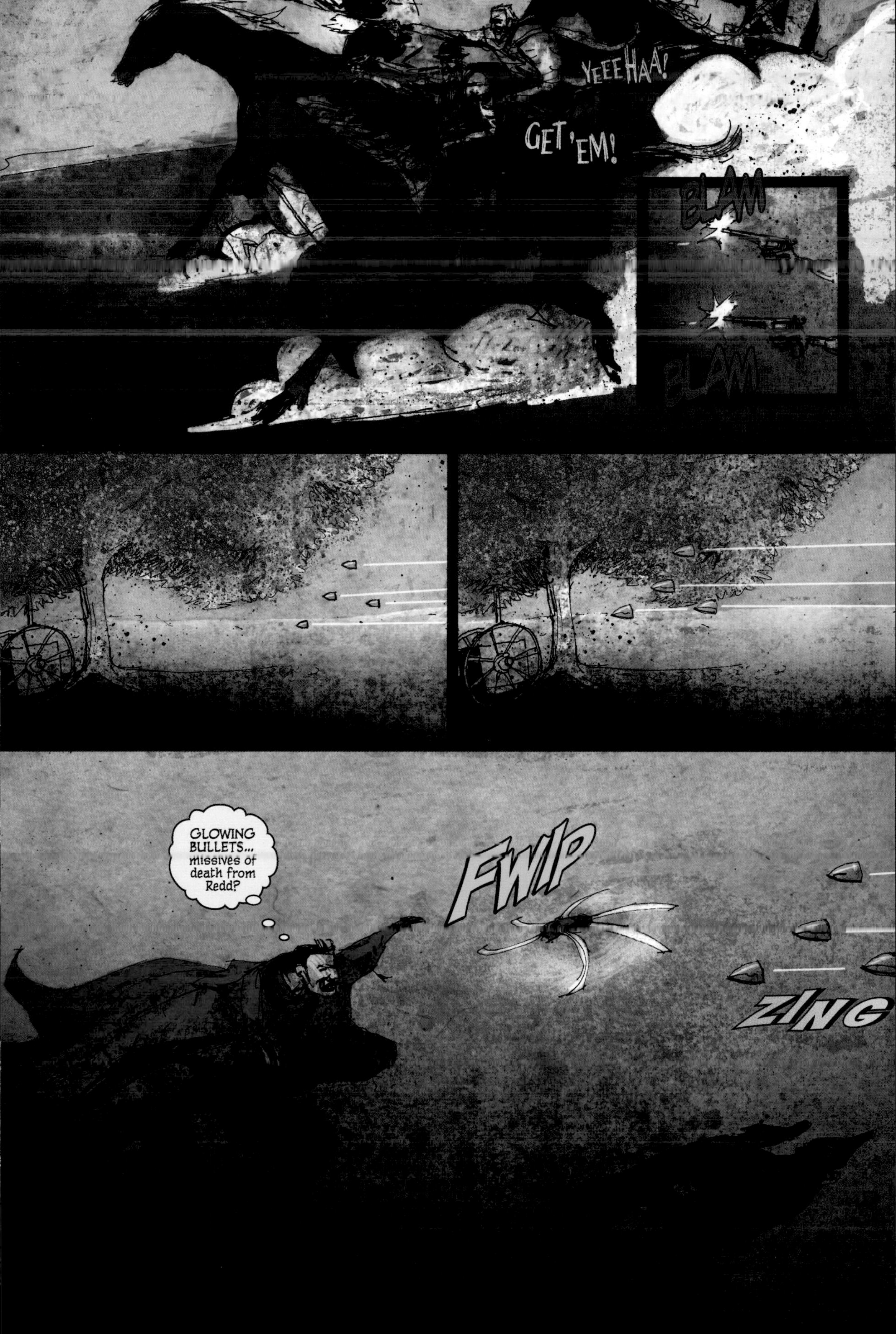
YEEEHAA!
GET 'EM!
BLAM
BLAM
GLOWING BULLETS... missives of death from Redd?
FWIP
ZING

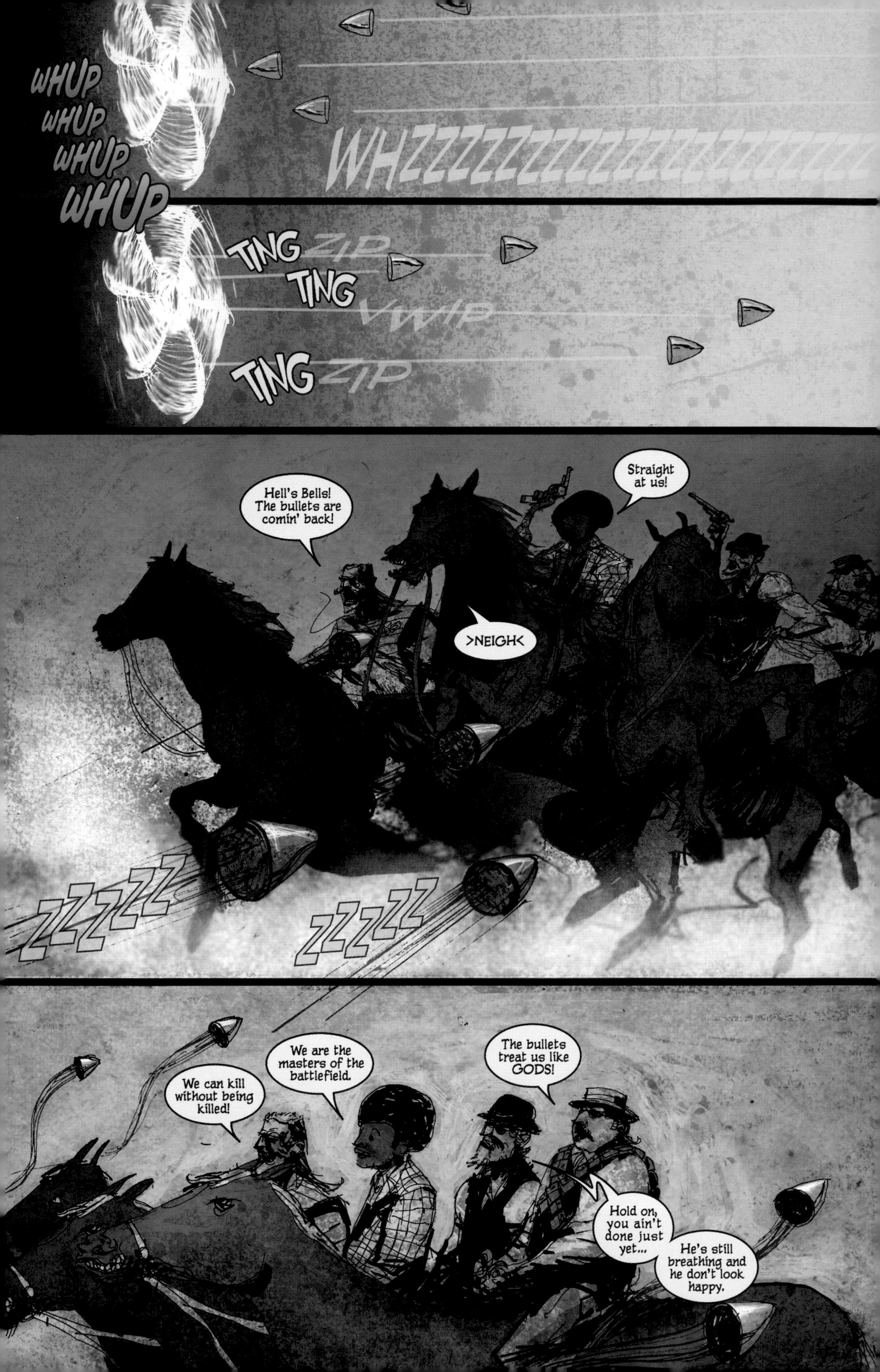
WHUP
WHUP
WHUP
WHUP
WHZZZZZZZZZZZZZZZZZZZZZ
TING
ZIP
TING
VWIP
TING
ZIP
Hell's Bells! The bullets are comin' back!
Straight at us!
>NEIGH<
ZZZZZZ
ZZZZZ
We can kill without being killed!
We are the masters of the battlefield.
The bullets treat us like GODS!
Hold on, you ain't done just yet...
He's still breathing and he don't look happy.

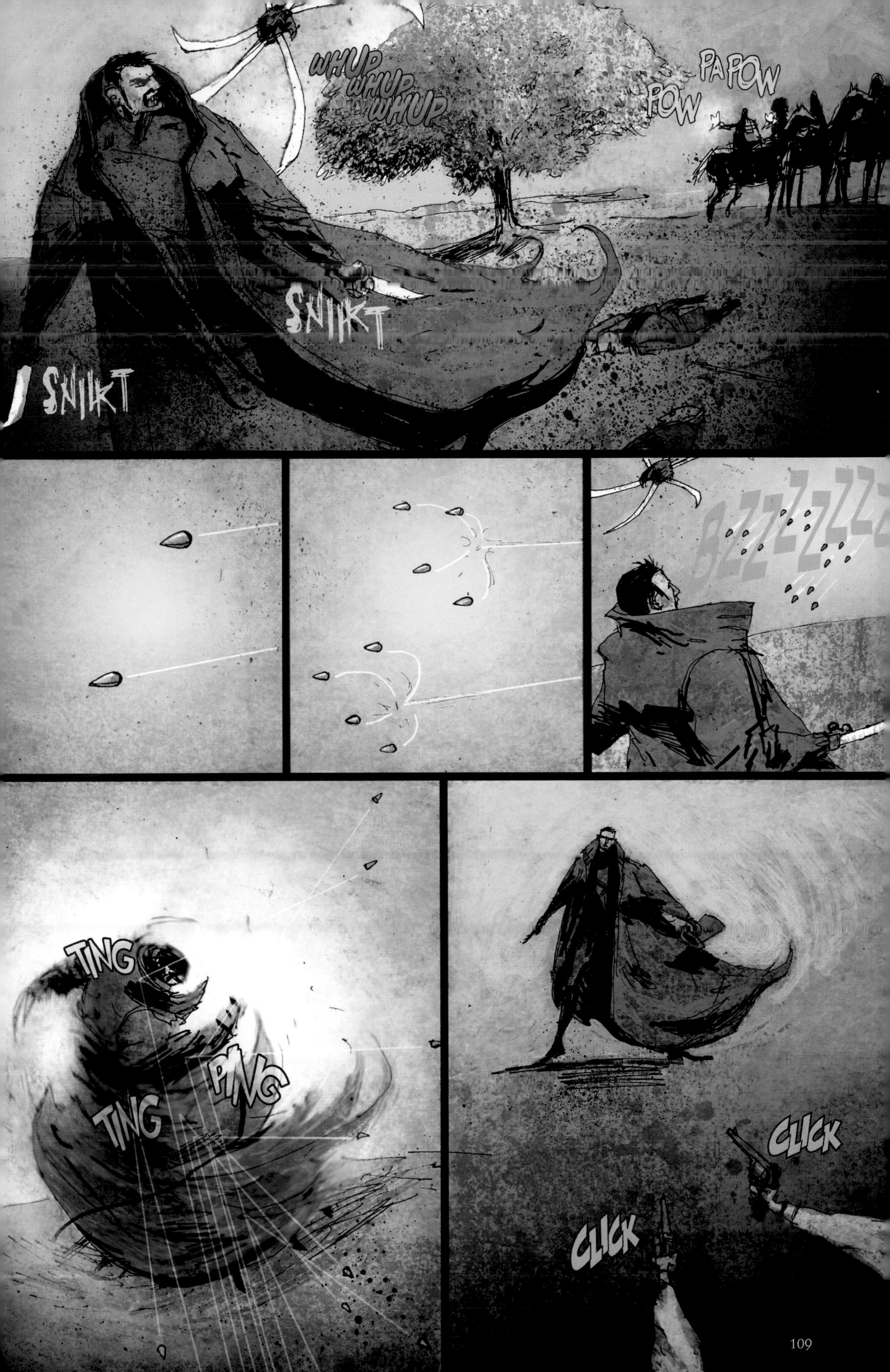
WHUP
WHUP
WHUP
PAPOW
POW
SNIKT
SNIKT
BZZZZZZZ
TING
PING
TING
CLICK
CLICK

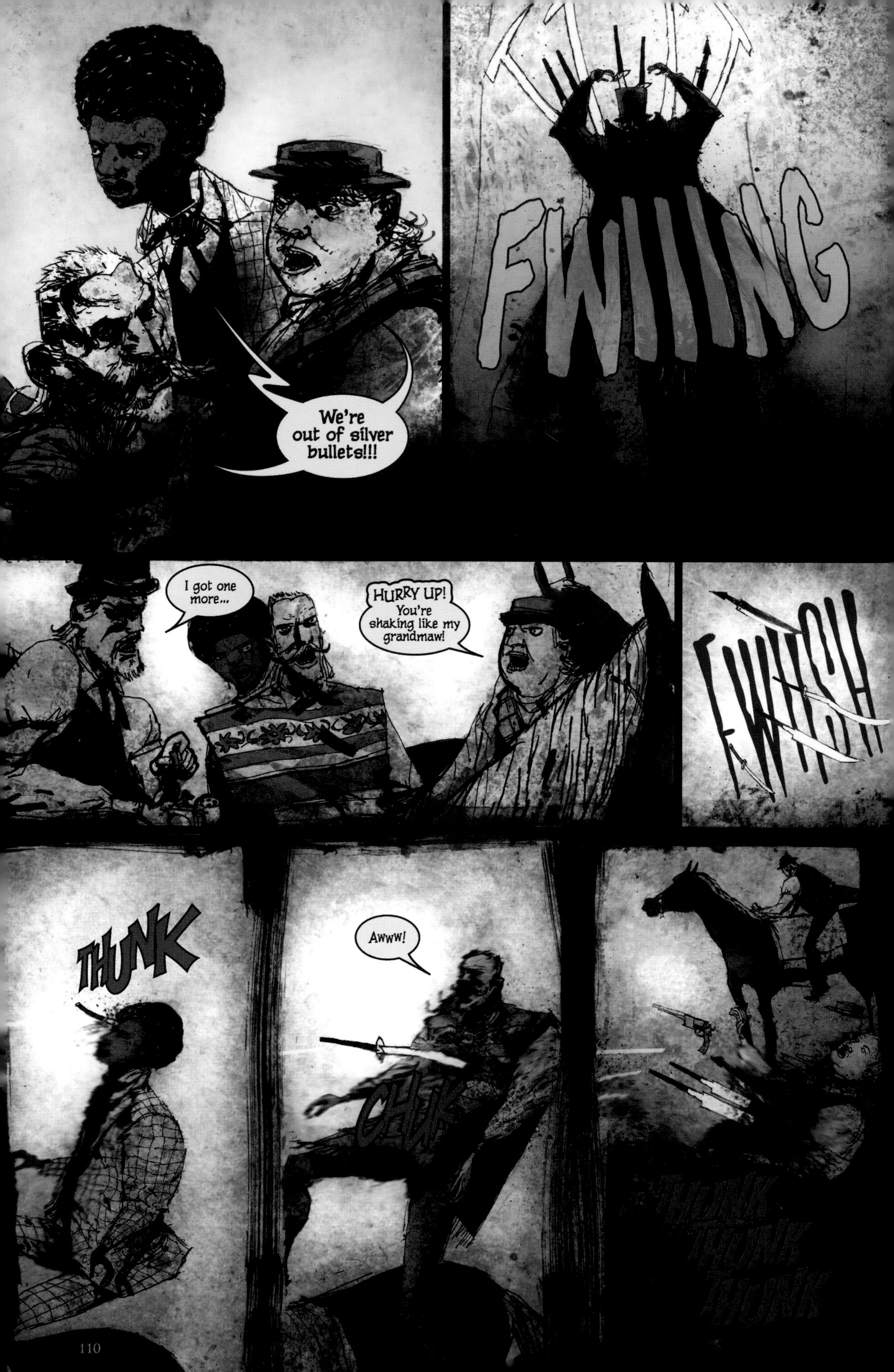
We're out of silver bullets!!!
FWIIIING
I got one more...
HURRY UP! You're shaking like my grandmaw!
FWISH
THUNK
Awww!
CHUK
THUNK THUNK THUNK

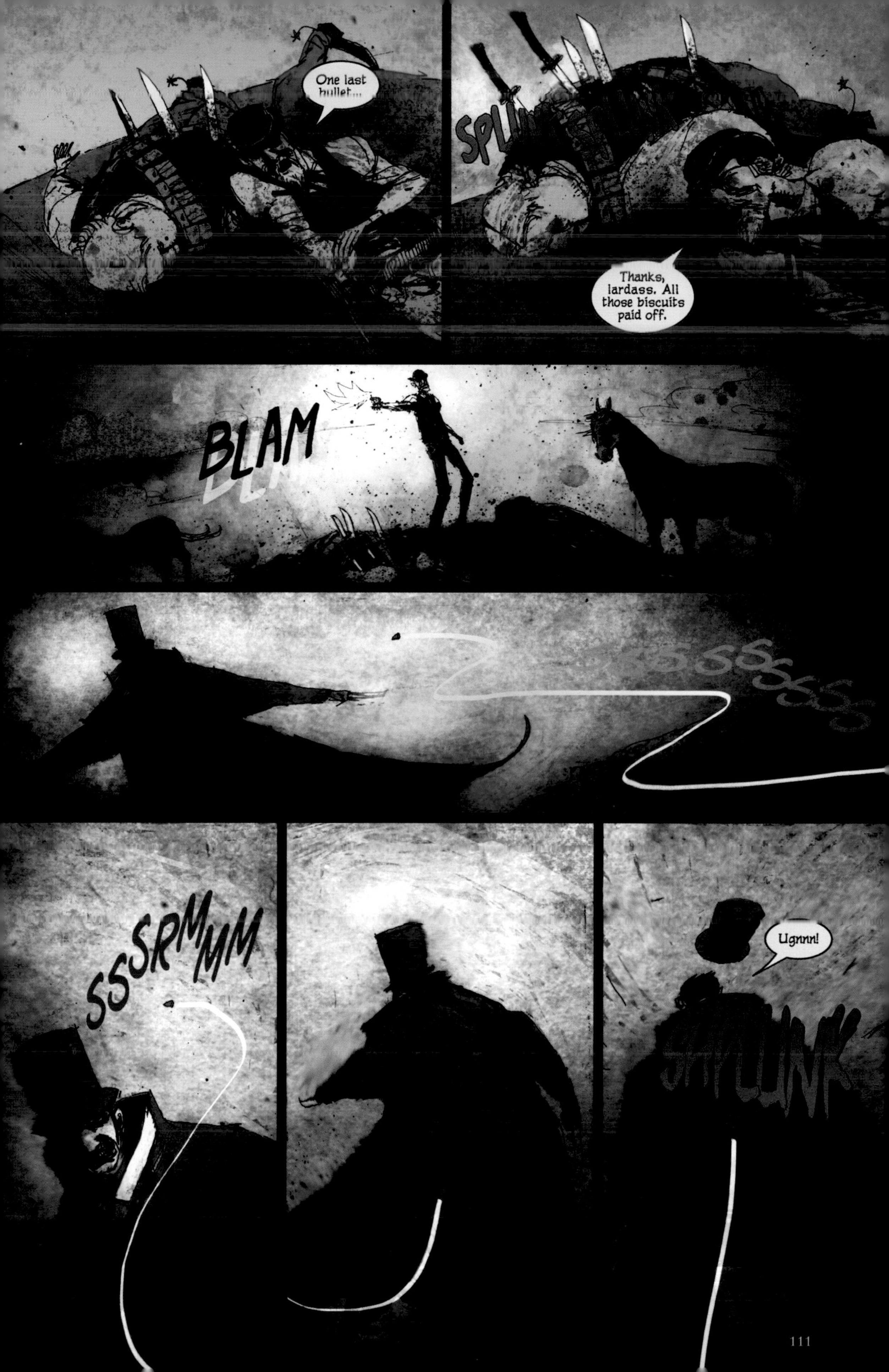
One last bullet...
Thanks, lardass. All those biscuits paid off.
BLAM
SSSRMMM
Ugnnn!

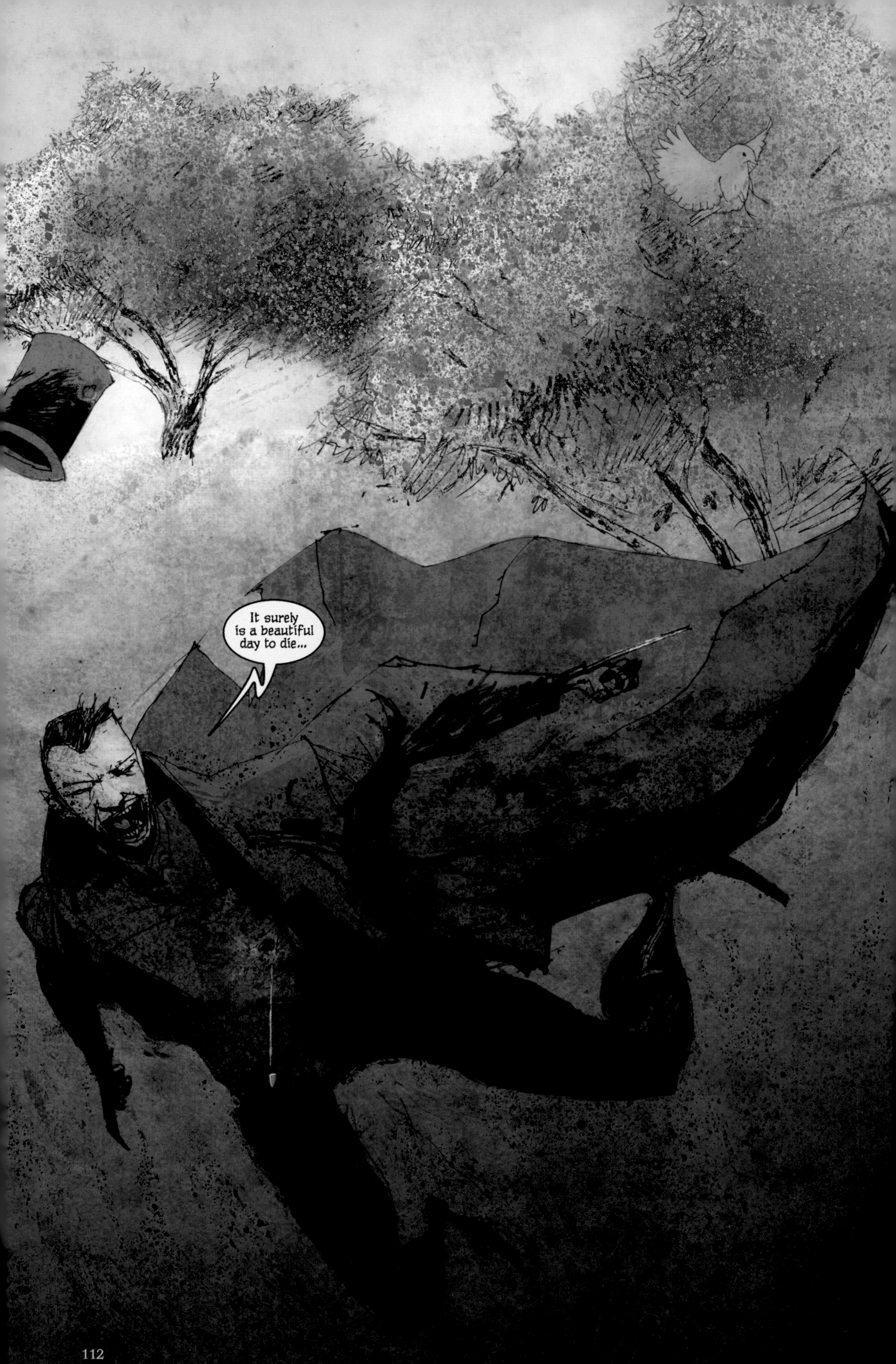
It surely is a beautiful day to die...

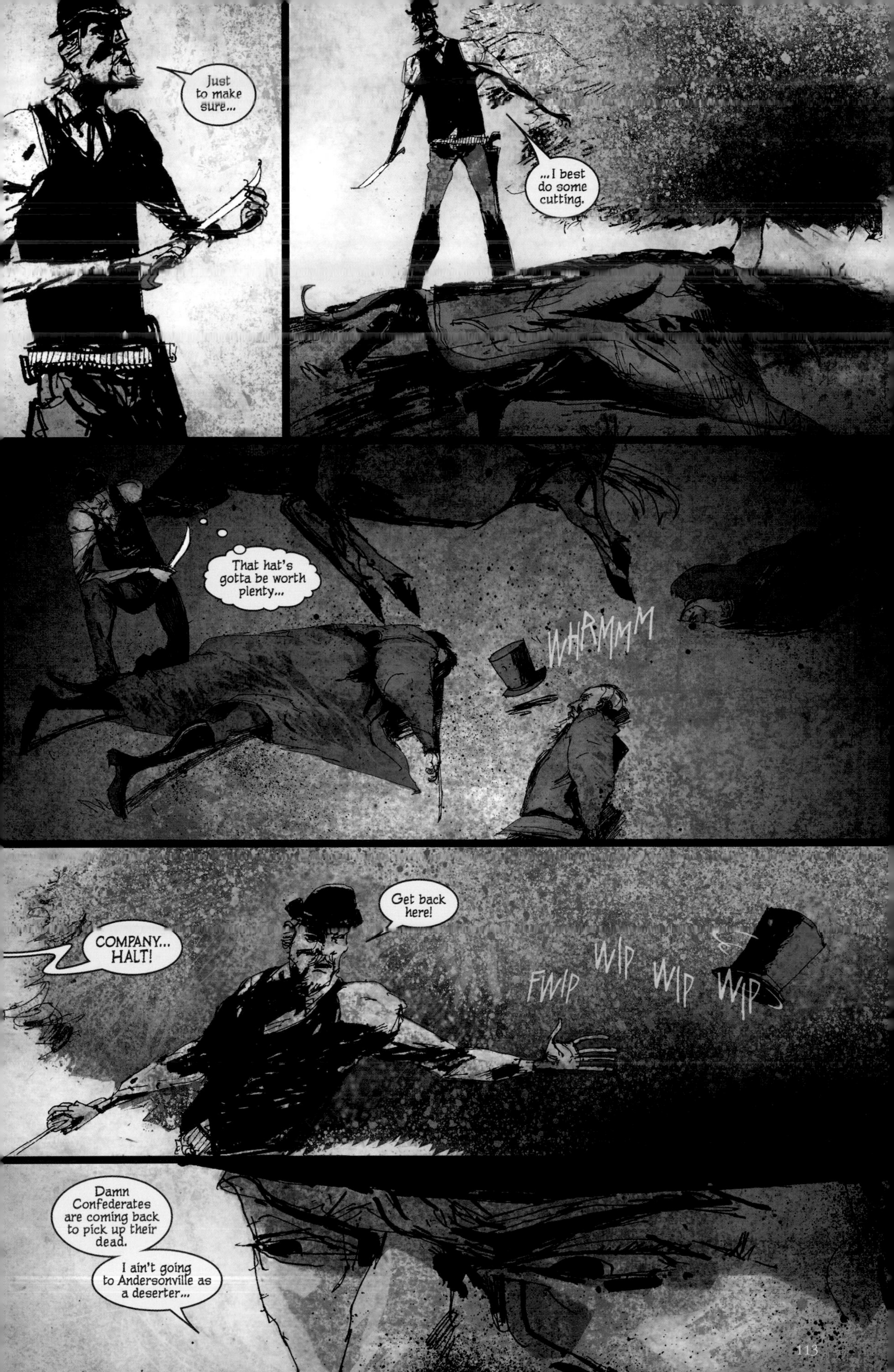
Just to make sure...
...I best do some cutting.
That hat's gotta be worth plenty...
WHRMMM
Get back here!
COMPANY... HALT!
FWIP WIP WIP WIP
Damn Confederates are coming back to pick up their dead.
I ain't going to Andersonville as a deserter...

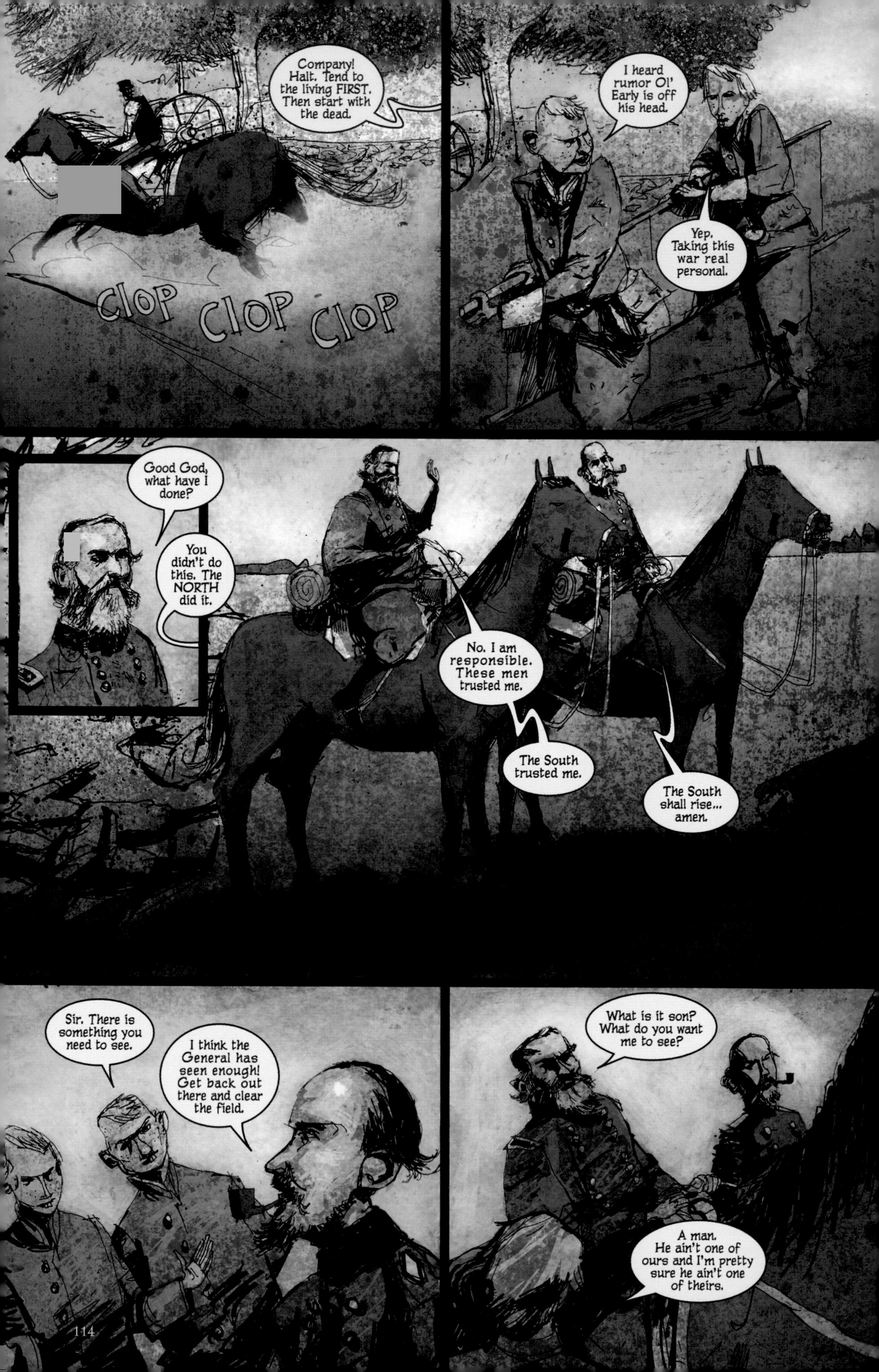
Company! Halt. Tend to the living FIRST. Then start with the dead.
CLOP CLOP CLOP
I heard rumor Ol' Early is off his head.
Yep. Taking this war real personal.
Good God, what have I done?
You didn't do this. The NORTH did it.
No. I am responsible. These men trusted me.
The South trusted me.
The South shall rise... amen.
Sir. There is something you need to see.
I think the General has seen enough! Get back out there and clear the field.
What is it son? What do you want me to see?
A man. He ain't one of ours and I'm pretty sure he ain't one of theirs.

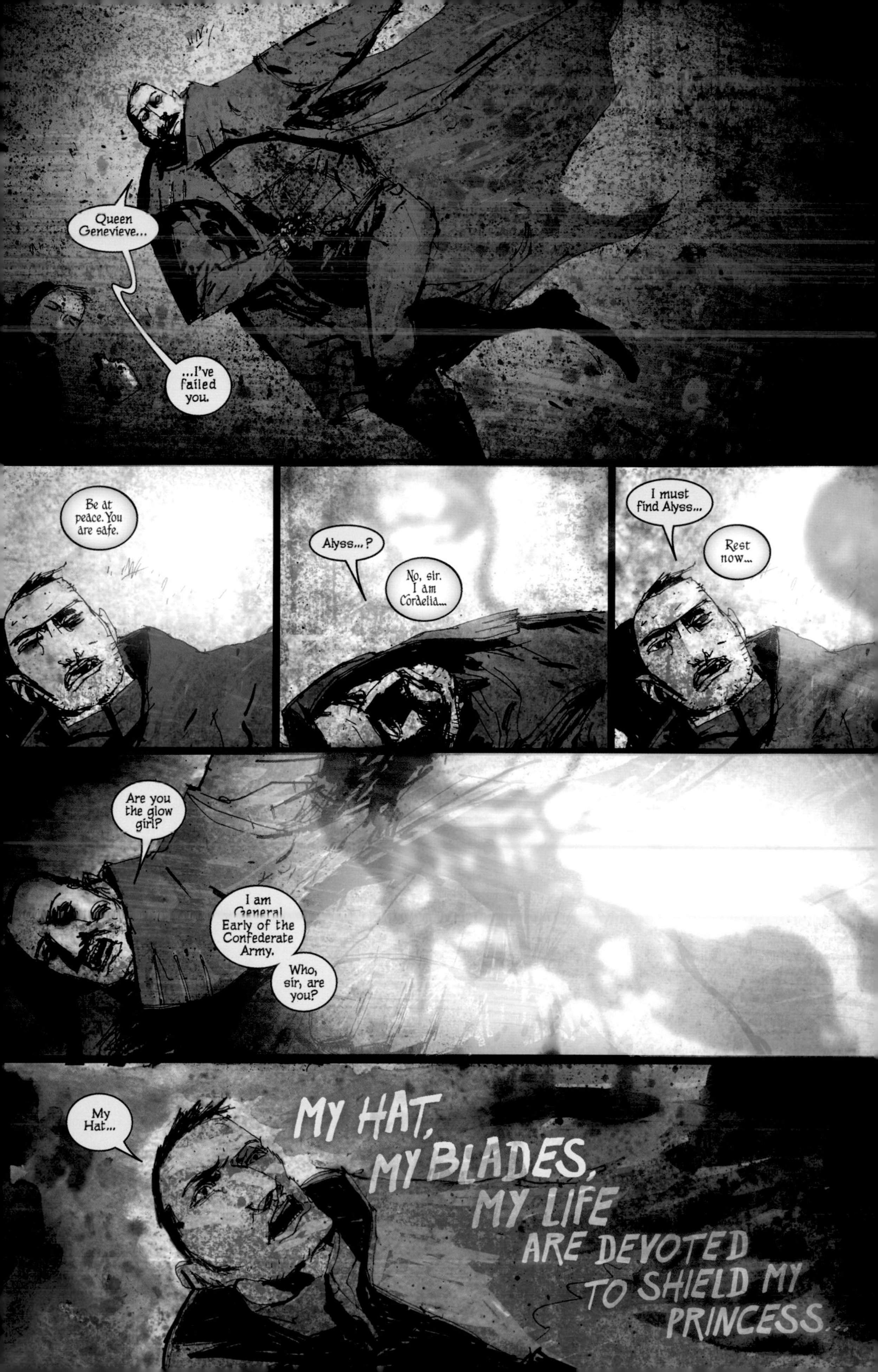
Queen Genevieve...
...I've failed you.
Be at peace. You are safe.
Alyss...?
No, sir. I am Cordelia...
I must find Alyss...
Rest now...
Are you the glow girl?
I am General Early of the Confederate Army.
Who, sir, are you?
My Hat...
MY HAT, MY BLADES, MY LIFE ARE DEVOTED TO SHIELD MY PRINCESS.

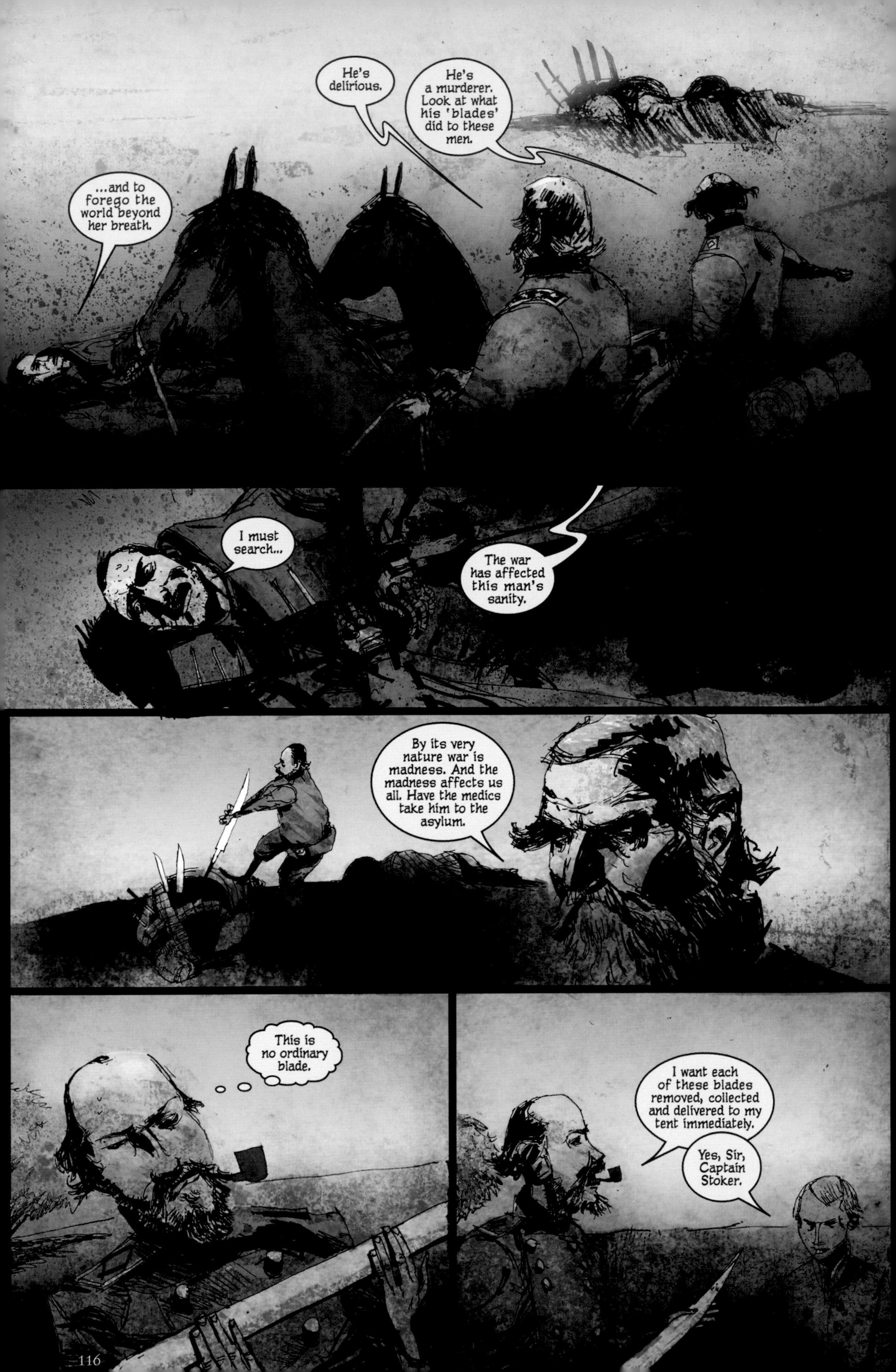
...and to forego the world beyond her breath.
He's delirious.
He's a murderer. Look at what his 'blades' did to these men.
I must search...
The war has affected this man's sanity.
By its very nature war is madness. And the madness affects us all. Have the medics take him to the asylum.
This is no ordinary blade.
I want each of these blades removed, collected and delivered to my tent immediately.
Yes, Sir, Captain Stoker.

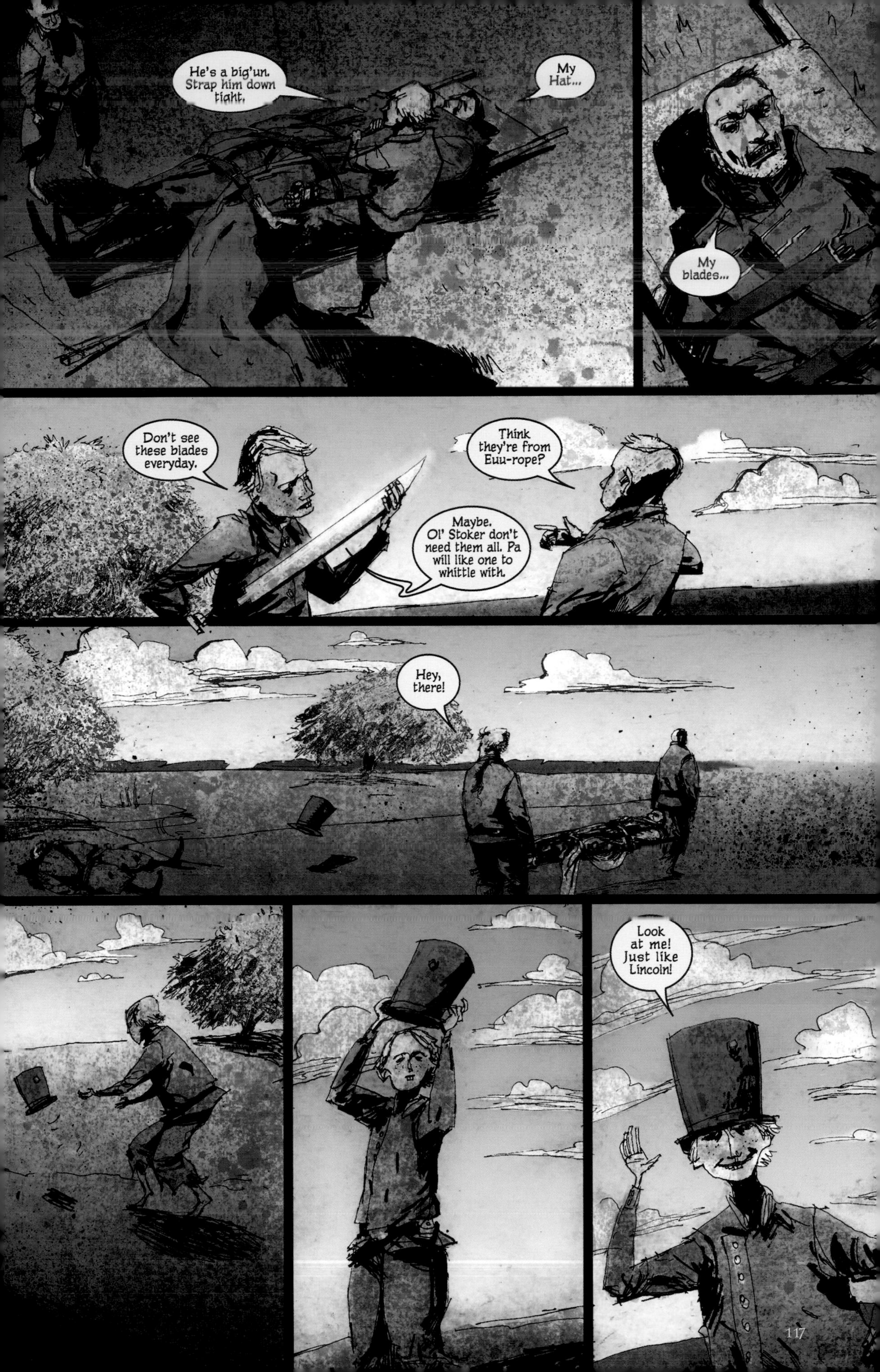
He's a big'un. Strap him down tight.
My Hat...
My blades...
Don't see these blades everyday.
Think they're from Euu-rope?
Maybe. Ol' Stoker don't need them all. Pa will like one to whittle with.
Hey, there!
Look at me! Just like Lincoln!

My name is Hatter Mad...Mad...Madigan...

"The only difference between me and a madman is that I am not mad." —SALVADOR DALÍ

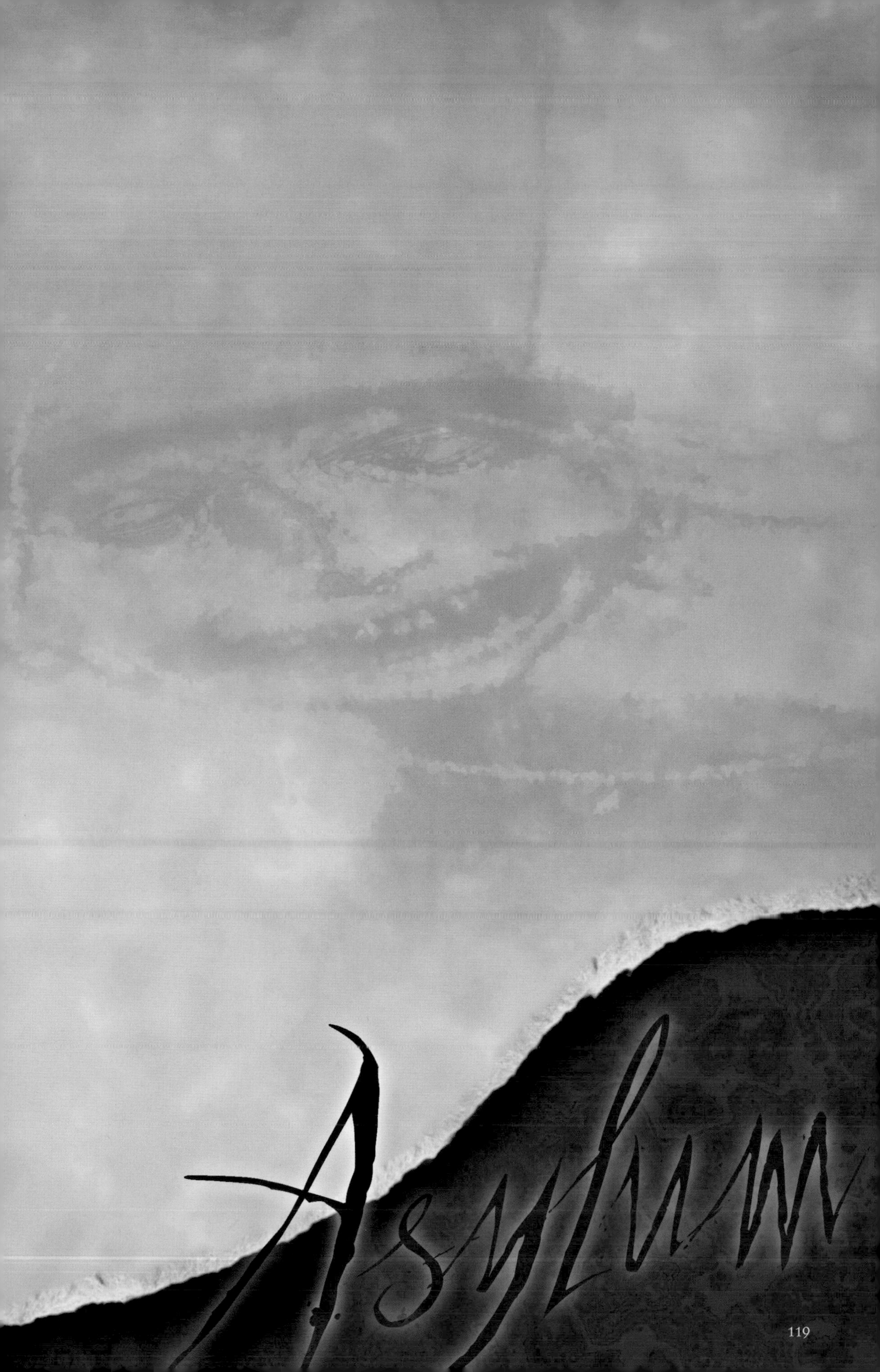

Asylum

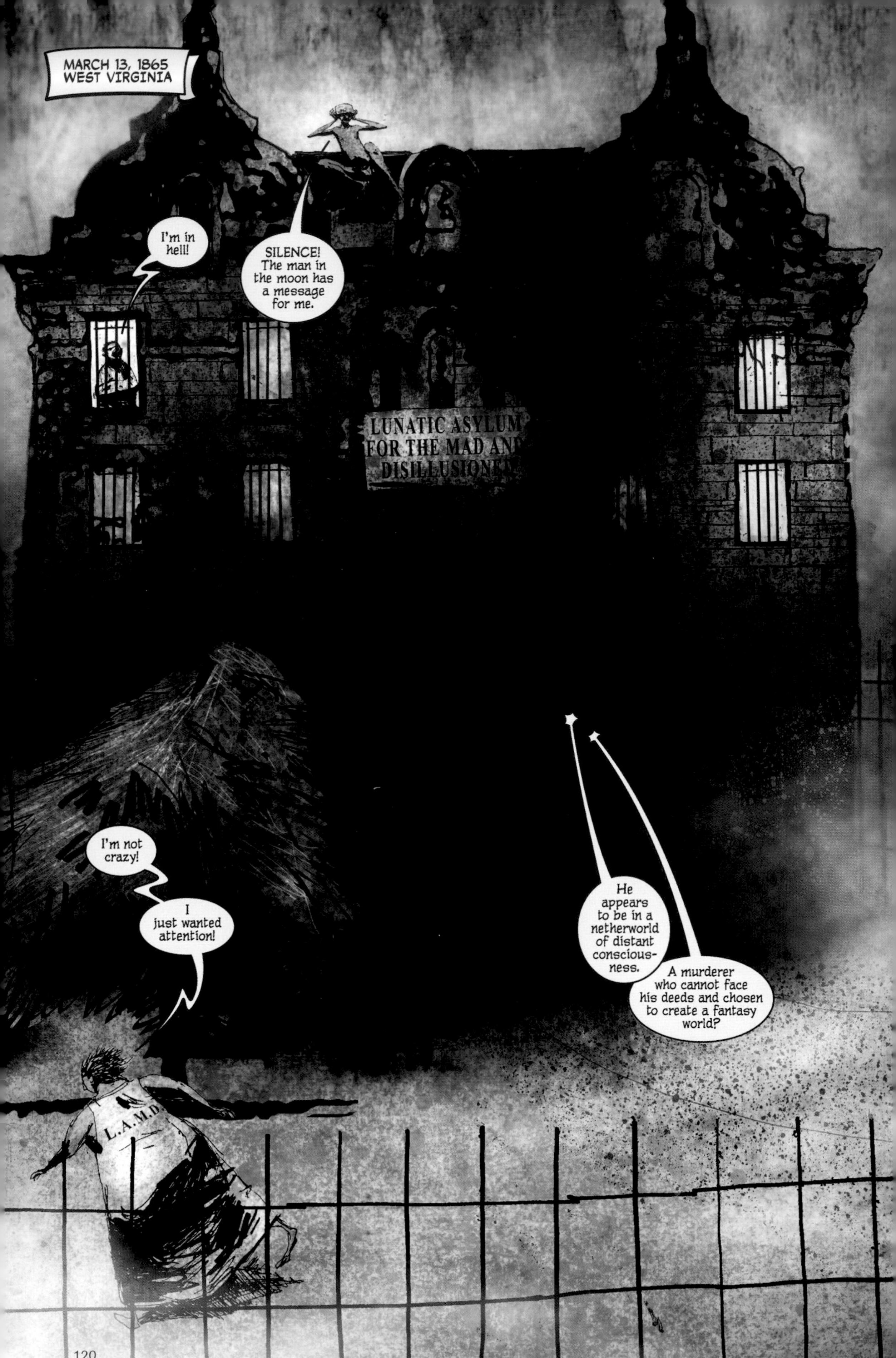
MARCH 13, 1865
WEST VIRGINIA
I'm in hell!
SILENCE! The man in the moon has a message for me.
LUNATIC ASYLUM FOR THE MAD AND DISILLUSIONED
I'm not crazy!
I just wanted attention!
He appears to be in a netherworld of distant conscious-ness.
A murderer who cannot face his deeds and chosen to create a fantasy world?
L.A.M.D.

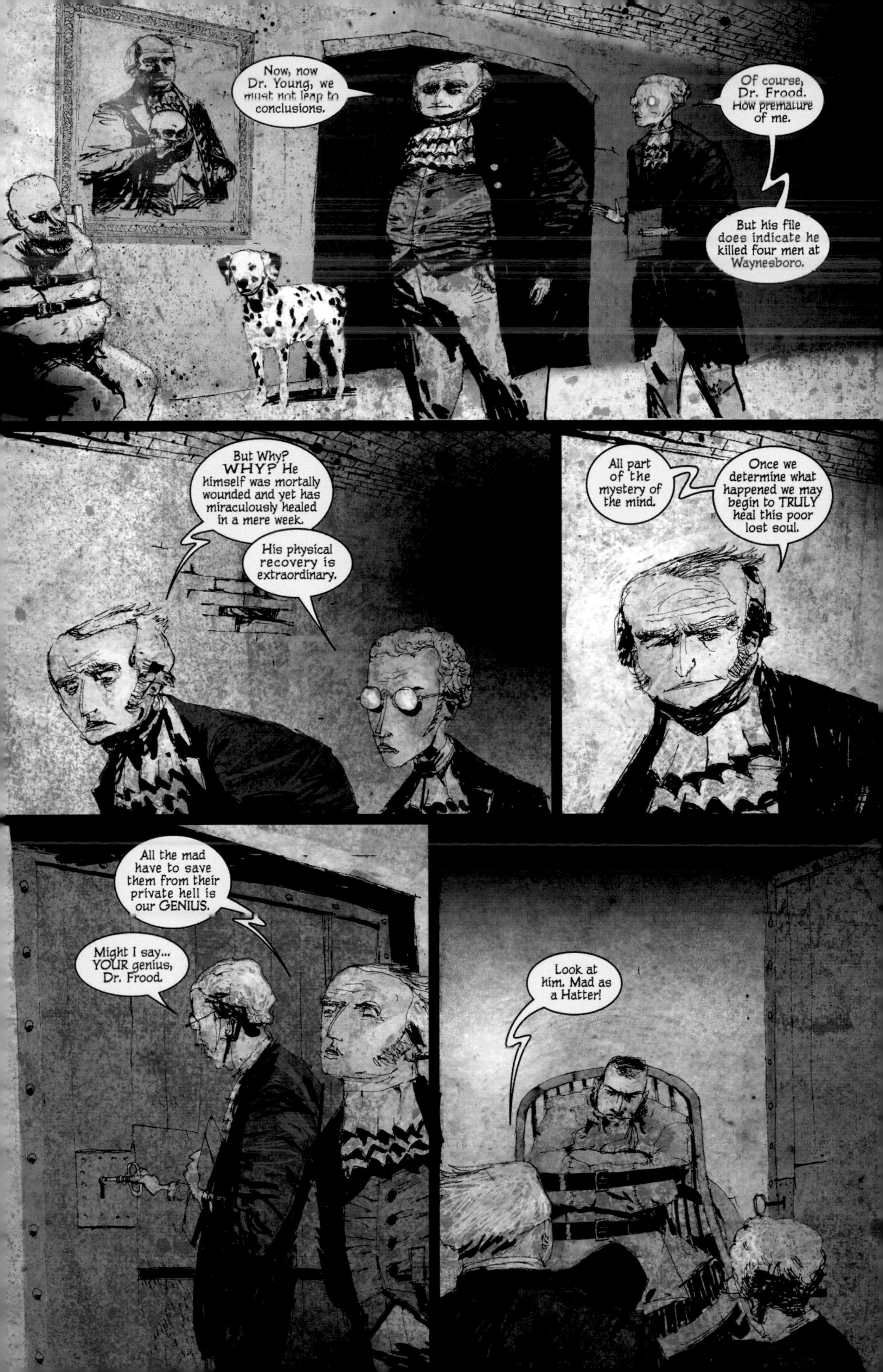
Now, now Dr. Young, we must not leap to conclusions.
Of course, Dr. Frood. How premature of me.
But his file does indicate he killed four men at Waynesboro.
But Why? WHY? He himself was mortally wounded and yet has miraculously healed in a mere week.
His physical recovery is extraordinary.
All part of the mystery of the mind.
Once we determine what happened we may begin to TRULY heal this poor lost soul.
All the mad have to save them from their private hell is our GENIUS.
Might I say... YOUR genius, Dr. Frood.
Look at him. Mad as a Hatter!

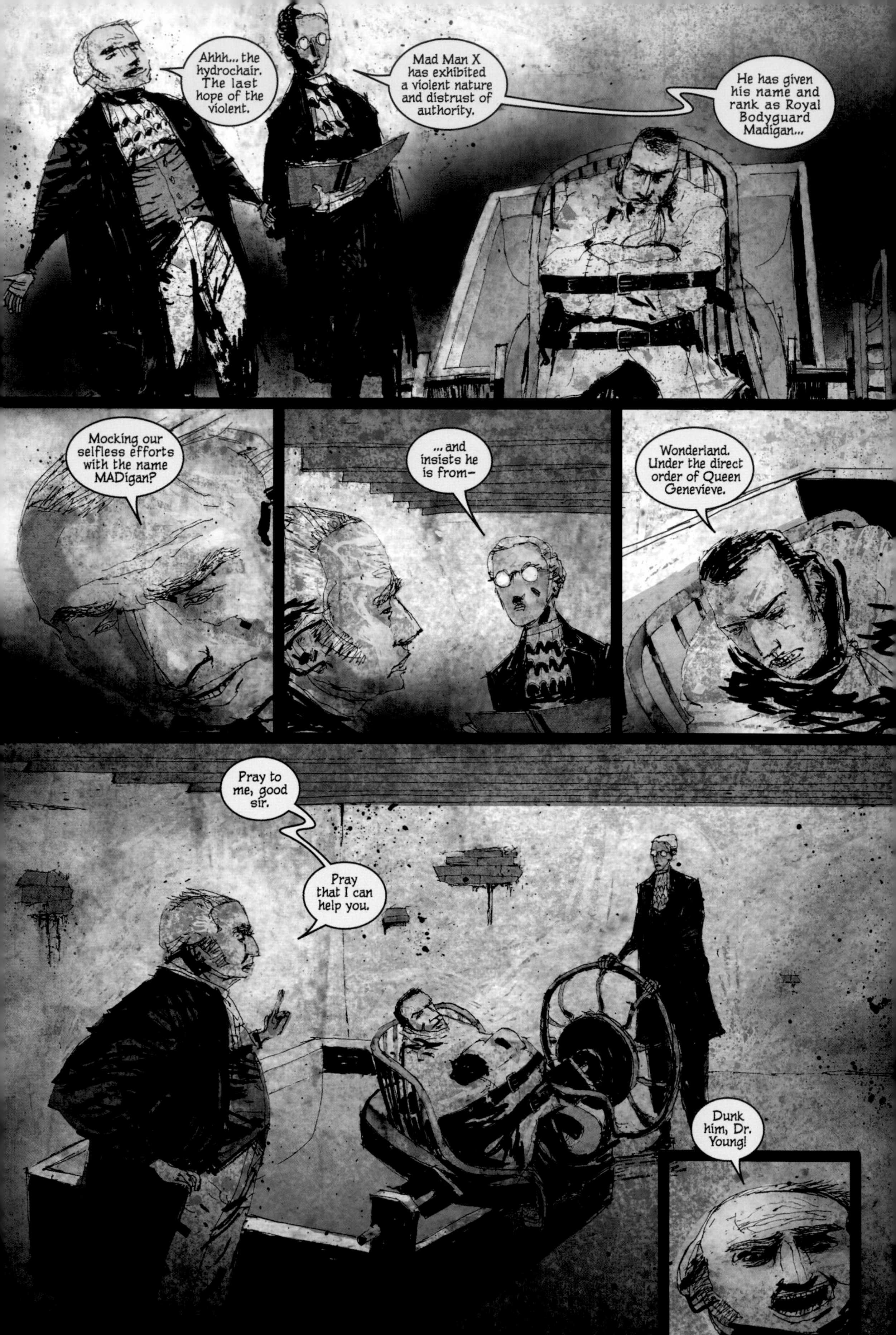

Ahhh... the hydrochair. The last hope of the violent.
Mad Man X has exhibited a violent nature and distrust of authority.
He has given his name and rank as Royal Bodyguard Madigan...
Mocking our selfless efforts with the name MADigan?
...and insists he is from–
Wonderland. Under the direct order of Queen Genevieve.
Pray to me, good sir.
Pray that I can help you.
Dunk him, Dr. Young!

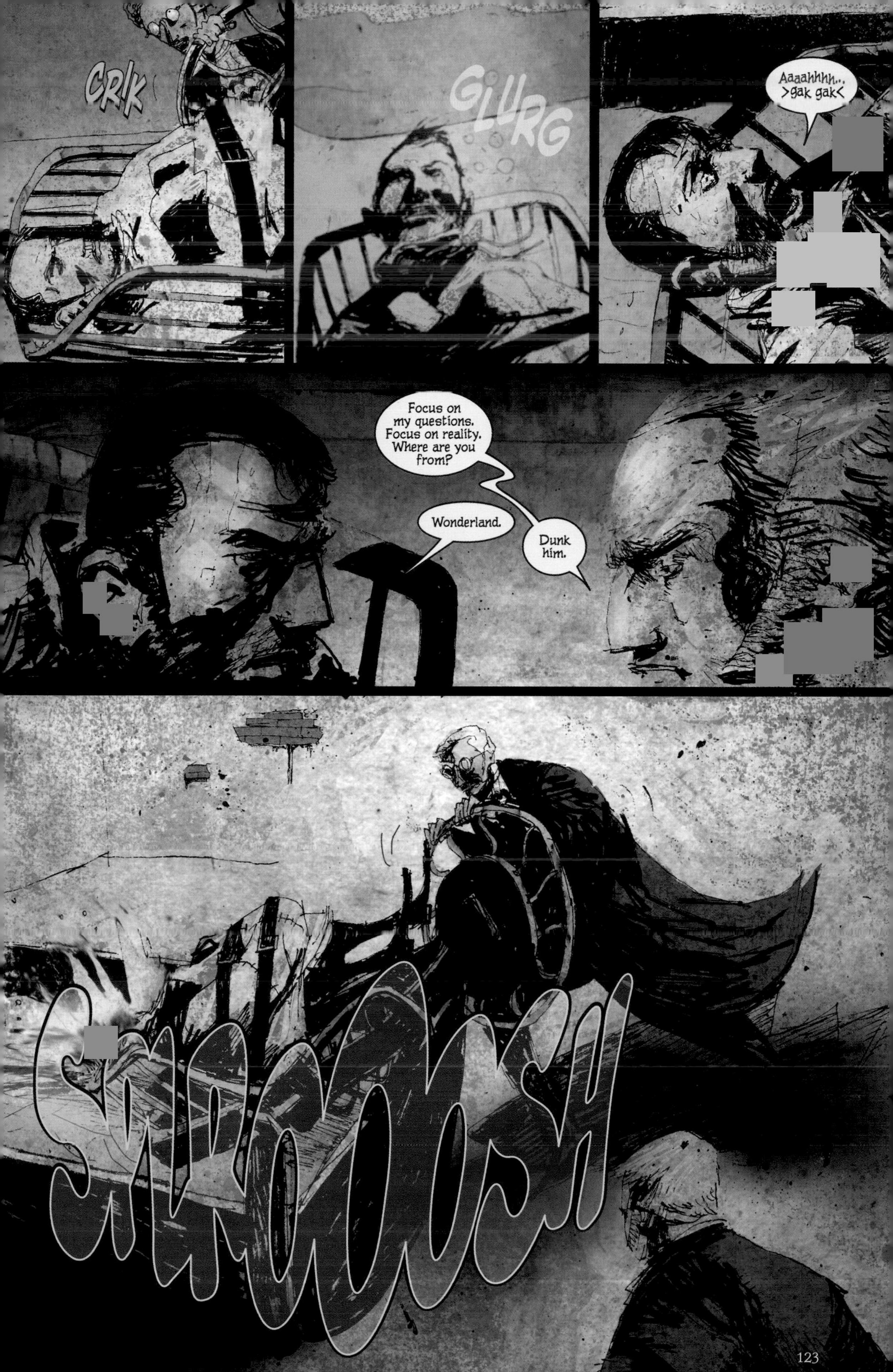

CRIK
GLURG
Aaaahhhh...
>gak gak<
Focus on my questions. Focus on reality. Where are you from?
Wonderland.
Dunk him.
SPLOOOSH

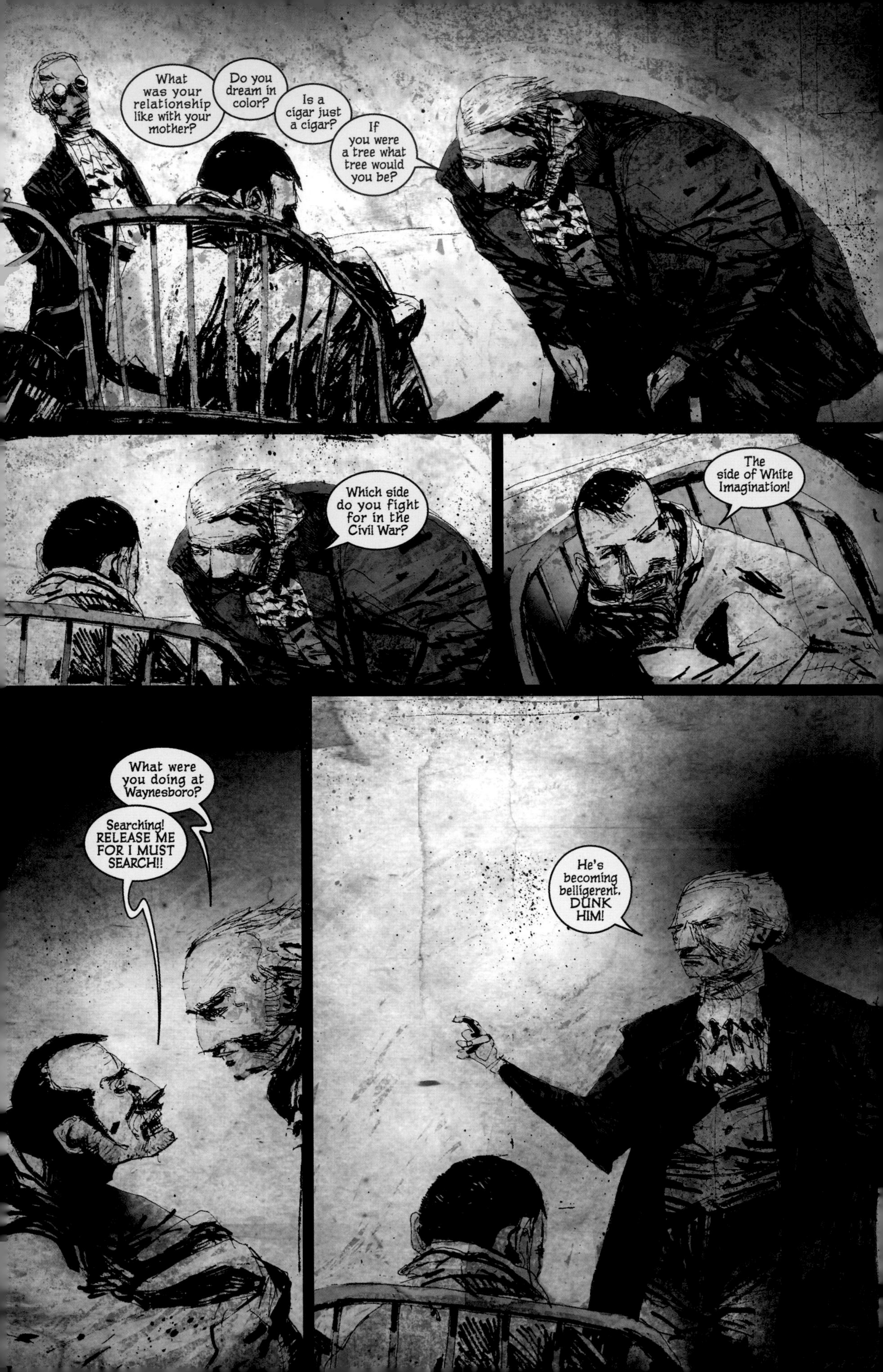
What was your relationship like with your mother?
Do you dream in color?
Is a cigar just a cigar?
If you were a tree what tree would you be?
Which side do you fight for in the Civil War?
The side of White Imagination!
What were you doing at Waynesboro?
Searching! RELEASE ME FOR I MUST SEARCH!!
He's becoming belligerent. DUNK HIM!

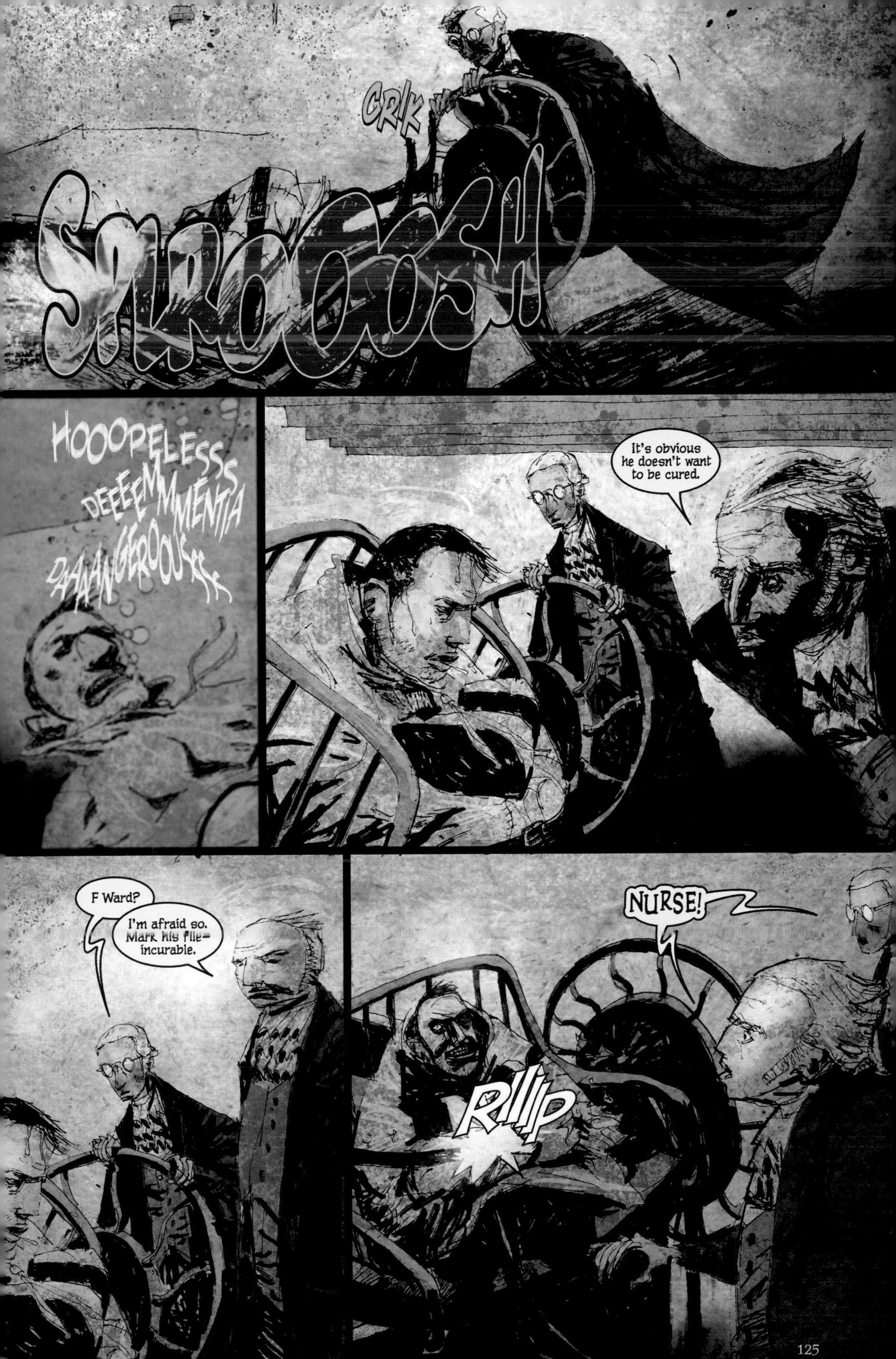
CRIK
SPLROOOSH
HOOOPELESSS
DEEEEMMMENTIA
DAAANGEROOUS
It's obvious he doesn't want to be cured.
F Ward?
I'm afraid so. Mark his file— incurable.
NURSE!
RIIIP

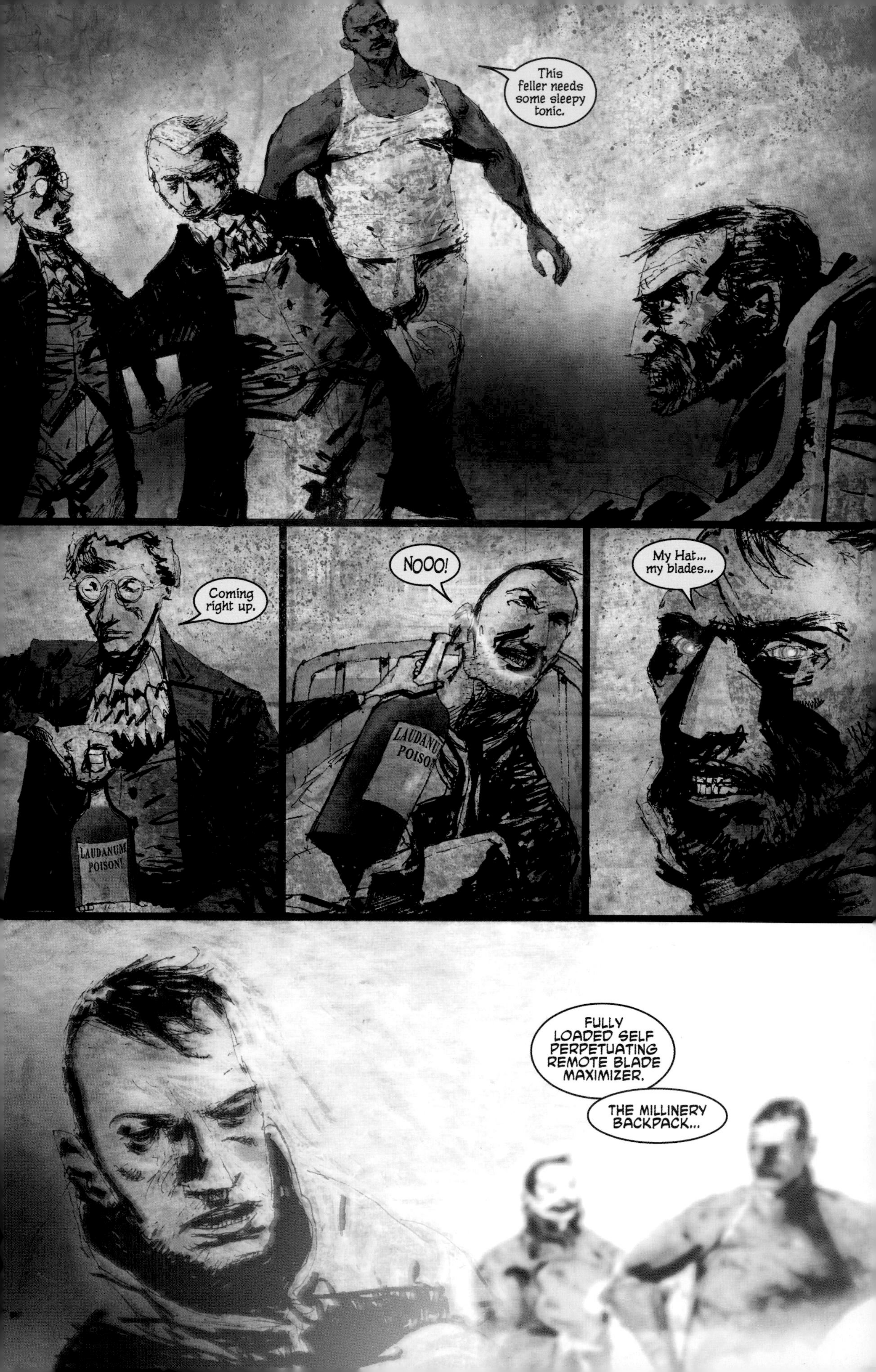
This feller needs some sleepy tonic.
Coming right up.
LAUDANUM POISON!
NOOO!
LAUDANUM POISON
My Hat... my blades...
FULLY LOADED SELF PERPETUATING REMOTE BLADE MAXIMIZER.
THE MILLINERY BACKPACK...

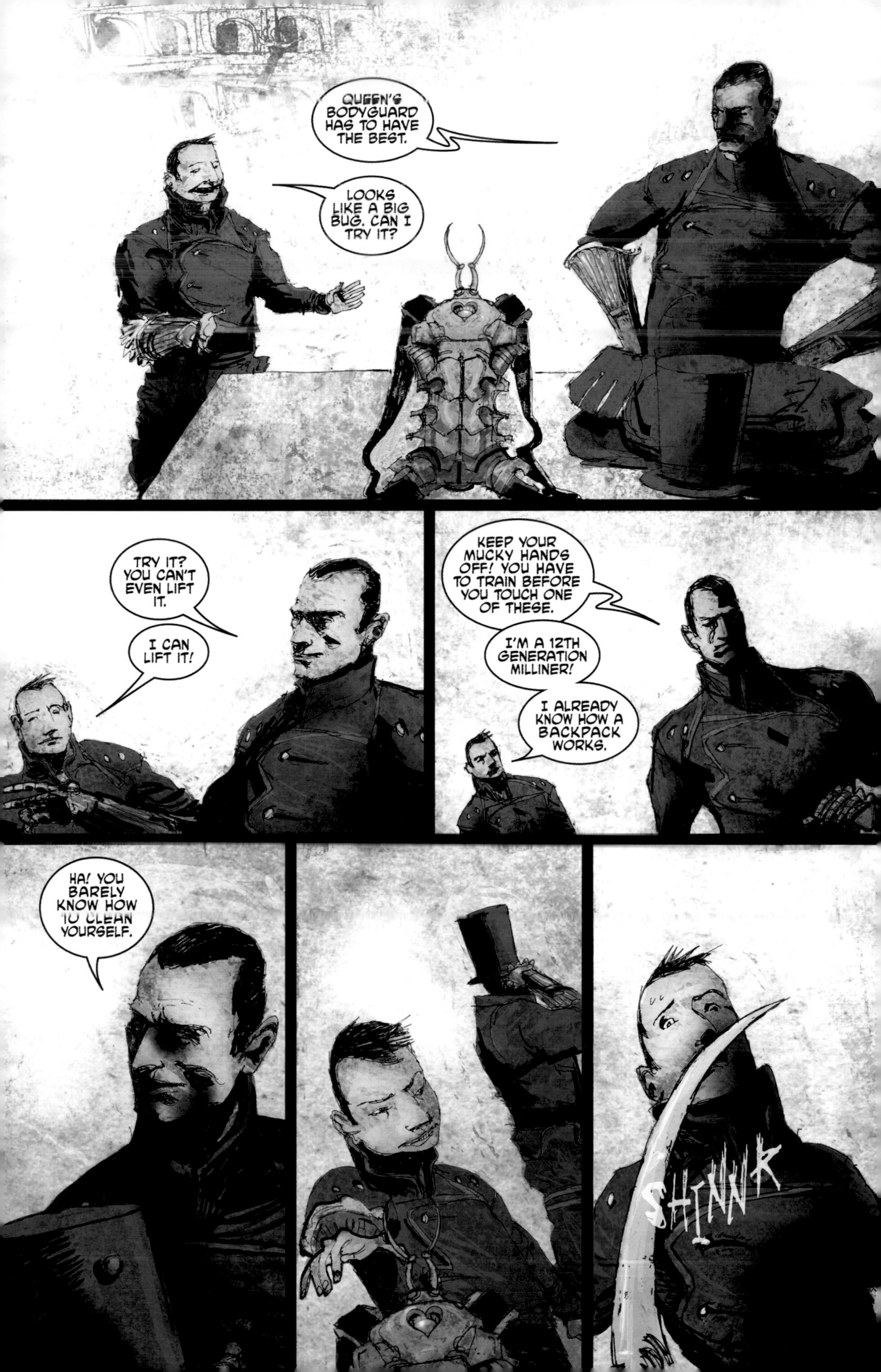
QUEEN'S BODYGUARD HAS TO HAVE THE BEST.
LOOKS LIKE A BIG BUG. CAN I TRY IT?
TRY IT? YOU CAN'T EVEN LIFT IT.
I CAN LIFT IT!
KEEP YOUR MUCKY HANDS OFF! YOU HAVE TO TRAIN BEFORE YOU TOUCH ONE OF THESE.
I'M A 12TH GENERATION MILLINER!
I ALREADY KNOW HOW A BACKPACK WORKS.
HA! YOU BARELY KNOW HOW TO CLEAN YOURSELF.
SHINNK

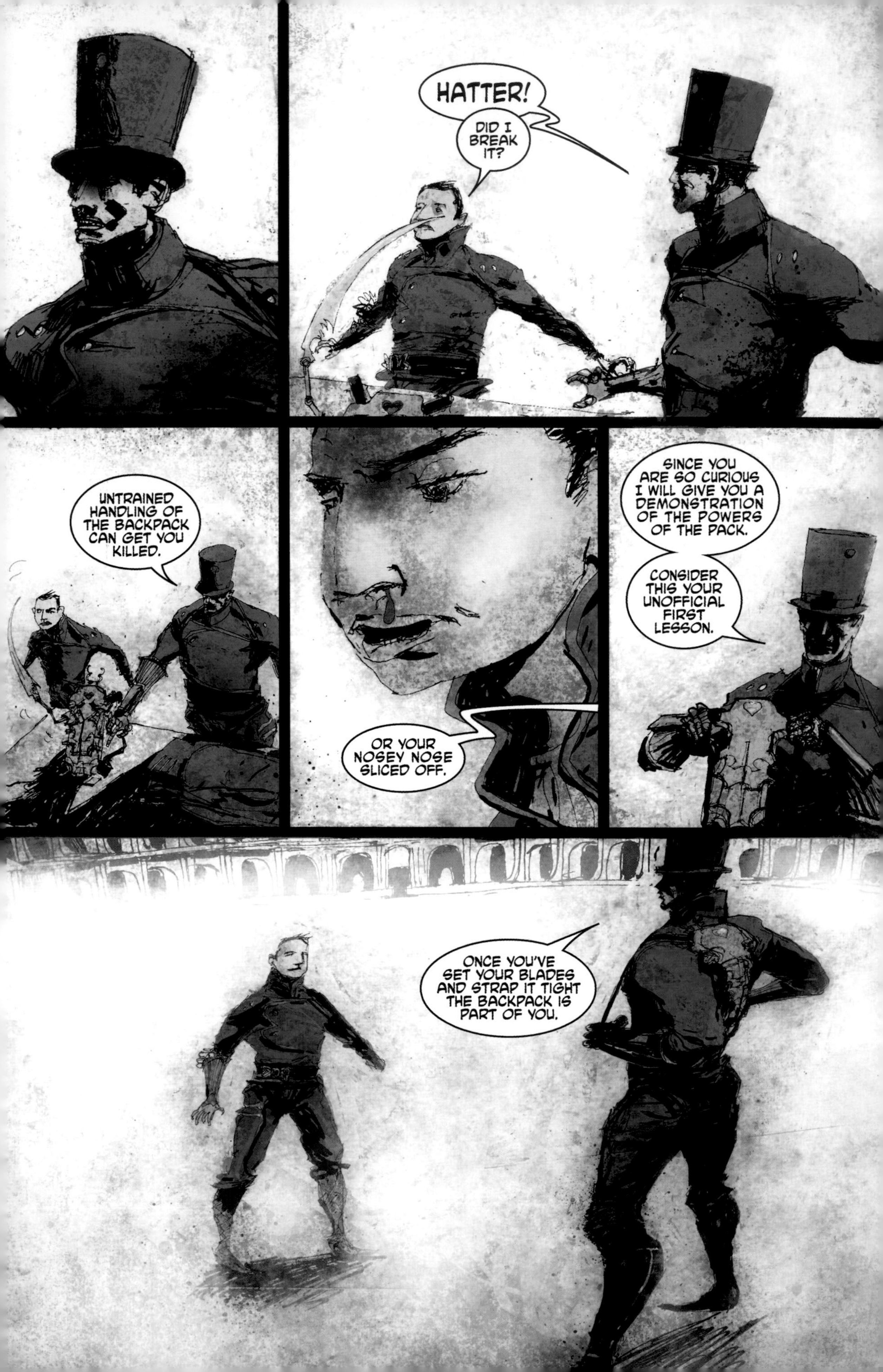
HATTER!
DID I BREAK IT?
UNTRAINED HANDLING OF THE BACKPACK CAN GET YOU KILLED.
OR YOUR NOSEY NOSE SLICED OFF.
SINCE YOU ARE SO CURIOUS I WILL GIVE YOU A DEMONSTRATION OF THE POWERS OF THE PACK.
CONSIDER THIS YOUR UNOFFICIAL FIRST LESSON.
ONCE YOU'VE SET YOUR BLADES AND STRAP IT TIGHT THE BACKPACK IS PART OF YOU.

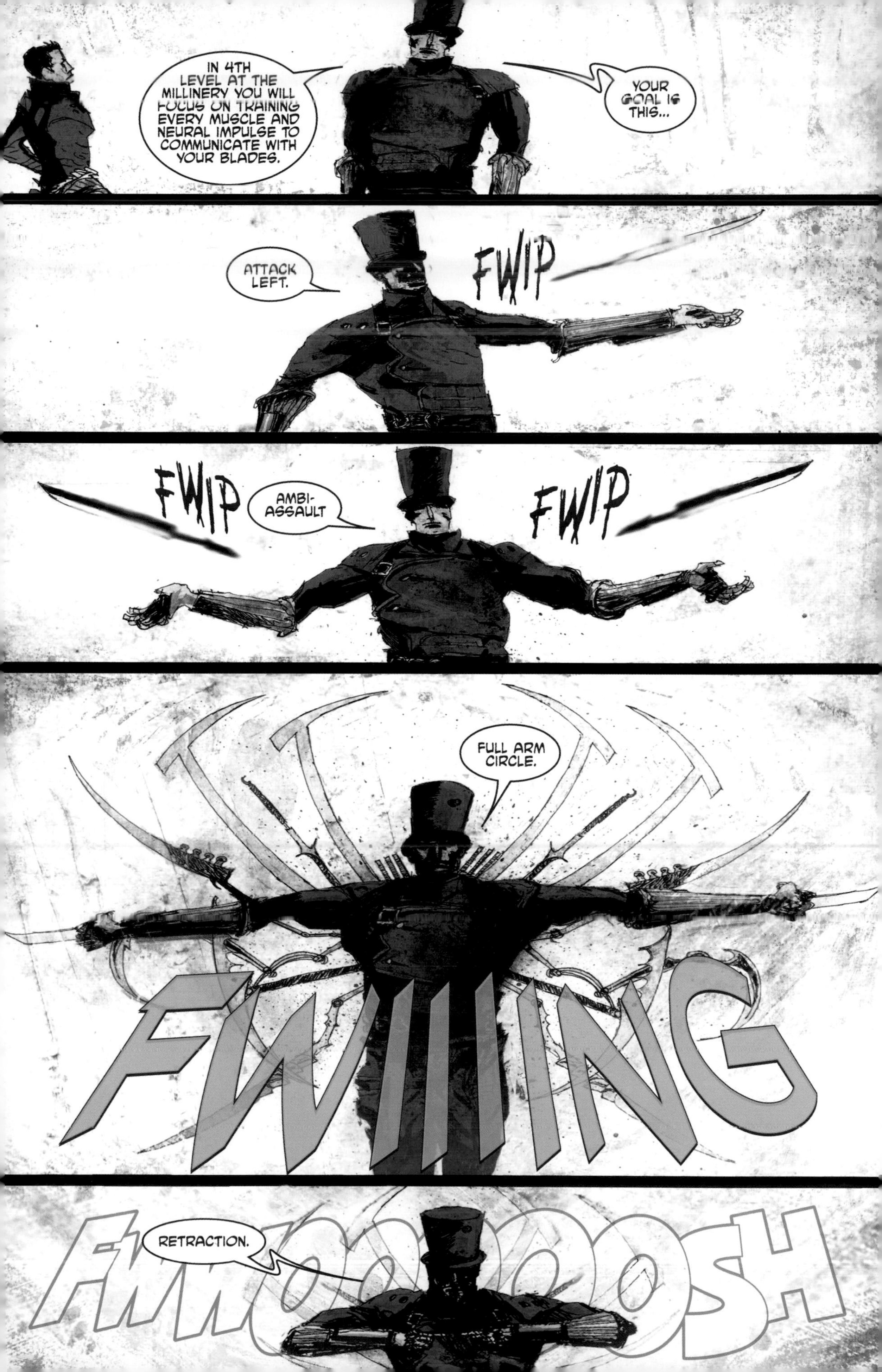
IN 4TH LEVEL AT THE MILLINERY YOU WILL FOCUS ON TRAINING EVERY MUSCLE AND NEURAL IMPULSE TO COMMUNICATE WITH YOUR BLADES.
YOUR GOAL IS THIS...
ATTACK LEFT.
FWIP
FWIP
AMBI-ASSAULT
FWIP
FULL ARM CIRCLE.
FWIIING
RETRACTION.
FWOOOOOSH

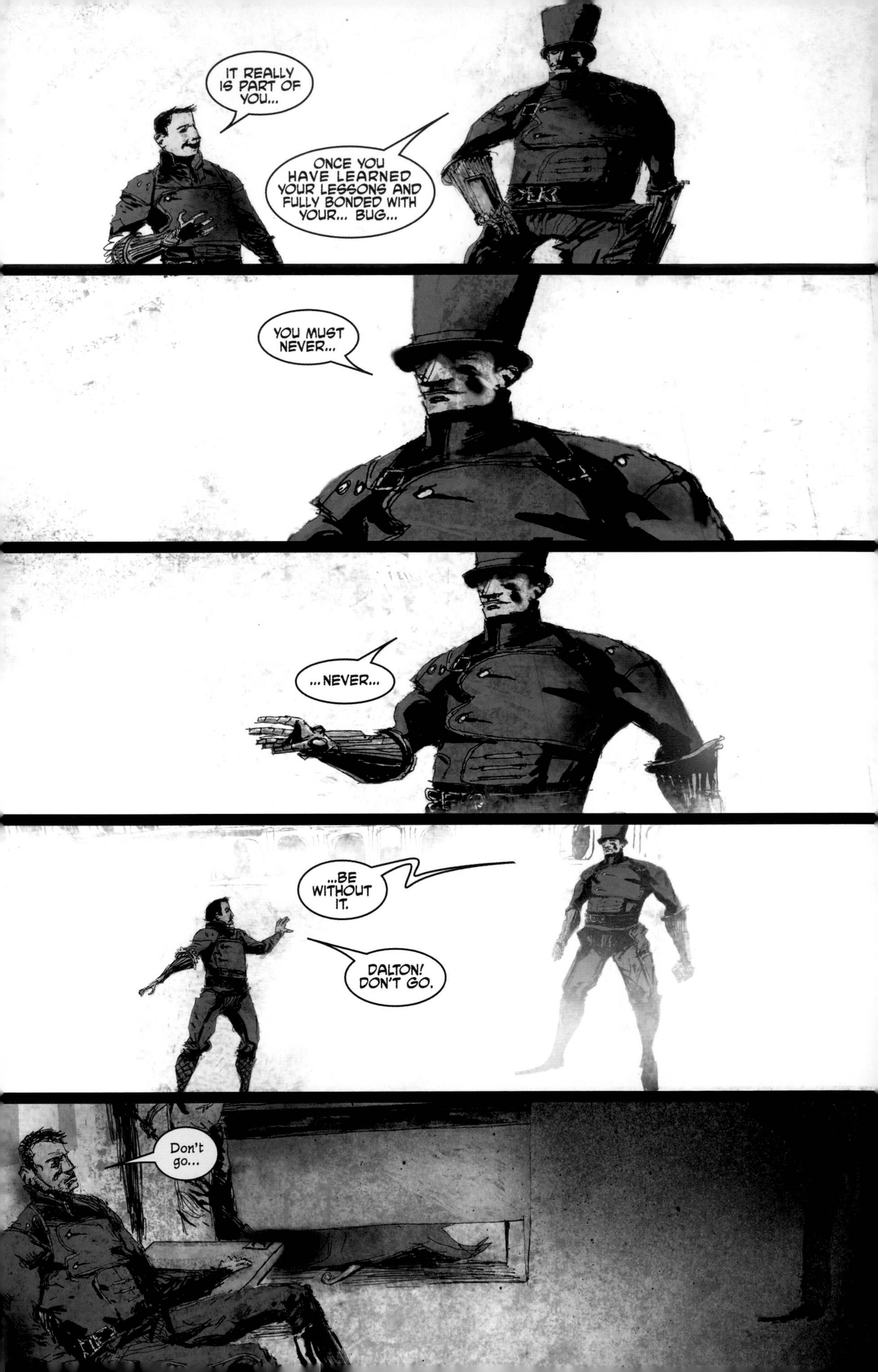
IT REALLY IS PART OF YOU...
ONCE YOU HAVE LEARNED YOUR LESSONS AND FULLY BONDED WITH YOUR... BUG...
YOU MUST NEVER...
...NEVER...
...BE WITHOUT IT.
DALTON! DON'T GO.
Don't go...

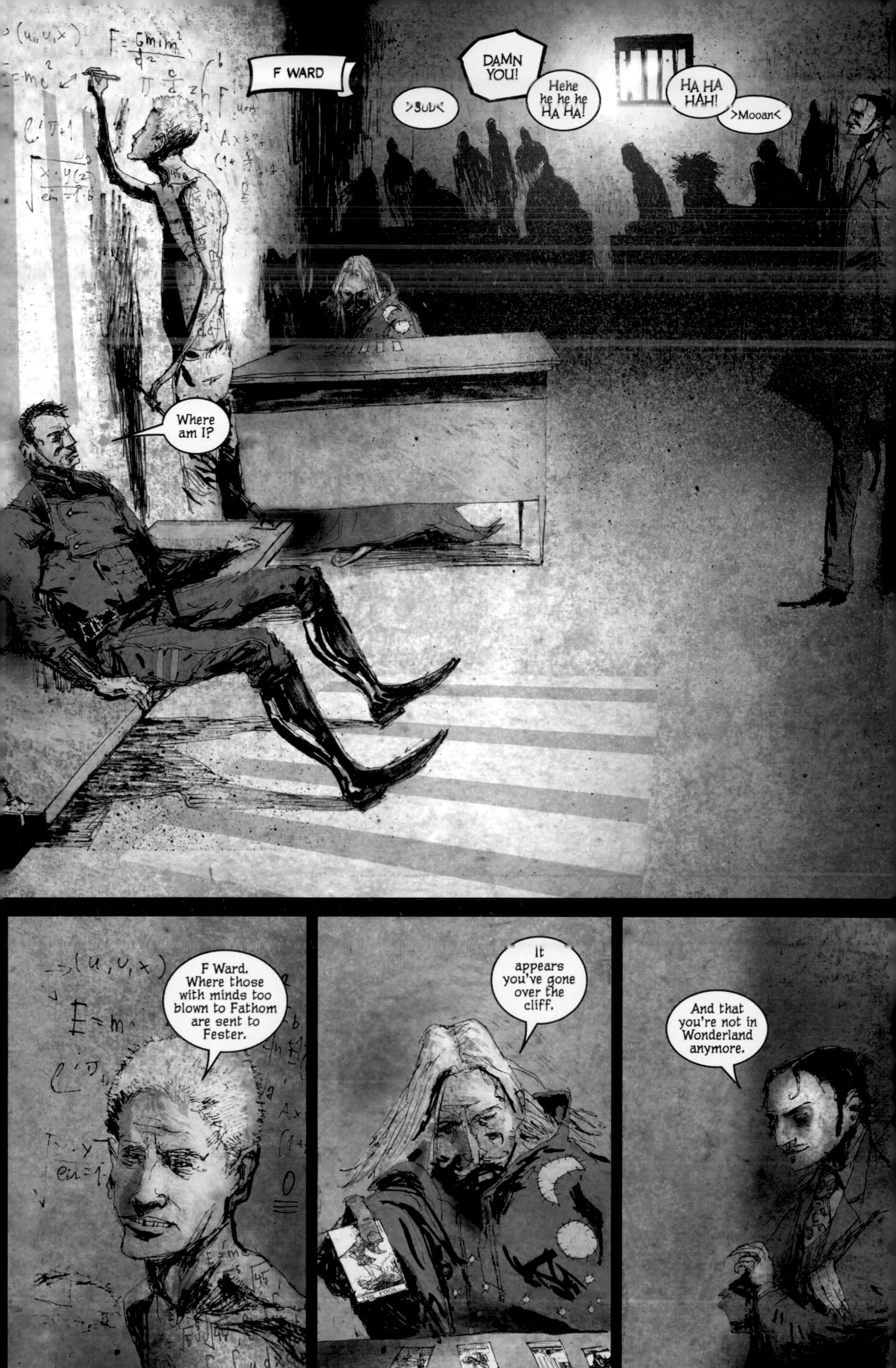
F WARD
DAMN YOU!
Hehe he he he HA HA!
HA HA HAH!
>Mooan<
Where am I?
F Ward. Where those with minds too blown to Fathom are sent to Fester.
It appears you've gone over the cliff.
And that you're not in Wonderland anymore.

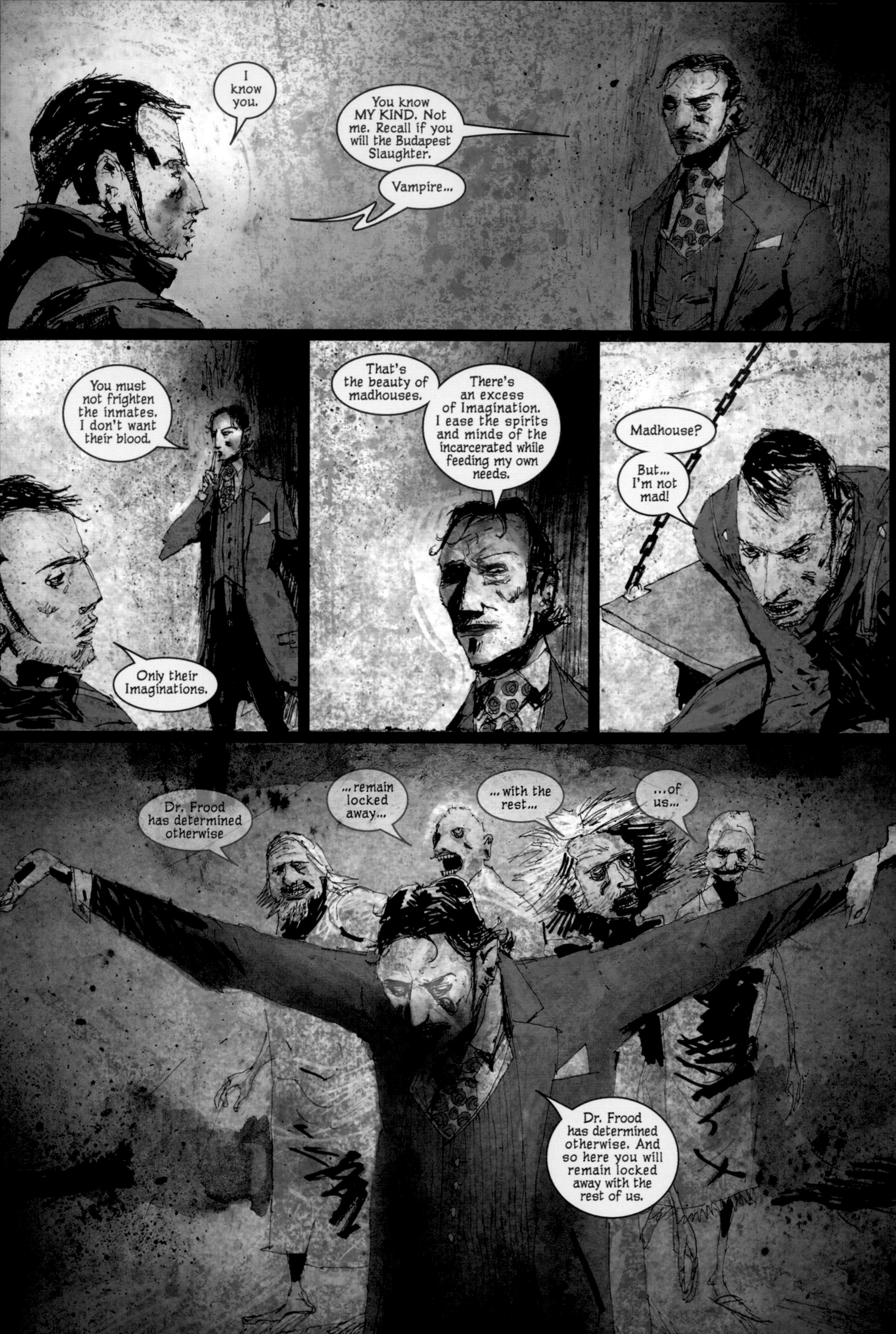

I know you.
You know MY KIND. Not me. Recall if you will the Budapest Slaughter.
Vampire...
You must not frighten the inmates. I don't want their blood.
Only their Imaginations.
That's the beauty of madhouses.
There's an excess of Imagination. I ease the spirits and minds of the incarcerated while feeding my own needs.
Madhouse?
But... I'm not mad!
Dr. Frood has determined otherwise
...remain locked away...
...with the rest...
...of us...
Dr. Frood has determined otherwise. And so here you will remain locked away with the rest of us.

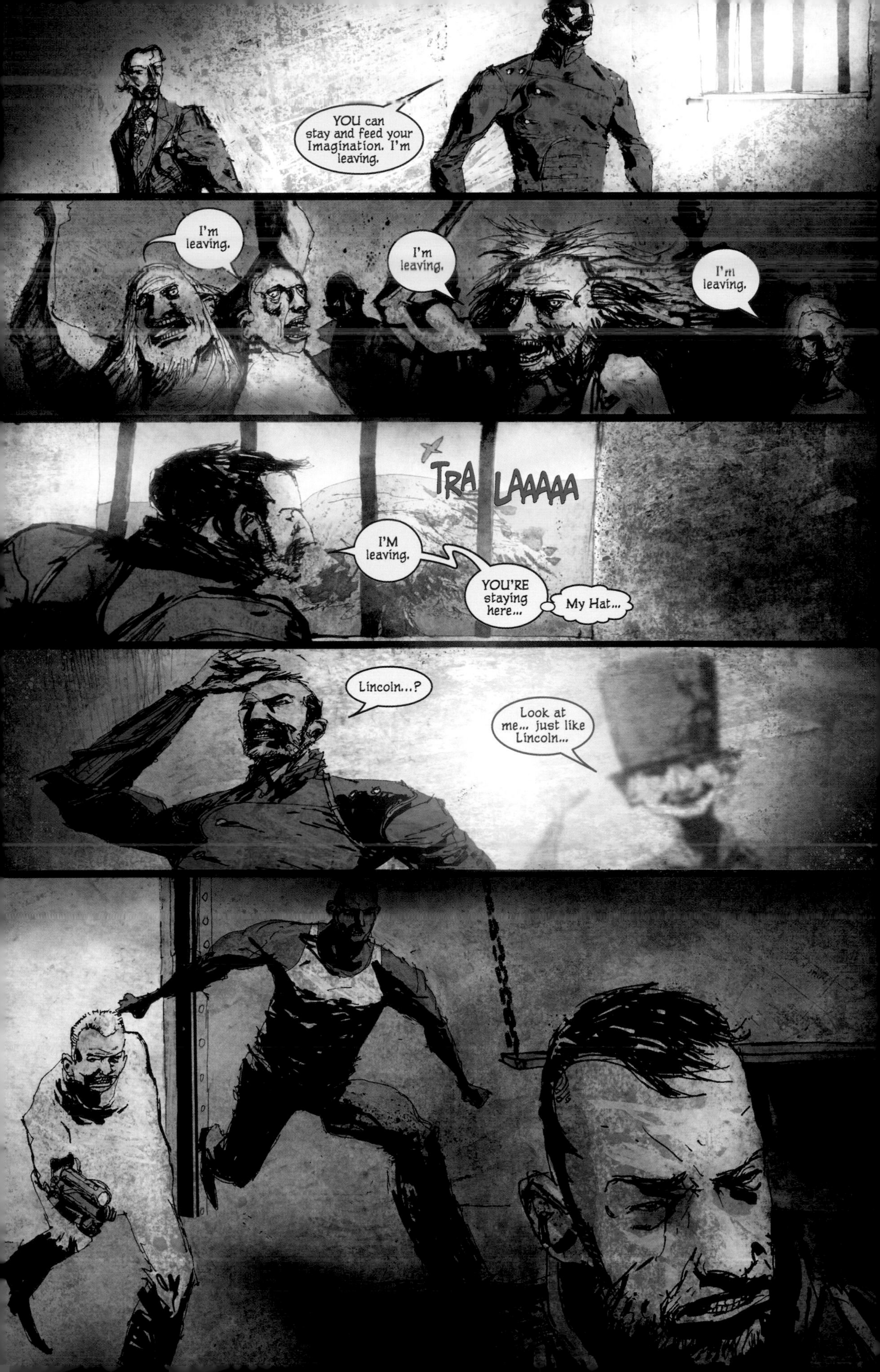
YOU can stay and feed your Imagination. I'm leaving.
I'm leaving.
I'm leaving.
I'm leaving.
TRA LAAAAA
I'M leaving.
YOU'RE staying here...
My Hat...
Lincoln...?
Look at me... just like Lincoln...

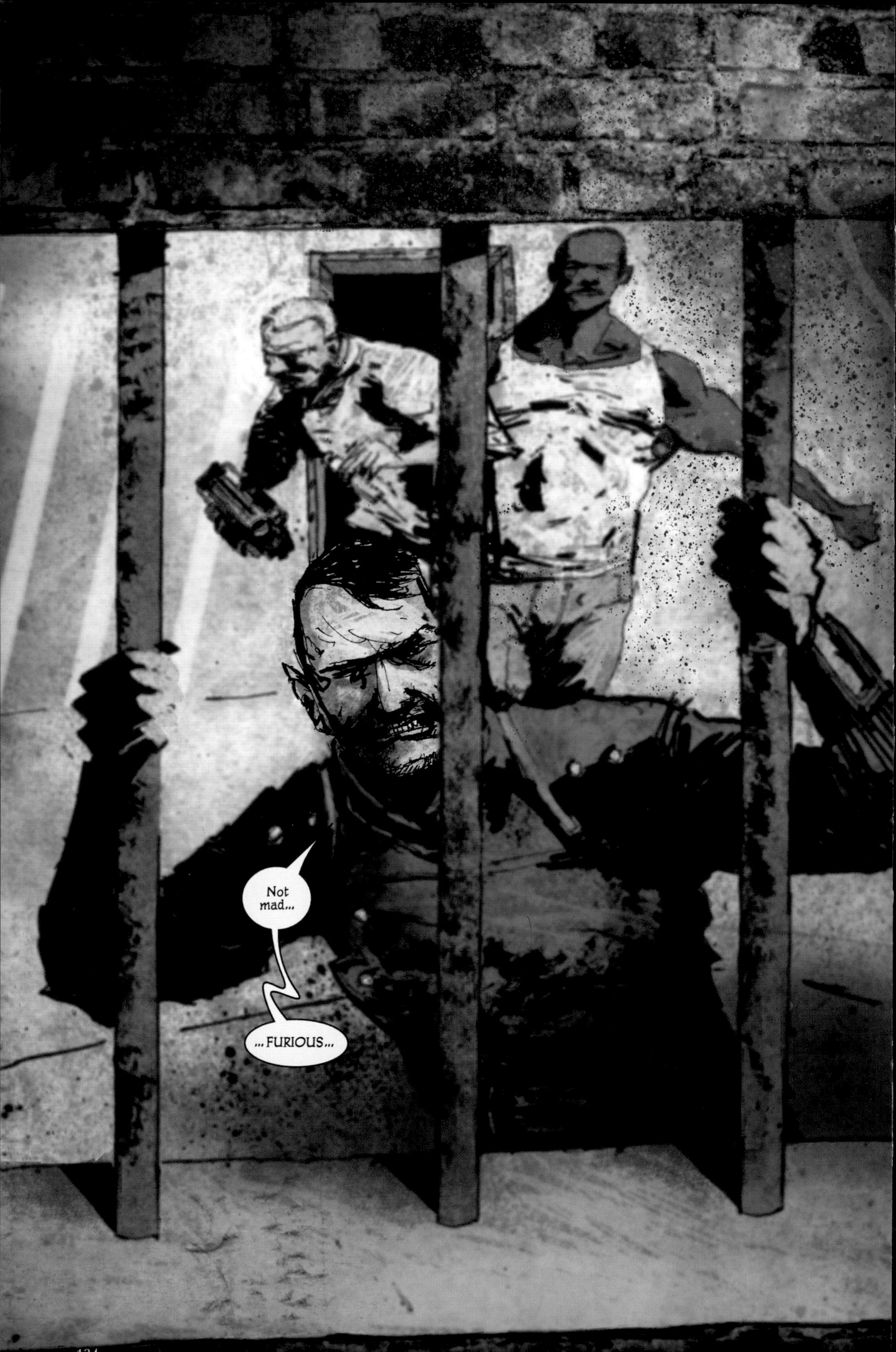

Not mad...
...FURIOUS...

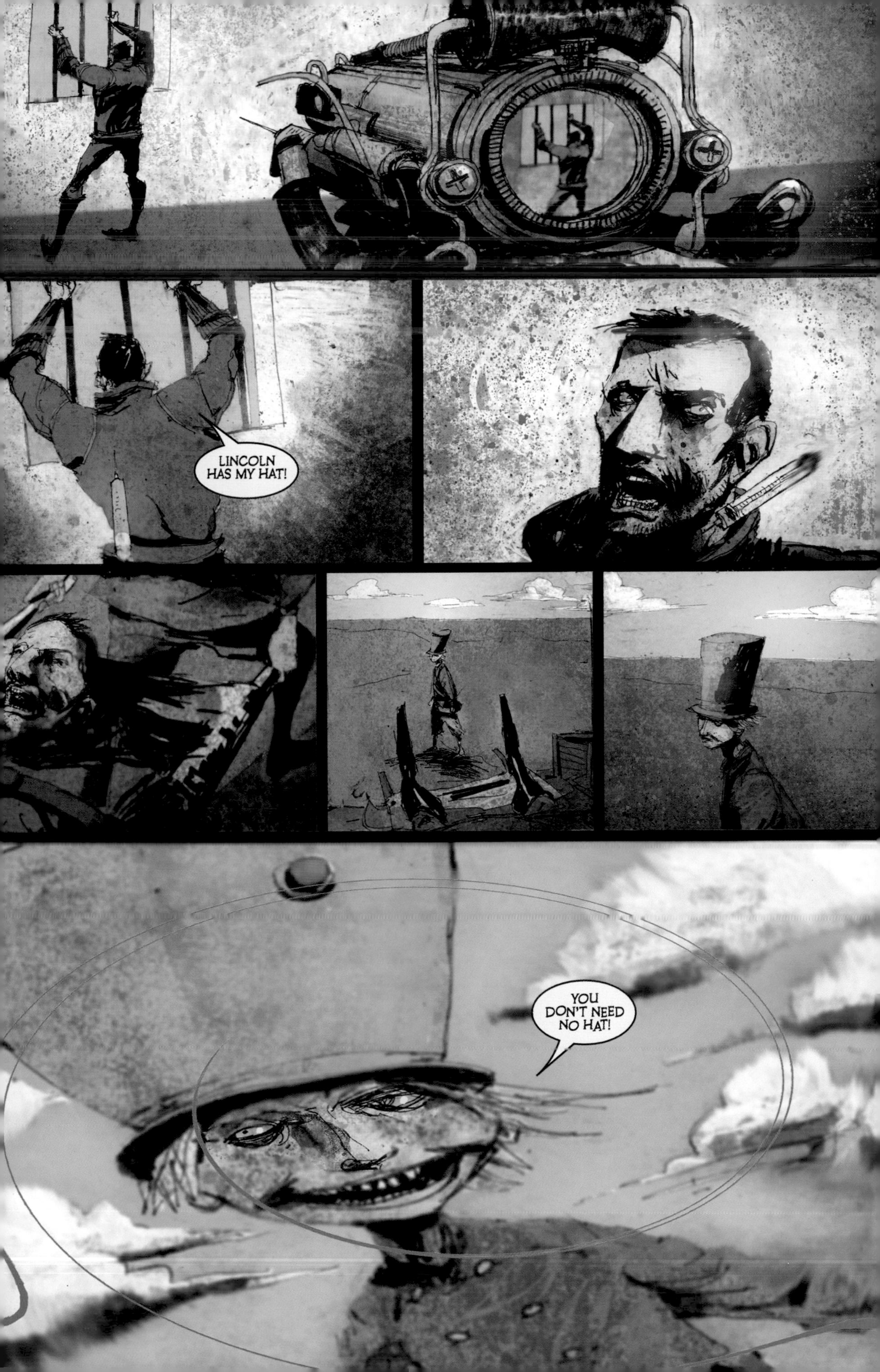
LINCOLN HAS MY HAT!
YOU DON'T NEED NO HAT!

Hat's free!

Aloft without the heaviness of consciousness.
No guilt propels me.

No loss haunts.

Hat is no longer separated from life by the
call of duty.

Hat flies free and soars knowing that moment
by moment...

Hat will be led back to him.

"A breath of wind from the wings of madness." —CHARLES BAUDELAIRE

Hat's Off!

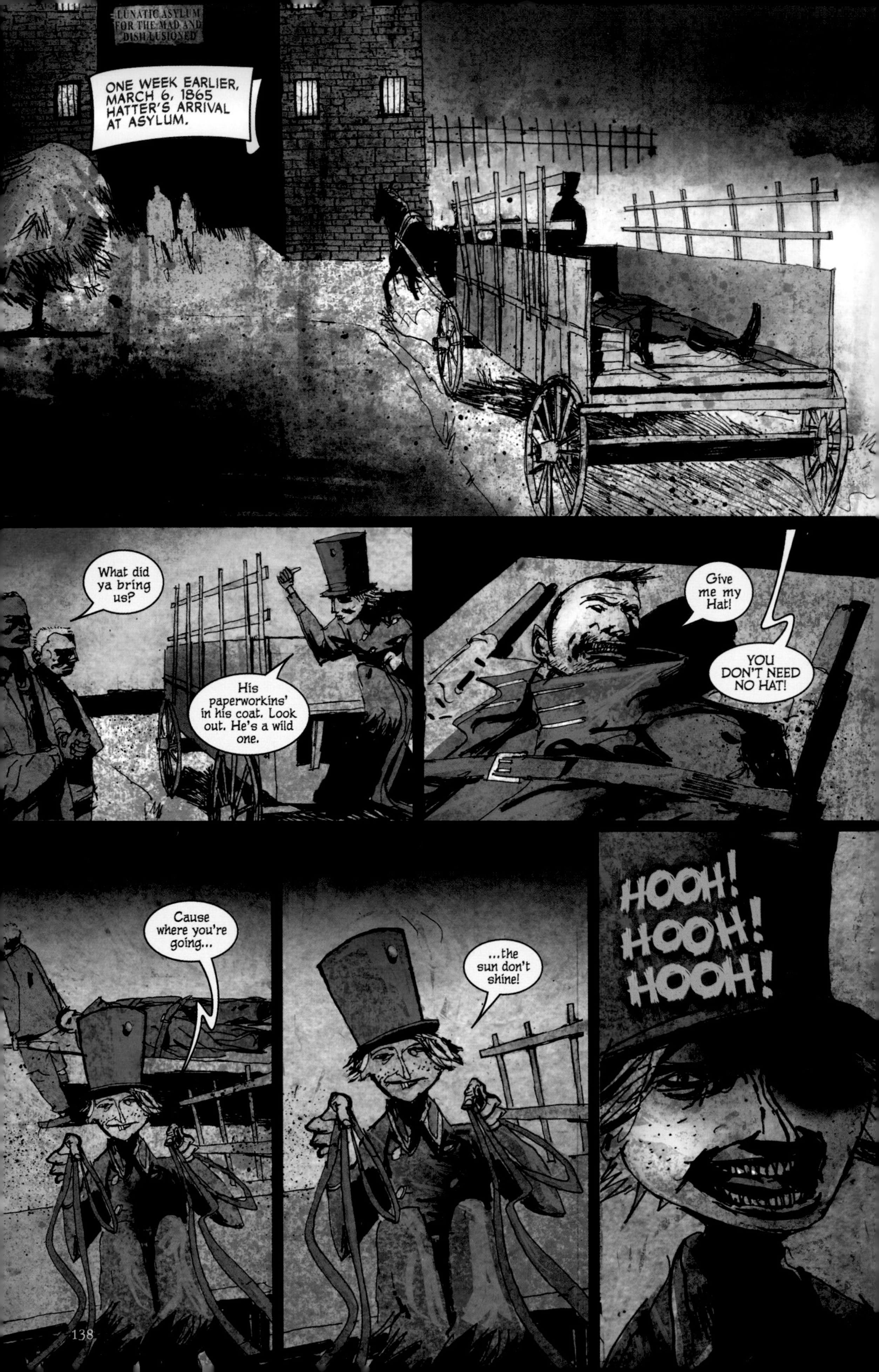
LUNATIC ASYLUM FOR THE MAD AND DISH LUSIONED
ONE WEEK EARLIER, MARCH 6, 1865 HATTER'S ARRIVAL AT ASYLUM.
What did ya bring us?
His paperworkins' in his coat. Look out. He's a wild one.
Give me my Hat!
YOU DON'T NEED NO HAT!
Cause where you're going...
...the sun don't shine!
HOOH! HOOH! HOOH!

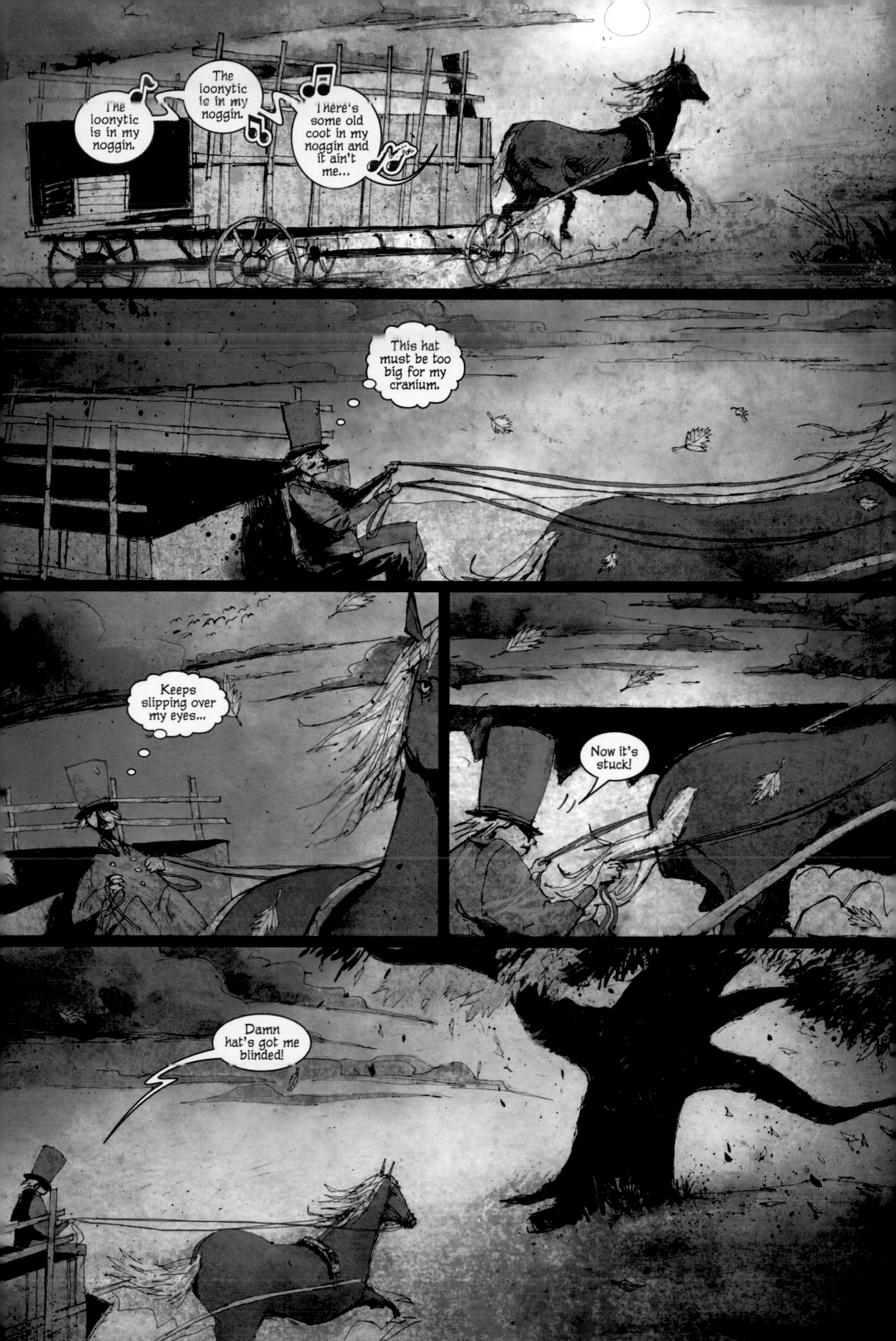
The loonytic is in my noggin.
The loonytic is in my noggin.
There's some old coot in my noggin and it ain't me...
This hat must be too big for my cranium.
Keeps slipping over my eyes...
Now it's stuck!
Damn hat's got me blinded!

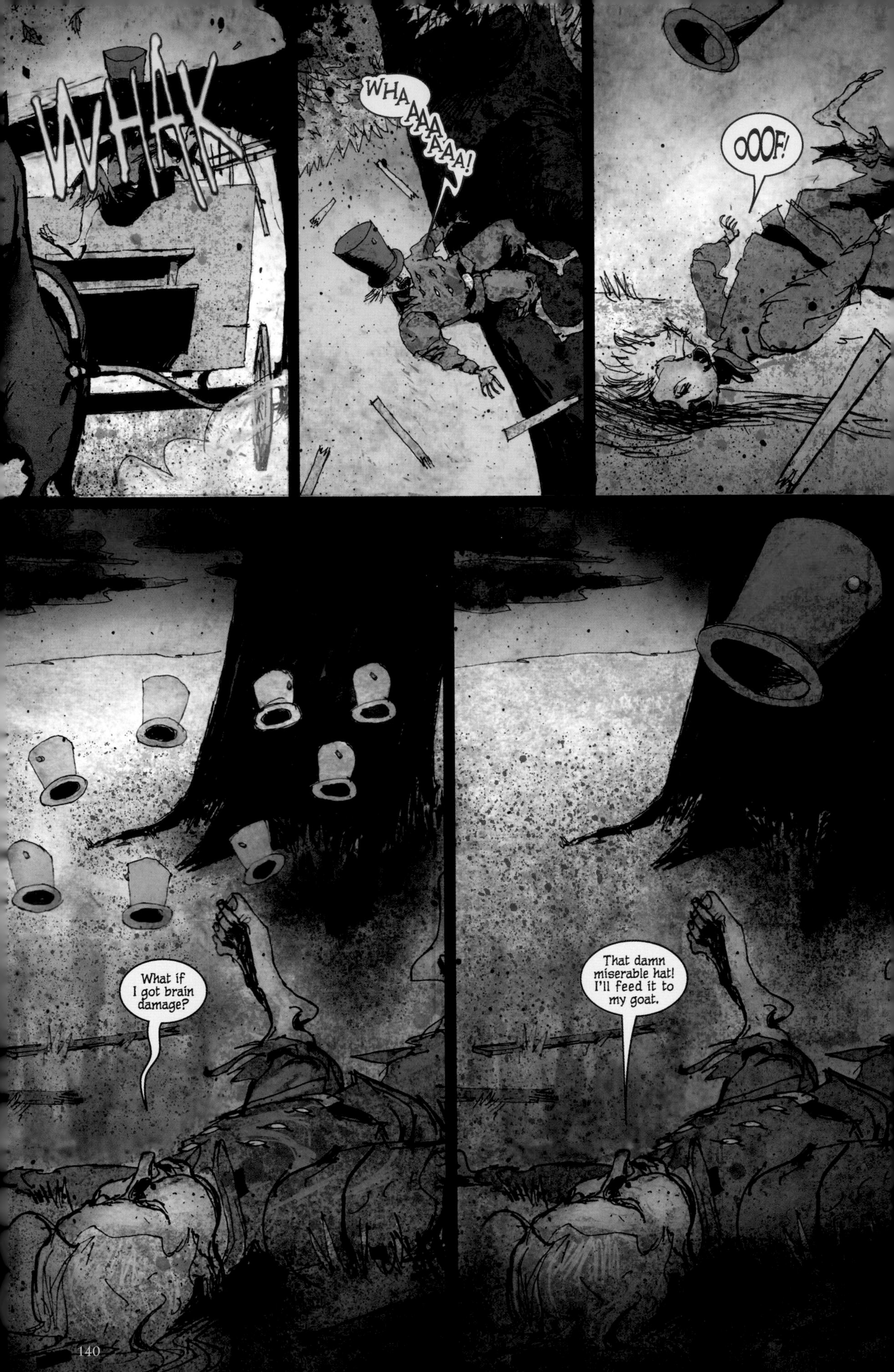
WHAK
WHAAAAAAAA!
OOOF!
What if I got brain damage?
That damn miserable hat! I'll feed it to my goat.

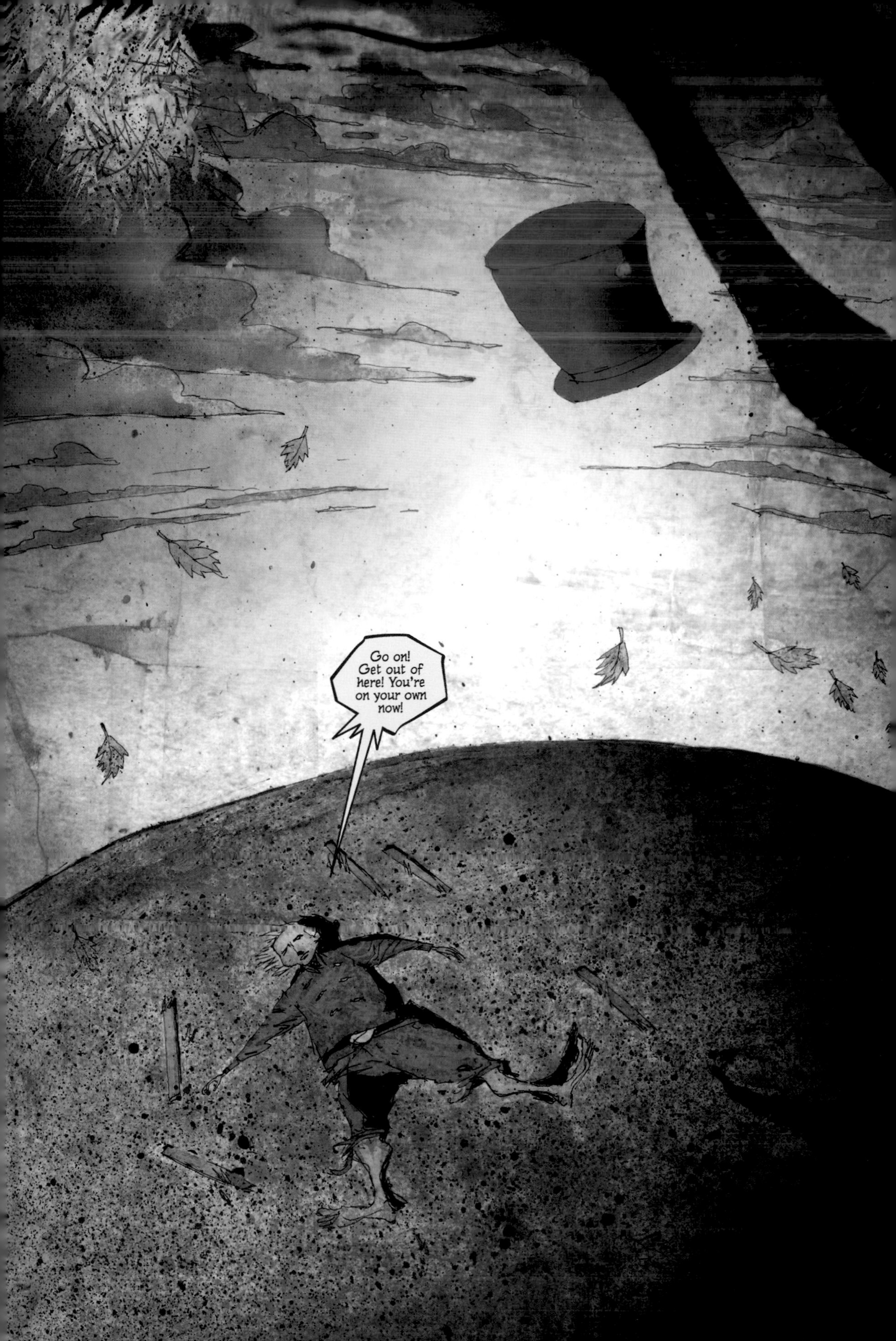
Go on! Get out of here! You're on your own now!

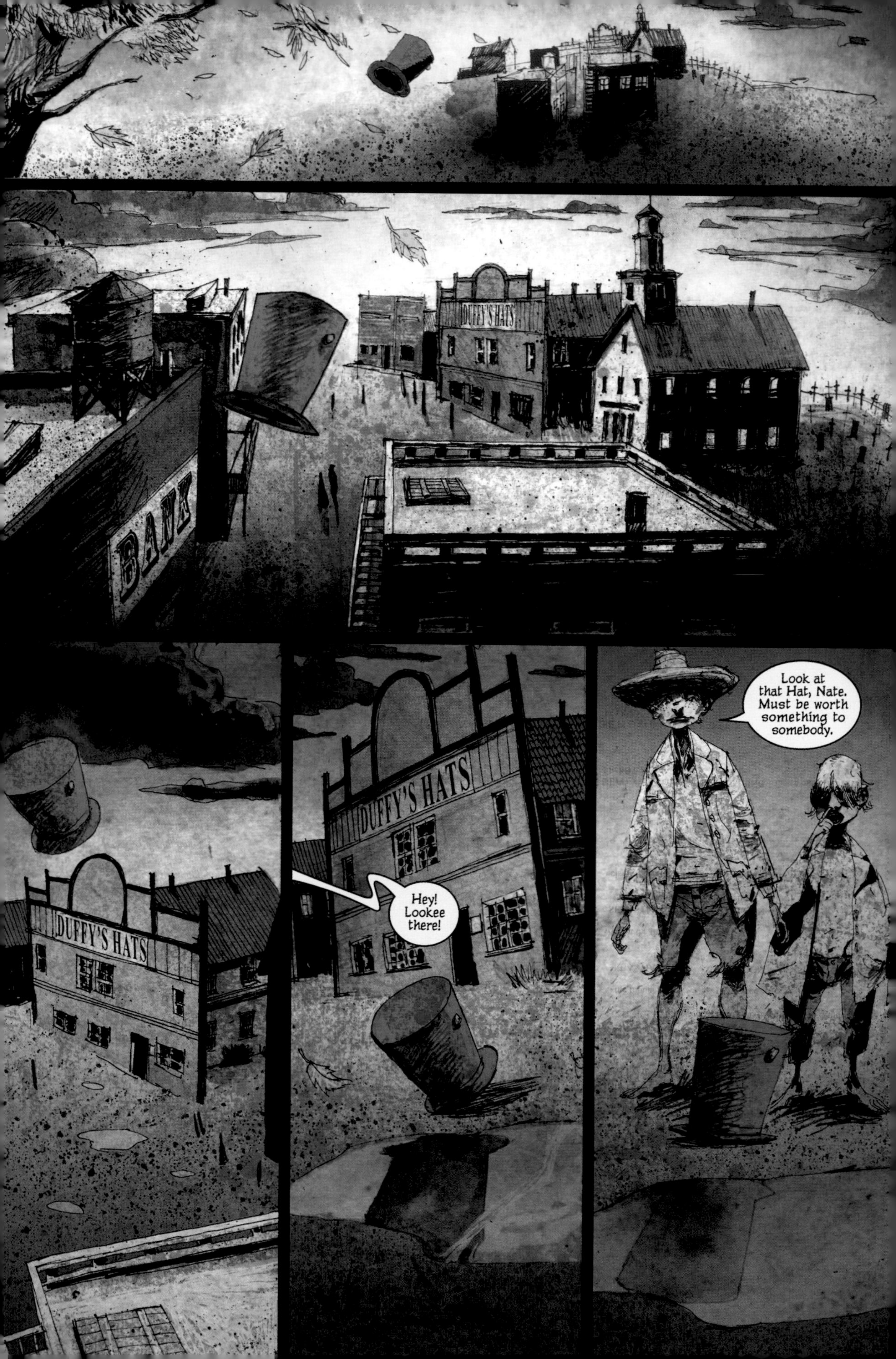

BANK
DUFFY'S HATS
DUFFY'S HATS
DUFFY'S HATS
Hey! Lookee there!
Look at that Hat, Nate. Must be worth something to somebody.

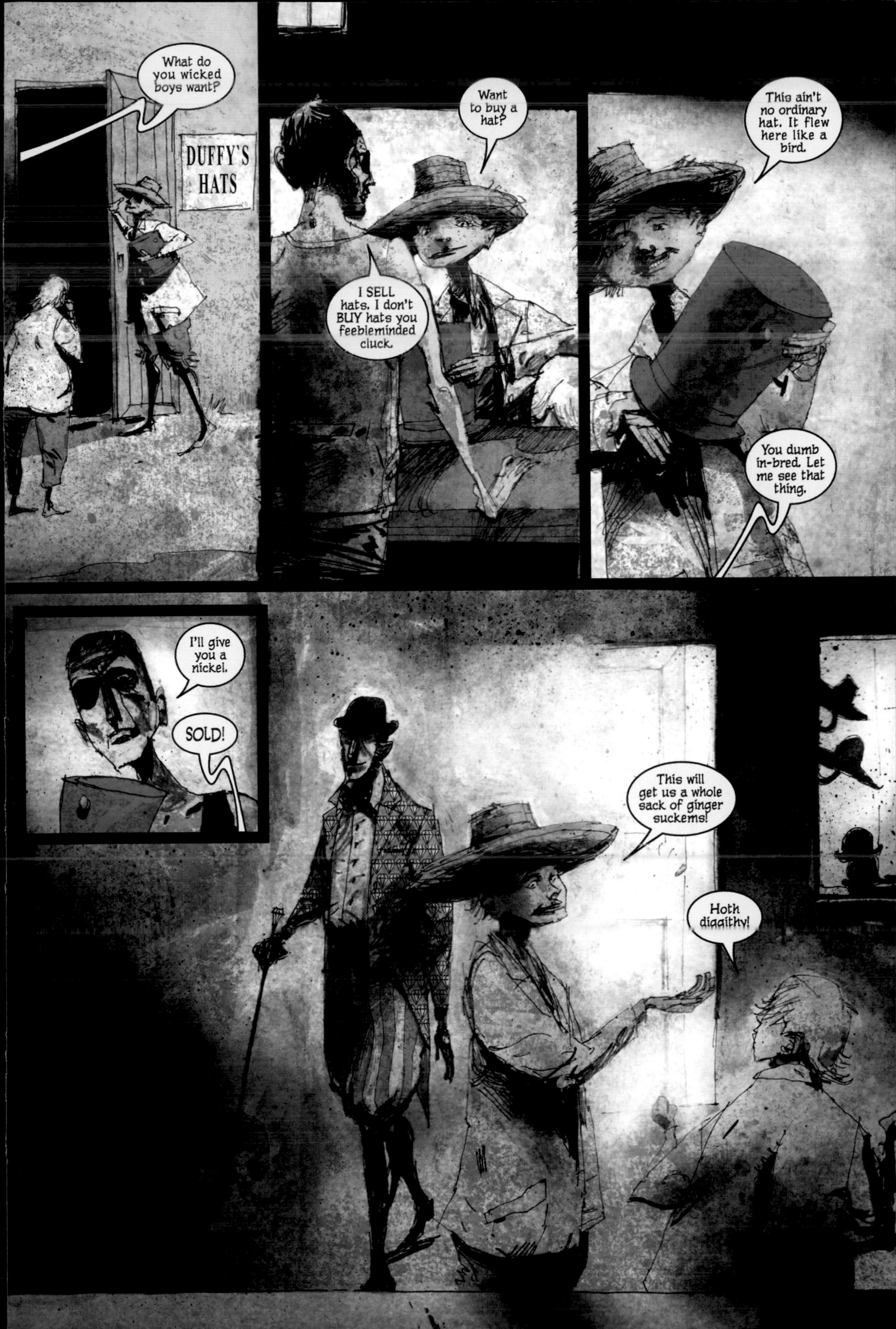
What do you wicked boys want?
DUFFY'S HATS
Want to buy a hat?
I SELL hats. I don't BUY hats you feebleminded cluck.
This ain't no ordinary hat. It flew here like a bird.
You dumb in-bred. Let me see that thing.
I'll give you a nickel.
SOLD!
This will get us a whole sack of ginger suckems!
Hoth diggithy!

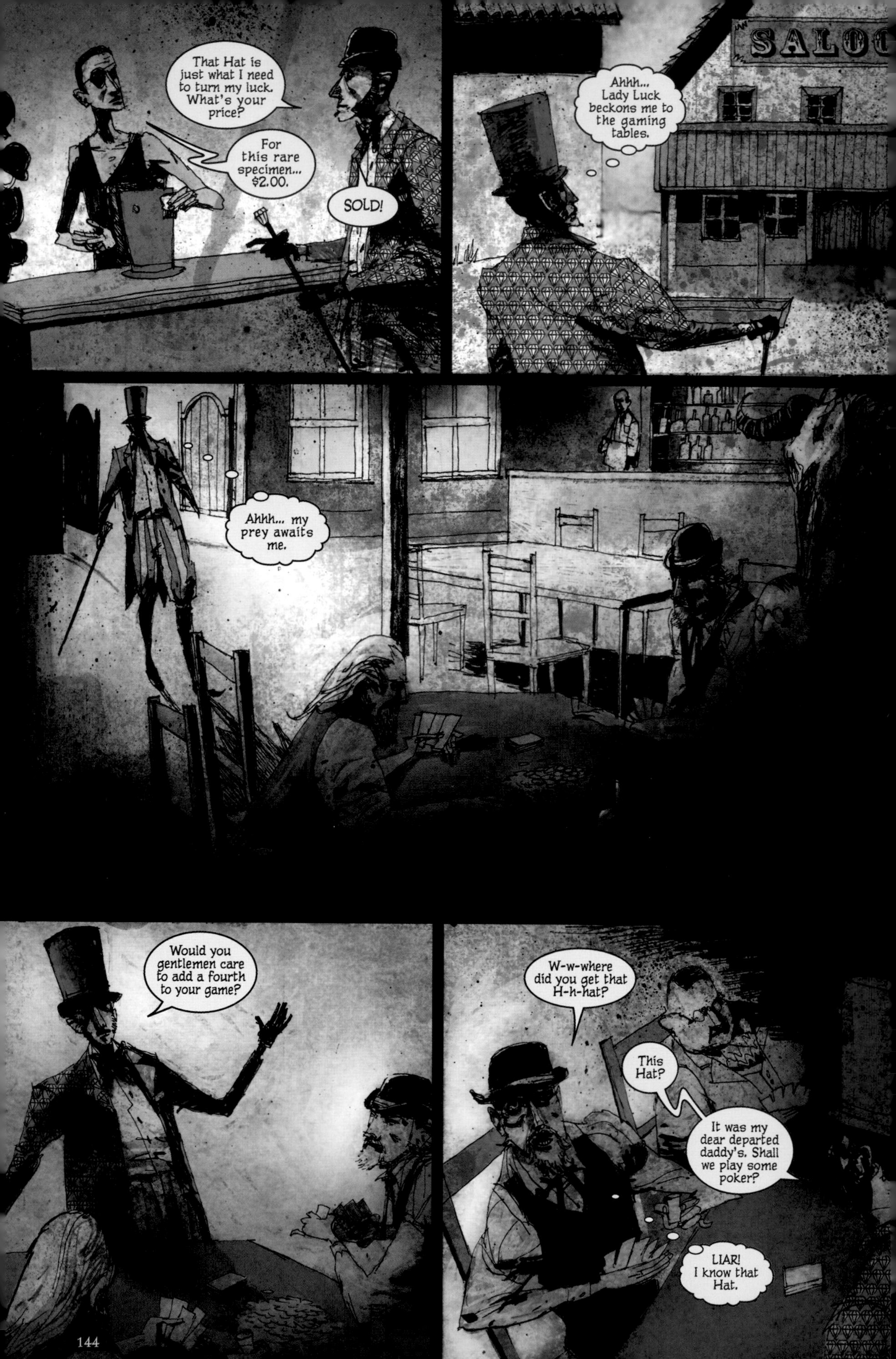

That Hat is just what I need to turn my luck. What's your price?
For this rare specimen... $2.00.
SOLD!
SALOO
Ahhh... Lady Luck beckons me to the gaming tables.
Ahhh... my prey awaits me.
Would you gentlemen care to add a fourth to your game?
W-w-where did you get that H-h-hat?
This Hat?
It was my dear departed daddy's. Shall we play some poker?
LIAR! I know that Hat.

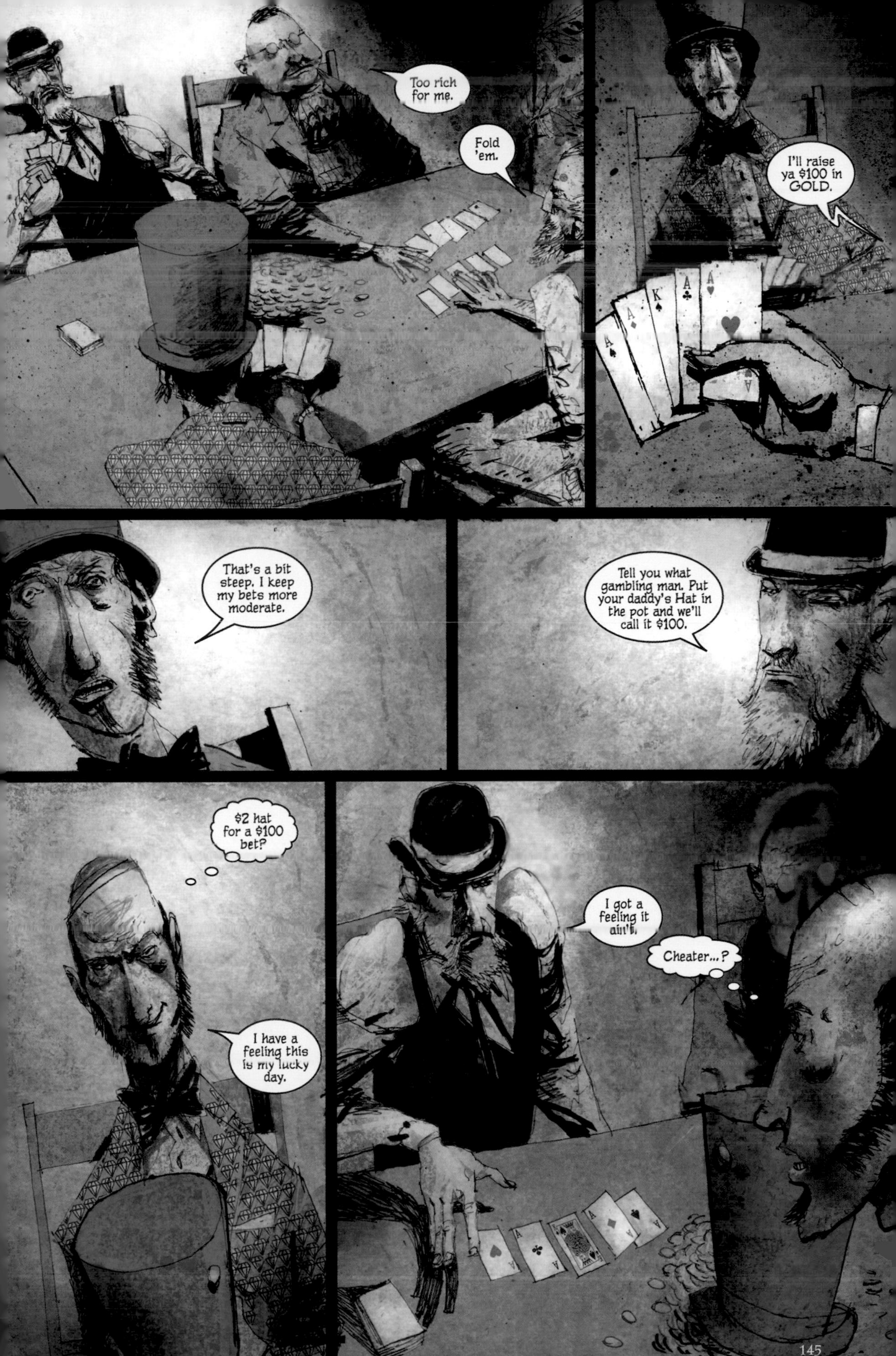
Too rich for me.
Fold 'em.
I'll raise ya $100 in GOLD.
That's a bit steep. I keep my bets more moderate.
Tell you what gambling man. Put your daddy's Hat in the pot and we'll call it $100.
$2 hat for a $100 bet?
I have a feeling this is my lucky day.
I got a feeling it ain't.
Cheater...?

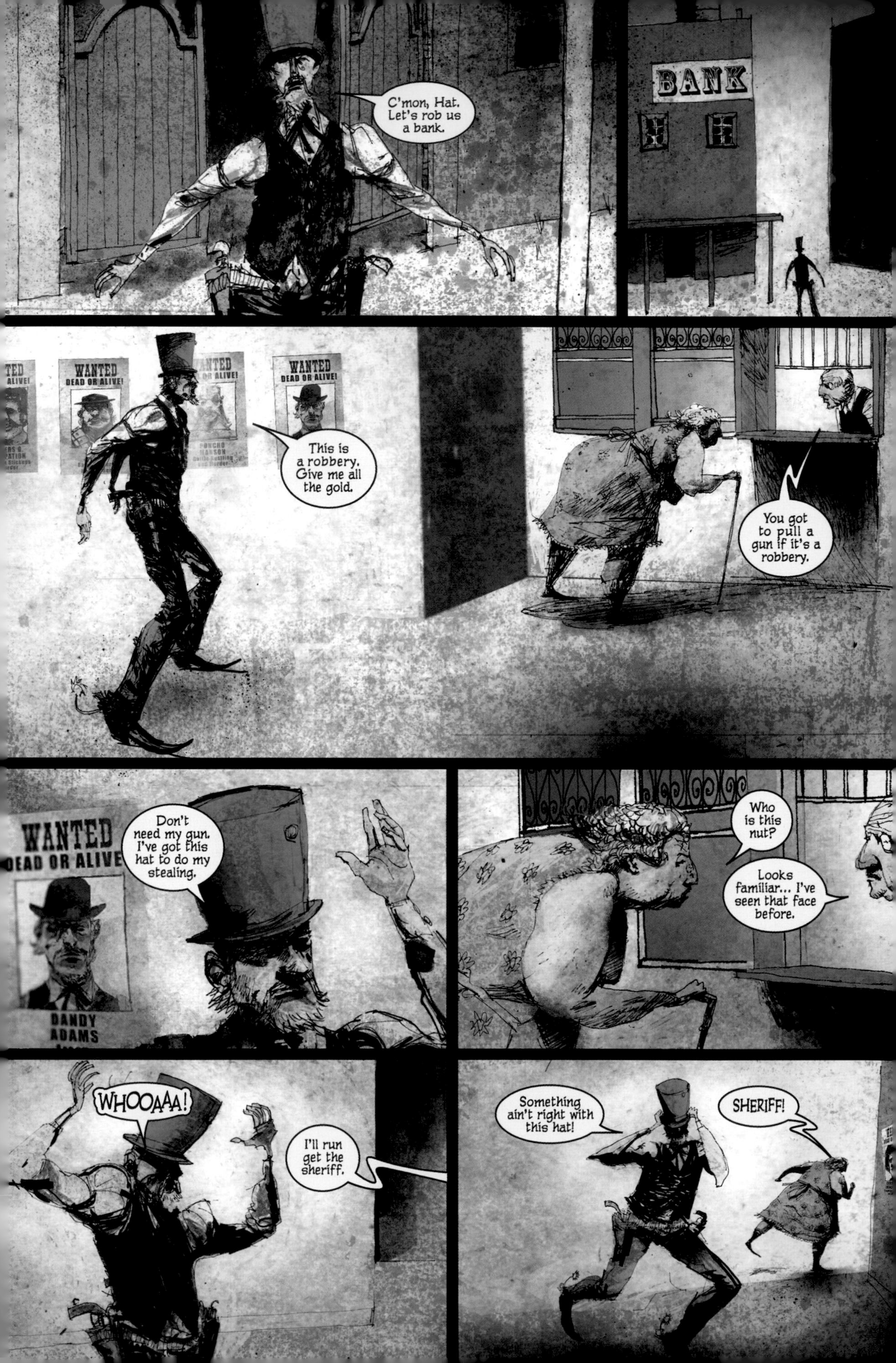
C'mon, Hat. Let's rob us a bank.
BANK
WANTED DEAD OR ALIVE!
WANTED DEAD OR ALIVE!
WANTED DEAD OR ALIVE!
This is a robbery. Give me all the gold.
You got to pull a gun if it's a robbery.
WANTED DEAD OR ALIVE
DANDY ADAMS
Don't need my gun. I've got this hat to do my stealing.
Who is this nut?
Looks familiar... I've seen that face before.
WHOOAAA!
I'll run get the sheriff.
Something ain't right with this hat!
SHERIFF!

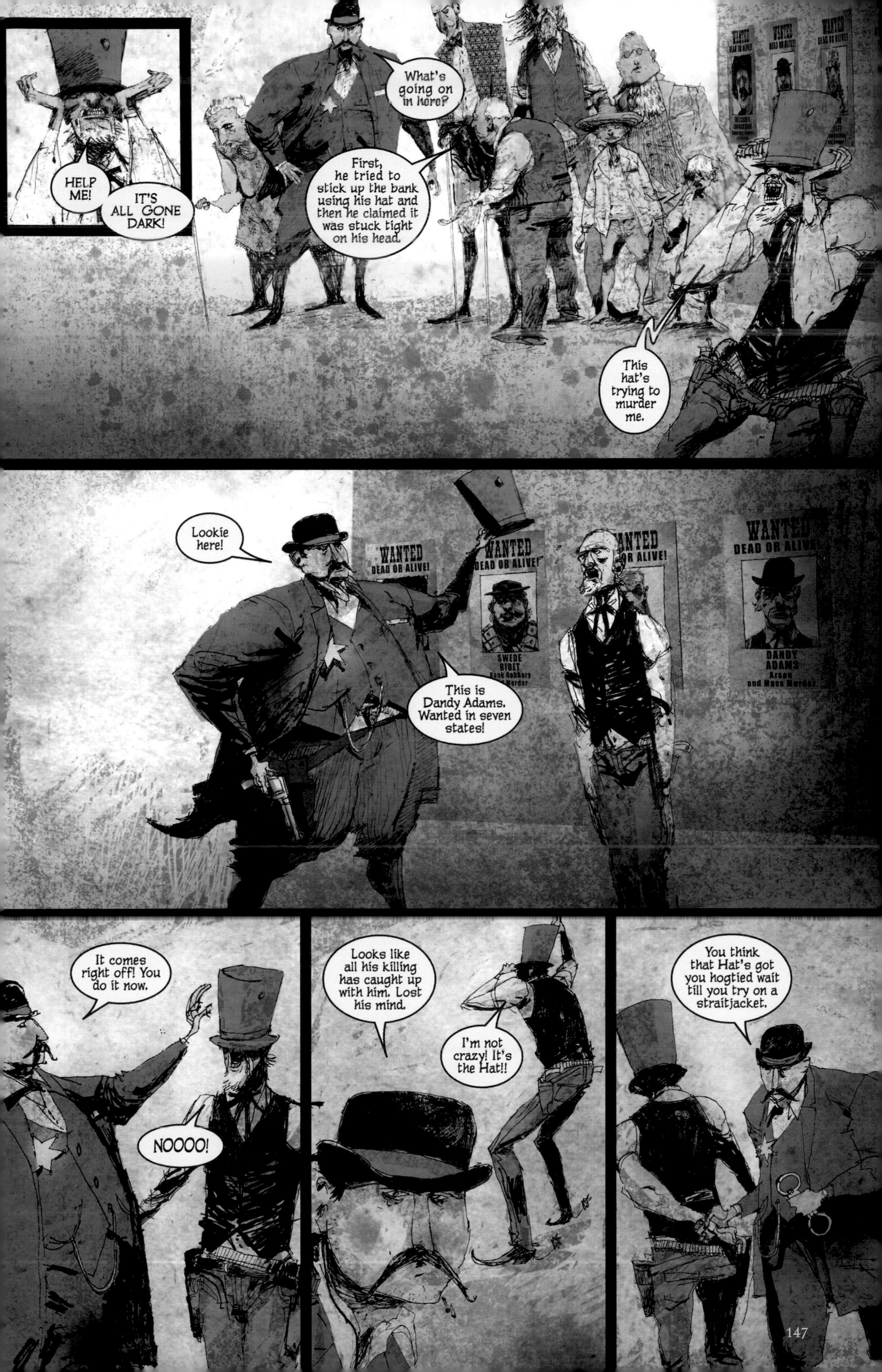
HELP ME!
IT'S ALL GONE DARK!
What's going on in here?
First, he tried to stick up the bank using his hat and then he claimed it was stuck tight on his head.
This hat's trying to murder me.
Lookie here!
WANTED DEAD OR ALIVE!
WANTED DEAD OR ALIVE! SWEDE BIDET Bank Robbery
WANTED DEAD OR ALIVE! DANDY ADAMS Arson and Mass Murder
This is Dandy Adams. Wanted in seven states!
It comes right off! You do it now.
NOOOO!
Looks like all his killing has caught up with him. Lost his mind.
I'm not crazy! It's the Hat!!
You think that Hat's got you hogtied wait till you try on a straitjacket.

I have learned that my search is not just the route
I follow but includes those individuals I encounter.
Each...if I choose to listen...has a word that will
assist me. My search will end in success when I am
able to put all of their words together.

"Madness need not be all breakdown. It may also be break-through. It is potential liberation and renewal as well as enslavement and existential death." – R. D. LAING

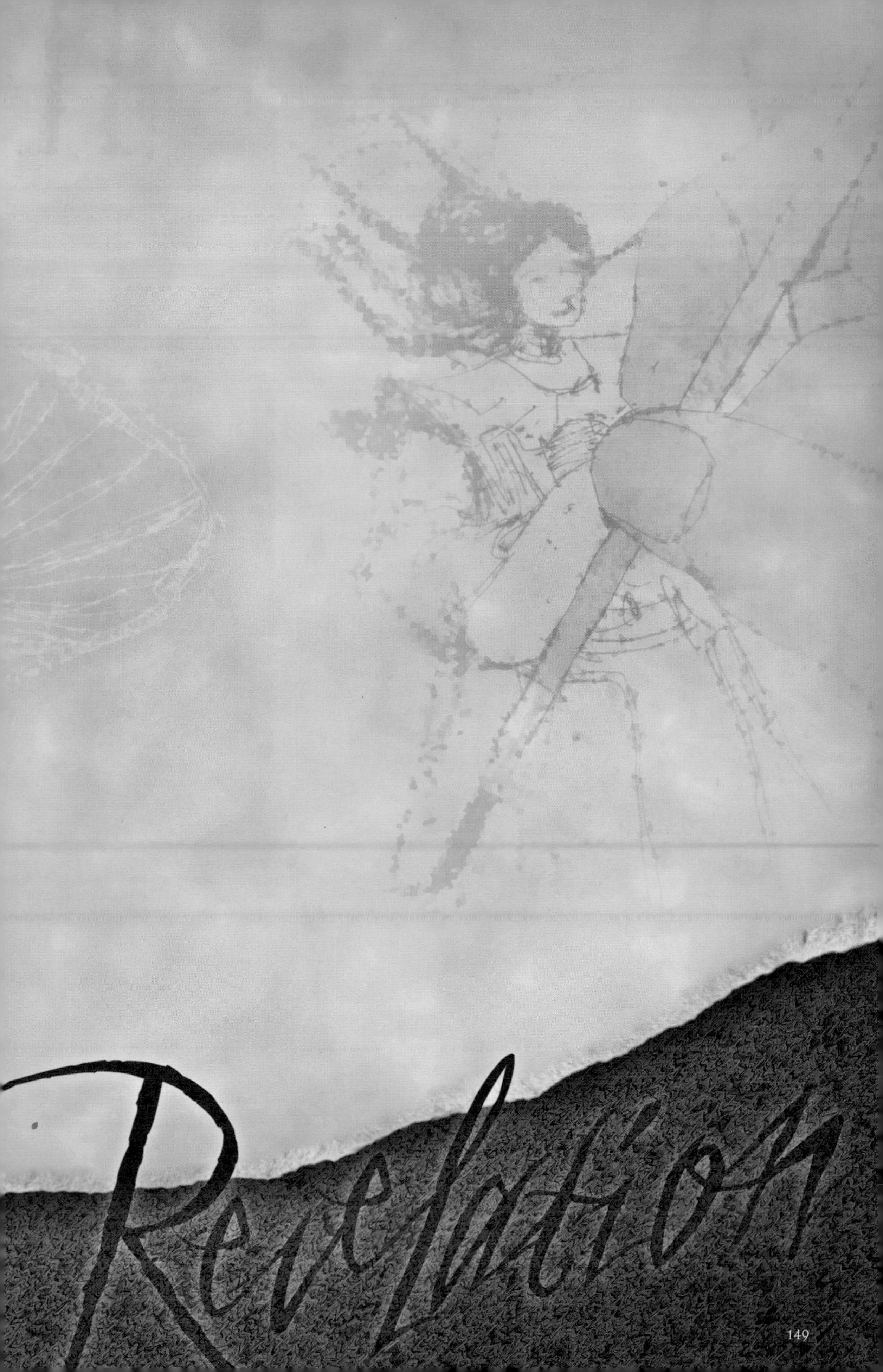

Revelation

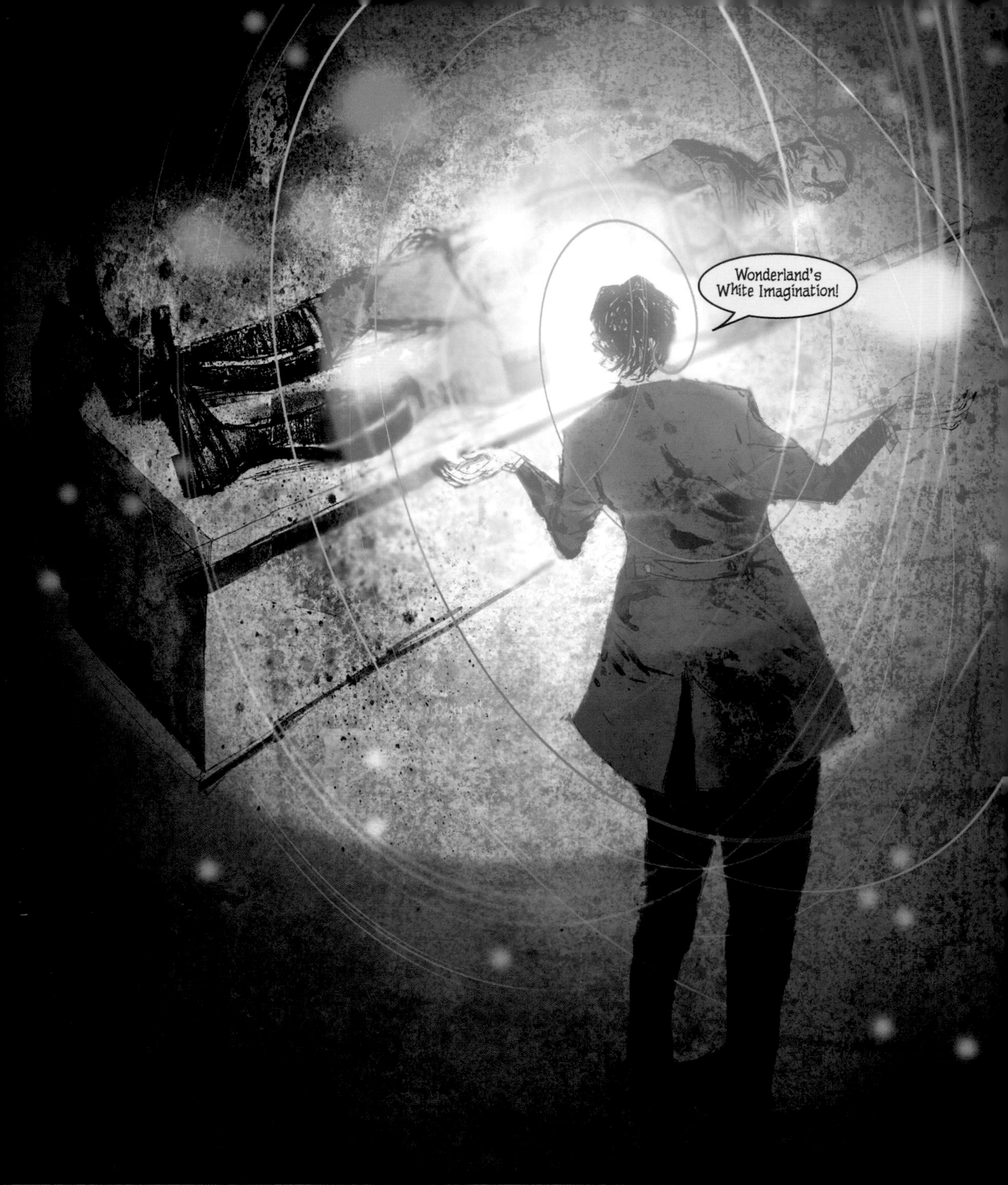
Wonderland's White Imagination!

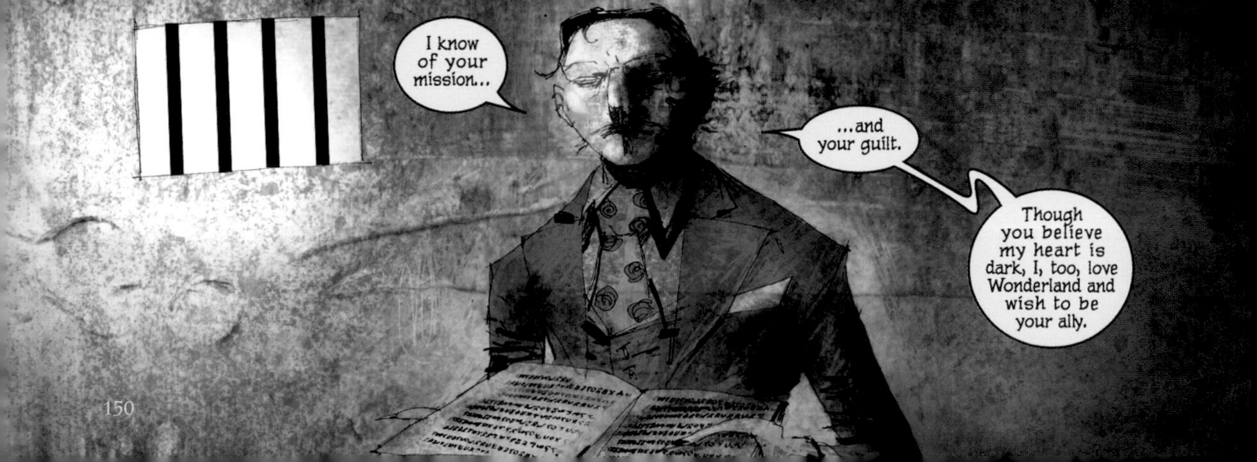
I know of your mission...
...and your guilt.
Though you believe my heart is dark, I, too, love Wonderland and wish to be your ally.

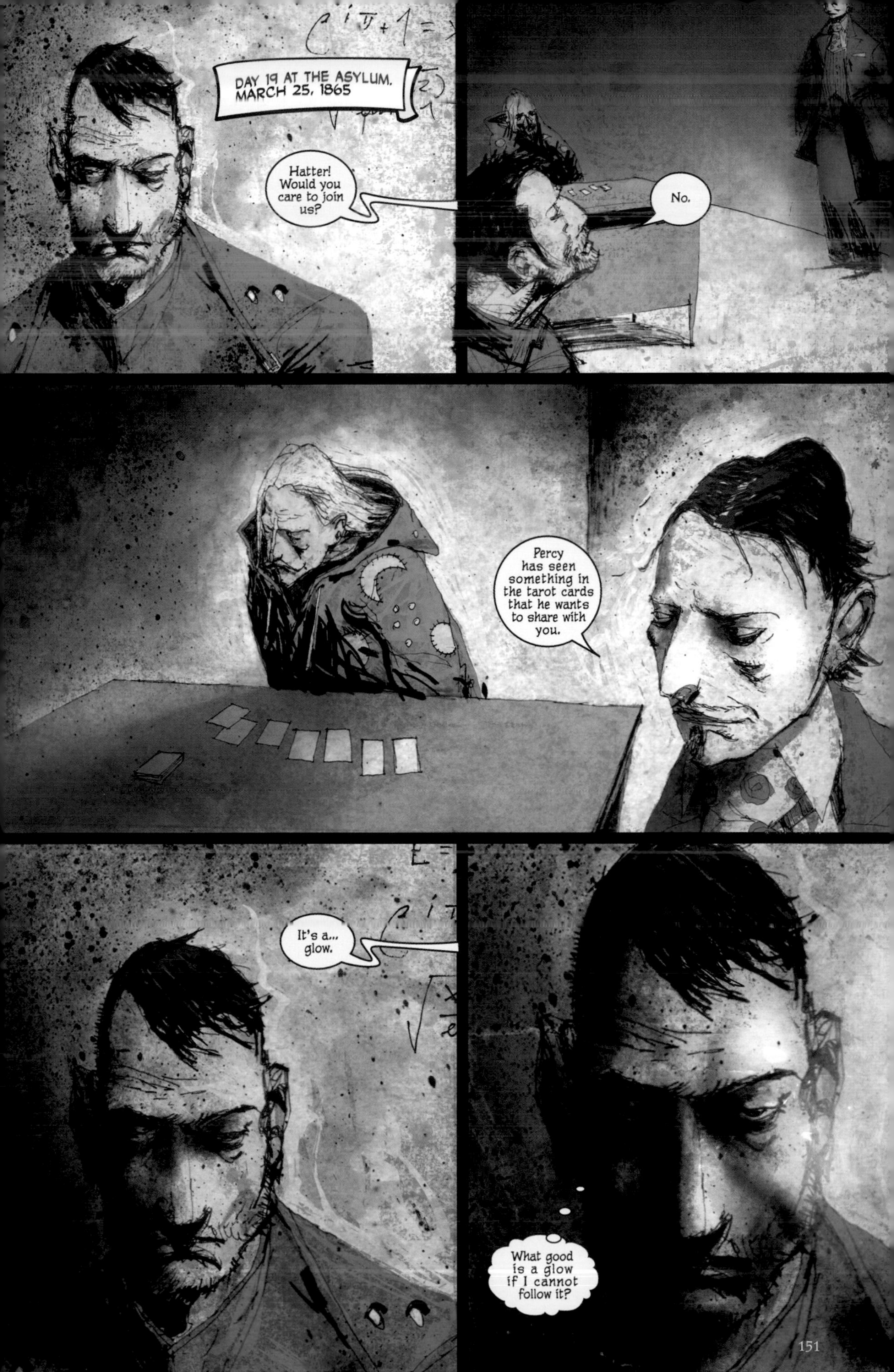
DAY 19 AT THE ASYLUM. MARCH 25, 1865
Hatter! Would you care to join us?
No.
Percy has seen something in the tarot cards that he wants to share with you.
It's a... glow.
What good is a glow if I cannot follow it?

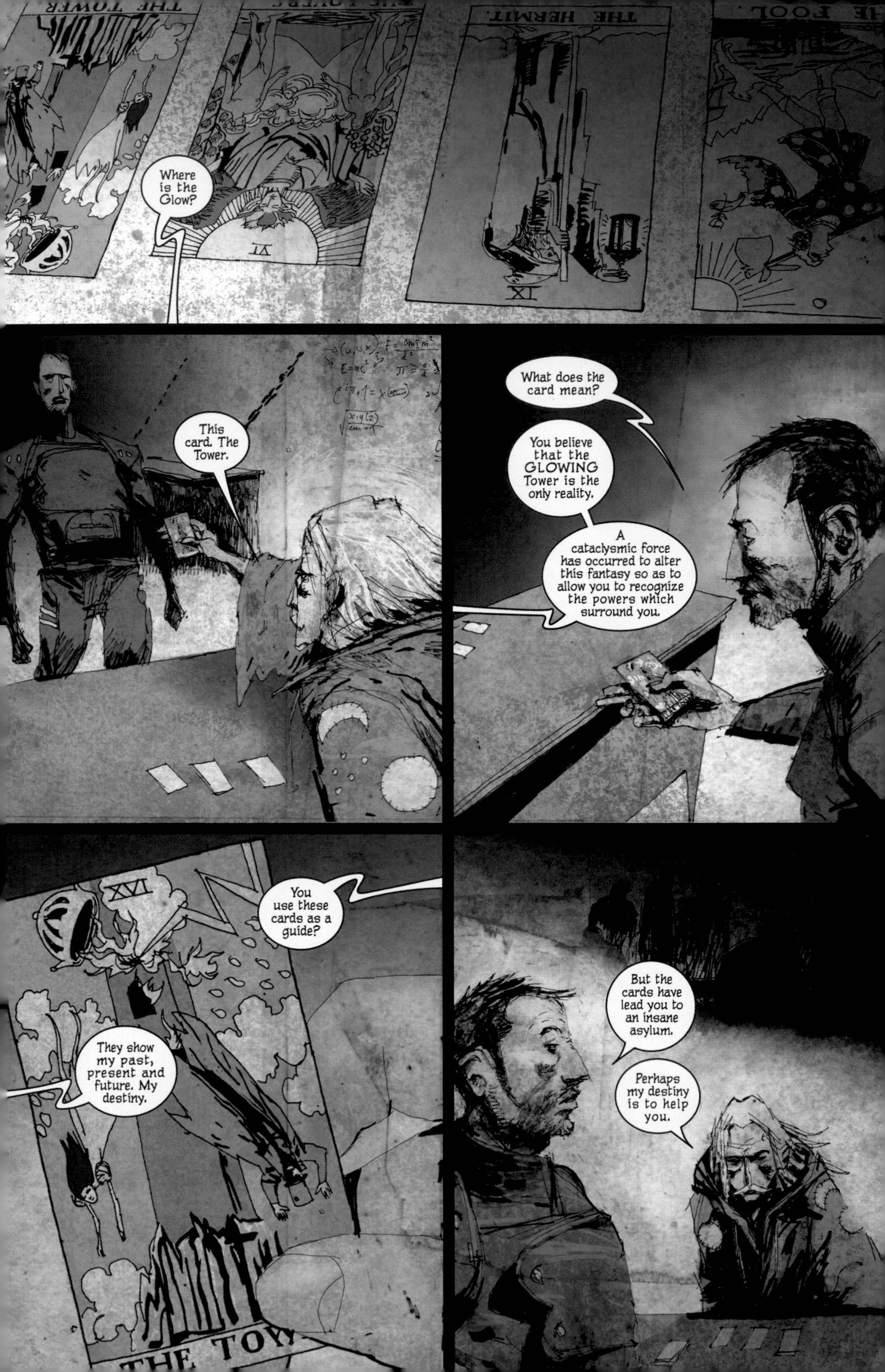
Where is the Glow?
This card. The Tower.
What does the card mean?
You believe that the GLOWING Tower is the only reality.
A cataclysmic force has occurred to alter this fantasy so as to allow you to recognize the powers which surround you.
You use these cards as a guide?
They show my past, present and future. My destiny.
But the cards have lead you to an insane asylum.
Perhaps my destiny is to help you.

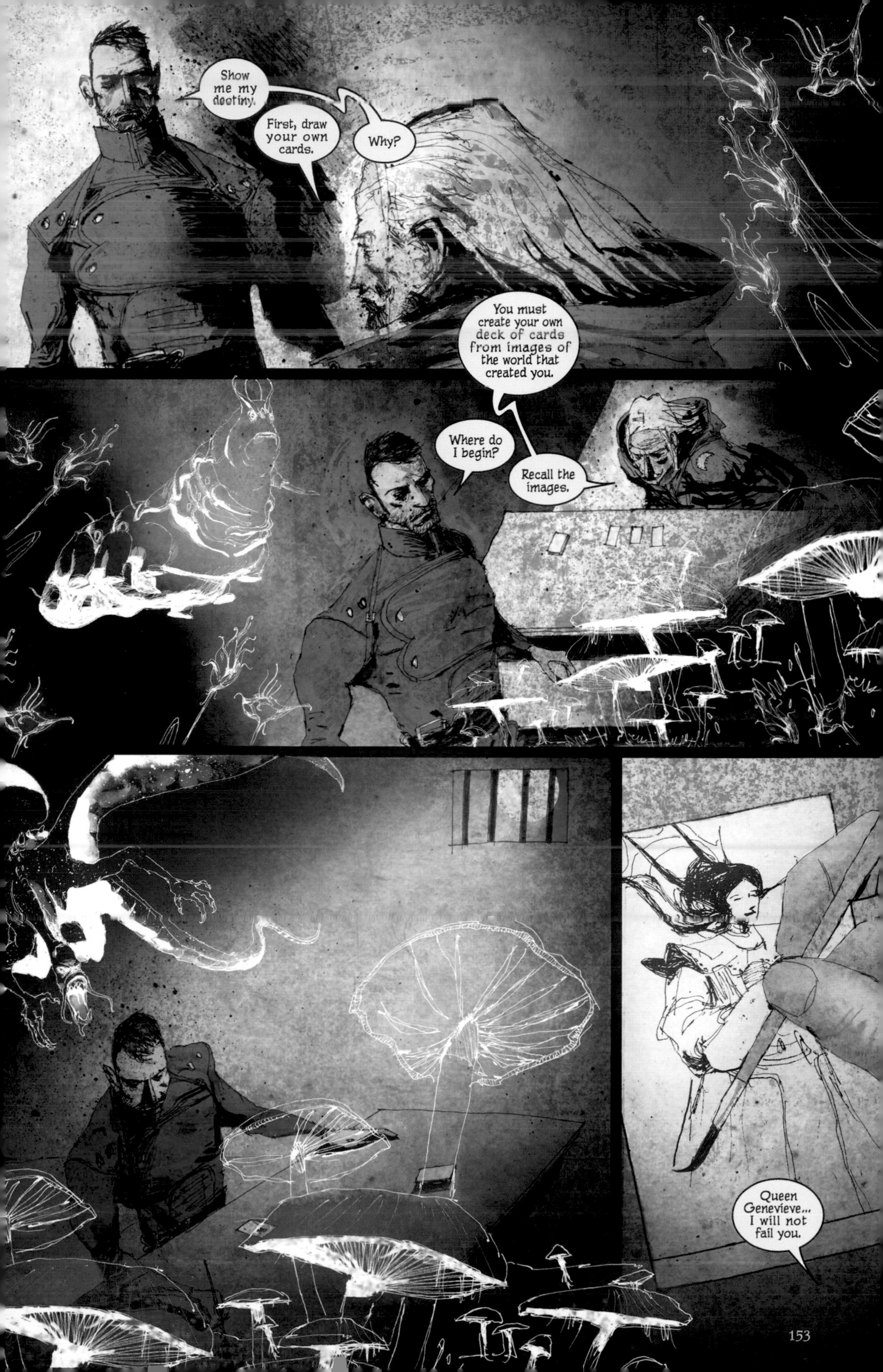
Show me my destiny.
First, draw your own cards.
Why?
You must create your own deck of cards from images of the world that created you.
Where do I begin?
Recall the images.
Queen Genevieve... I will not fail you.

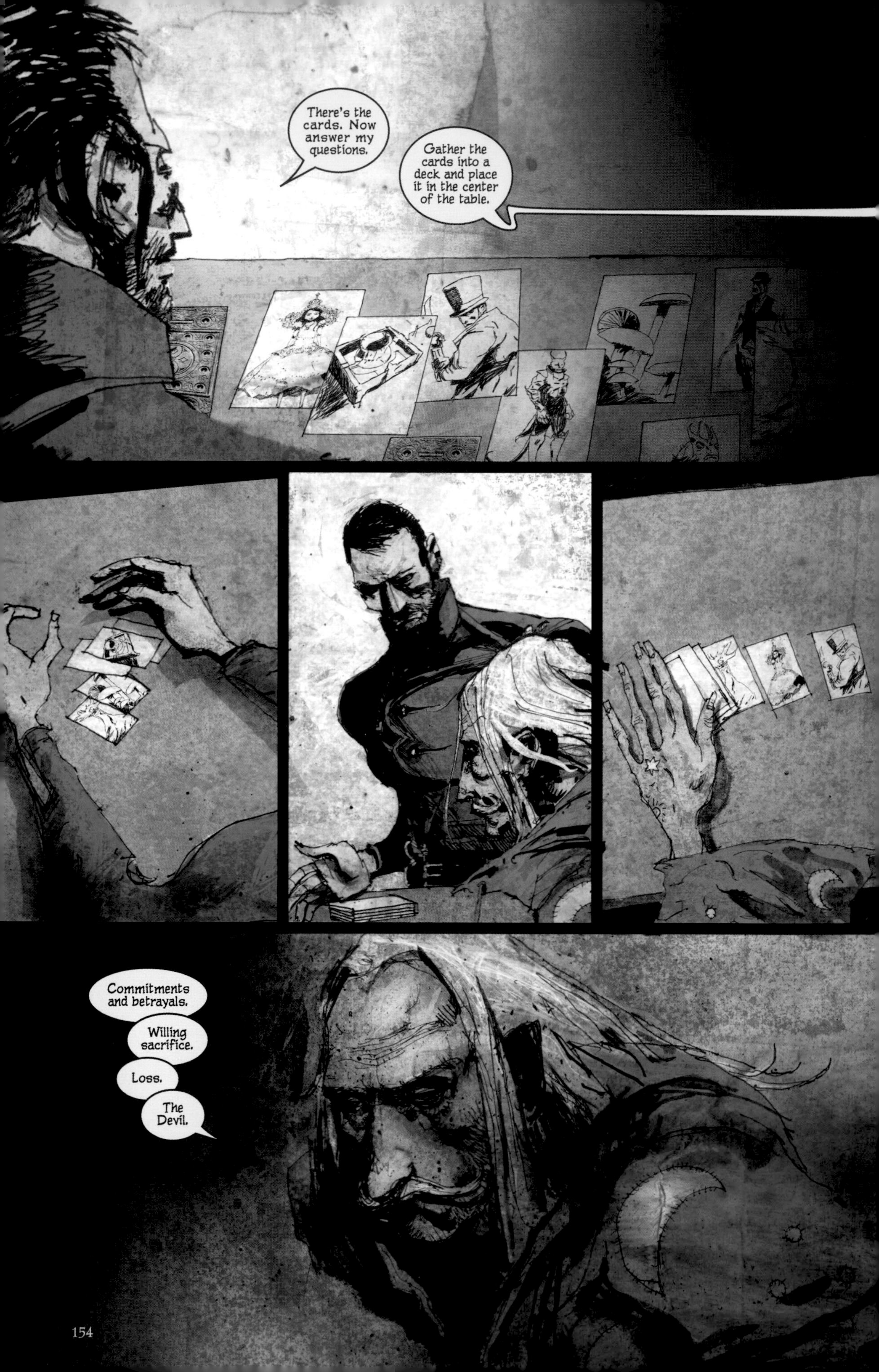
There's the cards. Now answer my questions.
Gather the cards into a deck and place it in the center of the table.
Commitments and betrayals.
Willing sacrifice.
Loss.
The Devil.

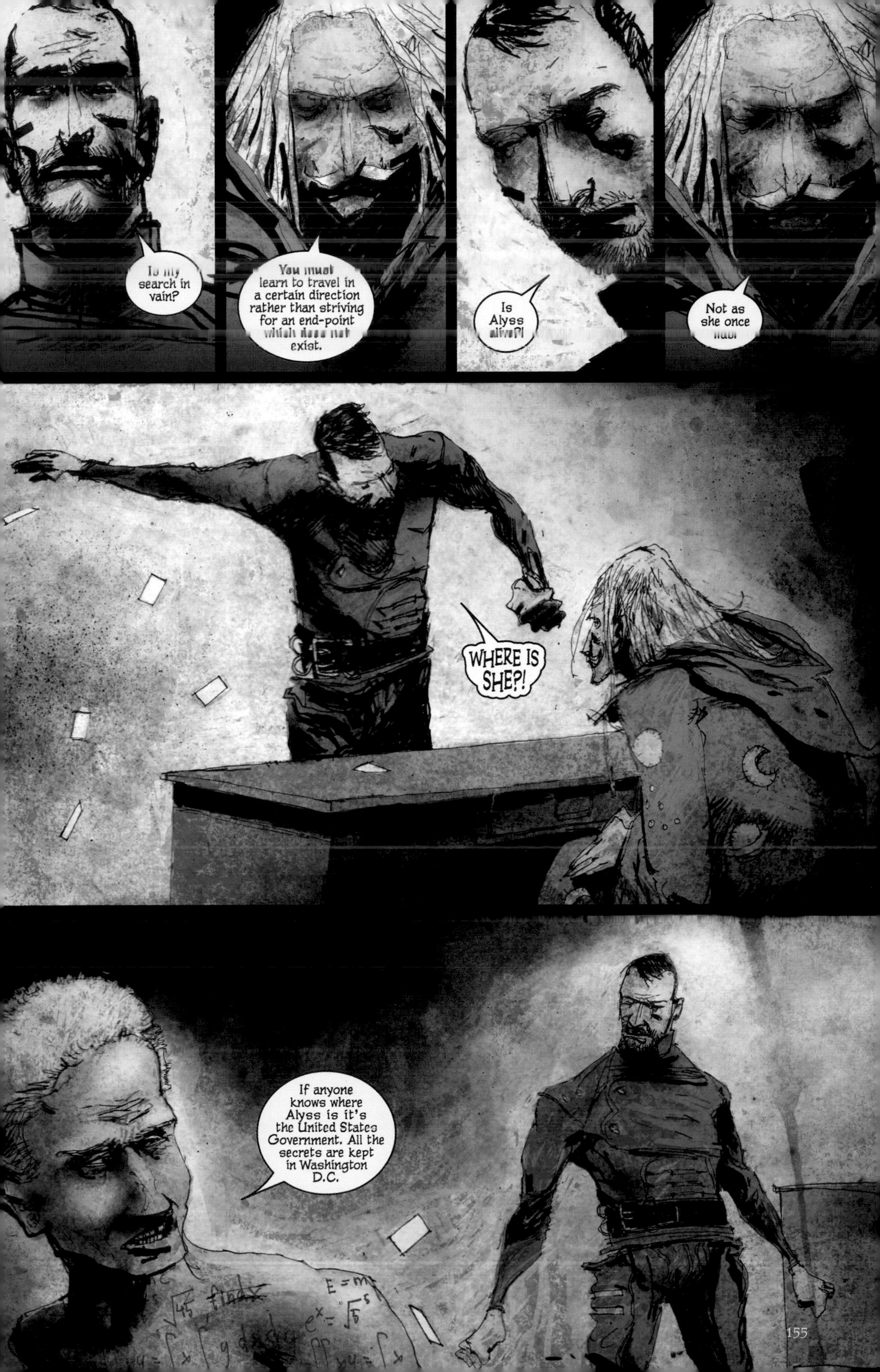
Is my search in vain?
You must learn to travel in a certain direction rather than striving for an end-point which does not exist.
Is Alyss alive?!
Not as she once
WHERE IS SHE?!
If anyone knows where Alyss is it's the United States Government. All the secrets are kept in Washington D.C.

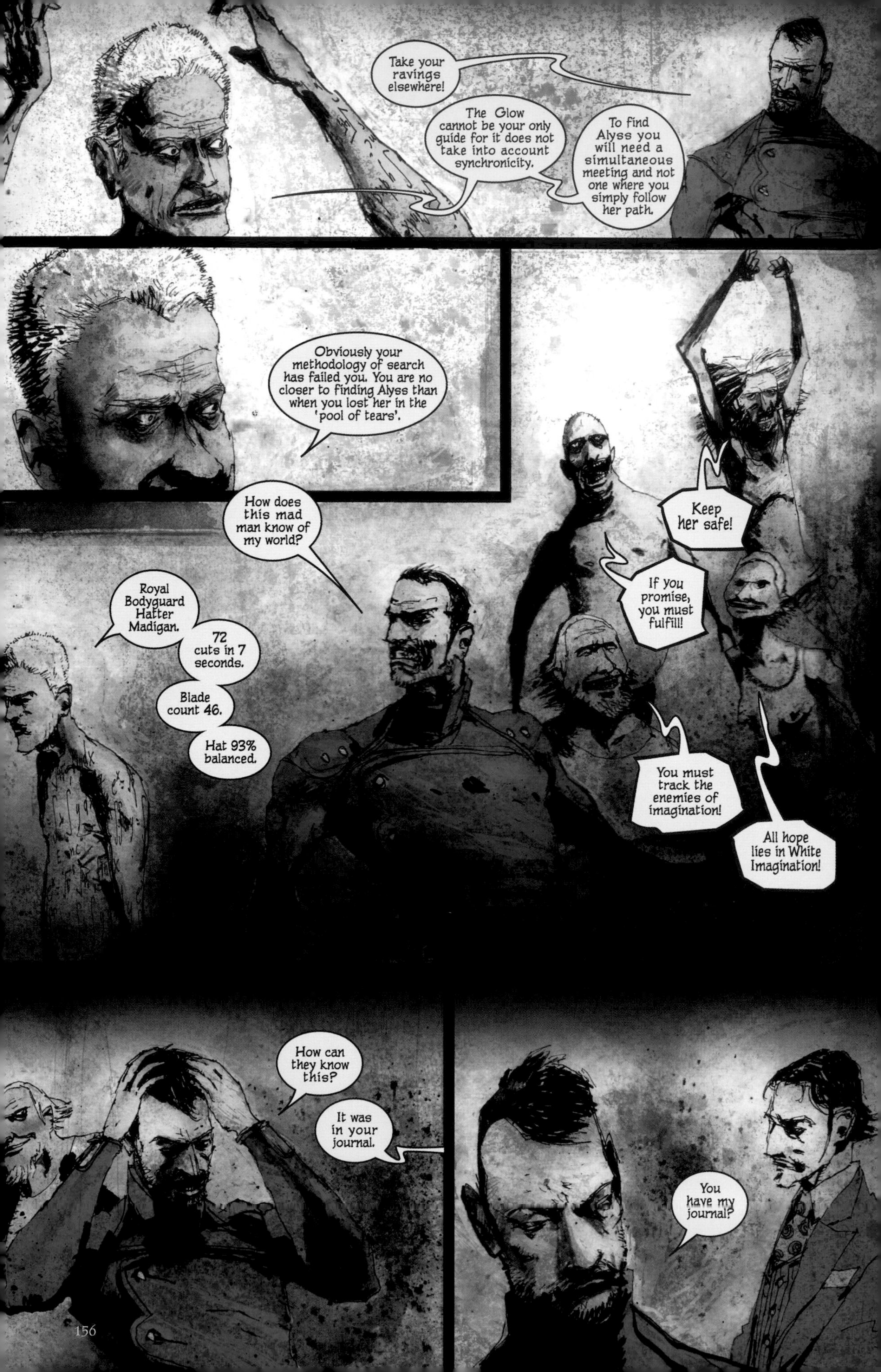
Take your ravings elsewhere!
The Glow cannot be your only guide for it does not take into account synchronicity.
To find Alyss you will need a simultaneous meeting and not one where you simply follow her path.
Obviously your methodology of search has failed you. You are no closer to finding Alyss than when you lost her in the 'pool of tears'.
How does this mad man know of my world?
Royal Bodyguard Hatter Madigan.
72 cuts in 7 seconds.
Blade count 46.
Hat 93% balanced.
Keep her safe!
If you promise, you must fulfill!
You must track the enemies of imagination!
All hope lies in White Imagination!
How can they know this?
It was in your journal.
You have my journal?

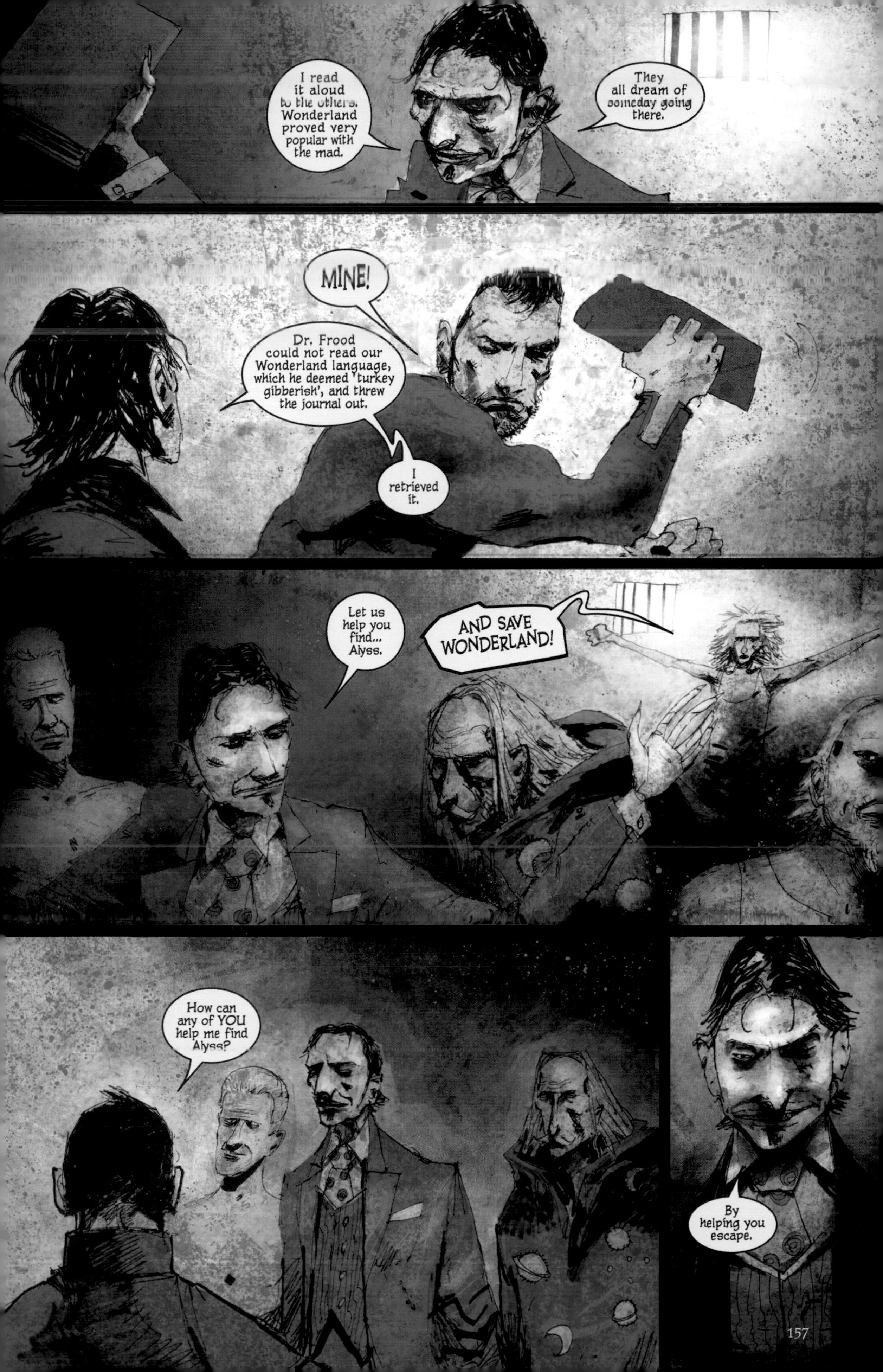
I read it aloud to the others. Wonderland proved very popular with the mad.
They all dream of someday going there.
MINE!
Dr. Frood could not read our Wonderland language, which he deemed 'turkey gibberish', and threw the journal out.
I retrieved it.
Let us help you find... Alyss.
AND SAVE WONDERLAND!
How can any of YOU help me find Alyss?
By helping you escape.

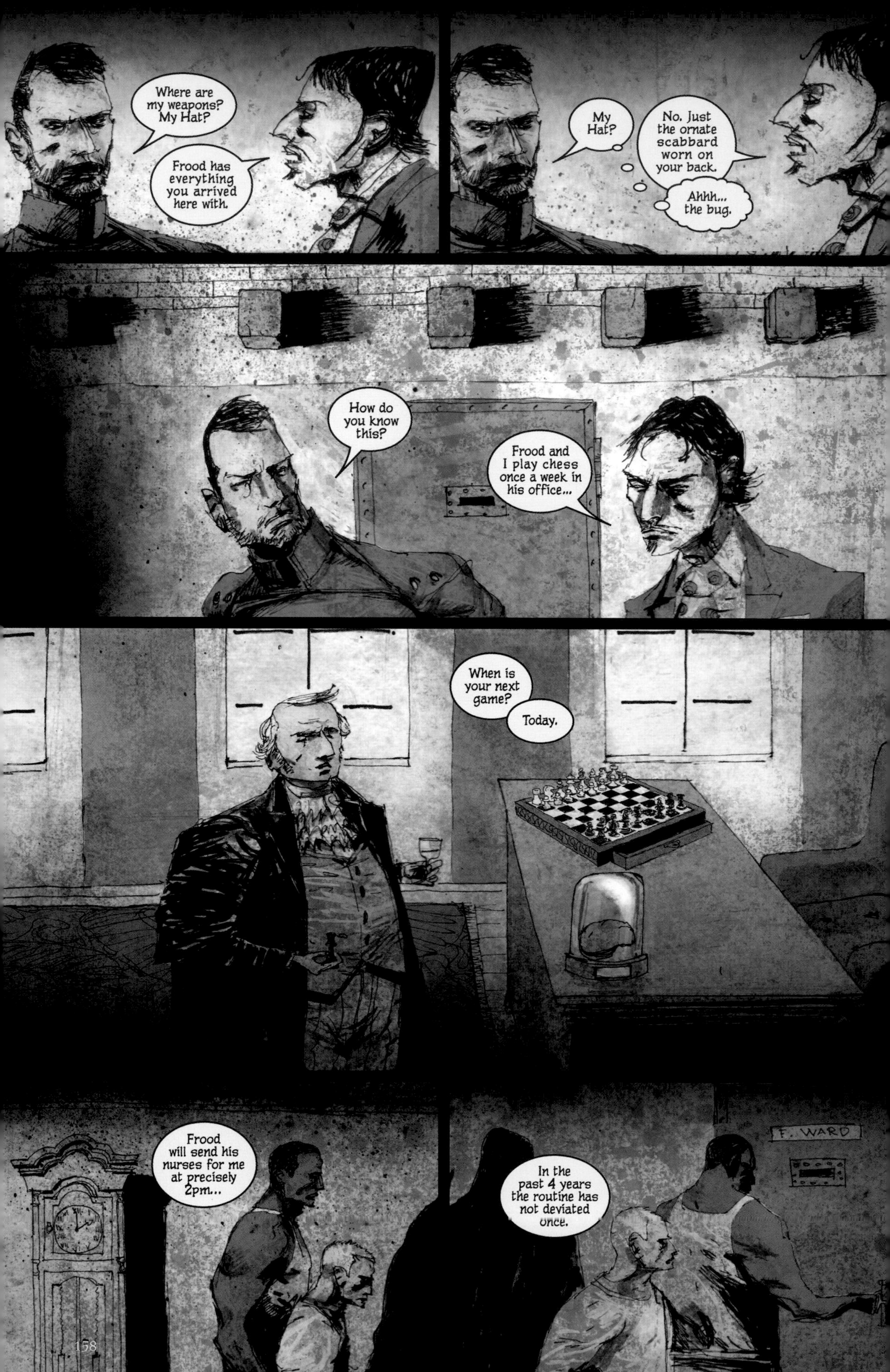
Where are my weapons? My Hat?
Frood has everything you arrived here with.
My Hat?
No. Just the ornate scabbard worn on your back.
Ahhh... the bug.
How do you know this?
Frood and I play chess once a week in his office...
When is your next game?
Today.
Frood will send his nurses for me at precisely 2pm...
F. WARD
In the past 4 years the routine has not deviated once.

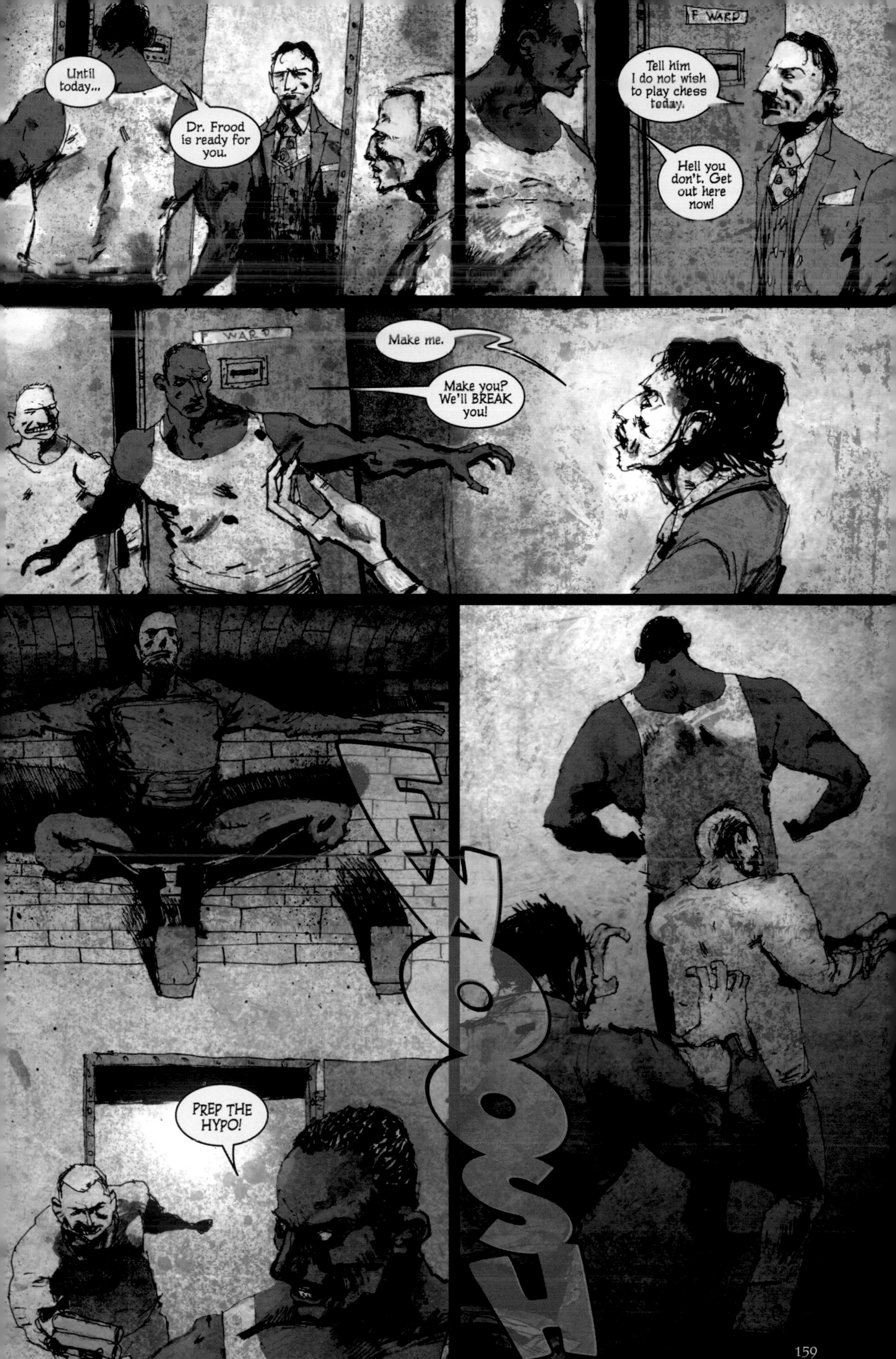
Until today...
Dr. Frood is ready for you.
F WARD
Tell him I do not wish to play chess today.
Hell you don't. Get out here now!
F WARD
Make me.
Make you? We'll BREAK you!
PREP THE HYPO!
FOOSH

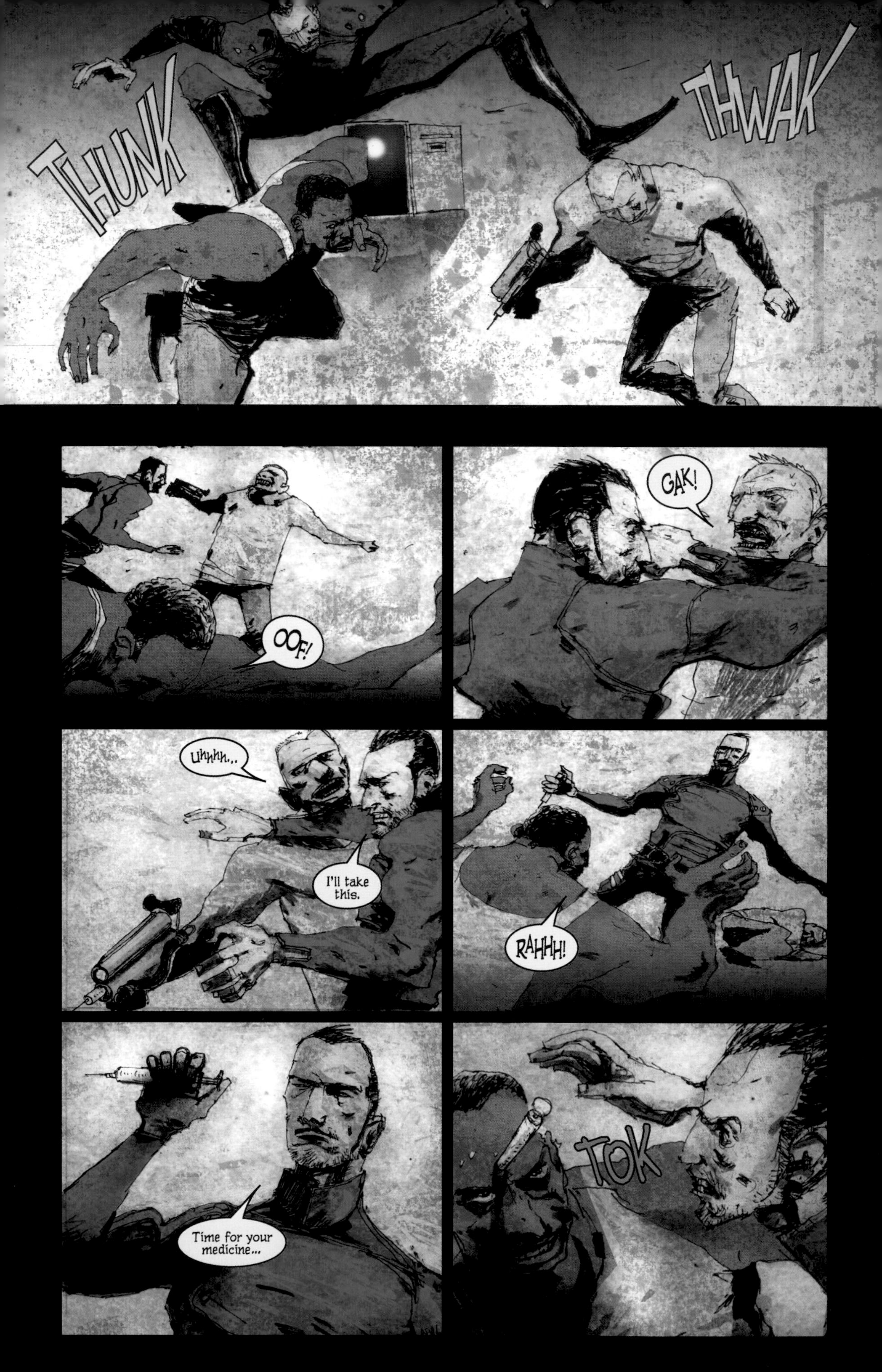
THUNK
THWAK
OOF!
GAK!
Uhhhh...
I'll take this.
RAHHH!
Time for your medicine...
TOK

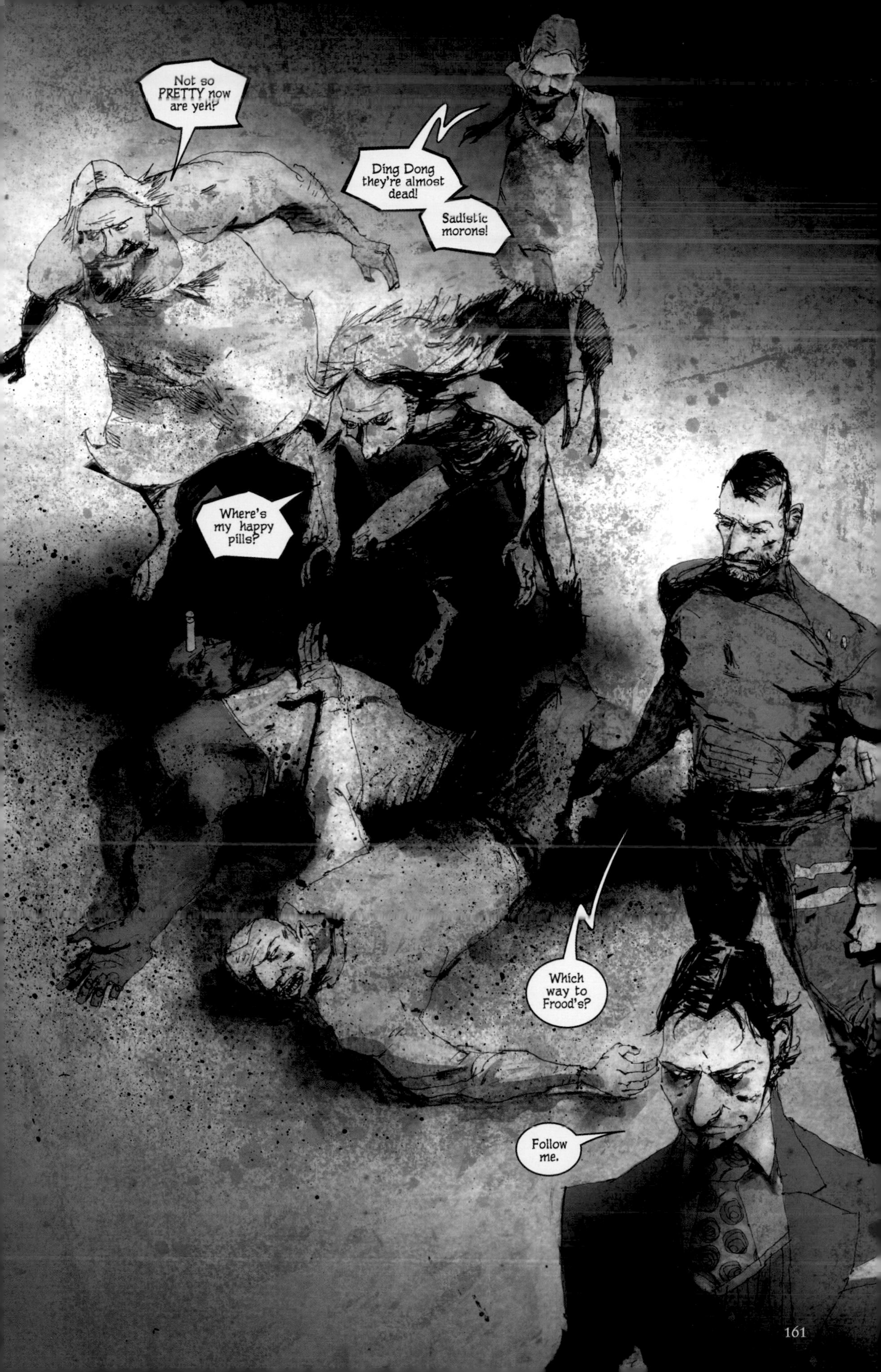
Not so PRETTY now are yeh?
Ding Dong they're almost dead!
Sadistic morons!
Where's my happy pills?
Which way to Frood's?
Follow me.

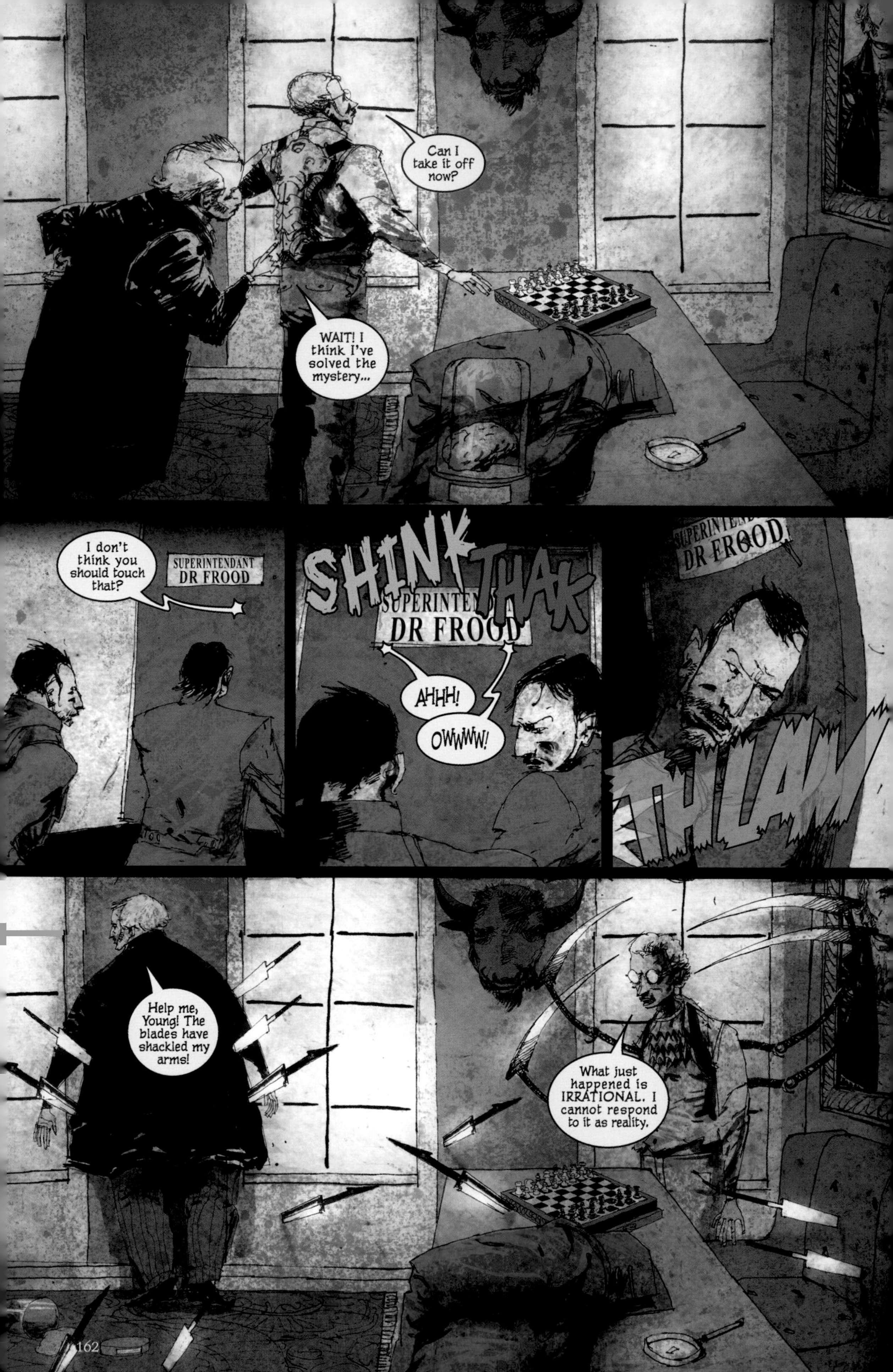
Can I take it off now?
WAIT! I think I've solved the mystery...
I don't think you should touch that?
SUPERINTENDANT DR FROOD
SHINK THAK
SUPERINTEND
DR FROOD
AHHH!
OWWWW!
SUPERINTEND
DR FROOD
THLAW
Help me, Young! The blades have shackled my arms!
What just happened is IRRATIONAL. I cannot respond to it as reality.

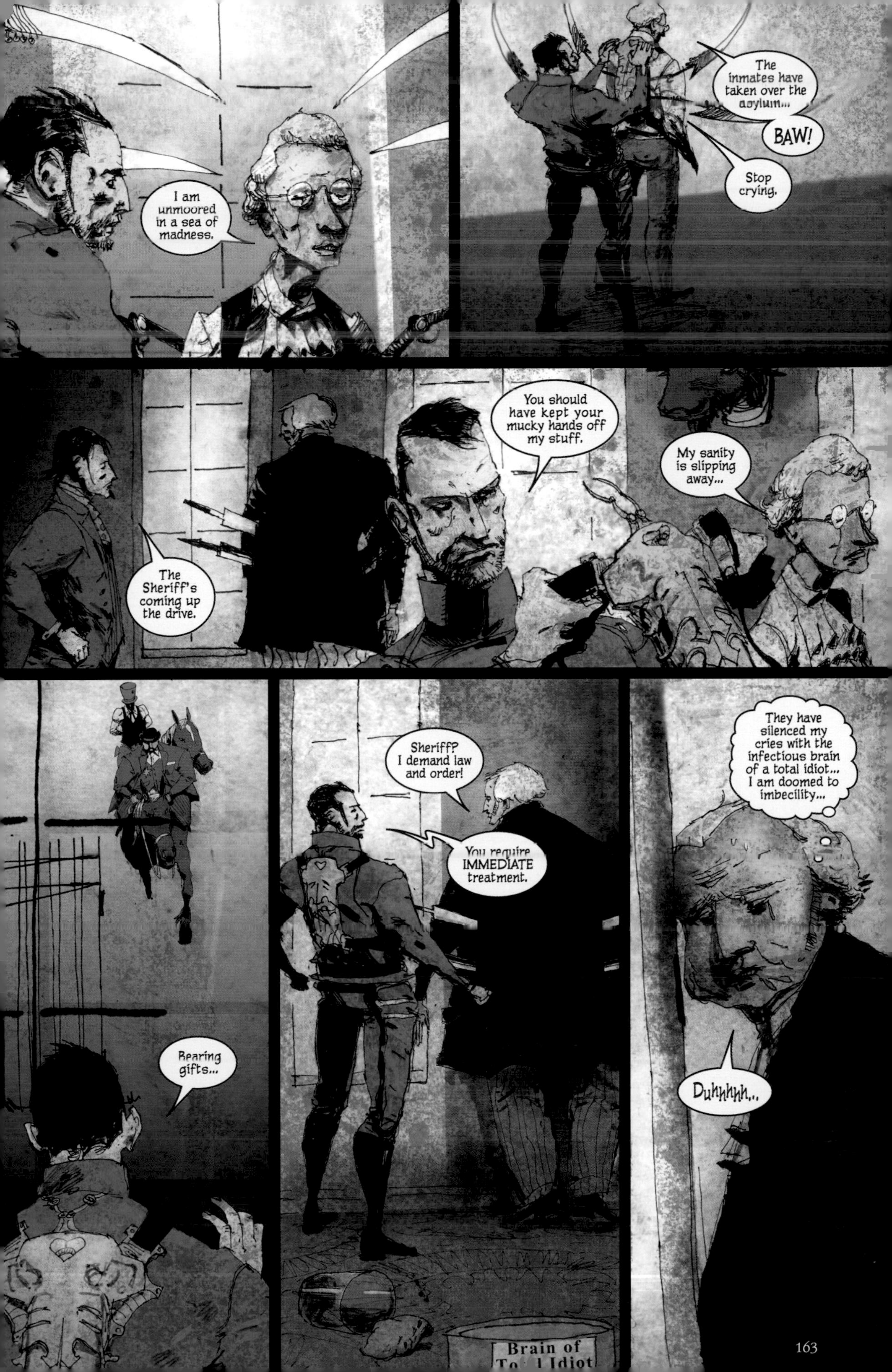
I am unmoored in a sea of madness.
The inmates have taken over the asylum...
BAW!
Stop crying.
You should have kept your mucky hands off my stuff.
My sanity is slipping away...
The Sheriff's coming up the drive.
Bearing gifts...
Sheriff? I demand law and order!
You require IMMEDIATE treatment.
They have silenced my cries with the infectious brain of a total idiot... I am doomed to imbecility...
Duhhhhh...
Brain of

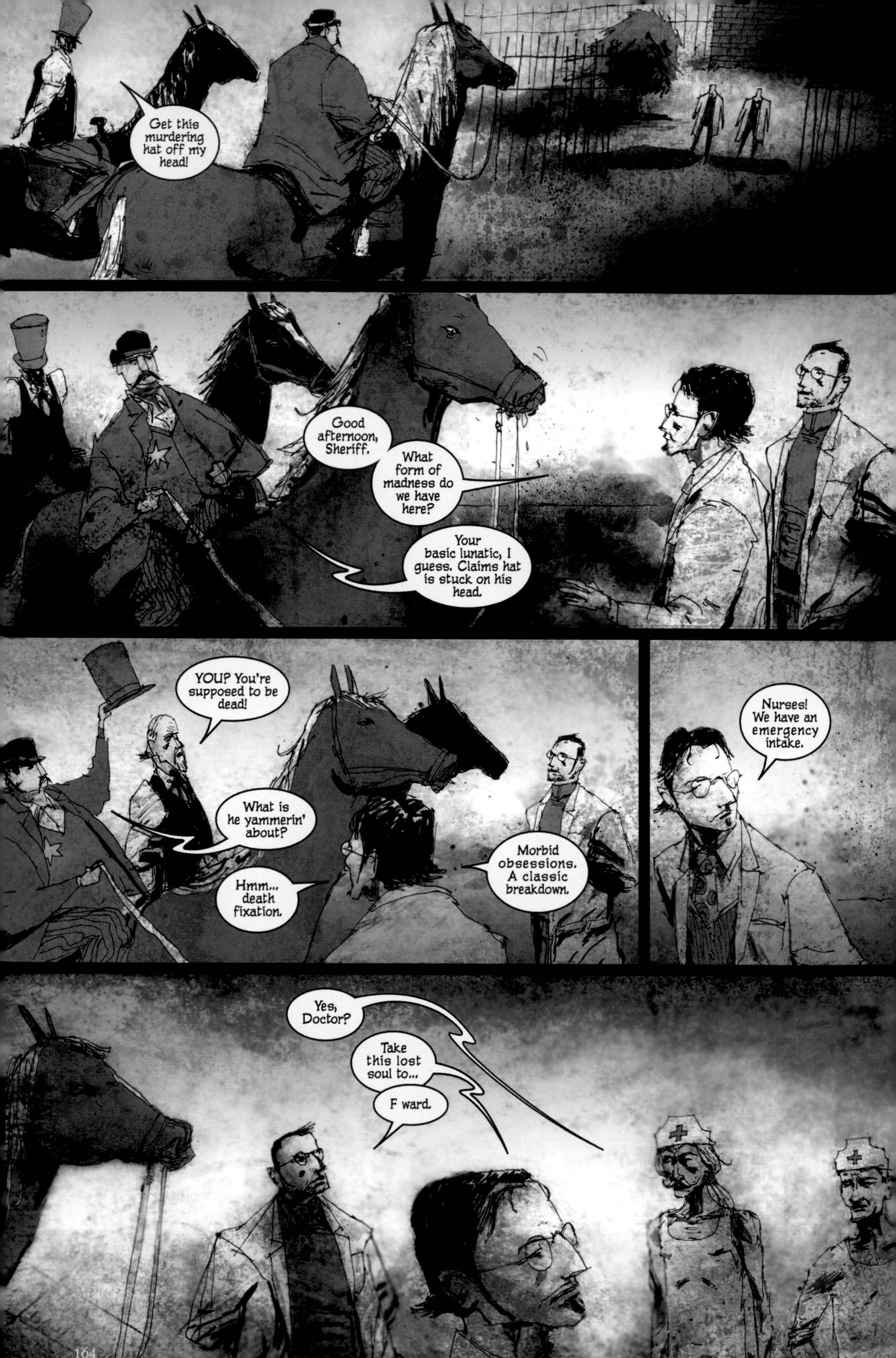
Get this murdering hat off my head!
Good afternoon, Sheriff.
What form of madness do we have here?
Your basic lunatic, I guess. Claims hat is stuck on his head.
YOU? You're supposed to be dead!
What is he yammerin' about?
Hmm... death fixation.
Morbid obsessions. A classic breakdown.
Nurses! We have an emergency intake.
Yes, Doctor?
Take this lost soul to...
F ward.

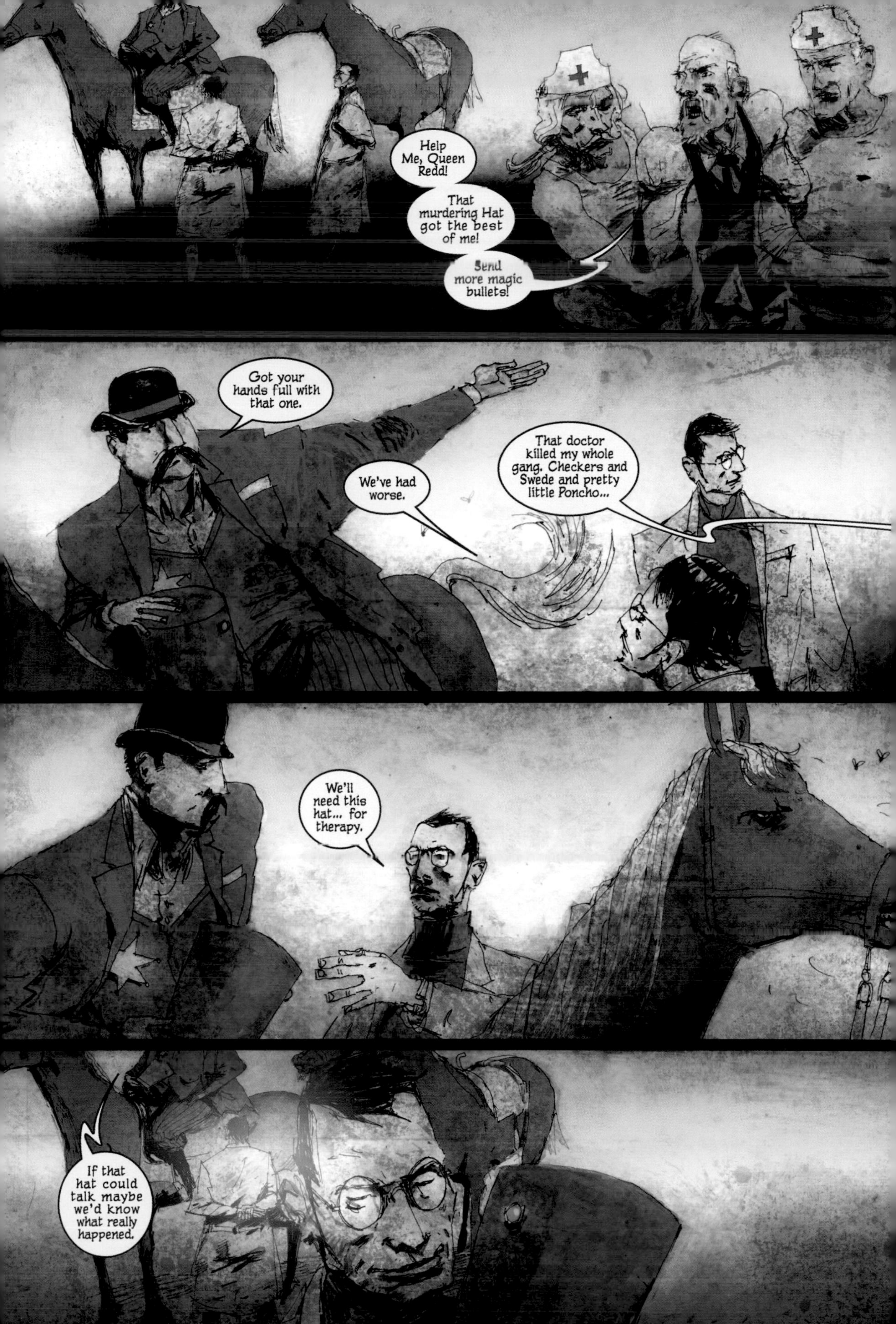
Help Me, Queen Redd!
That murdering Hat got the best of me!
Send more magic bullets!
Got your hands full with that one.
We've had worse.
That doctor killed my whole gang. Checkers and Swede and pretty little Poncho...
We'll need this hat... for therapy.
If that hat could talk maybe we'd know what really happened.

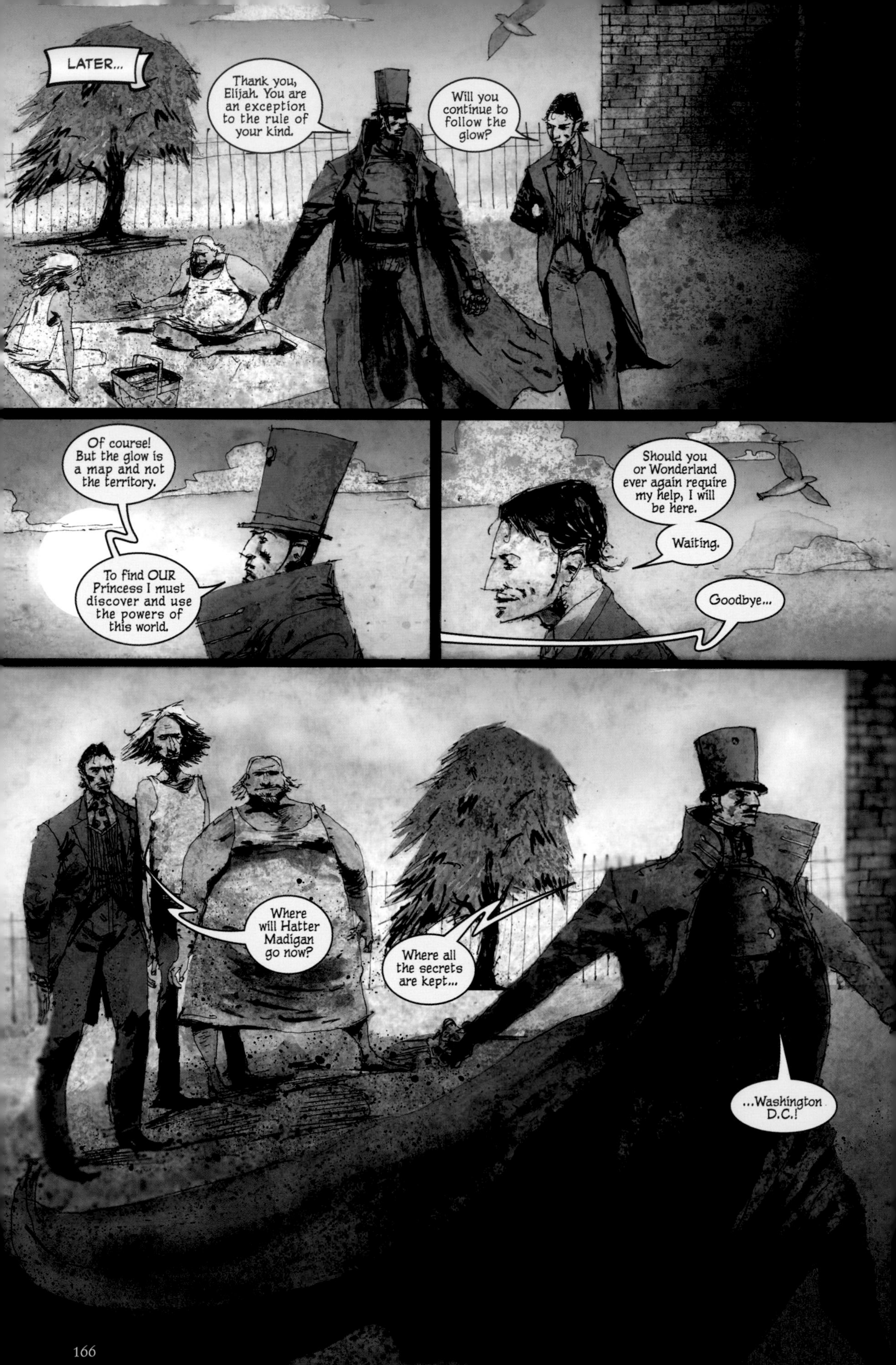
LATER...
Thank you, Elijah. You are an exception to the rule of your kind.
Will you continue to follow the glow?
Of course! But the glow is a map and not the territory.
To find OUR Princess I must discover and use the powers of this world.
Should you or Wonderland ever again require my help, I will be here.
Waiting.
Goodbye...
Where will Hatter Madigan go now?
Where all the secrets are kept...
...Washington D.C.!

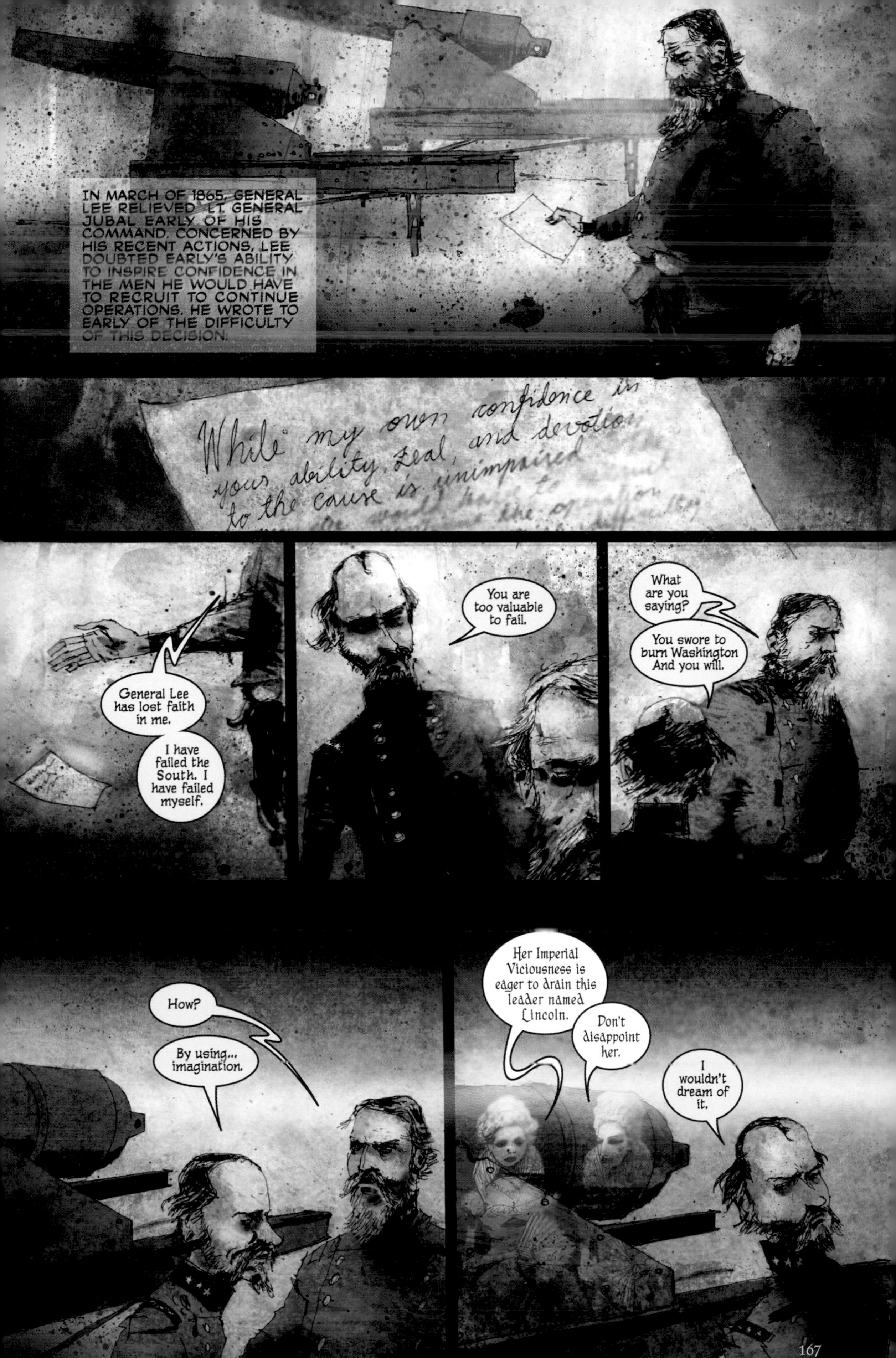
IN MARCH OF 1865, GENERAL LEE RELIEVED LT. GENERAL JUBAL EARLY OF HIS COMMAND. CONCERNED BY HIS RECENT ACTIONS, LEE DOUBTED EARLY'S ABILITY TO INSPIRE CONFIDENCE IN THE MEN HE WOULD HAVE TO RECRUIT TO CONTINUE OPERATIONS. HE WROTE TO EARLY OF THE DIFFICULTY OF THIS DECISION.
While my own confidence in your ability, zeal, and devotion to the cause is unimpaired
General Lee has lost faith in me.
I have failed the South. I have failed myself.
You are too valuable to fail.
What are you saying?
You swore to burn Washington And you will.
How?
By using... imagination.
Her Imperial Viciousness is eager to drain this leader named Lincoln.
Don't disappoint her.
I wouldn't dream of it.

*Enjoy a sneak preview of
Hatter M Volume 3*

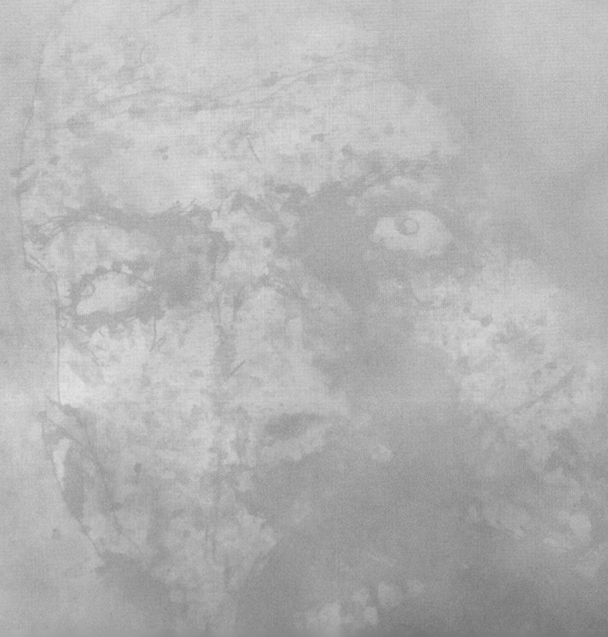

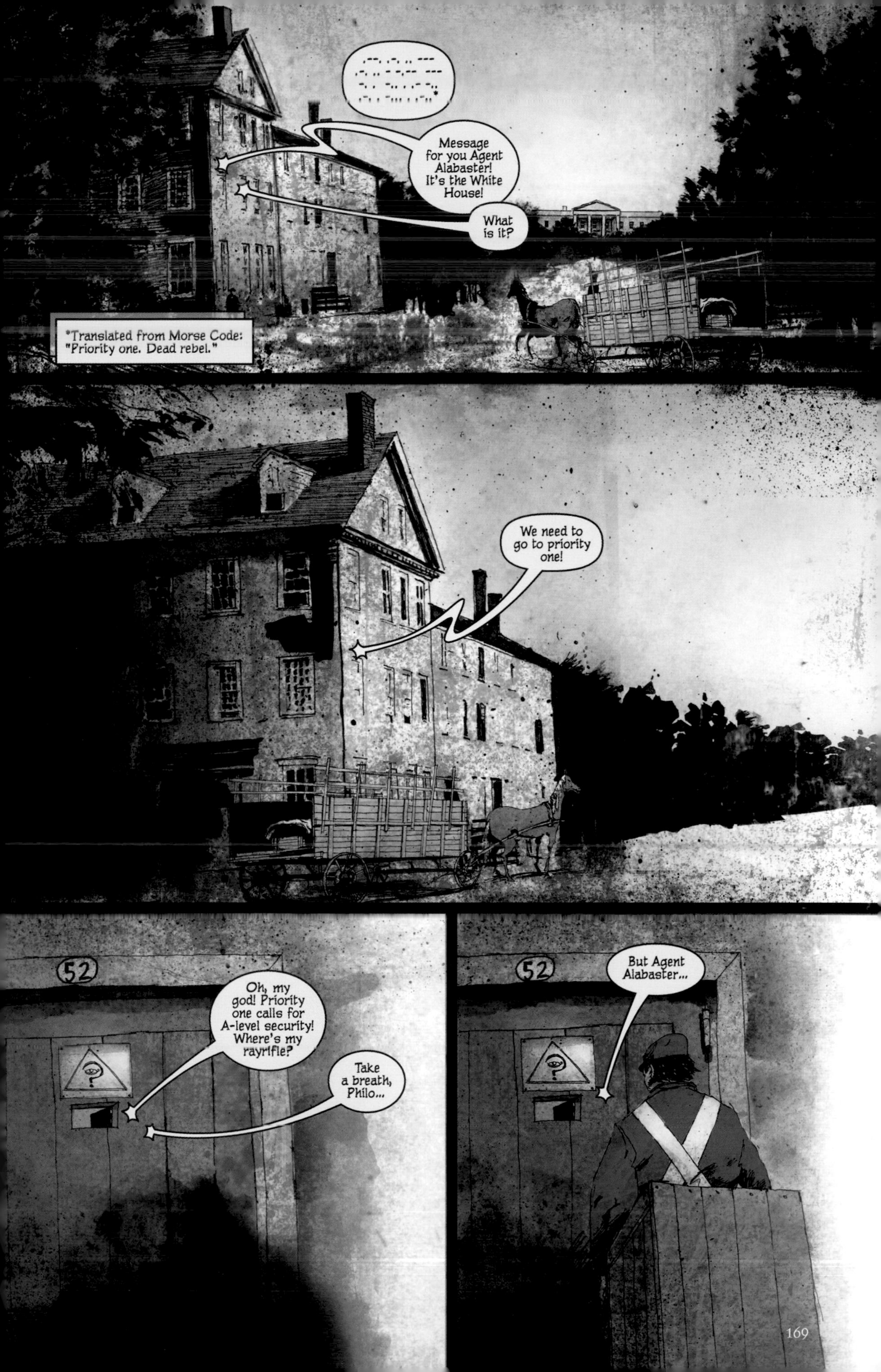
Message for you Agent Alabaster! It's the White House!
What is it?
*Translated from Morse Code: "Priority one. Dead rebel."
We need to go to priority one!
52
Oh, my god! Priority one calls for A-level security! Where's my rayrifle?
Take a breath, Philo...
52
But Agent Alabaster...

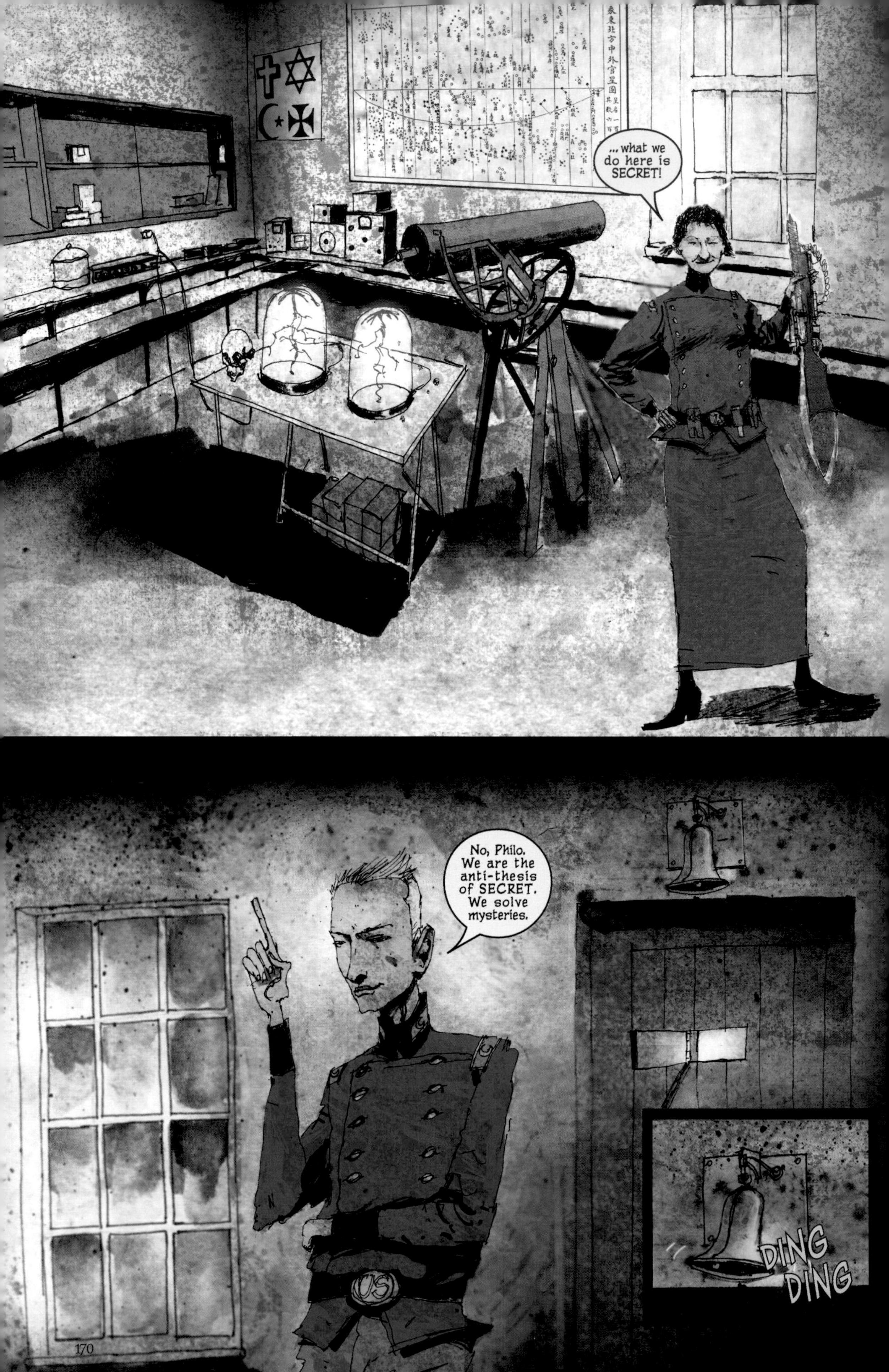
... what we do here is SECRET!
No, Philo. We are the anti-thesis of SECRET. We solve mysteries.
DING DING

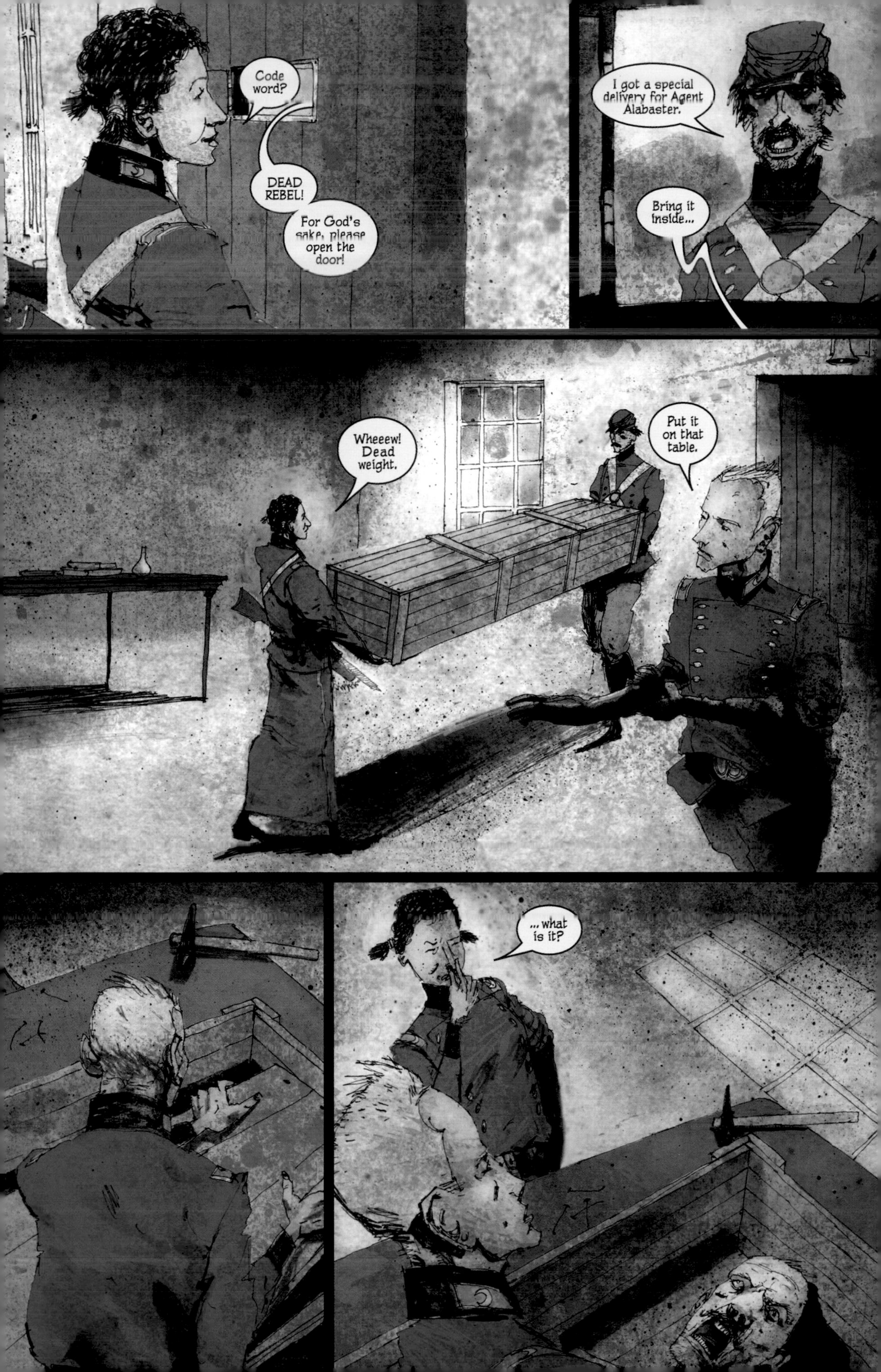
Code word?
DEAD REBEL!
For God's sake, please open the door!
I got a special delivery for Agent Alabaster.
Bring it inside...
Wheeew! Dead weight.
Put it on that table.
...what is it?

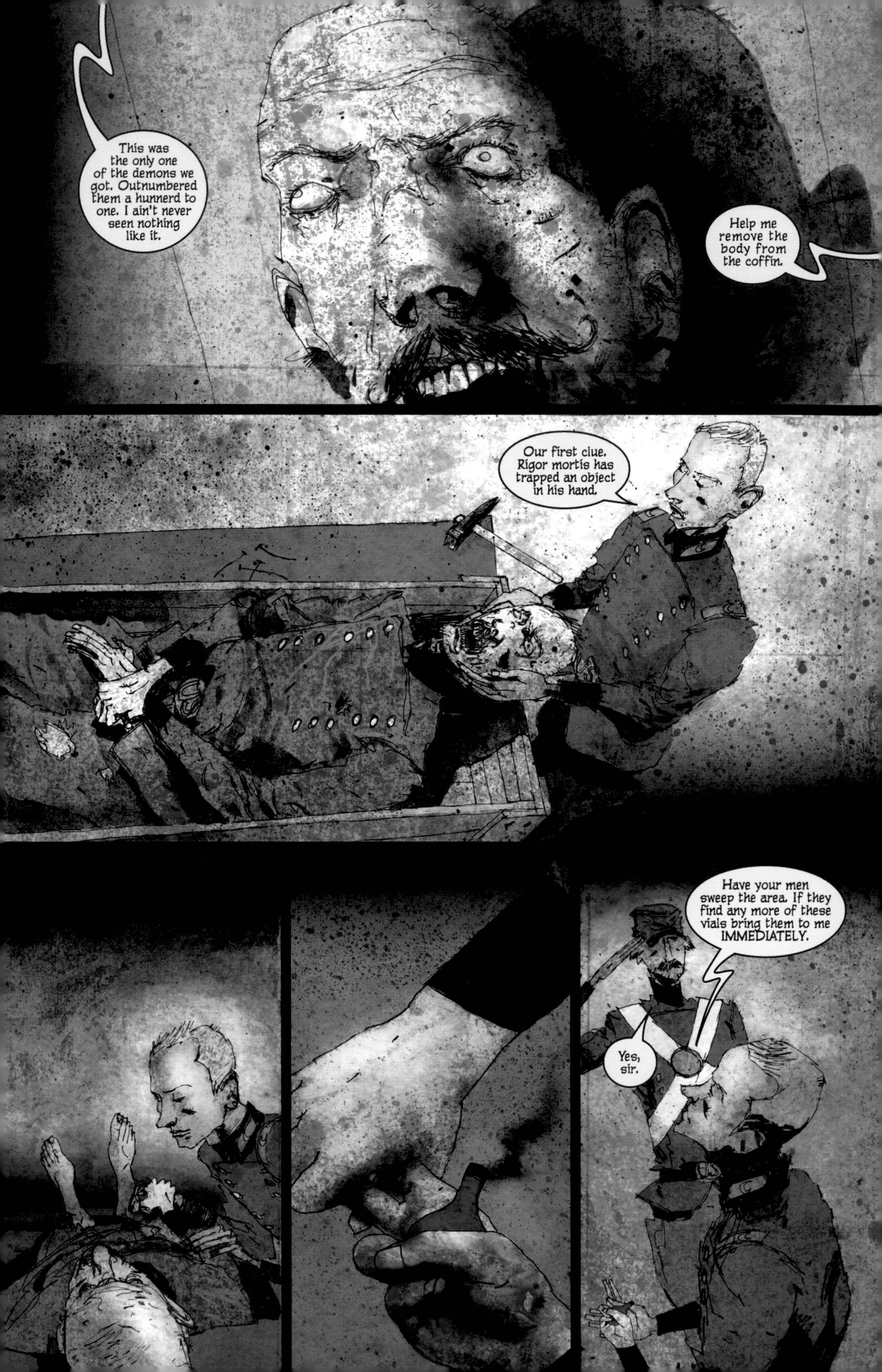
This was the only one of the demons we got. Outnumbered them a hunnerd to one. I ain't never seen nothing like it.
Help me remove the body from the coffin.
Our first clue. Rigor mortis has trapped an object in his hand.
Have your men sweep the area. If they find any more of these vials bring them to me IMMEDIATELY.
Yes, sir.

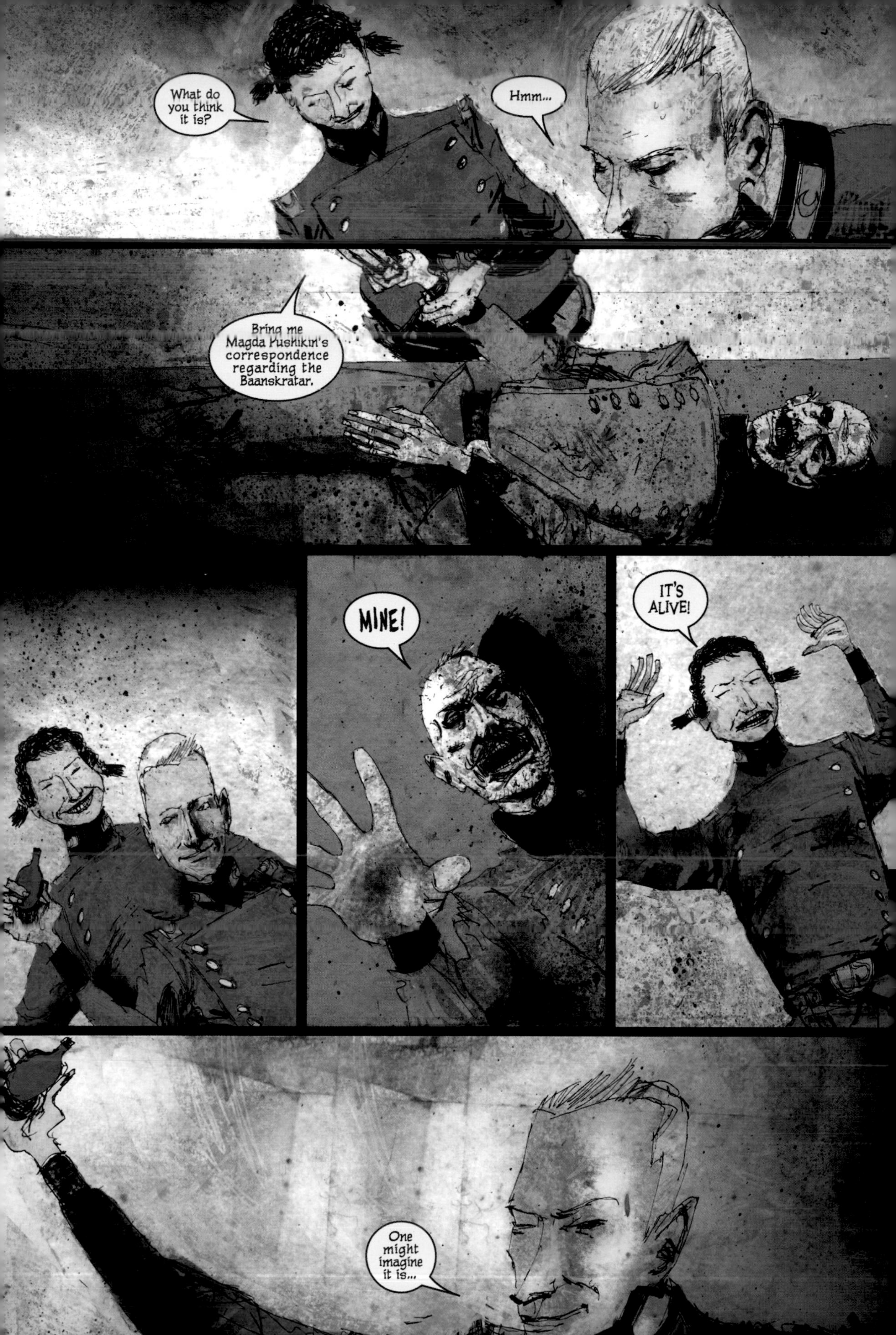
What do you think it is?
Hmm...
Bring me Magda Pushkin's correspondence regarding the Baanskratar.
MINE!
IT'S ALIVE!
One might imagine it is...

GREETINGS FROM THE Hatter M INSTITUTE FOR PARANORMAL

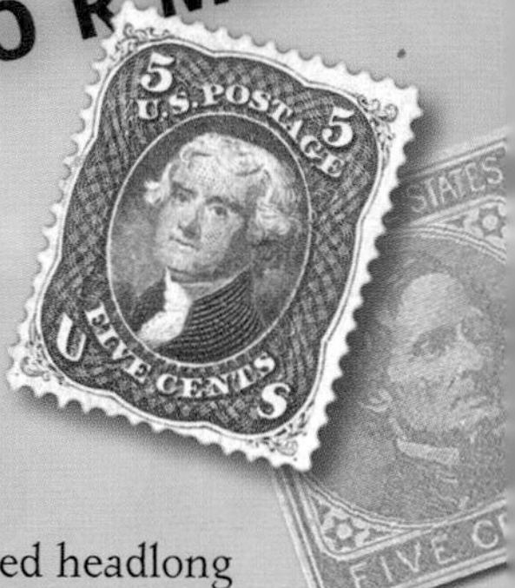

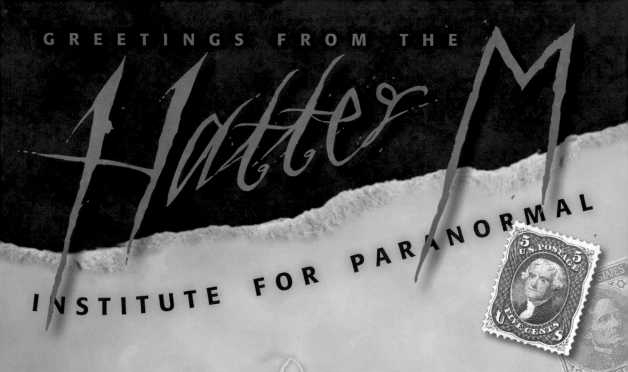

Take a moment and breathe deeply, we believe there is much to absorb from the preceding pages brought to you at the speed of Imagination. Researching, writing, illustrating and assembling geo-graphic novel *Hatter M: Mad with Wonder, Volume 2*, was an epic task for all of us here at the Institute. We chose to focus on the pivotal time period of 1864 – 1865 for Hatter's travels because in the course of our research we came upon several pieces of the intricate puzzle that forms the basis of the Looking Glass Wars saga.

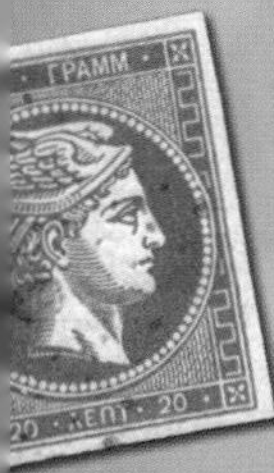

Beginning with chapter one we delved headlong into one of the most quotidian of mysteries. How did Royal Bodyguard Hatter Madigan finance his extensive travels for 13 years? Through the excellent sleuthing of our London office, headed by Dame Agnes MacKenzie, we were able to uncover the seemingly insignificant Sir Lucius Oliphant Wellesley. Wellesley's unabashed timbromania (if you haven't checked your French dictionary by now it is a mania for stamp collecting) as the geographical impetus for his occasional funding of Hatter's travels was verified by cross-referencing his stamp collection with Hatter's journal and other travel ephemera including tickets and maps.

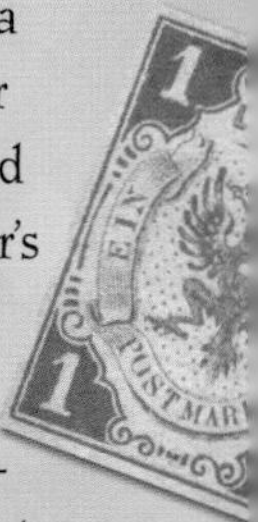

If the location of a stamp coveted by Wellesley coincided with Hatter's Glow ordained destination a deal would be struck whereupon Hatter's travel expenses would be paid in return for his assistance in procuring the desired stamp. This gentlemen's agreement was in itself fortuitous, but when Dame Agnes discovered that Sir Wellesley's full name was actually 'George Lucius Oliphant Wellesley' a whole other dimension of speculation opened given his initials now spelled G.L.O.W.! Dame Agnes has been an indispensable contributor to the Institute. As you turn a few more pages you will find an excerpt from her book, *Princess Alyss of Wonderland*, the art and letters from the lost journals of Princess Alyss Heart during her exile in our world.

Hatter's decision to follow the glow to the battlefields of the American Civil War led the Institute's Miss Emily

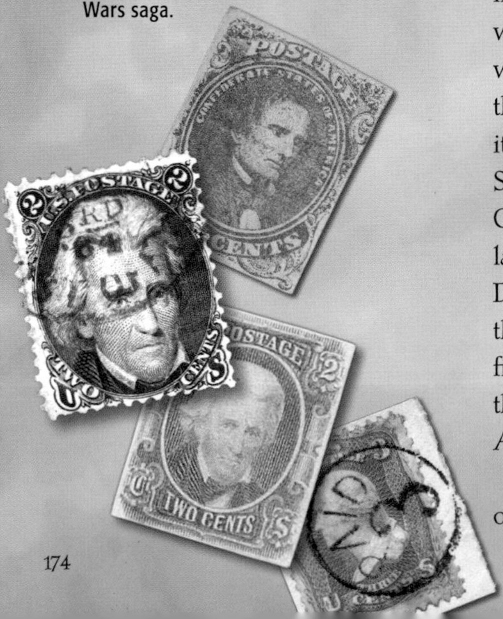

TRAVEL

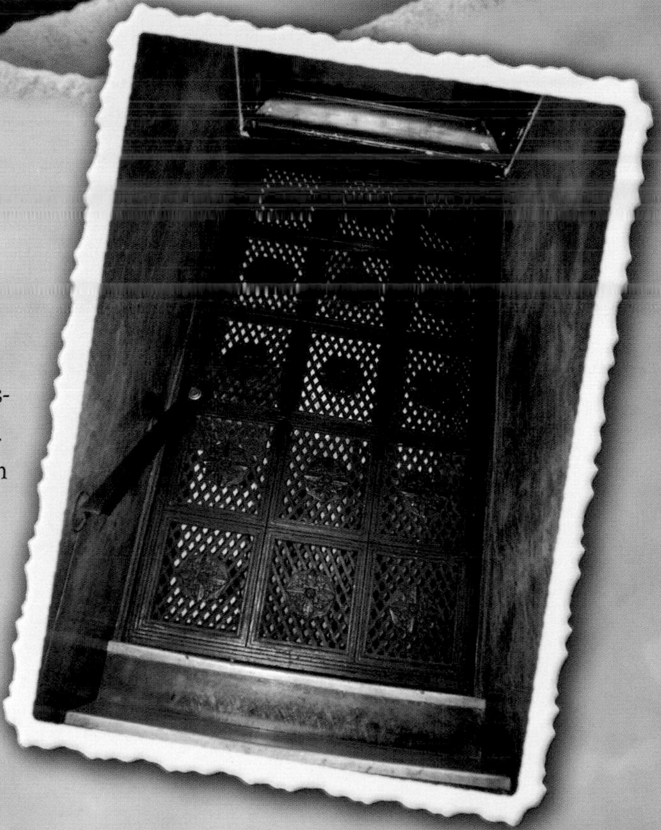

and Colonel Barlow on a merry chase through dusty antebellum archives researching Lt. General Jubal Early's obsessive fixation to invade Washington D.C. How Early and Hatter's paths collided in our nation's capital will be revealed in Hatter M Volume 3. But it was Hatter's stay at the West Virginia Hospital for the Insane that provided the most astounding revelation of all! Given access to the asylum's vaults, Colonel Barlow came upon a crumbling intake file dated March 1865 and labeled 'Mad Man X'. Upon opening the file he was rewarded with the details of Hatter's incarceration including Dr. Frood's notes on his mental state and prescribed treatment.

But surely the most startling find of all was an illustrated card tucked inside the file and matching the style and artistry of the illuminated deck of Wonderland cards that first inspired Frank Beddor's investigation into the Looking Glass Wars! The card found in the file has been meticulously carbon tested and verified as the missing link that finally answers the question of who was the creator of The Looking Glass Wars deck of cards. We can now accurately state that the artist was Royal Bodyguard Hatter Madigan. Turn the page to see this pivotal piece of history and the newest card of the H.A.T.B.O.X.

With the genesis of the deck now in our sights we will continue to track the paper trail of the Looking Glass Wars cards and how they came to be in the possession of both the British Museum and antiquities dealer Mr. Buffington.

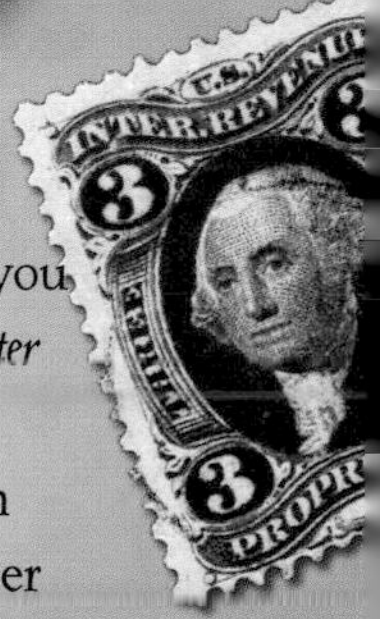

As a final note, dear reader, we hope you will share news of geo-graphic novel *Hatter M: Mad With Wonder, Volume 2,* with other dedicated followers of White Imagination as you prepare your psyches for the further adventures of Hatter M in the forthcoming Volume 3. Thank you for continuing to join us in following the glow!

The Hatter M Institute for Paranormal Travel

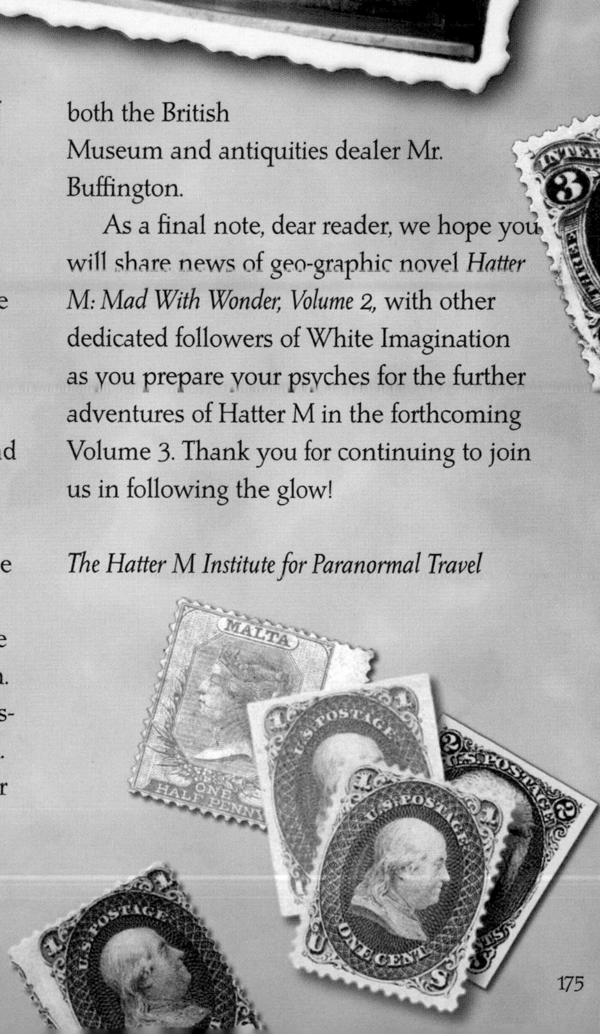
MALTA
U.S. POSTAGE
ONE CENT

Hospital for the Insane

The West Virginia Hospital for the Insane (currently known as the Weston State Hospital and declared a national historic landmark) has proven to be one our most fascinating discoveries. Colonel Barlow spent weeks combing through the remains of this crumbling, massive example of Gothic Revival architecture. In the course of his search he came upon a storeroom filled with rotting furniture, seemingly undisturbed since the days of the Civil War. In a roll top desk he found a newspaper article and photograph torn from the Weston Gazette dated April 1st, 1865. From what we can glean

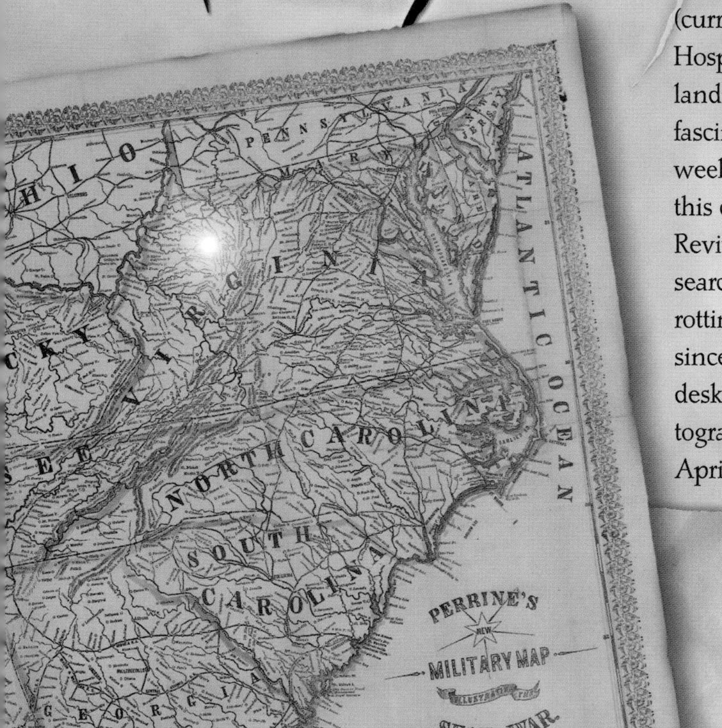

ATLANTIC OCEAN
NORTH CAROLINA
SOUTH CAROLINA
PERRINE'S
NEW
MILITARY MAP
SEAT OF WAR
SOUTHERN PART OF FLORIDA
SCALE OF MILES

Hatter's Map to the Asylum

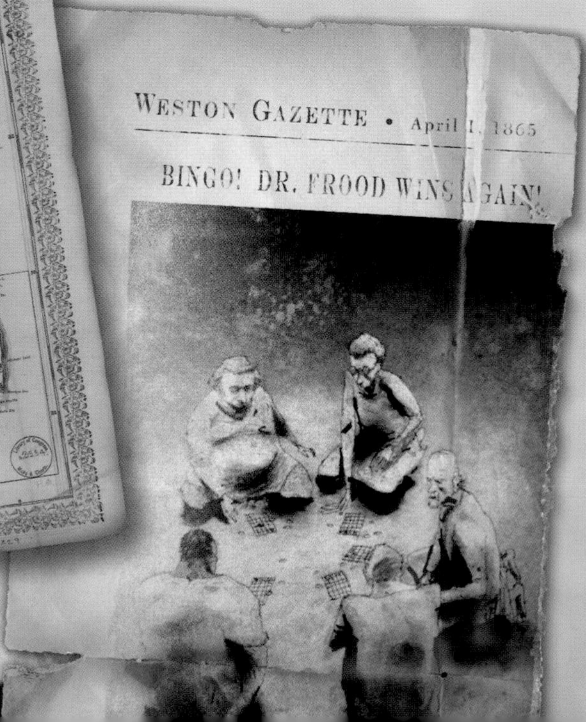

WESTON GAZETTE • April 1, 1865
BINGO! DR. FROOD WINS AGAIN!

"Madness in great ones must not unwatched go," —William Shakespeare

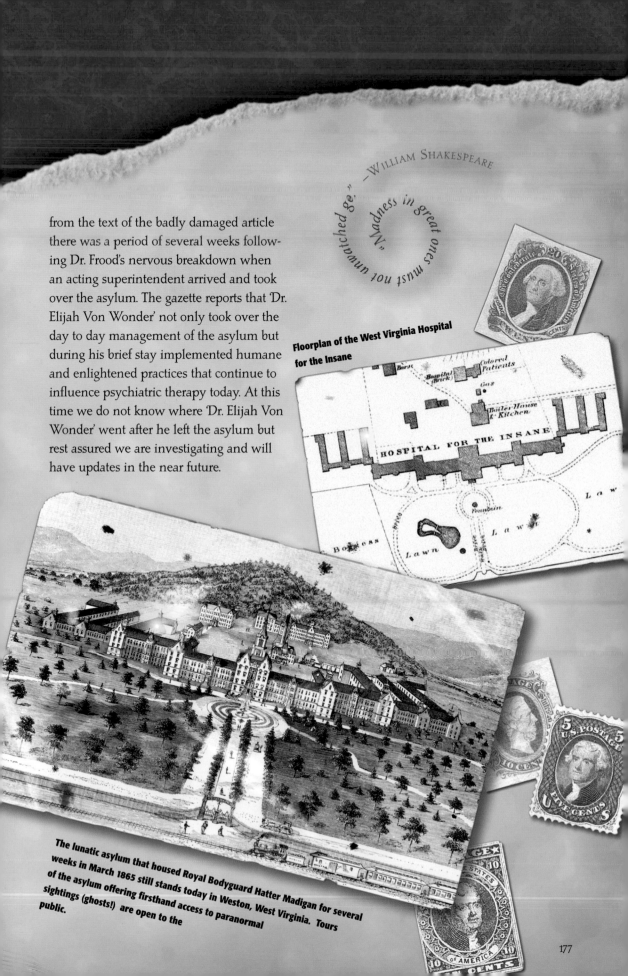

from the text of the badly damaged article there was a period of several weeks following Dr. Frood's nervous breakdown when an acting superintendent arrived and took over the asylum. The gazette reports that 'Dr. Elijah Von Wonder' not only took over the day to day management of the asylum but during his brief stay implemented humane and enlightened practices that continue to influence psychiatric therapy today. At this time we do not know where 'Dr. Elijah Von Wonder' went after he left the asylum but rest assured we are investigating and will have updates in the near future.

Floorplan of the West Virginia Hospital for the Insane

Hospital (Brick)
Colored Patients
Gas
Boiler House & Kitchen
HOSPITAL FOR THE INSANE
Fountain
Lawn
Law

The lunatic asylum that housed Royal Bodyguard Hatter Madigan for several weeks in March 1865 still stands today in Weston, West Virginia. Tours of the asylum offering firsthand access to paranormal sightings (ghosts!) are open to the public.

Mystery Solved

"I'd rather be mad with the truth than sane with lies." —An anonymous psychiatric patient and poet

Behold…the lost card. This card is the link connecting the Wonderland cards discovered by Frank Beddor in the British Museum and the deck collected by British antiquities dealer Mr. Buffington with Hatter Madigan, royal bodyguard and artist. For reasons unknown, this card depicting Wonderland's Millinery H.A.T.B.O.X. remained at the asylum while the other cards were moved. We wonder how many cards are in this deck and if any are still missing. How and why did the existing deck travel to England? Questions… questions. Evidently the mystery is not solved but more tantalizing. We will continue to search for other missing cards depicting as yet unseen images of Wonderland and share our discoveries in geographic novel Hatter M Volume 3.

We hope you enjoy the color art images inspired by Hatter Madigan's cards and rendered by our very own Institute artists.

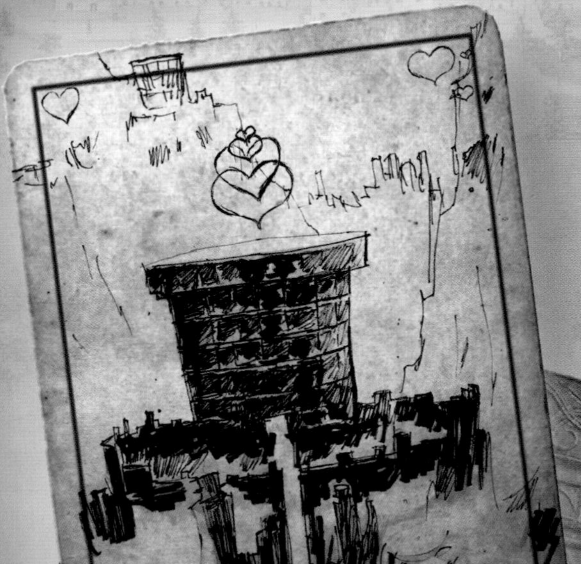

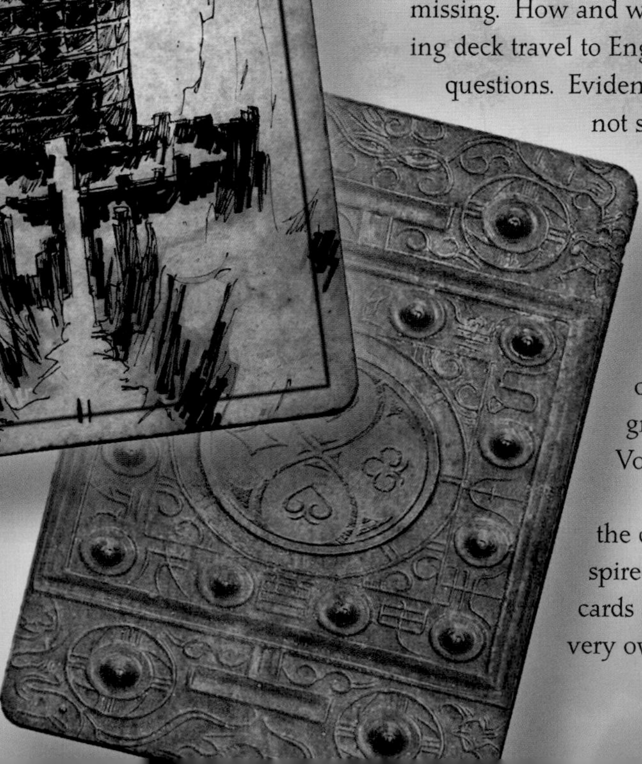

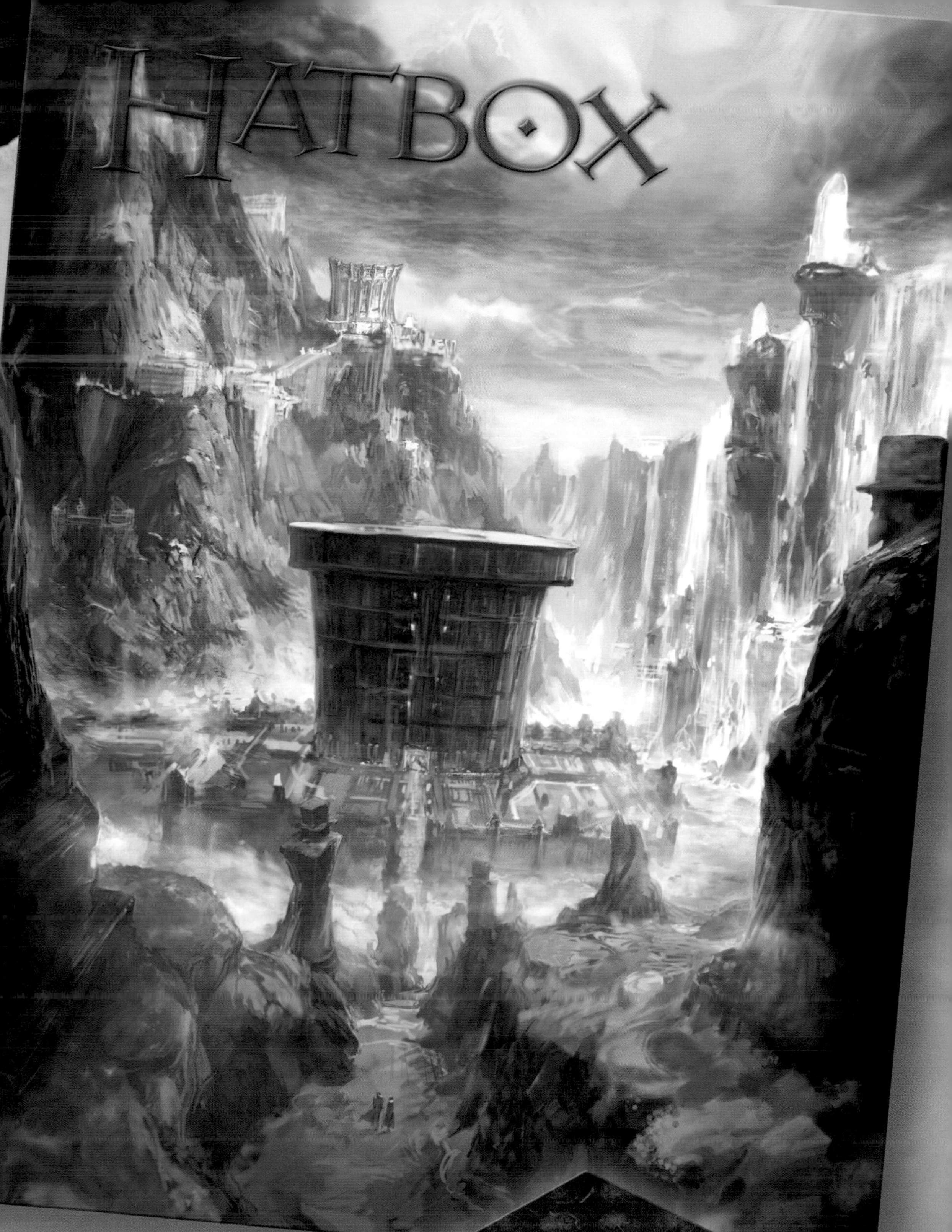
HATBOX

H.A.T.B.O.X.: Holographic and Transmutative Base of Xtremecombat: High vibrational training facility for Millinery Bodyguards.

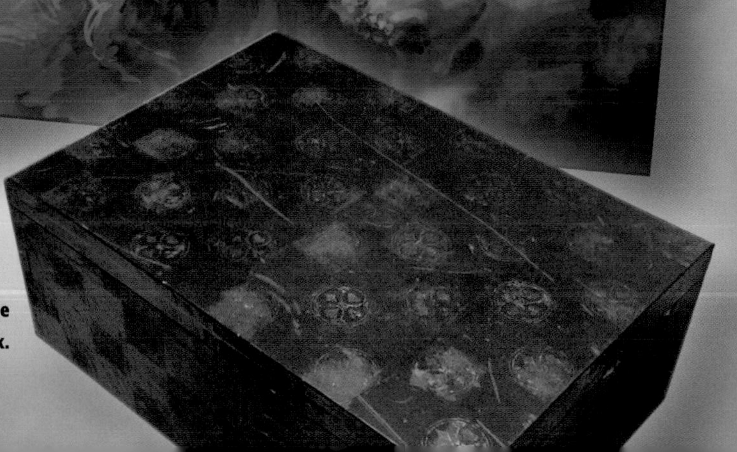

Now, after nearly 150 years, the cards can be reunited in their original box.

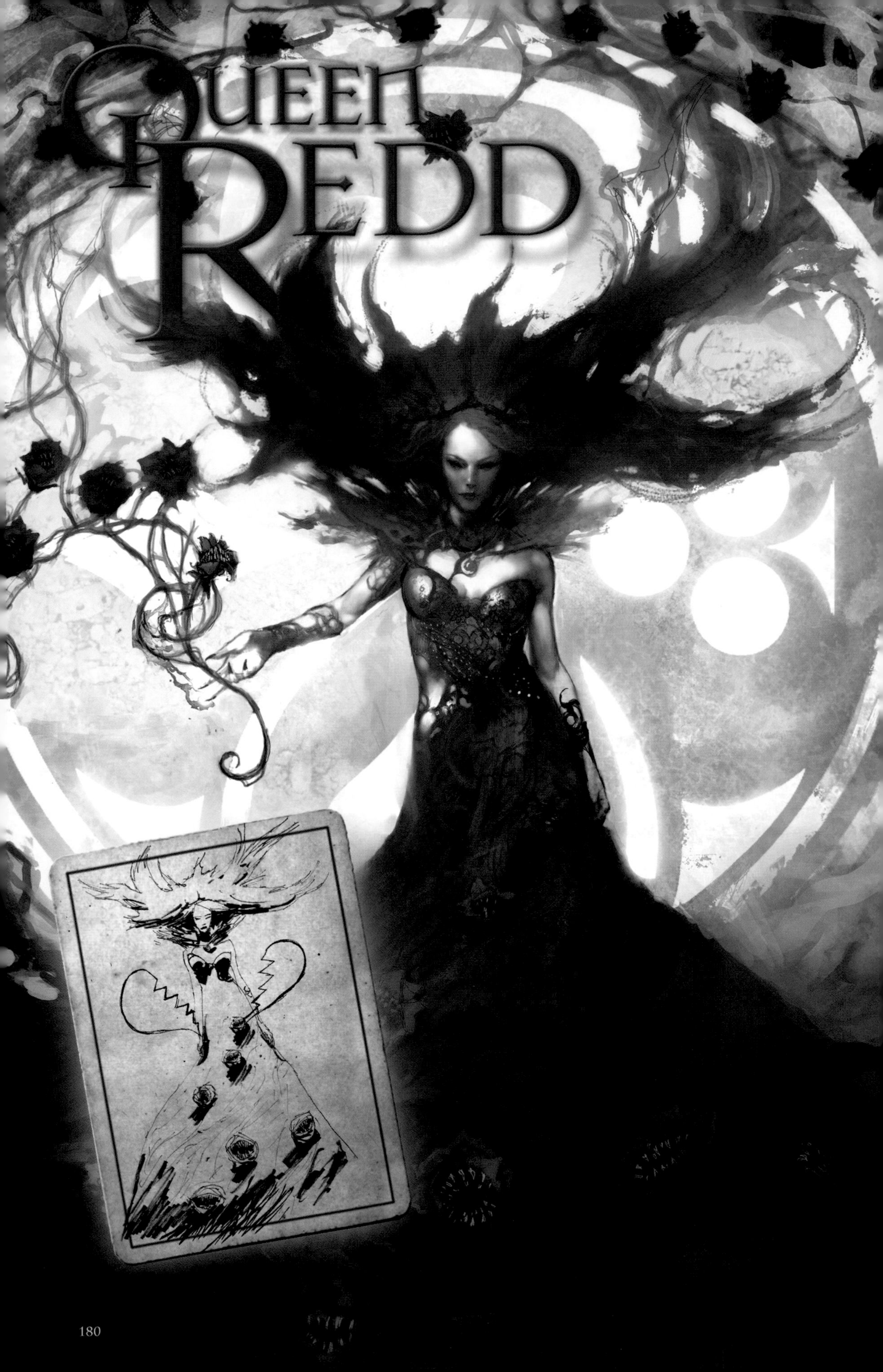
Queen Redd

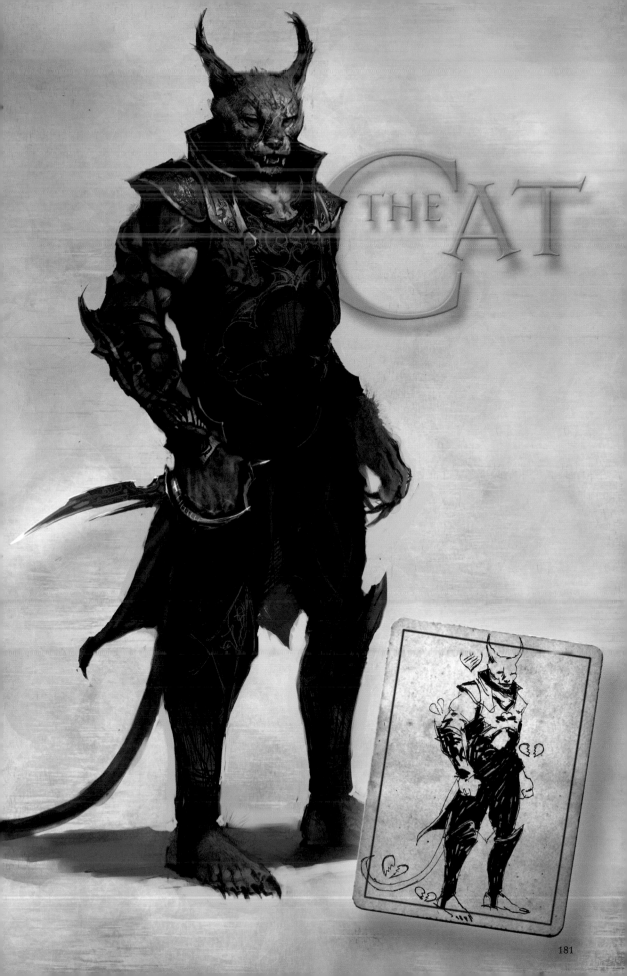

The Cat

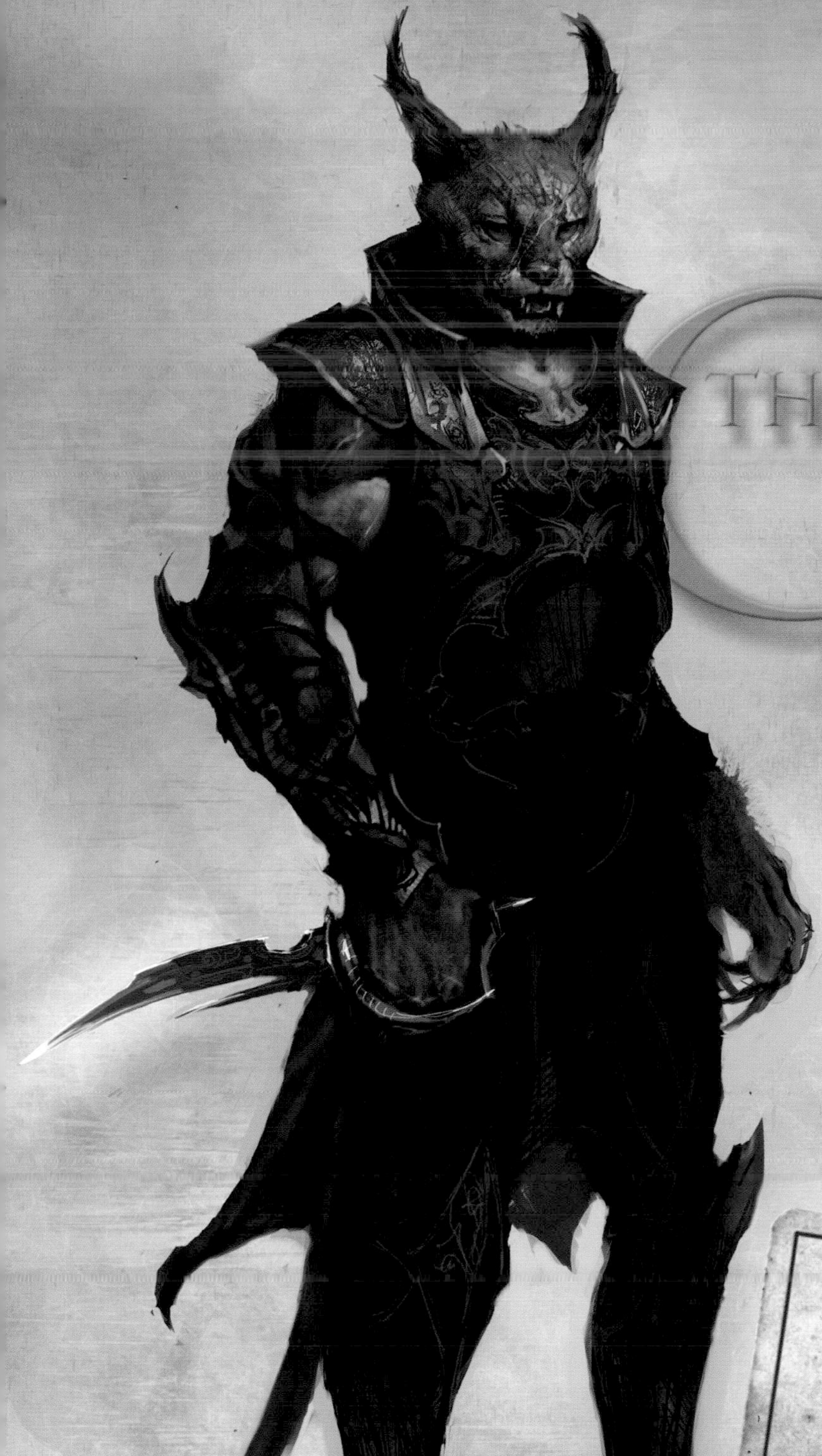

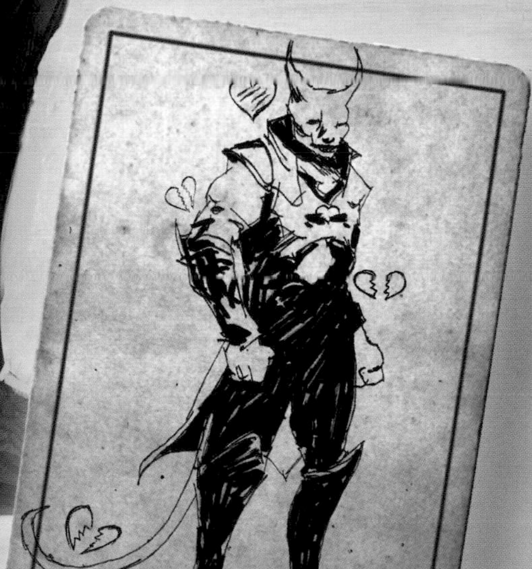

Princess Alyss

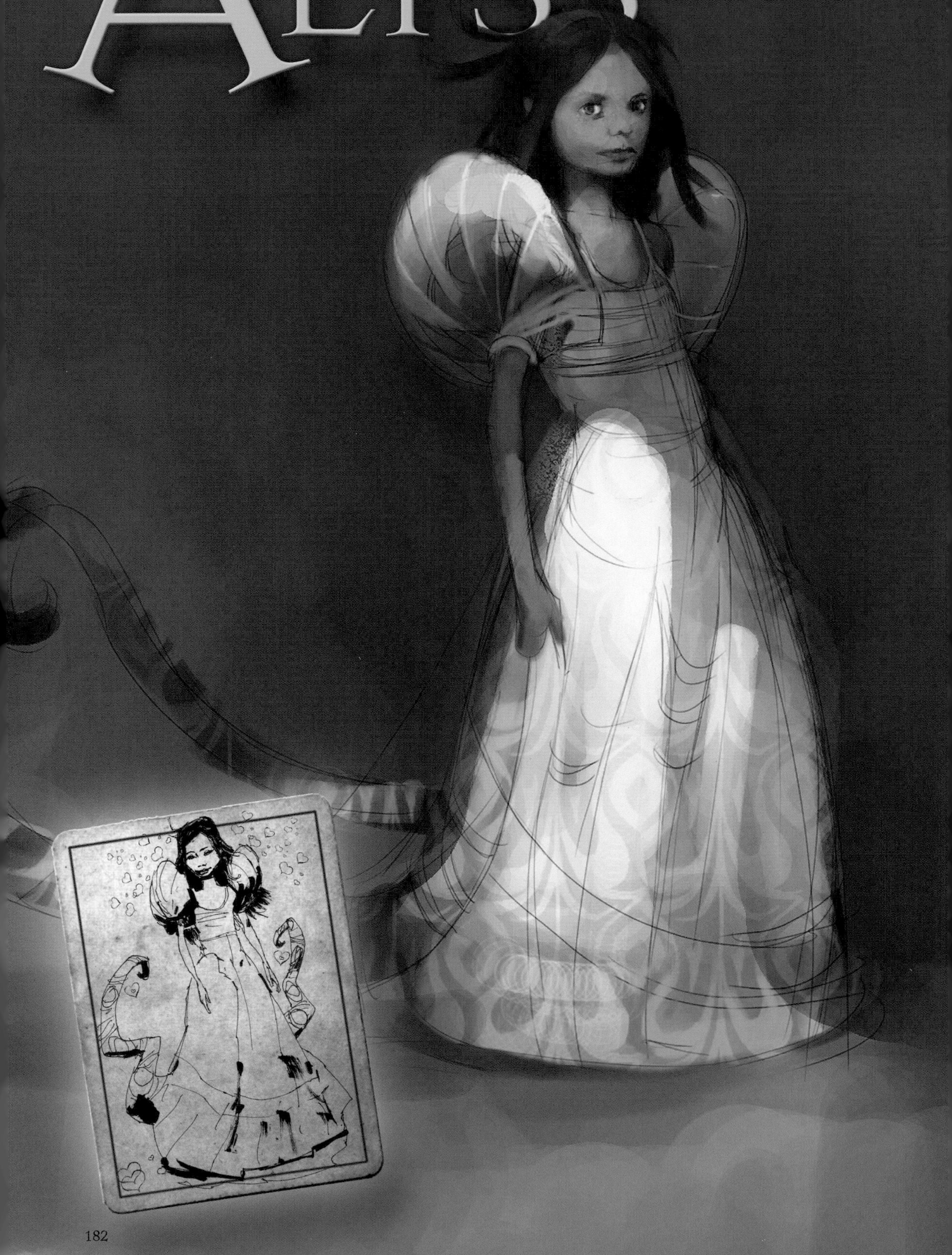

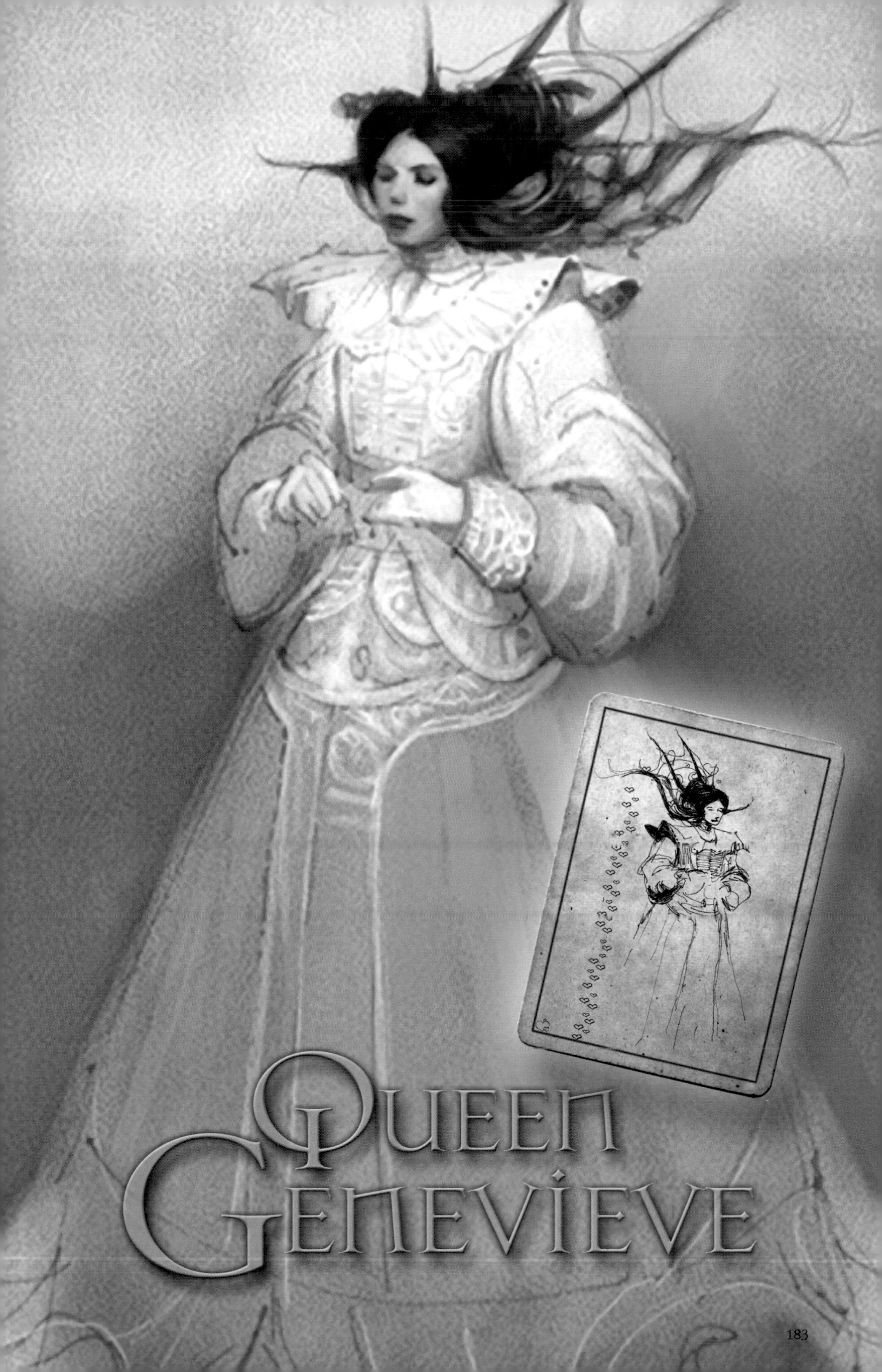

Queen Genevieve

The Chessboard Desert

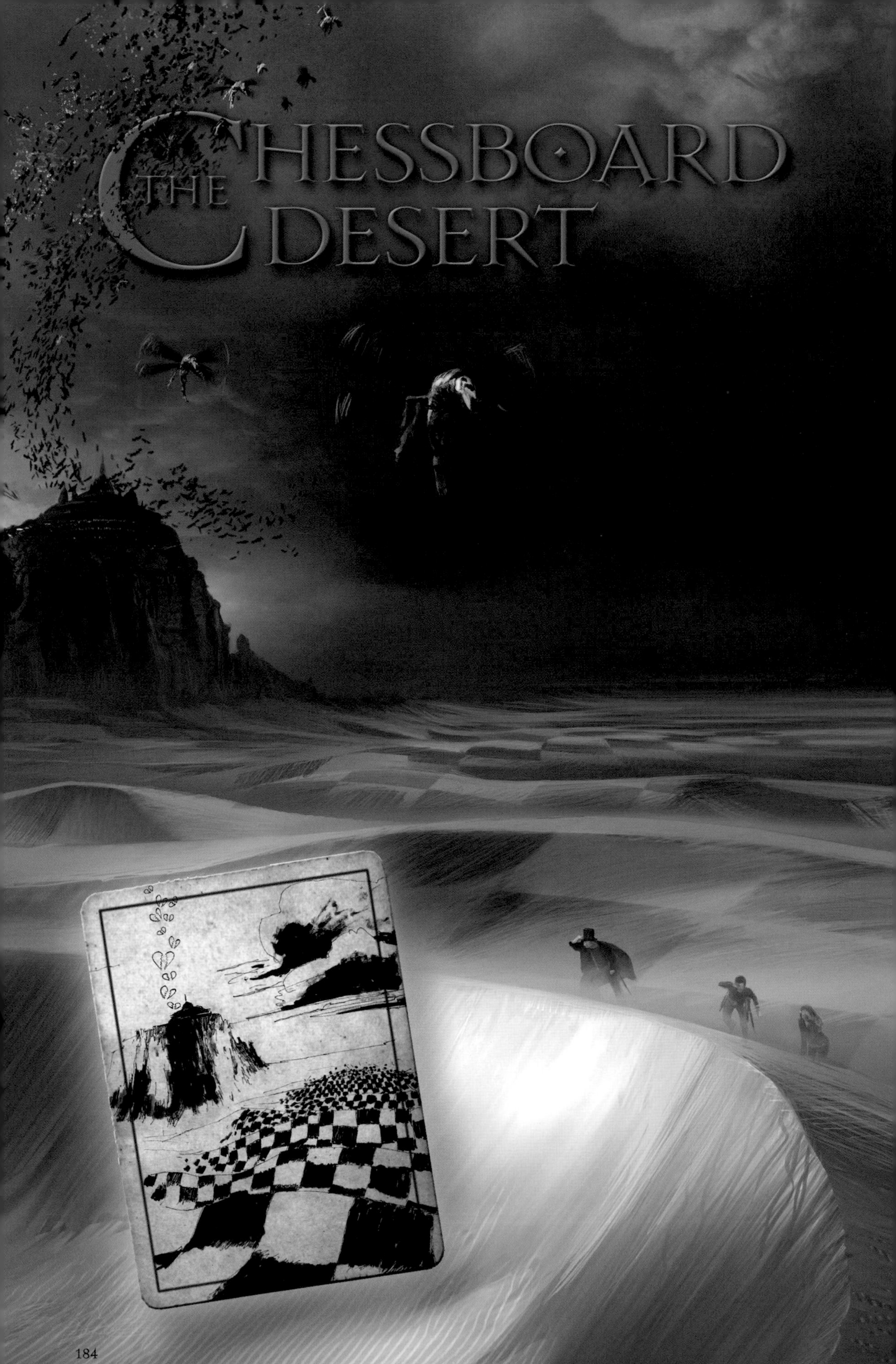

Valley of Mushrooms

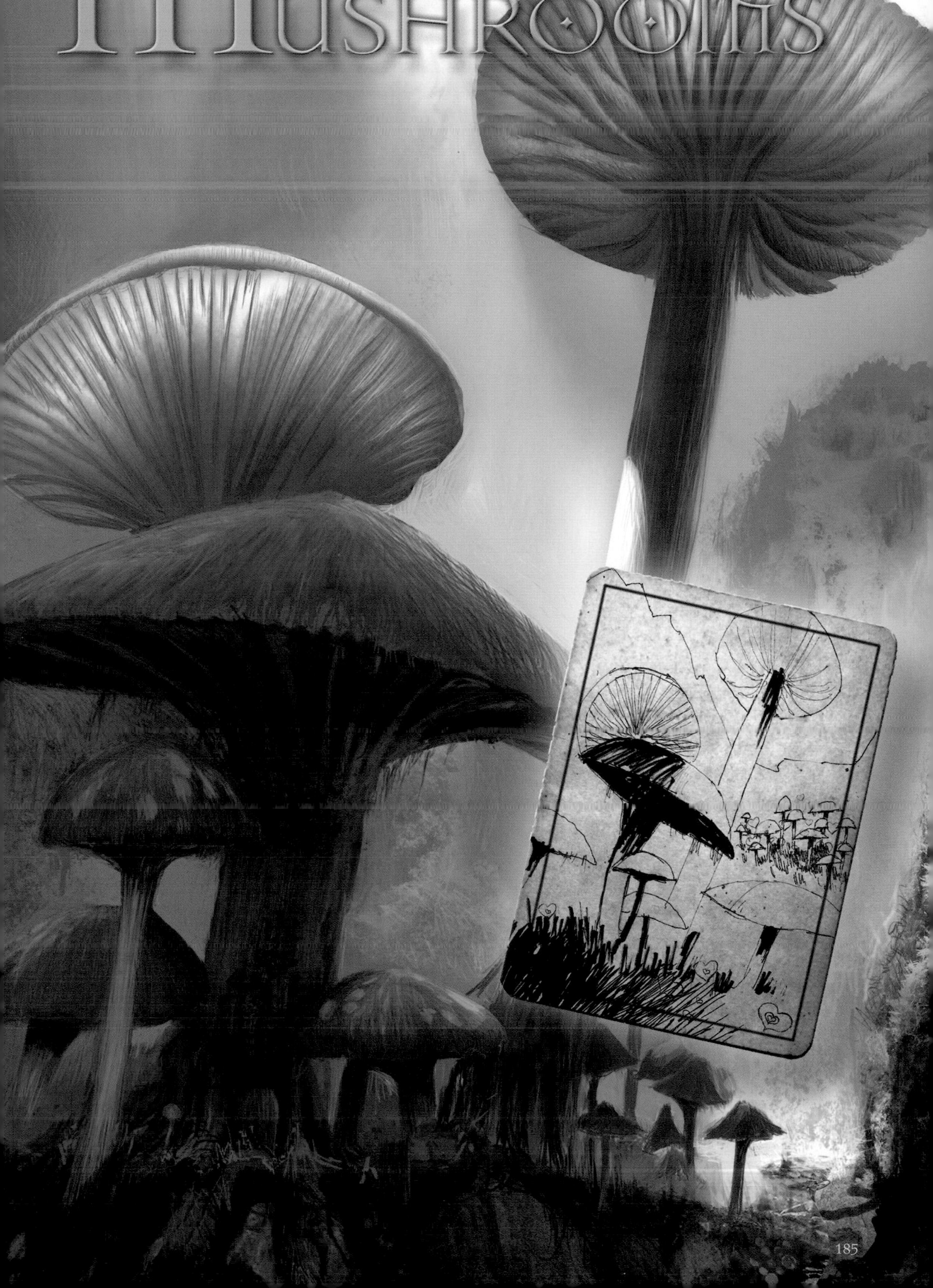

Alyss in Exile

WONDERLAND

Valentine's Day 1863

Mr. Charles Dodgson has promised to write a book telling of my harrowing adventures! He told me I must tell him every detail of my escape and exile, so I am putting it all down on paper. It will be a lot of work but I must do everything I can to help MR. DODGSON get it right!

It was nearly 4 years ago on my 7th birthday that my life completely changed for the WORST! My best friend DODGE and I had just returned from exploring Wondertropolis, a forbidden excursion outside the gates of the palace, when we came across the most peculiar kitten.

My squiglerry cake, and the birthday fairies who appear with every royal cake, to sing "Deliriously Happy Birthday to You." I wish I had been able to slice that cake open and discover what surprise the Royal Bakers baked inside. (I had hinted for a singing tiara).

HAPPY BIRTHDAY to me!

It was wearing a card that read "Happy birthday, Alyss" and since it was my birthday and everyone in the queendom was of course giving ME gifts, it only made sense that this kitten was for me. Unlike most kittens, who only hiss and purr, this kitten smiled.

And THAT is where ALL the TROUBLE began ...

Charles Dodgson's aptitude in the nascent art of photography made him a popular portraitist of children for Oxford's better families. Choosing their costumes for the various portraits was always left to the girls, and might I suggest that the photograph of Alyss in the white dress appears to be her tribute to her time spent with Quigley and the others as a street urchin. It is interesting to note that Charles Dodgson's custom of marking dates of great importance with a white stone may well have stemmed from the Wonderland custom.

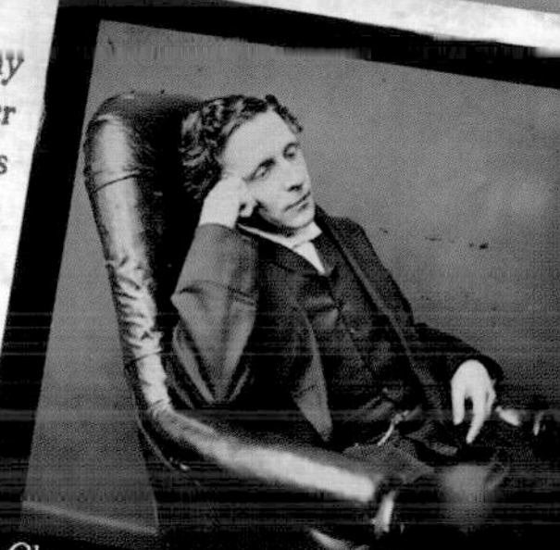

Charles Dodgson at age 25 photographed by Reginald Southey.

Monday Morning

I mark the date April 1, 1862 with a white stone, for it is when I first met Mr. Charles Dodgson! (In Wonderland it is custom to always mark days of great imagination with a white stone. When we were introduced I looked up and saw the kindest face I had seen since leaving Wonderland. I liked him immediately but it wasn't until Lorina introduced me very grandly as Princess Alyss Heart (mocking me, of course) that I knew he was to be my best friend in this world, for the man bowed quite seriously, took my hand and whispered, "Delighted to make your acquaintance, Princess Alyss Heart."

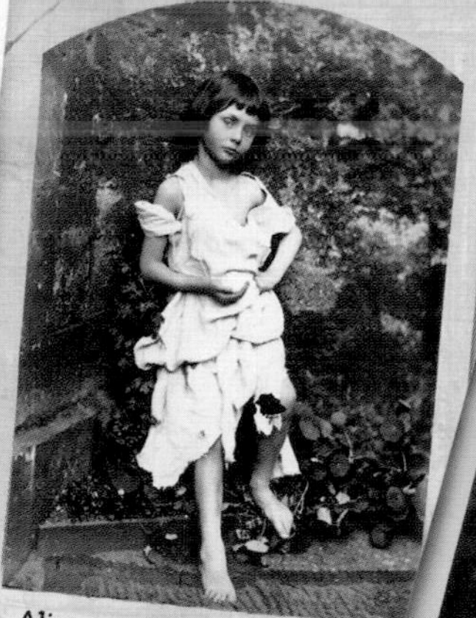

Alice as a beggar maid.

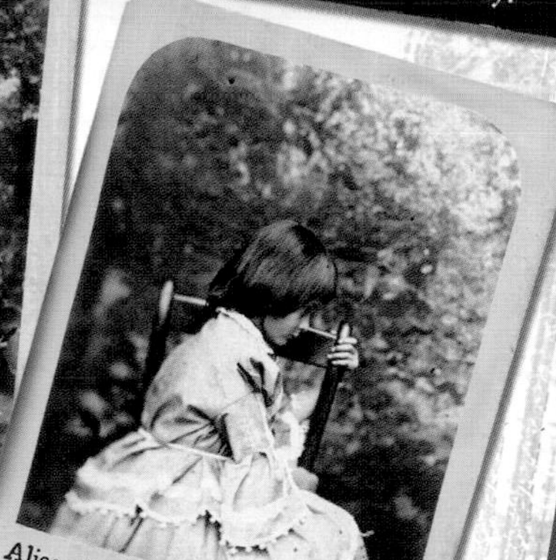

Alice photographed by Dodgson.

Tuesday

Soon after our introduction Mr. Dodgson invited Lorina, Edith and me to his studio for our first photographic portrait. What we all enjoyed most about the portrait setting was being able to try on the costumes that Mr. Dodgson had collected. I told him that I had not seen such imaginative costumes since I left Wonderland. He became very interested and said he would like to hear more about this land called Wonderland.

CDL

Dear Princess Alyss Heart,

I would be most honored if you and your sisters Lorina and Edith would join me for a day of boating and picnicking along the Thames. I am looking forward to hearing all about this world you call Wonderland.

Inquisitively yours,
Charles Lutwidge Dodgson

After the publication of the Looking Glass Wars, we were contacted by the British historian Dame Agnes Mackenzie who had some very interesting information to share. A trunk had been discovered inside a dilapidated carriage house in Oxford, England. It contained the art and journals of a young Victorian girl. After an intensive examination we confirmed the contents to be the property of Princess Alyss Heart of Wonderland. Alyss' art, letters and journal entries provide a haunting portal into the mind of a lost princess searching for a way home. Dame Agnes' book *Princess Alyss of Wonderland* beautifully displays Alyss' work along with her own meticulously researched notes and annotations to provide the reader with historical background and commentary. The excerpted pages follow the trajectory of Alyss and Lewis Carroll's great friendship, the collaboration on the promised book and the ultimate literary betrayal that forever separated muse and author. As The Looking Glass Wars first revealed, Lewis Carroll got it all wrong.

"But I don't want to go among mad people," said Alice. "Oh, you can't help that," said the cat. "We're all mad here."

—Lewis Carroll

26 November 1864

In November of 1864, Charles Dodgson proudly and dare I venture, a bit shyly, presented "Miss Alice Liddell" with his handwritten manuscript of ALICE'S ADVENTURES UNDERGROUND. This historic manuscript contained 37 illustrations also drawn by the versatile and prolific Mr. Dodgson. As you shall SOON DISCOVER, Alyss' reaction was not quite what the poor man had anticipated!

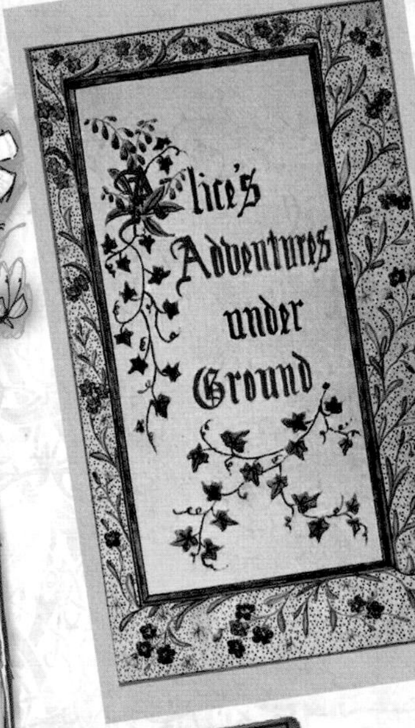

Alice's
Adventures
under
Ground

And at long last the promised book was delivered. What can I say?
HE GOT IT ALL WRONG
WRONG WRONG WRONG WRONG!!!!
He even spelled my name *wrong! What makes me want to scream* off with his head AND *both arms is the fact that he actually seems to believe* HE *told* ME *this nonsensical children's story when the truth is (and he knows it!) that* I told him.

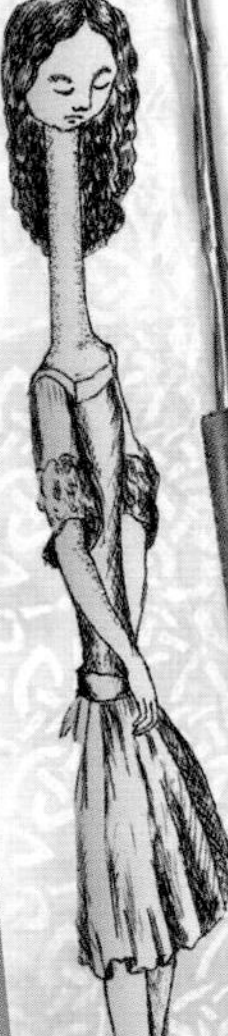

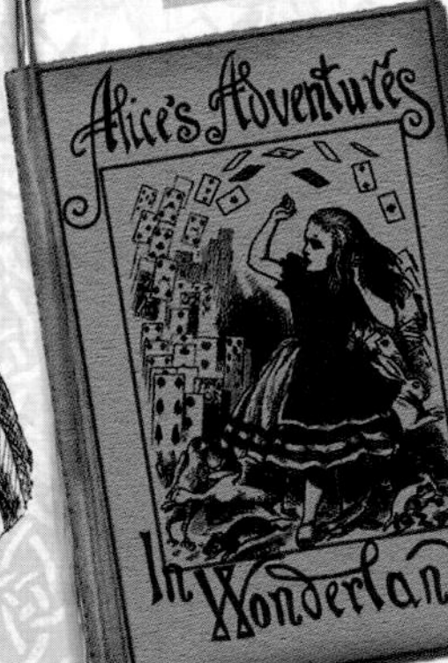

Alice's Adventures
In Wonderland

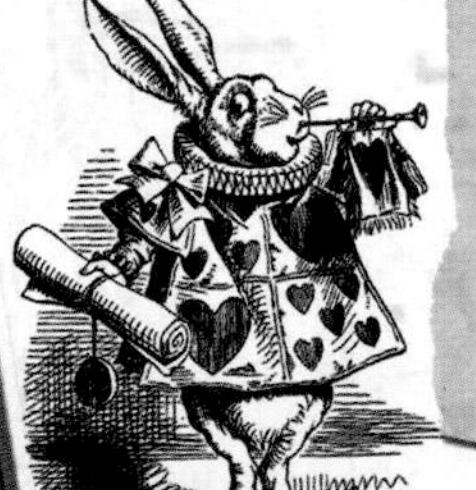

The first published edition of ALICE'S ADVENTURES IN WONDERLAND appeared early in July 1865 and featured illustrator John Tenniel's iconic artwork. Alyss now had to adjust to the fact that the betrayal was no longer an unpublished manuscript but an actual book that would soon find its way into the hands and hearts of the literate public.

To the Very CRUEL Mr. Dodgson,

How could you betray me with this pack of lies? If I were not so furious with you I would certainly be sobbing at the loss of what I believed to be my one true friend in this gray world. Be warned, for the sake of Wonderland and everyone I love, I cannot allow this book of lies to go unchallenged. And who is this "Lewis Carroll" that you are now calling yourself? Are you ashamed to put your own name on this book? I should hope so! As if a royal princess would ever travel through a rabbit hole! Thanks to your efforts my reality has now become this world's fantasy.

Your Un-Friend,

Princess Alyss Heart

PS. Now you shall never be invited to Heart Palace for tarty tarts! And no, strawberry jam tastes NOTHING *like the oh so delicious squigberry jam.* Your loss!

Friday Afternoon

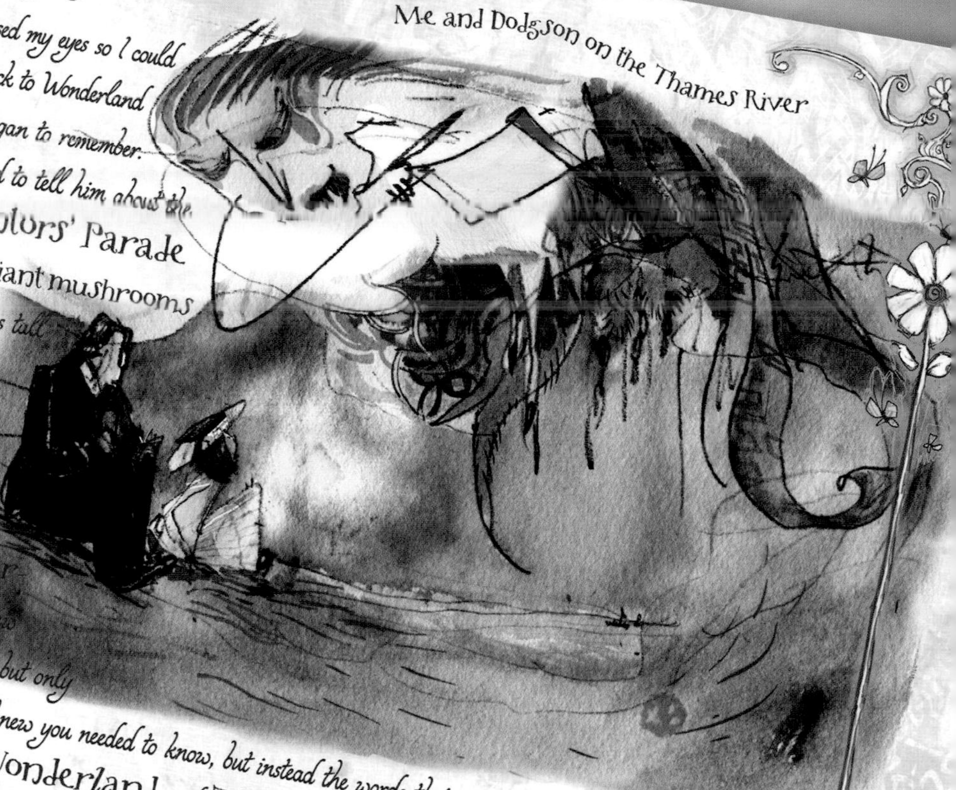
Me and Dodgson on the Thames River

I closed my eyes so I could see back to Wonderland and began to remember. I wanted to tell him about the Inventors' Parade and the giant mushrooms that were as tall as ten of London's greatest trees set end to end and the caterpillars who knew everything but only told you what they knew you needed to know, but instead the words that came out were the story of my last day in Wonderland and The Cat and Redd entering the palace and her ear-shattering cries of "Off with their heads!!!"

At this point I opened my eyes and saw poor Mr. Dodgson absolutely pale with fright.

He asked, "What, my dear, is so WONDERFUL about WONDERLAND???" I smiled and told him there was much, MUCH more to tell . . .

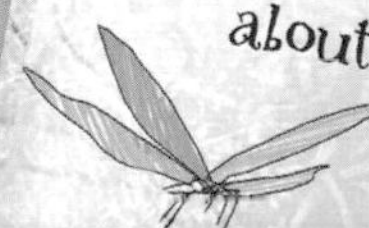

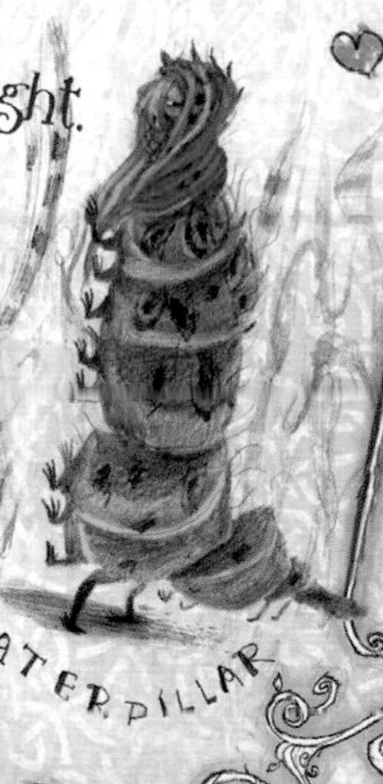
CATERPILLAR

I cannot help but be moved by the beauty of the friendship shared by Charles Lutwidge Dodgson and Alyss Heart. As devastating a betrayal as the eventual outcome may have been, for a period of time two kindred spirits found each other in the same world and proceeded to have a riotous good time. Charles Dodgson was a young mathematics don at Christ Church when he first met the daughters of Dean Liddell and, as history has voluminously recorded, he was particularly in awe of the daughter supposedly named "Alice."

"O! that way madness lies; let me shun that." —William Shakespeare

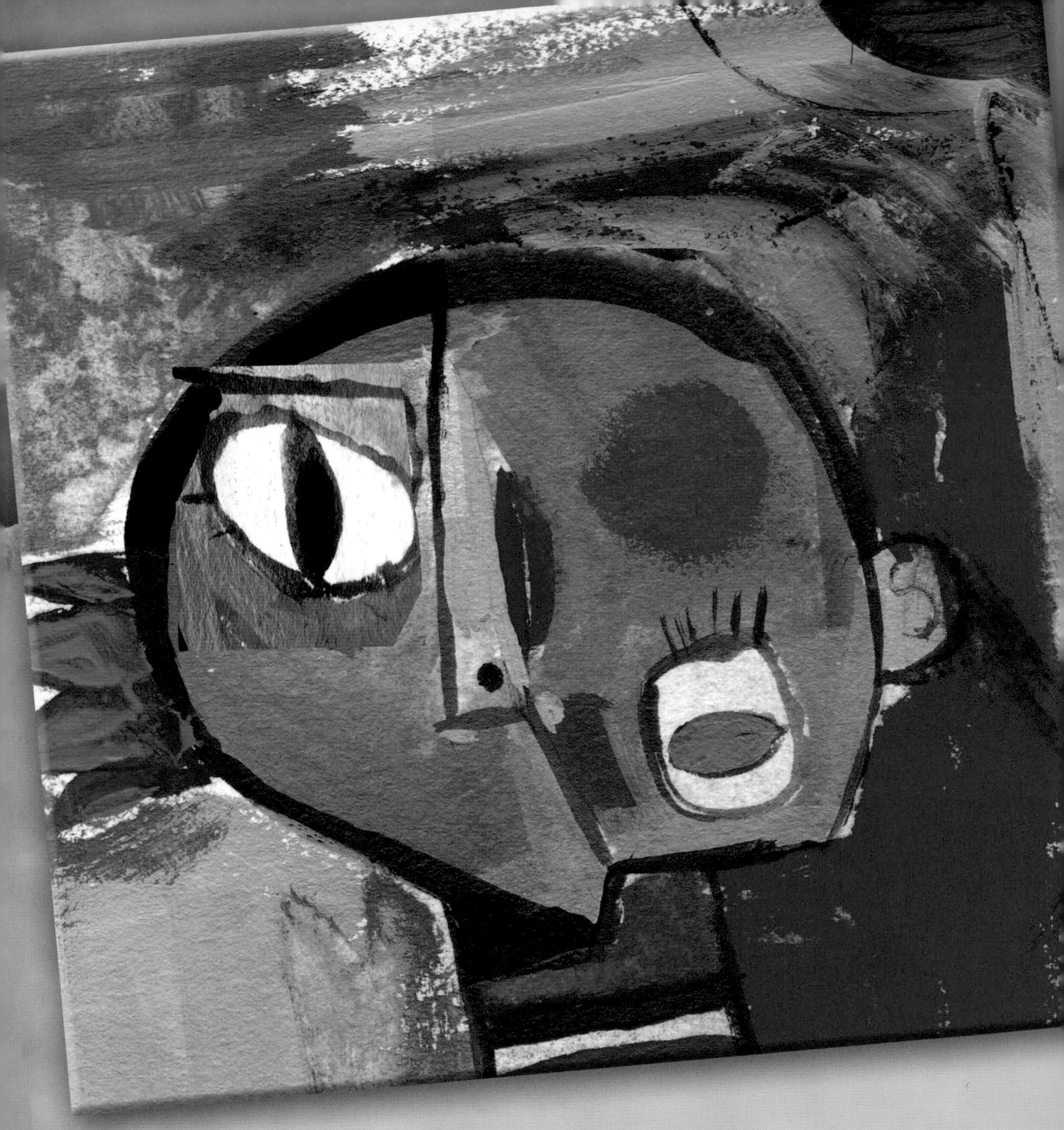

Following the publication of *Princess Alyss of Wonderland,* Dame Agnes received a tip regarding an unusual painting that could be traced back to Buckingham Palace circa. 1872. Upon investigation she discovered these facts:

As an engagement gift, Alice Liddell took up the brush and palette to paint a self-portrait at the request of her fiancé Prince Leopold. The result of her artistic self-examination yielded a strange fractured portrait of someone obviously unsure of who she is and what she wants! Is it child or is it a woman? Is it Alice or is it Alyss? The cubist style precedes that particular art movement by over 30 years. Could it have somehow inspired the painters of the early 20th century? After Alice Liddell's disappearance in the midst of their royal wedding, Prince Leopold disposed of the painting (never having liked it in the first place) which began a circuitous trek across Europe until coming to Malaga, Spain in the year 1881 to hang on the wall of an old school house until now.

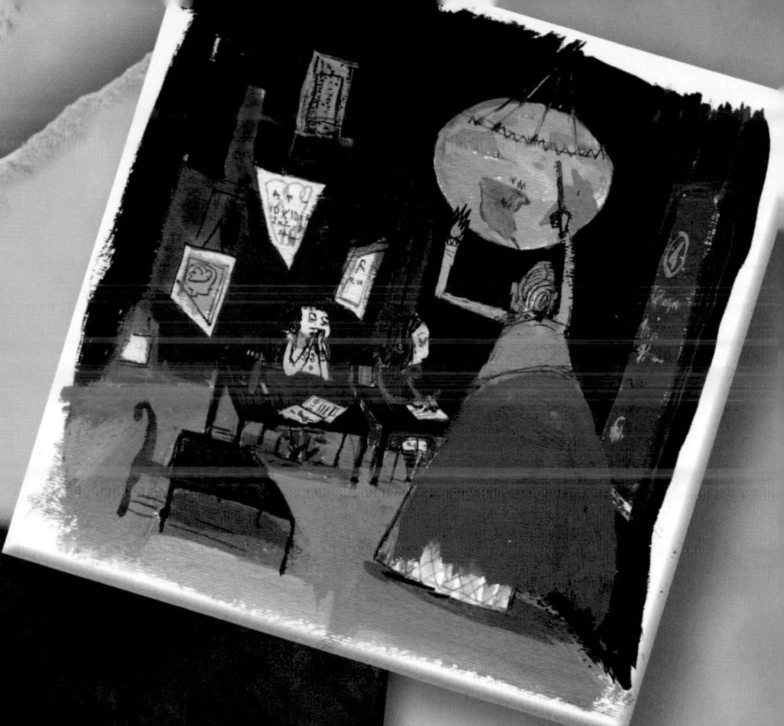

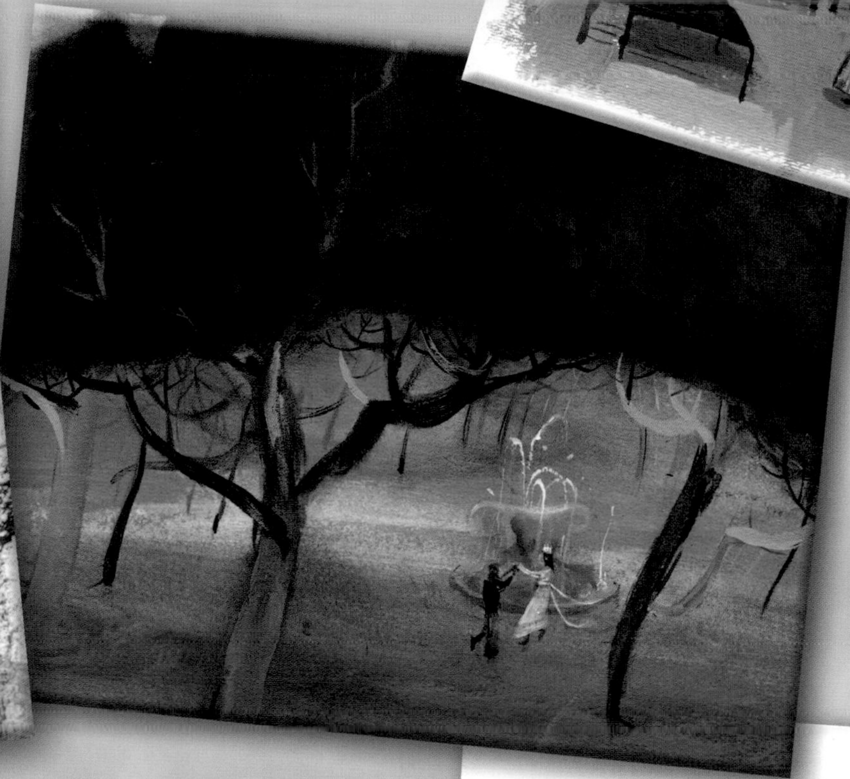

"No excellent soul is exempt from a mixture of madness." —Aristotle

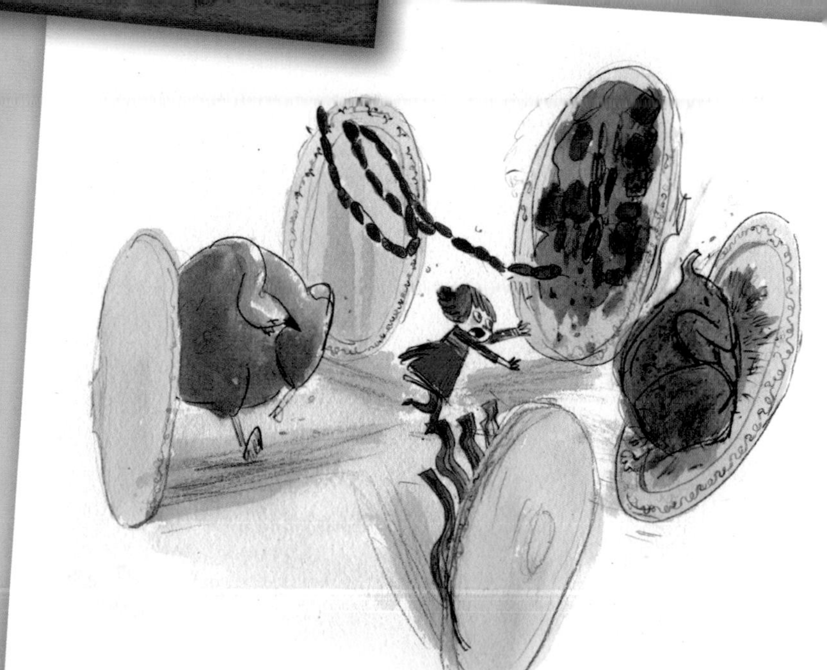

Awaiting Verification!
We recently received these three pieces of possible 'Alyss' art from Dame Agnes. All three are from a private collection and are currently on loan to the Institute for forensic testing and authentication. We will have the results of our ongoing Alyss art investigation in geo-graphic novel Hatter M Volume 3.

Process Gallery

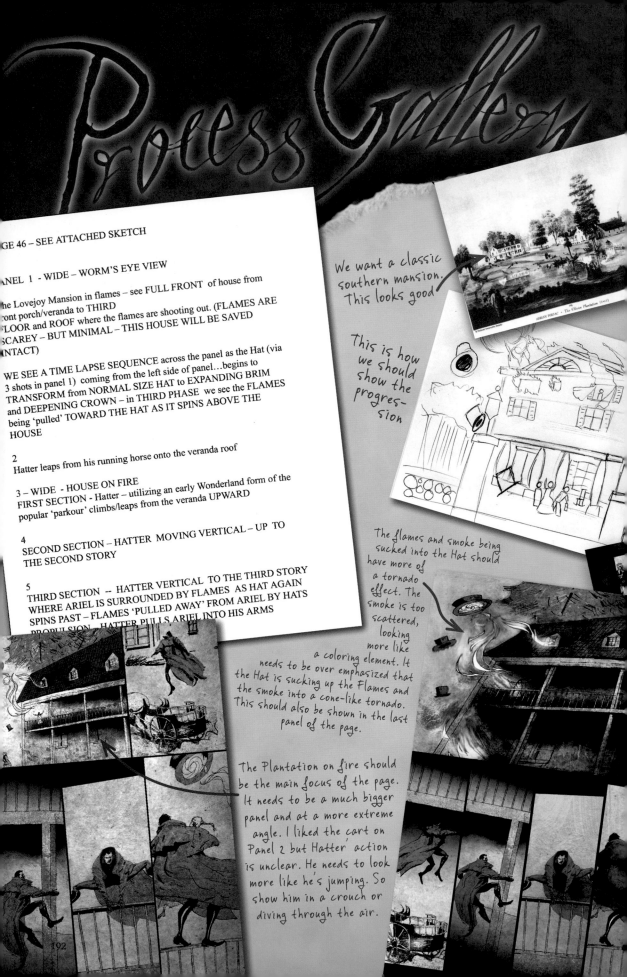

GE 46 – SEE ATTACHED SKETCH

ANEL 1 - WIDE – WORM'S EYE VIEW

he Lovejoy Mansion in flames – see FULL FRONT of house from
ront porch/veranda to THIRD
FLOOR and ROOF where the flames are shooting out. (FLAMES ARE
SCAREY – BUT MINIMAL – THIS HOUSE WILL BE SAVED
NTACT)

WE SEE A TIME LAPSE SEQUENCE across the panel as the Hat (via
3 shots in panel 1) coming from the left side of panel…begins to
TRANSFORM from NORMAL SIZE HAT to EXPANDING BRIM
and DEEPENING CROWN – in THIRD PHASE we see the FLAMES
being 'pulled' TOWARD THE HAT AS IT SPINS ABOVE THE
HOUSE

2
Hatter leaps from his running horse onto the veranda roof

3 – WIDE - HOUSE ON FIRE
FIRST SECTION - Hatter – utilizing an early Wonderland form of the
popular 'parkour' climbs/leaps from the veranda UPWARD

4
SECOND SECTION – HATTER MOVING VERTICAL – UP TO
THE SECOND STORY

5
THIRD SECTION -- HATTER VERTICAL TO THE THIRD STORY
WHERE ARIEL IS SURROUNDED BY FLAMES AS HAT AGAIN
SPINS PAST – FLAMES 'PULLED AWAY' FROM ARIEL BY HATS
PROPULSION – HATTER PULLS ARIEL INTO HIS ARMS

ADRIAN PERSAC • The Olivier Plantation

We want a classic southern mansion. This looks good

This is how we should show the progression

The flames and smoke being sucked into the Hat should have more of a tornado effect. The smoke is too scattered, looking more like a coloring element. It needs to be over emphasized that the Hat is sucking up the Flames and the smoke into a cone-like tornado. This should also be shown in the last panel of the page.

The Plantation on fire should be the main focus of the page. It needs to be a much bigger panel and at a more extreme angle. I liked the cart on Panel 2 but Hatter action is unclear. He needs to look more like he's jumping. So show him in a crouch or diving through the air.

anel 1 – wide of the ballroom in the mansi
ith scarred floors -- only the humanity and energy of the people make it

BACKGROUND
Kate plays the piano. Hayward plays the fiddle. Ariel and Lulu waltz together around the once elegant – now scarred and stripped ballroom. Very formal – funny and cute.

FOREGROUND
Hatter and Rosalind waltz together. Very formal. Elegant. But there is also something very personal between them.

ROSALIND
The war has changed our lives forever.
Lovejoy was built by artisans to stand
a thousand years.
If you could only IMAGINE how beautiful this once was…

HATTER
I can…I can imagine it all.

2 - INSERT 'IMAGINATION ' PANEL OVER PART OF PANEL 1 – this panel can be a 'bleed' that progresses (left to right) beginning with Hatter's POV across the page beginning in the grays and muted colors of Panel 1's REALTY and progressing into the HYPER-REAL WONDER-LAND COLORS AS IT COMES FROM HATTER'S IMAGINATION

Hatter 'sees' the ballroom transformed and at the main focal point 'sees' Rosalind dressed in a flowing gown – the image is reminiscent of the beauty and fantasy of Wonderland. Rosalind's hair and gown has a Wonderland fantasy to it as do Hatter's imagining of the room, the candelabra – more vivid, surreal than anything Earth could create.

SEE ATTACHED REFERENCE IMAGE OF QUEEN GENEVIEVE FOR ROSALIND 'IMAGI-NATION' LOOK

NOTE: PANELS 3 AND 4 – BOTTOM OF PAGE – CAN BE POSITIONED OVER THE IMAGINATION 'BLEED' OF PANEL 2 AS IT SPREADS TOWARD THE BOTTOM OF THE PAGE

3 – SMALL PANEL
TWO SHOT HATTER AND ROSALIND HEADS CLOSE TOGETHER

ROSALIND
In the South it is considered very
bad manners to ask personal questions of guests…

4 – SMALL PANEL
CLOSE UP – ROSALIND'S EYES BOLD – STARING INTO HATTER'S FACE AT SIDE OF PANEL

ROSALIND
But I beli… u told me
…e from.

Page layout needs a shake up, a full bleed for the main panel of interest.

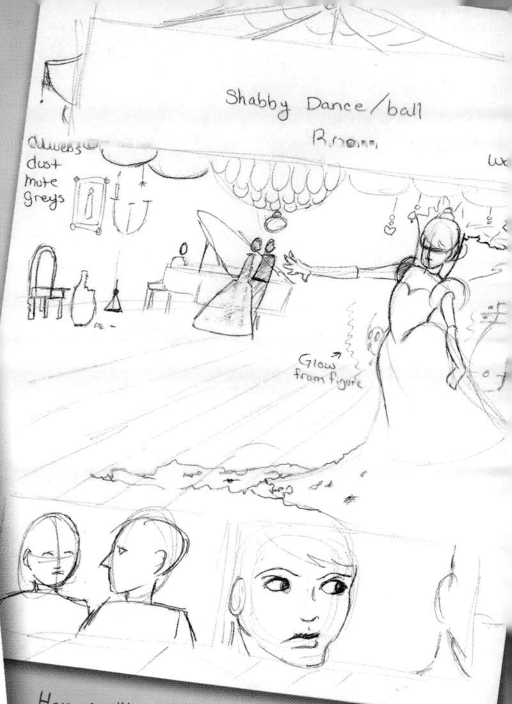

Shabby Dance/ball Room
Cobwebs dust mute greys
Glow from figure

Here is Miss Emily's sketch with some changes. Pull back from Rosalind. Take out Wonderland objects behind Rosalind.

"Follow your inner moonlight; don't hide the madness." –Allen Ginsberg

Add notes, swirling in Wonderland colors to feel the sweep of the music.

Emphasize the colored glow of Wonderland as reality bleeds into Hatter's vision of Rosalind.

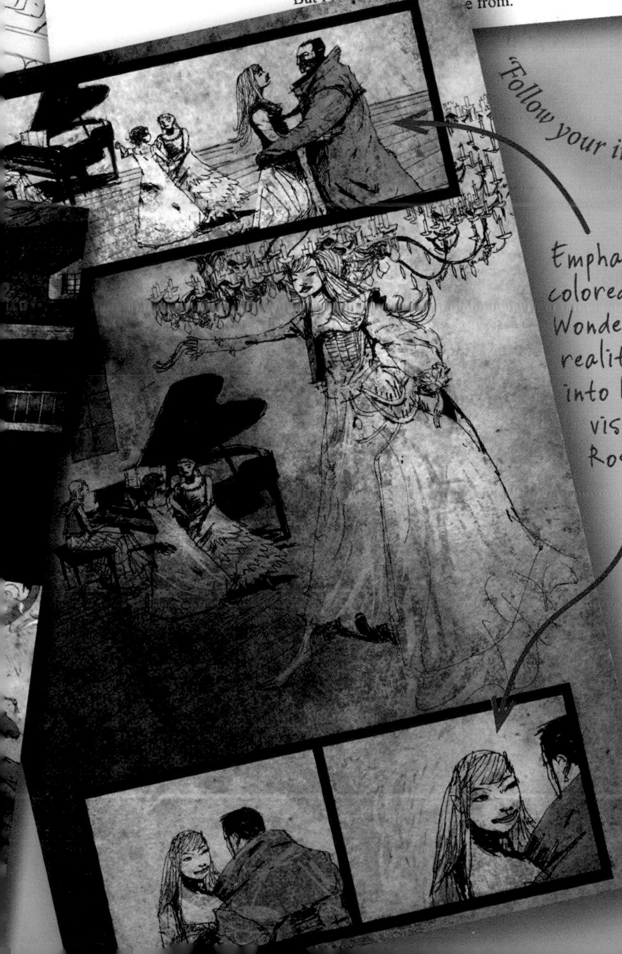

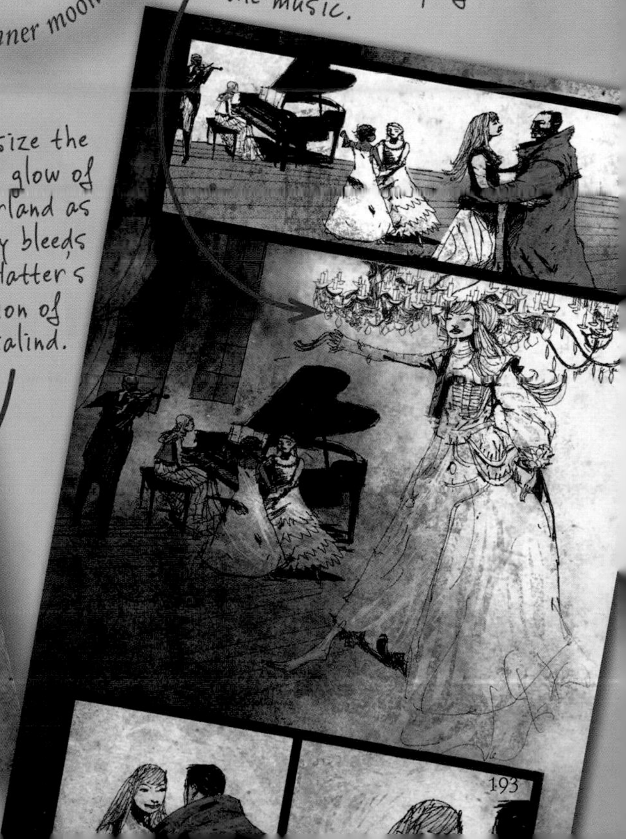

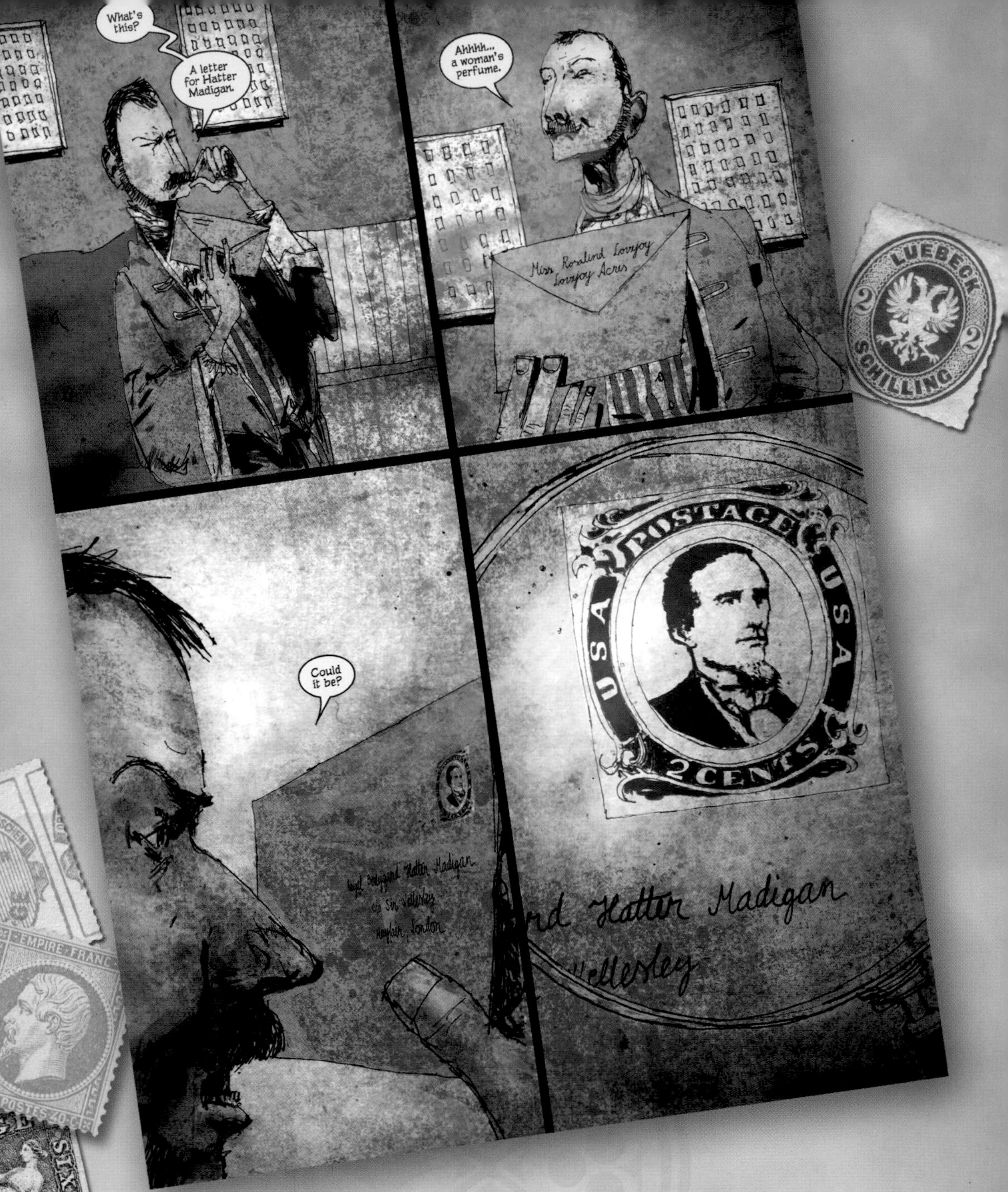
What's this?
A letter for Hatter Madigan.
Ahhhh... a woman's perfume.
Miss Rosalind Lovejoy
Lovejoy Acres
Could it be?
POSTAGE
USA
USA
2 CENTS
Hatter Madigan
LUEBECK
2
SCHILLING
2

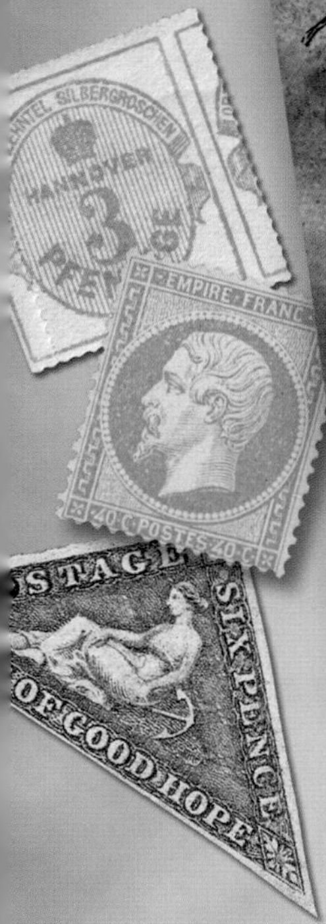
HANNOVER
3
EMPIRE FRANC
SIX PENCE
OF GOOD HOPE

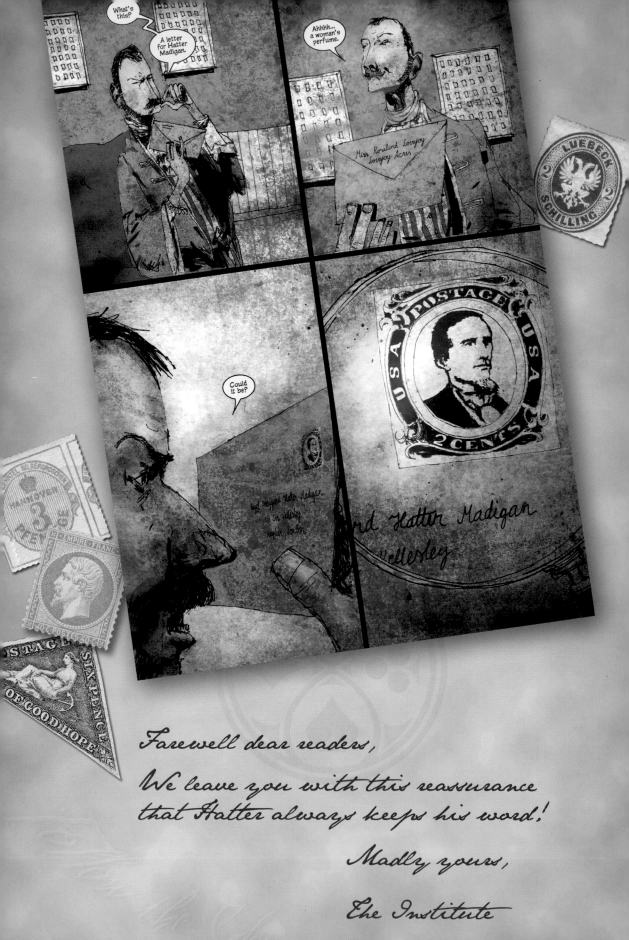

Farewell dear readers,

We leave you with this reassurance that Hatter always keeps his word!

Madly yours,

The Institute

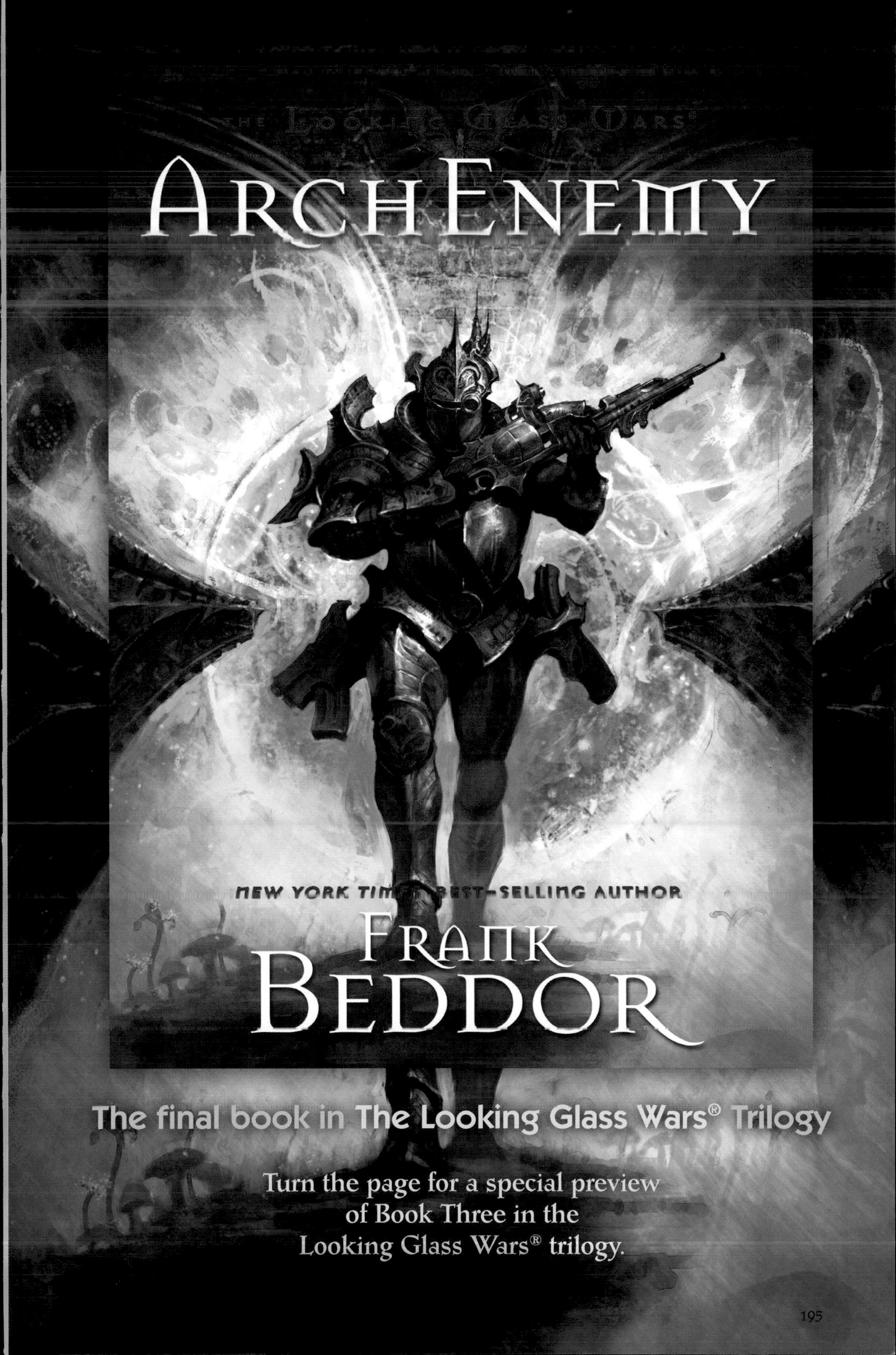
THE LOOKING GLASS WARS®
ArchEnemy
NEW YORK
BEST-SELLING AUTHOR
FRANK BEDDOR

The final book in The Looking Glass Wars® Trilogy

Turn the page for a special preview
of Book Three in the
Looking Glass Wars® trilogy.

CHAPTER 8

BOARDERLAND: WONDERLAND'S largest, most powerful neighbor, consisting wholly of nomadic towns and cities,
any one of which might be situated amid the sandy dunes of
Duneraria one week but spread out alongside Bookie River
the next; an uncultivated, expansive place where itiner-
ant settlements had always been separated by large tracts of
unpopulated, rugged terrain; a land where, except for clashes,
tribes used to keep to themselves, allowed to observe their
own customs and rituals so long as they submitted to Arch
as king of *all* Boarderland.

But that was before Arch had been reunited with an
old friend and his practice of perpetuating hostilities among
the tribes revealed for what it was: the method by which
he maintained his authority, stoking animosities so that the

Astacans and Maldoids and others wouldn't unite to form an army his own could not hope to rival.

That was before Redd Heart.

"WILMA was *not* activated as she should've been, but I recognize her effects," the former king whispered to one of his intel ministers, who was crouched behind an orb cannon to avoid notice. "I'm willing to bet Redd is without her powers. We wouldn't be returning to Boarderland if she had them."

"You don't know for sure she's without imagination, my liege."

"Not yet. But I will."

The military caravan had halted in Outerwilderbeastia before the final push back into Boarderland. With the prospect of it before him, the country Arch had so recently ruled suddenly seemed inhospitable and miserly, a dusty landscape of wind-battered tenements and few natural resources. It had never been enough. He didn't want to be king again, not if it meant being king of Boarderland alone.

"Nor can you know if such a loss of imagination is permanent," the intel minister said.

Arch looked off to where Redd lounged beneath a canopy at the edge of the sparring arena, an open space surrounded by tribal warriors and Earth mercenaries. Sitting with Mistress Heart in the shade along with the rest of her top military rank was The Cat—half feline, half Wonderlander, total assassin; and Vollrath, that member of the tutor species devoted to Black Imagination. All unengaged troops had been ordered to gather for a series of brawls. It was supposed to be entertainment.

"You see how Redd pretends to give no thought to the fact that even now," Arch said to his minister, "both in front of us and behind, her recruits are fighting Alyss' forces? She's overacting. With this leisurely retreat of ours, she's trying to prove that clashes with her niece's armies are nothing and she can go where she likes, Wonderland is as good as hers. I don't believe it."

Arch knew Redd's impatience too well: In taking back the crown, in putting an end to Alyss Heart, Redd would never have been leisurely if she could help it.

"Had WILMA wreaked what she was supposed to," the minister said, "Boarderland and Wonderland would already be yours, my liege."

Arch nodded. "If Redd's without her imagination, so is Queen Alyss. I have to take a chance and make my move while they're without their powers."

Shouts rose from the troops around the sparring arena. Hoofs and fists pumped the air. The first brawl had begun.

"Arch!" Redd's voice cut through the cheers and catcalls, her eyes on the former king.

Arch dipped his head, the closest he would ever come to a bow. "Coming, Your Imperial Viciousness!" Turning away to take his position at Redd's side, keeping his lips as still as possible, he told his minister, "You're going to pay a visit to

the Glass Eyes' tent and you're going to do and say exactly as I instruct . . ."

~

It could not have been going worse for her niece, chessmen succumbing to slashing blades, card soldiers falling a pack at a time under a barrage of orb generators and cannonball spiders. How invigorated Her Imperial Viciousness had felt, watching Alyss' pathetic defensive maneuvers as Boarderland's twenty-one tribes, under *her* command, stormed into Outerwilderbeastia, each tribe wielding the weapons they most favored: gossamer shots (Awr), mind riders (Maldoids), kill-quills (Scabbler), death-balls (Gnobi), knobkerries (Astacans), and the crude tools of less developed tribes hardly worth her notice. No, her attack on Wonderland couldn't have been going better. Her Boarderlanders and Earth recruits had laid flat shuffle after shuffle of Heart soldiers, rampaging through Outerwilderbeastia into the Everlasting Forest and the Chessboard Desert, converging on Wondertropolis. How she had frowned with appreciation as The Cat swiped claws across the chests of Six Cards and swatted down pawns! How she had grimaced with pride as her foremost military rank, the most gifted of her Earth recruits, proved their worth: Sacrenoir, who raised the bones of the dead into skeleton-zombies desperate to satisfy their insatiable hunger for live flesh; Siren Hecht, unhinging her jaw to release high-pitched screams that sent platoons squirming to the ground in pain; Alistaire Poole, the surgeon/undertaker who conducted autopsies on living card soldiers; and Mr. Van de Skülle, dexterously lashing chessmen with his spike-tipped whip.

And at last she'd been making her way down Heart Boulevard, toward Heart Palace and a final victory over her presumptuous upstart of a niece! But that's when things had gone instantly, horribly—

Odd.

She awoke, lying in the middle of the boulevard, her head hazy, her soldiers splayed about in various stages of unconsciousness. She had tried to view Alyss with her imagination's eye but saw only blackness. Whether or not her niece had harnassed some sort of reserve power from the Heart Crystal, as Arch had suggested, Redd didn't know. The infusion of strength she'd experienced when nearing the Heart Crystal had gone in a moment. She'd been barren of imagination ever since.

"Not bad," she said, applauding listlessly as Ripkins dragged a defeated Glass Eye from the sparring arena.

She had called for the fights in order to boost morale. The tribes were fitful, having never remained in such proximity to one another for any length of time and not understanding why they hadn't stormed Heart Palace when they had been so close. But she couldn't have risked entering the palace when Alyss might have had her powers while she . . . no, she hated to admit it even to herself. Besides giving her

an opportunity to observe what Arch's bodyguards were capable of, the sparring matches would distract the troops from their unease.

Redd nodded in Blister's direction. "Your turn."

The bodyguard stepped into the sparring arena, pulled off his elbow-length gloves and placed them neatly in his pocket. Her Imperial Viciousness glared out at the troops.

"Anyone wishing to earn my special regard, which should be every one of you, will step forward and earn it!"

Blister waited for an adversary, but none came forward.

"Are this Doomsine's talents so great that you'd all risk *my* wrath as cowards?"

"Let me fight him."

The Cat's words had come out as a growl. He was standing between Redd and Arch in humanoid form, erect on two heavily muscled legs, his strong arms reaching down past his waist, his paws unsheathing claws sharp and long enough to run through an average-sized Wonderlander. His fangs showed beneath his flat pink nose, his twitching whiskers.

"You've only one life left," Redd reminded him.

"And it's worthless if I don't risk it doing what I do best."

"I like your rashness, feline. Take your position."

The Cat leapt into the sparring arena. He and Blister eyed each other, unmoving.

"Is this supposed to be impressive?" Redd snorted.

Like one warming up for more strenuous exercise, Blister

tossed a whipsnake grenade, but The Cat easily sidestepped its slithering, snapping electric coils. Blister would try to work his way in close, The Cat knew. Every swipe of a paw could prove as deadly to himself as to Blister. He should be careful. But he wasn't here to be careful, so he ran straight at his adversary, his powerful legs carrying him forward with such thrust and purpose that anyone else would have tried to flee, but Blister merely remained where he was.

The Cat pounced—a low, perfectly horizontal leap forward. He morphed into a kitten in mid-air, ducking Blister's outstretched hands, and transformed back into a humanoid as he passed, raking his claws across Blister's shin. He came to a stop three spirit-dane lengths away, a full-formed assassin again.

Blister showed no sign of feeling the bloody gash in his leg. He produced an AD52 from somewhere beneath his coat and held down its trigger, shooting a full deck of razor-cards at The Cat and stalking after it. The Cat avoided what projectiles he could and batted down others, smacking the tops of them without touching their sharp edges, but Blister was able to get within arm's reach and—

The Cat hissed, leapt back. Blister had grazed his shoulder with a finger. The fur immediately swelled; the skin underneath it bubbled. The Cat popped the swelling with a claw and spat.

Beneath Redd's canopy, Arch leaned toward his mistress, smiling and flirtatious.

"You're looking particularly grim, Your Imperial Viciousness."

"Flatterer."

"I *was* going to woo you with lies, Redd, but I have to say, the blurriness that's been part of you and The Cat since your return to our world—"

"What of it?"

"I know you said something about its being the result of your unprecedented journey through the Heart Crystal, but . . . well, it's pretty much gone."

Redd crinkled her nose in what was supposed to be a teasing manner. "Again I ask: What of it, Archy? Does it surprise you that I used my powerful imagination to rid myself of a loathsome blurriness? It's just taken longer than I'd liked. What the Heart Crystal gives isn't so easily done away with . . . even for me."

"Hm," Arch said.

Blister and The Cat stood breathing heavily in the middle of the sparring arena, each waiting for the other to make the next move. Blister's clothes were shredded, thin lines of blood showing where The Cat's claws had dragged across his chest, back, leg, and arms. The Cat's shoulder and forearms were leaking—wherever Blister had even lightly touched him, yellow pus dribbled from popped bubbles of skin.

"Caterpillar," Vollrath noted, his ashen finger pointing at a series of green smoke rings drifting out from behind a fried dormouse hawker's stall.

In the sparring arena, Blister threw a dagger at The Cat. The feline dropped into a crouch, about to spring forward.

"Enough!" Redd shouted. "As much as we're all dying to see the outcome of this little dalliance, I may still have use for *both* of you."

Though she'd always deemed caterpillar-oracles to be ugly, annoying creatures, Her Imperial Viciousness stomped toward the dormouse hawker's stall, leaving Blister and The Cat to believe they had lost their sole chance to prove which of them was the greater fighter. They couldn't know there would soon be another.

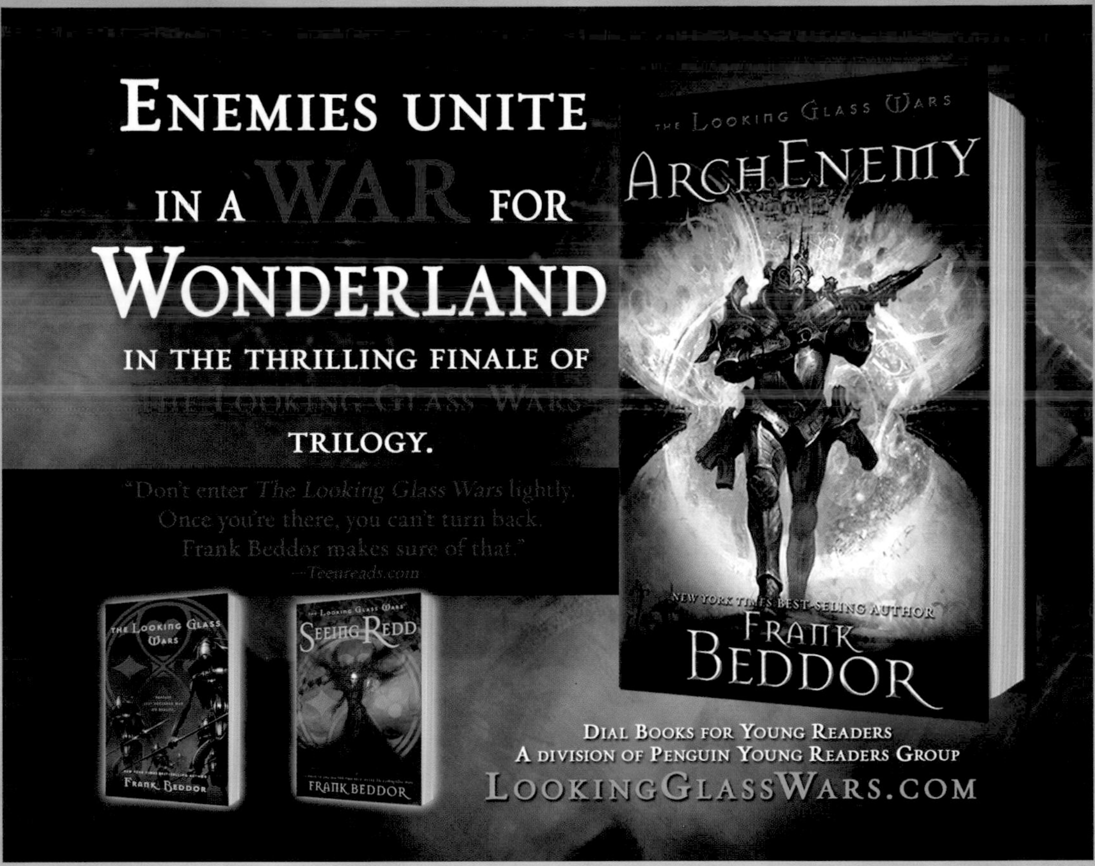

Enemies unite
in a WAR for
Wonderland
in the thrilling finale of
The Looking Glass Wars
trilogy.
"Don't enter The Looking Glass Wars lightly.
Once you're there, you can't turn back.
Frank Beddor makes sure of that."
—Teenreads.com
The Looking Glass Wars
Frank Beddor
The Looking Glass Wars
Seeing Redd
Frank Beddor
The Looking Glass Wars
ArchEnemy
New York Times Best-Selling Author
Frank Beddor
Dial Books for Young Readers
A division of Penguin Young Readers Group
LookingGlassWars.com

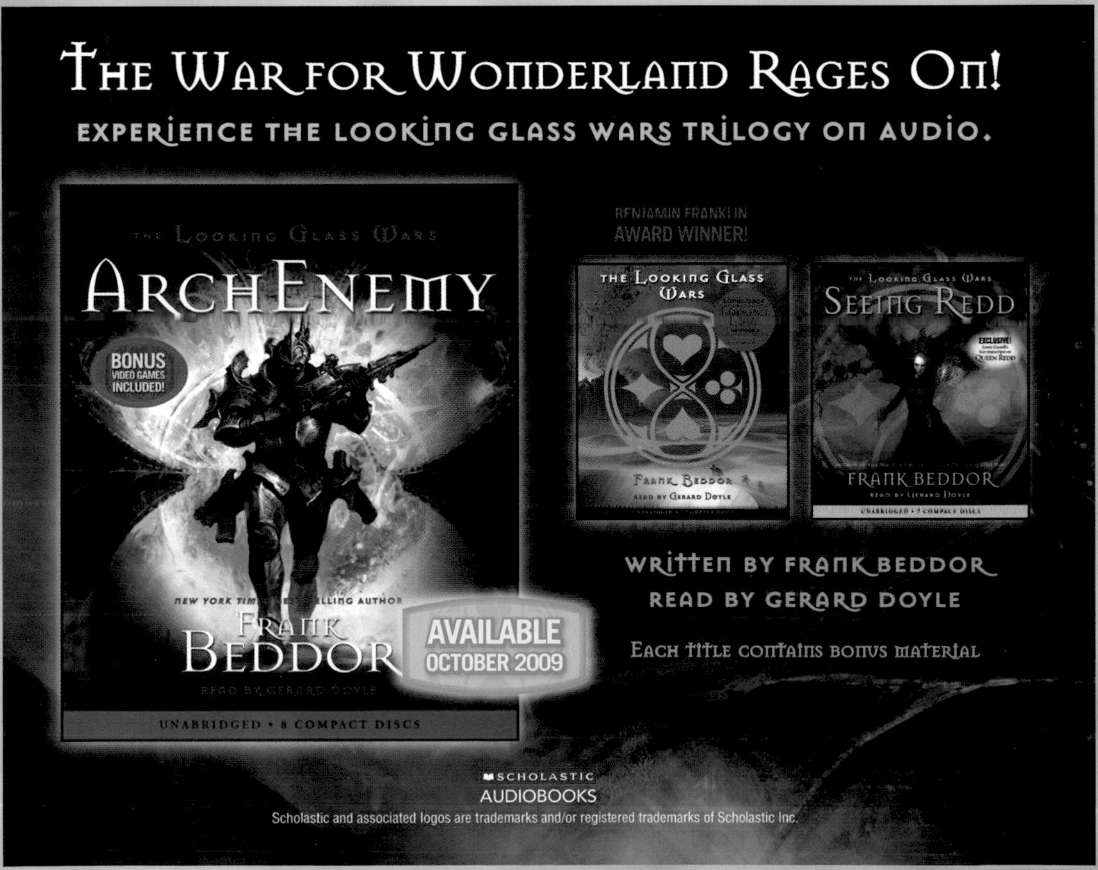

The War for Wonderland Rages On!
Experience The Looking Glass Wars trilogy on audio.
The Looking Glass Wars
ArchEnemy
Bonus video games included!
New York Times Best-Selling Author
Frank Beddor
Read by Gerard Doyle
Unabridged • 8 Compact Discs
Available October 2009
Benjamin Franklin Award Winner!
The Looking Glass Wars
Frank Beddor
Read by Gerard Doyle
The Looking Glass Wars
Seeing Redd
Exclusive!
Frank Beddor
Read by Gerard Doyle
Unabridged • 7 Compact Discs
Written by Frank Beddor
Read by Gerard Doyle
Each title contains bonus material
Scholastic
Audiobooks
Scholastic and associated logos are trademarks and/or registered trademarks of Scholastic Inc.

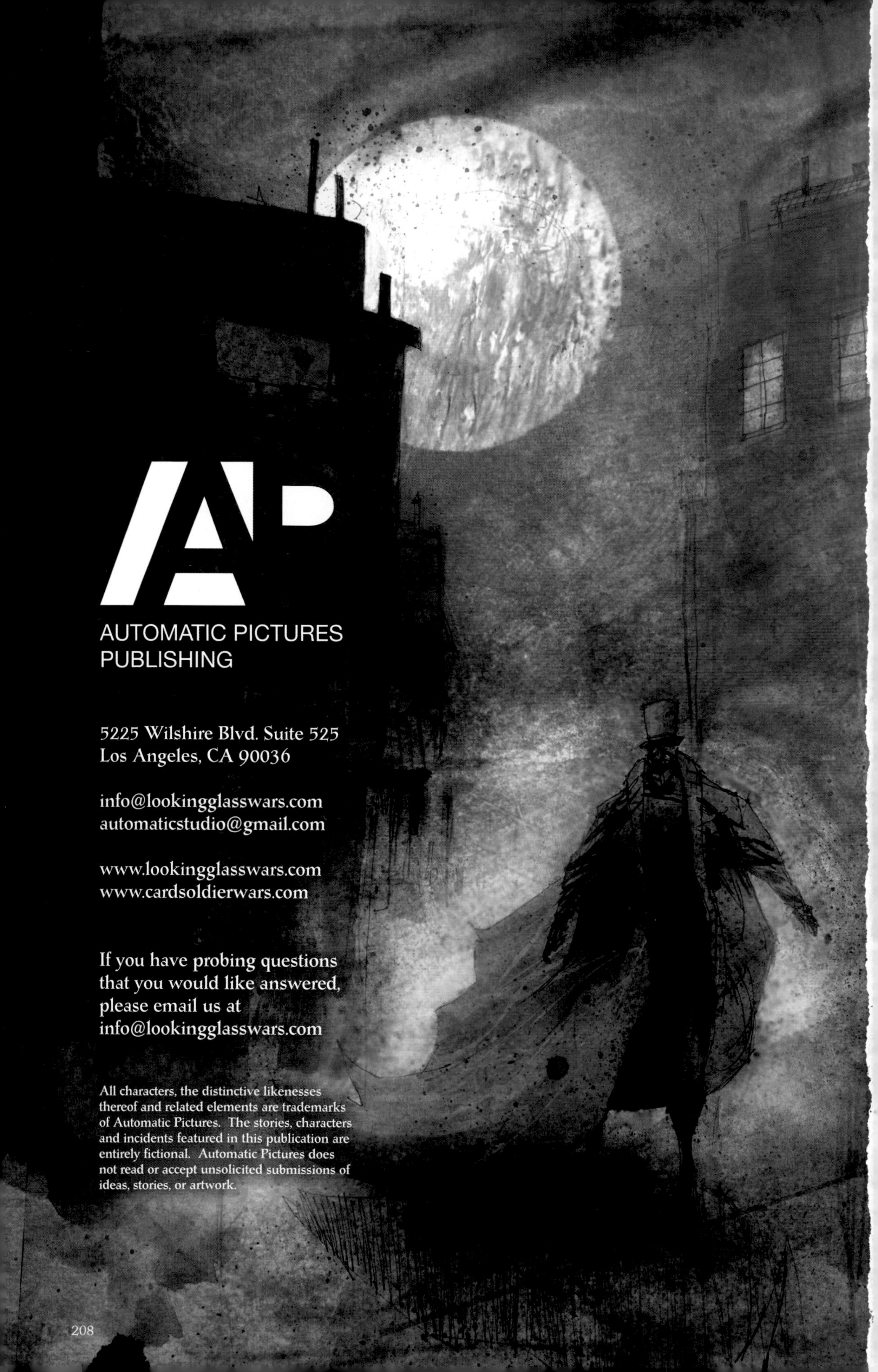

AUTOMATIC PICTURES
PUBLISHING

5225 Wilshire Blvd. Suite 525
Los Angeles, CA 90036

info@lookingglasswars.com
automaticstudio@gmail.com

www.lookingglasswars.com
www.cardsoldierwars.com

If you have probing questions that you would like answered, please email us at info@lookingglasswars.com